PEOPLE
YOU'VE BEEN
BEFORE
not a memoir

dedicated to the work

of

Bill W. and Dr. Bob
*and all who help
along the way*

and

To the joys and suffering
of my friend, Tommy

Works by Tim Jollymore

Listener in the Snow

Observation Hill,
a novel of class and murder

The Advent of Elizabeth

Lake Stories and Other Tales

People You've Been Before,
not a memoir

The Second Confession
of St. Augustine (2021)

Correspondence of characters

People You've Been Before	*Twelve: Lives With(out) Drink*

The Living

Els	Moe
Racine	De Lorr
Gabriella (Gabby)	Linda
Gael	Jude
Ona	Roxie
Dwayne	Muckey D

The Dead
(so presumed)

Tom	Tom
Burt	Burt
Glenn	Glenn
Maggie	Maggie
(Len)	Len
(Susan)	Susan
(Toady)	Toady

Els's Children

Ella, his goddaughter (Gabby's daughter)	[Roburta] Burta
[Annette] Nettie, adopted (Raci's daughter)	Tilla
Michael Siiri (with Raci)	Michael Siiri

PEOPLE
YOU'VE BEEN
BEFORE
not a memoir

A NOVEL BY

TIM JOLLYMORE

FINNS WAY BOOKS

PEOPLE
YOU'VE BEEN
BEFORE
not a memoir

Between the Bars

Drink up, baby, stay up all night
With the things you could do, you won't but you might
The potential you'll be, that you'll never see
The promises you'll only make

Drink up with me now and forget all about
The pressure of days, do what I say
And I'll make you okay and drive them away
The images stuck in your head

People you've been before that you
Don't want around anymore
That push and shove and won't bend to your will
I'll keep them still

Drink up, baby, look at the stars
I'll kiss you again, between the bars
Where I'm seeing you there, with your hands in the air
Waiting to finally be caught

Drink up one more time and I'll make you mine
Keep you apart, deep in my heart
Separate from the rest, where I like you the best
And keep the things you forgot

People you've been before that you
Don't want around anymore
That push and shove and won't bend to your will
I'll keep them still

Elliott Smith, 1997

Morning

Drink up one more time and I'll make you mine
Keep you apart, deep in my heart
Separate from the rest, where I like you the best
And keep the things you forgot

Elliott Smith, from "Between the Bars"

"Ella, is that you?" I yelled from bed, although I knew it was.

Forgot her key. Any neighbor'd let her in downstairs, I suppose.

She knocked again. "Hold on, hold on."

Why not use the street buzzer? In a hurry. Emergency with Gabby? No, she would have called from hospice.

I threw on my robe and, barefoot, shuffled to the door. "Locks, locks, and more locks," I mumbled. It *is* New York City, after all, but still no burglars in ten years. Ready to harangue and hug her both, I flung the door wide.

The woman standing there smiling at me was *not* my goddaughter, Ella.

"Raci! What . . ? How . . ? What time is it?"

It was my ex-wife, Raci.

She was passing through New York City on a trip to County Cork, and I had promised to take her to lunch. Also, I had, reluctantly, agreed to meet at my apartment, "Where the [writing] magic happens," she'd said.

I'd warned her over the phone, "No arguments."

Now, here she was, early. I would have to quell my annoyance. "I just got up," I confessed. "It isn't noon already, is it?"

She looked me over, laughed, and shook a newly-styled bob. "I'm a little early. Just a couple hours."

It was 9:30! I stammered, "Well, *you* look wonderful!"

She smiled and put on her old apologetic smirk. "Sorry, Els. You know how I am with time."

"Yes, I remember." I swept my arm toward my hallway. "You're here, so come in."

No arguments, indeed! Now she'd arrived hours early, and, to boot, was stunning and youthful in gray wool sweater and smart skirt.

Still in my bathrobe, I raked my bedhead with my fingers and, following, watched her drift down the hall to the kitchen.

Yes, she did look fine, all right. Almost too good.

I pressed dark coffee and foamed milk for her, trying to come fully awake amid her chirping banter. "Don't be so miffed, Els. I just wanted to soak up the literary ambiance awhile."

"I'll leave you to it, then," I said. I left her perched on a stool in the kitchen, sipping her cappuccino while I shaved and threw on my clothes. I was feeling uneasy, pushed off center, yet found myself whistling in the shower.

She'd nose around the place, of course. I'd hidden the pictures of Gabby and Ella, but I'd left the manuscript of *Twelve* on the desk in plain sight.

When I ducked into the bedroom, Raci was in the my study, singing. I dressed quickly and joined her.

"Is this the 'blood money' desk?" Raci turned to me and ran her fingers over its darkened cherry-wood grain. She shook her bob. Even after twenty years, I admired her look. She pleased me, but as I had suspected and feared, she could still pack two decades of bile into a sentence of six words. I wouldn't rise to her bait.

"No, actually, I bought that when *Careless* came out." I pushed back a blunt truth. Then, I rallied to appear more agreeable. "Of course, Tom did make it all possible."

Though it wasn't the real reason for our tenuous antipathy, my fame provided a convenient wrangle.

"Oh, Tom. Dear old Tom."

"Yes. He was generous in the end."

Raci crossed her arms and turned to look out the window. There were deeper, more crushing issues Raci couldn't bear to unearth—the loss of three children, abandonment, divorce, a pain-filled rehab—and as a totem of those she instead tiptoed around her resentment of my success.

Raci's was my second marriage. It ended in a crash.

Just after Christmas in 1986, I was in LA on an alcoholic-rescue jaunt. That finished, I'd planned a surprise return on New Year's Eve. Raci who'd been alone with restive kids since late Christmas night, took the three kids, Nettie, Siiri, and Michael, on a desparate sojourn from Oakland to central Oregon to visit her parents. She didn't make it.

The trip and Siiri's and Michael's lives were cut short at an intersection just outside Redding, California by a drunken driver. He plowed into them broadside, killing Michael and Siiri. Raci was left in a coma. Somehow, Nettie escaped without injury.

I was devastated. At the time, I thought Raci was leaving me, taking the kids with her. Though I had been the one to flee the family just two years prior, I was so hurt and confused that I divorced Raci even while she lay in the hospital, unconscious. Raci, the woman I loved, woke to a shattered life. I thought she would never forgive me. I'd always wondered if I could acquit *myself* of guilt.

Still, a year after Raci left me with our kids, I was able to publish Tom McIntyre's book, *Tunnel Rats*, a novel he bequeathed to me as co-author. Afterward, when my writing took off, I pretended not to care about my losses. And after *Tunnel Rats*, I couldn't write a book that wasn't well received. Perhaps the manuscript sitting on the desk—Raci now toyed with it, turning over the cover sheet—would be my first bomb, too ragged and philosophic.

"Not ready to be seen," I said, moving behind her, putting my hand on it. Her familiar scent–something like cinnamon over melted butter, wholesome and sweet–swelled a longing that had crept over me even before opening the door to her that morning. Her coming to New York offered me new hope.

I slid the manuscript off the desk into the top drawer.

Had she turned the next page, she would have seen her own name. Raci had been around for most of the action of the book, and I had dedicated it to her.

"Twelve: lives with(out) drink. Am I in this one?"

"Racine, it's fiction. Your name doesn't appear anywhere in the story."

"Like *Falling* and *Careless*? I was in those."

She couldn't leave it alone. "No, you certainly were not. It is spelled F-I-C-T-I-O-N."

I touched her arm. "How about we go early to lunch? I'm starved."

"You're right," she conceded. "While we're eating, I'll tell you all about that daughter of ours."

I knew all Nettie's news already, but said, "I'll get my jacket." I turned the drawer key on *Twelve*, securing it for now.

Years before in an interview, I foolishly called what I'd received from *Tunnel Rats* "blood-money." I'd intended to be its editor. Tom, however, named me co-author in his will, a move to shut out his sister, who, he felt, had treated him "like a dirty gook." Sis fought for and received Tom's half.

None of it—the money, the notice, the door open to more—felt right to me. Guilt, back then—a broken family, two divorces, my determination to stay sober while watching friends die in multitudes, my struggle to write without Tom who had been more inspiration than I could admit—yes, guilt and shame were my roommates. They'd been with me all the years I'd boozed and had hung around after I'd quit.

Maybe that's why I wrote *Twelve*: to purge guilt. Pathetic as a mewing kitten lapping up milk spilled on shag carpet, I tried to explain how I wasn't to blame for Tom's dismal end or the destruction at my recovery meeting, *Today*. I penned my regret for turning my back on so many, for abandoning some, and for leaving others to languish and disappear. *Twelve* was my amends, especially to Raci.

For a year I'd sat at my blood-money desk, gazing out on the leafy green space behind my brownstone along West

11th, seeing them all: my savior, Burt, my benefactor, Tom McIntyre, and my ex, the aquiline-faced Racine Davis. Staring out, I wrote much of the fiction from memory:

. . . My name is Moe, alcoholic, and habit was my habit.

In my early drinking days, the 70s, I had stopped for a bottle of wine on the way home. Daily. Sharon, my first wife, helped me finish it at dinner. Later, when DeLorr, wife number two, and I emptied a bottle even before eating, I started buying two.

The habit, really though, was the stopping at the glass and aluminum liquor store that had been a small supermarket in earlier days. The car turned into the lot, it seemed, on its own. The swish of the automatic entry door whetted my thirst, the clink of two bottles together (one red, one white, for who knew what was for dinner?) spirited my mood, the ring of the register, and pop of the paper bags the clerk expertly whipped open formed part of what I called ritual. But, truly, it was habit.

You enter a ritual consciously. Even after years of performing one, it remains a deliberate and knowing act. One does not grow owly if he misses the thing. On the other hand, habit, once formed, springs up unconsciously and proceeds without thought. Most inveterate smokers, for example, have fired one up only to find a previously lit cigarette freshly burning in the ashtray, the impulse to smoke coming from habit. I suppose for some, wine at dinner forms a ritual, but those are not drinkers like me.

The real test of whether it was ritual or rut proved to be going without, when life impinged

7

on rota: department meetings, detours, customer lunches and such, wherefore I grew testy, liable to fly into argument, to practice horn blowing, and to participate in head and often fist shaking, all the while having absolutely no conscious idea what it was that agitated me: unfulfilled, habitual cravings. At these times I actually believed people purposely debated me, droned on, wrongly cut into my lane, and, therefore, deserved my wrath.

Worse was when habit impinged and pushed daily life to the side: drinking twice as much as others at a business lunch, empty bottles rolling from beneath car seats, missing a home-cooked meal while getting cooked at a bar with the secretaries.

No ritual would bring me to these passes. Habit drove. Eventually, it devoured.

The phone rang. I took it in the bedroom. This time it *was* Ella, calling as was her wont from Gabby's hospice.

"Everything all right?"

"Situation normal. I just stopped in before work. She's asking when you'll come."

I looked toward the hall down which I could hear Raci stirring.

"No pressure. We know you're expecting a guest."

Yes, both Ella and her mother had been informed. My daughter Nettie knew, too, and *she* was ecstatic. "Actually, Raci has been here for quite a while."

"Oh. Early. That's good. Time enough to catch up." Ella paused. I could hear her draw a long breath. "Papa, I think Mom is fading. *Can* you come later?"

"Of course. I'd planned to do just that." It was a fib, but I usually did go every day.

"I'll be back in the evening, so see you then, Papa Els."

"Papa Els," she had called me from the time she was eight and just getting acquainted with both Nettie and me. She needed a father then—her own having been forever absent. Gabby named Ella as my goddaughter. And even though it was late in her childhood, that allowed us all four something we each needed. Ella gained a father she could rely on. Nettie got a younger sister to share everything with and to help ease the loss of Siiri. I again had two daughters and a close but not erogenic connection to Gabby—her choice. She herself gained more freedom to build her career with the Riverside Symphony and a contentment that Ella would grow up well. We maintained but liberally shared separate households. It wasn't a marriage, but maybe I'd already had enough of that.

. . . Incomprehensible demoralization comes to the careless among drinkers, those like me, Moe, without a plan, or much of a plan for life, or to some who simply move fast, running from the pain they've inevitably caused and who, looking over their shoulders, do not notice the disaster toward which they flee. We inevitably crash, usually with passengers aboard.

If lucky, as was I, these reckless souls wind up at some version of the place where I grew sober: *Today* at 29th and Telegraph in Oakland. Those fortunate drunks, unlike some such as my co-author pal, Tom, fall into the able, if somewhat unsteady hands of the tarnished saint and savior of my sorry soul, Burt C, and enter into the company of a constant, if constantly shifting, cadre of supporters whom they will never forget nor can ever sufficiently thank. Un-alone at last, allowed, finally, to tell their truth, they straighten their paths, some briefly, others in

9

prolonged stints, and a few for the rest of their lives. Many, though, die trying.

Never mind that my life would be entirely changed now, but I would cede today what fame I've garnered and all my goods had my benefactor, Tom, lingered with Burt C at *Today*. Tom, like many another I'd met inside that meeting and out, had the wrong stamp upon him.

I realize now that this mark, a dried stain of liquid life—without the kind of transformation that happened to me at *Today* on 29th and Telegraph—comes over soldiers like Tom, plentifully during wars, depending so deeply on one another for their very lives. Similarly, the fire that brewed the drips into Burt C's spilled cup of life—his grandmother or the absence of mother and father—besmirched his sight then blinded him with smoke. What condensing drip of habit may come to any of us begins its trembling fall in childhood, as for Burt, or in catastrophe, as it did for Tom in Vietnam.

Tom and I spent early boyhood together in company so tight-knit as to create a world complete unto itself. Our camaraderie fixed and clarified a living sentiment, quickly fermented, settled, and thinly solidified like uplifted, vertical sediment onto the background of our lives, a layered, unrecognized film, so subtle, so usual and comfortable that it hardly occupied any space at all, though all the while it colored each and every act and thought of our existence by the light that passed through it, as sunshine through thinly sliced onyx. Were that early bond enough to save us both.

Raci appeared at the bedroom door.

"Editor. She's chomping at the bit to get that manuscript."

Raci pursed her lips. "She. Sounds like you're friendly."

She was always probing, pushing lightly.

"Best to keep on good terms in this business." Raci looked like she was buying my story, and that in itself brought up old guilt and some new as well.

"Just business, then."

Was she jealous? "No. *Strictly* business." The least I could do was to quell suspicions for her.

"I bet you're sweet on her."

"Raci, please. The woman is happily married."

I'd kept Gabby and Ella, our life in New York with Nettie, all secret from Raci. But now that she was here, right in front of me, I felt I owed her something more than deceit. "Anyway, she doesn't hold a candle to you. Did I tell you how good you look?"

"Flatterer. Are you ready?"

. . . Three of us, Tom, Burt, and Moe, became who we were without one of us really choosing, desiring, or understanding the process, as if molded early on then colored by life's sap, each in particular company, in singular places, during peculiar times.

In the 1960s, Tom crawled through Viet Cong tunnels, proving himself both *semper fidelis* and completely ruined.

Likewise, I wandered, after college, through cold, weird corporate hallways far from my home town near Lake Superior into what I had hoped would be a warmer, more hospitable climate, the north of California. By 1985, as an outcome of my corporate-stoked hubris, I sought salvation at *Today*, in an unheated, second-floor meeting room above a store that sold artificial limbs.

That particular gathering that a peculiar man,

Burt C, founded for all comers, including me and, in a brief encounter there, Tom, formed a passage through those rooms above the human-appliance store, to become the-without-which-nothing of the balance of my already careworn life. They, Burt, all who came, and Tom, too, shaped my life and gave me, Moe M, this story, *Twelve*.

Much of *Twelve* is Burt's scenario and his whirlwind affair with Maggie, but I tell, too, the tale-eccentric of that outrider, Tom McIntyre, who neither knew nor was known by the little group of boozers who saved my life upstairs at *Today*. Tom, my friend, my school and scouting chum, dabbed the canvas of my adult life in oils mixed in that jungle-tunnel world that had indelibly blotched his own. Having tinted my childhood, years later he colored red my understanding and my fortune as much as had Burt in his own waywardness. Perhaps more.

Both Tom and Burt appear to me now, alternately beacons and stain, *las luces y la mancha*, over my memory, lightly pressing into me a design and coloring my view of myself, of my now scattered family, of my rescue gang at *Today*, and most hauntingly, of the inexplicable desire within us all to destroy our haunts and ranges, the others living there, and ourselves as well.

The trees out front were budding. Raci and I stepped into the fresh Aprilness of the Village. She took my arm, watching her feet down the brownstone steps to the sidewalk. She cuddled against me at the bottom waiting for me to lead. Raci was lighter now, distanced from childbirth and stresses of rearing kids, approaching a fine-looking fifty-five, slim and jaunty. I enjoyed her closeness but resisted drawing her nearer.

"Down the block." I pointed, steering her toward 5th Avenue. "The quieter route."

She swung tight on my arm, looking about. "Such a lovely neighborhood. I love it here."

"Watch your step." I dropped the arm and pointed to the canted slab by the maple. I put my hands decidedly into my pockets.

"A bit chilly, too."

We walked slowly. Raci gazed all around, again exclaiming and pointing like a Midwesterner. Of course she would like to live on my street, but I could not let that happen. I kept my gaze on the corner ahead.

A chef friend had invited us for lunch. The Hill opened for dinner at five, but Greg was testing a few dishes including a version of my favorite pizza. On the way, I was taking Raci through Washington Square not only to impress her, I suppose, but also because I enjoyed getting off the gridiron of the city.

Raci tried her line once more, "Such a bustling place. I love it here." I ignored her salvo.

We paused at the monument to take in the crowd. We watched skaters, a boy band setting up, and students striding to class or home for a noon nap. I stood aside, my eyes following Raci. She strolled the periphery, stopped, chatting with one of the musicians—she cherished boys—and watched a photo crew adjust a light screen for their shoot. I gazed at her, petite against the swirl of people, enjoying this temporary presence in my life.

Something about a group of men lined up, all facing me, all smoking cigarettes at a juncture of three angled paths intersecting the plaza sent me, perhaps because of Raci's presence, back through years and across the whole continent.

. . . None in our knot of drunks, with the exception of Maggie, ever mentioned the crooked corners, but then there they were, off just little enough from square to seem like nineties, but when you thought about it that was impossible, somewhat like us. All of us were impossible. Under the meeting house awning Maggie was saying, "Just look, Moe, how wide the sidewalk is at one part, and grows narrow at the other." She pointed to one couldn't-be-square corner. The rain danced on the pavement beyond our shelter.

I leaned out past her and the line of smokers pressed up against the building to look. Maggie's hair dripped in curls. "Sure enough. Out of whack." Across the street the sword ferns drooped with the weight of water.

Twenty-ninth and the intersecting avenue we called Ferny, after those giant sword and delicate angel ferns, each ran into Telegraph but were askew from each other. They met off-kilter at Telegraph which itself was platted diagonally from downtown out to the University. Ferny and 29th came into Telegraph catawampus, like a broken femur, the numbered street something like ten feet south of Ferny which joined to the west, right across Telegraph from the door of the artificial limb store on the first floor of our building. Twenty-ninth ran down from the hilltop behind our place, meeting the big street opposite the steps of the red-painted clapboard Oakland Methodist Church kitty-corner from the prosthesis shop.

Today, everyone was pressed up against the barred windows away from the rain. Maggie, Muckey D, and I waited for Burt to open up, discussing the streets.

"I wonder," Muckey said, "if some crazed drunk ever run his car down the hill, through a red light, and up the twelve steps of that church."

I laughed at my program-friend.

But Maggie considered it. "Any one of us could have done it at certain times in our lives."

The avenues made a crooked crossing at the diagonally cut Telegraph, so two corners just had to be acute and, kind of like Muckey, the others obtuse.

On the facing out-of-square corner, across 29th from us, was the brick three-story that housed a cafe with a picture window looking out on Telegraph Avenue. The torn shades in the windows above accented the shabby look of the apartments. Surprisingly, we never knew anyone who lived up there. On the uphill side of the cafe, another big window had been painted over in brown enamel on the inside to keep the people walking by from looking in, peeking down on the diners to ape them or to beg, either of which was something anyone would do there. It was that type of neighborhood.

"Burt told me," Muckey said, "that the paint saves the cafe owners a lot of window cleaning."

Maggie shook her head. "Well, the front window is none too clean. So I doubt much effort is really conserved."

"I wonder if they're hiding the kitchen behind that painted window," I added.

I suspected Burt knew nothing about squeaky-clean windows, and a bit later I was forced to witness proof of it. Of course, in front of Maggie, who admired Burt, I said nothing. Later when I knew, I told no one about seeing Burt's windows, out of shame and respect both.

Burt. You'd be walking along with him, and suddenly he'd just blurt out that kind of stuff, "Saves on elbow grease." That's how Burt was—

15

unpredictable, surprising, erratic—and then, he'd
grin wide as Telegraph Avenue. That smile won me
over immediately. It seemed healthy, expansively
friendly, and kindly irreverent. That was how he
reached the wayward. Anyway, I drank the terrible
coffee in that painted-window cafe only once and
that was with Burt and a woman friend of his, a
cellist in the city symphony, whom I had seen
next door a couple of times. Linda was a woman
so beautiful she made you afraid. She had that
effect on me, and I soon discovered, had on Burt,
too. That had been a bit before Maggie appeared
on our scene and long before she took a shine to
Burt and he to her.

Diagonally from the cafe, behind the jungle of
ferns on one edge and a three-foot high chain-
link fence running along the other on Telegraph
Avenue, was the parking lot serving The Racquette,
a gym specializing in racquetball which was at the
height of its popularity then. In the mid '80s it
seemed like courts were springing up everyplace
in town. Where that fence made the corner you were
certain that the angle was not square because
the weave of the chain-link also added to the
obtuse, visual oddity of the place. The lot was
always half-full of cars when, waiting for Burt
to arrive with the keys for *Today*, we stood lined
up against the building opposite the Racquette
and its parking spots across the street.

Those of us lucky enough to still own a car, no
matter what vintage or condition, eyed the empty
spaces jealously but never dared to park there.
After all, we were here to reform ourselves,
and those slots did not belong to us, even on a
part-time, occasional, or emergency basis. So,
if you had a car, you parked on the street,
and if you were lucky, up Ferny alongside the
church where parking was unmetered and good for

two hours. As in most poor neighborhoods, part of city hall's revenue plan required eagles to police the parking of the citizen churchmice, and if you were expired or a second over the two-hour limit, *bam*, you found an orange welcome card grinning at you from under your windshield wiper. We had a whole collection of them among us. I paid mine, since I had a job and I owned the car with DeLorr, my working wife, who was monitoring my new, responsible lifestyle. Like *she* had invented propriety.

Anyway, you parked up Ferny, you'd spend an hour with Burt at *Today*, and still have time for a waffle up the street afterwards. Parking tickets, though, were better than having The Racquette haul your junker to the car pound. If that happened, you paid a bigger ticket. Meters and curb parking both started at eight o'clock, just before the meeting. Drop in your coin, turn the handle, and run up the stairs for a fix of sobriety.

Even in an enlightened age, if that's what we have here, it is nearly impossible to eat out absent the proliferation of drink.

"You don't mind if I have a glass of wine, do you?" Raci asked. She had drunk "moderately," she assured me, even in my abstinence during our last years married, though, according to my adopted daughter—Raci's first born, Nettie (who I called Tilla in *Twelve*)—"Mom is lighting-up" now, frequently and expansively, too.

Greg, who knew my restraint as well as his own, was still eager to show off his cellar despite the place being closed at this hour.

"A nice Napa Valley Chardonnay to start, I think," Greg told her. Raci smiled and palmed her cashmere sweater in pleased anticipation, it seemed, and easily bent to his will.

"A box wine with a water chaser for me." I drummed my finger nails on the table, smiling with a sardonic twist.

Greg rolled with my joke. "Mais oui, Mr. T."

Raci tilted her head and frowned. "Mr. T-totaler," I told her. She didn't even smile.

My ex talked of life and of teaching in California, of her trip to Ireland, and of Nettie. She only considered Greg's handwritten menu halfway through her second Chardonnay.

"You're thin. You should eat more," Raci said.

"I've been ready to order for half an hour. Are you?"

"Oh, my bad." She picked up Greg's list with a serious flair.

"I'm having a big dinner," I said, "so that small kale pizza will be fine."

Greg was working on his spring lamb dish and came by to suggest a Pinot Noir with it. I had to forgive my friend; it was his profession.

So, Raci ordered the lamb and switched to a "nice light red" to complement.

"Imagine, lunch without wine," I quipped for Greg's amusement.

"You can have the turnip and my spinach," she said. As it turned out I could have the lamb as well. Raci had kept to her liquid diet. She raised her Pinot in a toast, "To our dear old Tom McIntyre, who split us up and, now, has brought us together again."

I refrained from quibbling and said only, "Just for lunch, Racine."

Raci had not changed. She was still alluring–gold-flecked brown eyes sparkling–but she also moved mostly between cajoling and pushing. I could survive the hour or so of the midday meal by dissembling. So despite my phone conversations with Nettie and a week-long visit from Minneapolis the previous month, I posed innocently and asked Raci about our dear daughter. "Now, tell me all about Nettie." Let Raci feel especially in charge, I thought. Already knowing all Nettie's news as well as the secrets she kept from her mother, I didn't have to listen.

Instead I was thinking about Tom.

. . . Who would have known where an active imagination, as it was called in those days, the 1950's, would lead? Tom had one, and it did not end well.

That is not to say everyone whose fancy flies at the stirring of the slightest breeze is in danger of tumbling far below from the top of his tree. And some sustain the fall. It is just that Tom wouldn't be one of them.

Maybe it had much to do with his mother who, steadied by bourbon and barbiturates, took her last drive inside the family garage. Only now can I appreciate his mother's logic: she saw her only son off to school first, then made her exit before her physician husband came home for lunch.

I see him pulling his black sedan to the curb and hobbling through the front door, almost a guest at home. Thoughtful to the last, she had left a vegetable soup simmering on the stove. Eventually, maybe after crumbling a few saltines in the bowl, Doc McIntyre may have wondered where she was. Or perhaps the soup was too hot, and he looked to admonish her. Then, standing at the sink puzzled, he might have, too late, heard the car running, then seen the garage door spewing exhaust at its edges.

In that way, Tommy's mother spared her son the discovery but not the inheritance of her despair. Her wordless farewell made its mark. Tom, in his father's abeyance of all but work, became the ward of that sister he later abhorred, living with an overweening guilt doubled by Sissy's senses of loss and duty. Nurture vanished like the leftover Seconal, down the toilet. Bereaved surveillance reigned over Tom's life. He did not rebel, maybe out of reverence for his mother. But Tom could not carry the load and the loss forever.

Imagine. "Off to school, well fed on Grapenuts."

If stature counts for anything, Tom's matched his life. Short. And like his mother, he made up for any shortcomings speaking in a deep and sonorous and oftentimes gravelly voice.

In this always outsized, bombastic *vox magnus* he frequently announced his incipient belligerent actions. All friends knew Tom's preoccupation with war-play. In a Winchellesque voice he'd say, "Take that Nazi machine gun nest. Our lives depend on you." Then supplying sound effects, Tom pulled the pin on an invisible grenade, and lobbed the device beneath the muzzle of the gun. He spoke rapidly and loud. Even in the midst of outrageous pretend, he did not fear scorn, placing or taking it on, but I never scoffed at his talk.

It was usual that we'd be walking side by side along the Pinhurst Park path that connected our houses over half a mile, Tom descanting incessantly about Operation Overlord (D-Day) or the taking of Guadalcanal. He became a soldier in those battles. Suddenly he leapt into the air, expressed bursts of rifle fire followed by an oral mortar blast out of proportion to his voice, at which he toppled to the grass and rolled halfway down the hill adjacent to the sidewalk. You never knew when he would explode into his wartime exploits—we'd been born just after World War II, and the Korean conflict was barely over. I cannot count the number of deaths by explosion Tom had suffered. Machine-gun attacks were likewise deadly and somewhat more amusing: Tom staggered back and reeled with the rapid and repeated impact of the hail of lead on his body, finally bringing him to the ground, where his soon-to-be-corpse jolted and flapped around, his deep voice rat-tat-tating all the time. That was imagination, or what we took fancy to be in those days, but neither did Tom simulate nor, perhaps, fantasize the tunnel warfare that was all too soon to become his reality.

It did not seem to matter to Tom that I knew little about war, only feigned interest in history or the recent hostilities. My amazement at the power of war and its pageantry was sufficient audience for him. Perhaps my willingness to play Hitler against his Truman won him over. Tom supplied the uniforms and insignias from his father's collected Nazi paraphernalia, and I combed my hair over my high forehead and penciled on a cropped mustache. As long as this was confined to his attic playroom or the copses of lilacs in the park, no one seemed to mind. Youth is allowed. Let the boys experiment. It's innocent fun.

Between bites of my pizza, I listened only with one ear to Raci rambling on about our daughter and thought that if Tom had stumbled into *Today*—not that I didn't try to bring him in—his harmless juvenile entertainments may have quieted in time, even after Vietnam. But he never really came in, and his unbridled amusements grew wild and dangerous in the war, and self-destructive thereafter.

"You aren't listening," Raci said.

"I am. Nettie is thinking of marrying her Englishman."

"You're half-listening. He's Irish."

I smiled. "The man, for God's sake, was born and raised in Nottinghamshire."

Raci tasted her wine, ignoring my correction.

With a gesture I encouraged Raci to talk on even though her lamb was getting cold, and I would have to eat some of it to avoid Greg's displeasure and my own embarrassment. As she rolled on, telling me what I already knew, I entertained myself, watching people passing the single, subterranean window, knees, calves and feet.

That view—like the one which had been painted over at the terrible-coffee cafe—and the colonial look of buildings up and down Washington Place, as Raci sipped and spilled her hoard of news, stirred thoughts of my time with Burt.

. . . The Racquette stood tall and alone on Telegraph Avenue, looking very colonial: red faux brick and fake white columns, a cornice with a golden eagle over the double entry doors, looking like the big house on a plantation, a weird kind of joke seeing that the neighborhood was comprised of West-African, African-American, Somalian and Ethiopian renters. No one said much about it, maybe because The Racquette took all fee-paying comers. Burt C himself, as poverty stricken as he seemed, belonged. He fit in, too. Not dark but meriney: light-skinned, freckled with hair of an orangish tinge.

Across from the club on our own acute corner, *Today*'s building ran two stories, offices strung above, storefronts below with windows reaching nearly to the sidewalk, protected by racks of square iron bars bolted top, bottom, and sides into solid brick. Outside of the church and racquetball businesses, times were not so good there. The ground floor corner store displayed crutches, mechanical arms and legs, whoopee-cushions, wheelchairs and walkers: necessities in up times and down. The store always seemed closed. Of course, only able-bodied people (this was before the ADA days of the nineties) climbed up our steep stairs.

We gathered early, rain, shine, or fog. The awnings over the second-story windows kept us dry unless a storm drove in off the ocean. The plentiful smokers gravitated to the open-air corner to bum one or get a light. They could puff upstairs too, but most couldn't wait for Burt to get that first nicotine jolt of the day. The non-indulgers leaned back against the window bars.

There were waves of mumbled greetings, sometimes cheering when long-absent personages sauntered up. We lounged there, watching people pull up curbside by the church and meander across Telegraph, not always waiting for the light, until those spaces on Ferny were filled, forcing the later-comers to pay the meters right in front. They'd dig into their pockets for change or beg us for coin. Sometimes these had to run down during the meeting to add a plug to the meter. Change always came available when the pink can went around. Those may have been thirty-minute meters. I don't remember mainly because I always came early; it got me out of the house, away from DeLorr's watchful eye.

We assembled, waiting for Burt.

I wondered what people driving by on their way to work in a downtown office or City Hall thought was going on with fifteen or twenty people huddled up under the awnings, a ragtag bunch mostly of men, peppered by a small number of women, with a few of each in suits and ties. No commuter would guess this bunch were there to get themselves straight for the remainder of the day. We were white, black, mongrels, and were occasionally joined by a couple of *trabajadores* who hadn't yet found work for the day. A mixed bag, all waiting for Burt to save them.

On any given day Burt would appear as if from nowhere, stride up to the door, key in hand, joking, saying something that had a double edge like, "Oh, yes, you've waited your whole life for this moment," and then would leap up the stairs to open the doors to the meeting room above. He was always striding or leaping or jaunting around, his tall, thin figure built for long, smooth movements he made appear effortless, his head held high, maybe a little gawky to the right or left depending on who was dogging him, his bony-looking chest erect no matter what the lower parts were doing. Only his arms swung along with or opposite of his legs, though often he crooked books or newspapers at one elbow, letting the other slue along with the momentum of his canter. All his movements looked easy, his manner inspired. You'd think he had no cares. Then again, perhaps he kept moving to avoid being caught.

Often he'd come up with someone, rambling along gabbing like mad, exercising those arms plenty, books or no. Most of the time it seemed that he'd be agreeing with whatever had just been said to him, laughing, nodding, and smiling big. "Oh, yes, I got that number. Don't you know!" Then he'd be going straight ahead following his forehead, only his eyes shifting to the side he was talking to and, usually, down on the person he was agreeing with. Burt was quite tall.

In rain, Toady would drive Burt, sweeping into the curb to let him off, then roaring up Telegraph to find a free, safe spot to stow his BMW. Nice days, those two walked together like Mutt and Jeff all the way down the block.

Toady's nickname—the only moniker he ever answered to since no one seemed to know his given or family name—was, he said, a badge of honor. "In Philly every one had a handle. Mine was the best, and I brought it with me to Oakland."

Toady looked, well, like a toad: a massive jaw and big belly making up most of who he was, supported on short limbs, bowlegged below the weight of his stomach. He'd hop along beside or often behind Burt, and the pair resembled, seen a way down the street, a man walking his jumpy, yipping little dog.

Occasionally, we'd see Burt emerge from the front door of The Racquette, stepping right into Telegraph without appearing to look and stretching over four lanes, making his own crosswalk. It was enough to make any mother scream, but none of us thought a thing about it. We'd all been playing in traffic for years. Besides, Burt was special in a walking-on-water way. He saved souls.

However he arrived, we were waiting. When he turned the key, capering up the steps, we followed, climbing the narrow staircase made tighter by the picture-of-walnut paneling and wooden railings on both sides, into the meeting room adjacent to the organization's central office, bare besides thirty-six metal folding chairs and eight collapsible tables set up in a square, a few hope-instilling wall placards, and a thousand coats of stale cigarette smoke painting every surface. Some immediately hung on the l-shaped counter waiting for the first cups of Folgers, or whatever else had been on sale last week, to drip on down. It didn't take long. The organization owned a commercial-style Bunn with four pot-warmers.

The room, despite the heavy scent which I could

now smell thanks to having quit a 24-year smoking habit, was pleasant enough but not homey. Snug and warm were comforts none of us could stand anyway. Our nerves were shot, and just the idea of home gave us palpitations or led to obsessions. Hard and cold surfaces were what we needed to remind us of how we'd gotten there.

On the second story ran a bank of windows, laid out harmoniously in two sets of three wide panes, each clad in wooden shutters painted the same shade of institutional tan as the walls, posts, and ceiling of the room. The awning-style windows being on the second floor were left open in an effort to freshen the room. The floor and the Formica coffee counter were the only truly clean surfaces, one being swept three times a day, mopped each afternoon, and waxed weekly, the other being wiped so frequently that the pattern had long ago worn thin overall and in spots had completely disappeared.

In that fusty meeting room I first saw Burt. There I turned over my heart to him in exchange for each day sober.

I find that nearly impossible to explain. Burt and I were as near to polar opposites as two men could be, but maybe that is why he had a calming and, I suppose, magnetic effect on me. What he said and did made little sense—his cavalier attitude toward almost anything belied his deep belief in almost everything, especially in people's hopes and dreams—so when he captivated one it seemed so strange, so unlikely, that everyone was sure it was a miracle. How can one not give his heart to a man performing miracles? Especially when that stunning feat, *la increible milagra*, was the removal of the long-standing and ungovernable desire to booze until absolutely everything around one had fallen to utter ruin.

At first I observed from afar, and I sensed Burt did the same. He could be a messiah only at a distance. Up close, the savior-veneer would show the cracks none of us wanted to see. At the time, I wasn't looking for saving exactly, just relief.

My first visit I came right on time, but things had started rolling fifteen minutes before. The coffee was on. Glenn, a bulky, balding guy, was spreading out pamphlets on a small table that punctuated the line of chairs at the windows. A short pink-faced man, Len, seeming to appear only in profile and who walked like a sailor, feeling the cant of the floor with every step, slid clean ashtrays down the tables. Burt C was just then sitting down at the head of the front table, under the portraits of Bill W and Dr. Bob, looking tall even seated, erect, head bobbing around, his mile-wide, gat-toothed smile sweeping everyone with joy, seeming to speak, sending ironic messages out even before he uttered a word. And just as I took a chair in the very back of the room by the rear exit, although there were plenty further forward, Burt rapped the pink can he held three times on the picture-of-mahogany table and began, "This is the *Today* group of . . ." something I would hear five times a week for the next two years, and, in place of Burt C, would eventually say myself.

This was December, months before Burt fell in love—he liked to say it was Valentine's Day—and, when that was over by the following Thanksgiving fled to LA, back when he was still walking down to the college three days a week, taking classes in something like business or community organizing or politics or something that fit him like two left-footed shoes. For Burt wasn't a business man, or an organizer, or very much political even in a common-sense understanding of trade, demonstrations, candidates, elections, or voter turnout, because he hadn't room for any of that. Burt was pure minister.

Still, though he might have been raised by his grandmother to be Baptist, he wouldn't fit into any pulpit like the one we never saw across the street in the red Carpenter Gothic church. Fire and brimstone, blame, and big hopes weren't in Burt's lexicon. He knew very well we were suffering in this life, enough to fill a hundred hells and at the same time loving so much in this world to flood a hundred heavens. He need never speak about anything but today, this minute, the very breath he was taking and never the next one which might not come. He was a preacher of the now, never to pontificate in the church-y sense. He witnessed. Burt was our paraclete. Told it as it came to him. Some thought he made it up on the spot, but he didn't and mostly stuck to what he'd experienced or been told directly, much of it by his grandmother who'd raised him. He witnessed without explaining, scolding, or predicting, and never mentioned sin though he knew, as he had done already, that we all would sin aplenty.

One at a time, Burt stayed in the day. He rose hopeful and energetic like the morning. Regret was left in yesterday. Dawn brought another chance for sober living. Maybe that's why he named the group *Today*, although some joked it was a misreading of Toady that stuck as soon as it slipped off a tongue. Others cited the NBC show of the same name that was just then getting popular. In any case, we felt centered in *Today*.

Burt and Toady ran the group out of one of the twelve stacked two by two by two-foot deep plywood lockers, one of that dozen that lined the back wall of our meeting room—stained to the color of walnut though the whole bank of storage was pine plywood. There they kept literature, coffee and supplies, and, as I later learned, the coffers that the baskets passed around five times a week fed. That was the main thing that connected Burt C with the church across Telegraph Avenue, the offerings. And it wasn't until he was on his way to being lost in LA that anyone bothered to ask where the money went or how much. That spoiler would be Jude.

If a person needs soothing and direction at the same time, there is nothing as good as routine. *Today* was a regimen for us all no matter what we drove or how we got there or, really, what we'd done before, how much or how many we had wasted along the way, either money, or friendships, or lives.

"My grandmother taught me to get up and make my bed," Burt said, "to keep life simple." Of course, if you rose as early as he seemed to, there better not be someone still sleeping in the bed because he had to make it. Maybe that was why he needed to get to LA, to start making his bed again.

I always had someone out-sleeping me, so my mantra was different: "Always have breakfast before leaving the house." Still, like much in sobriety, I learned "first things first" from Burt.

Routine: Our knot on the crooked corner. The Racquette across the street. The red-painted Ferny Street church that never seemed to be open. The prosthesis outlet downstairs. The acid-coffee cafe. They stood sentinels to our operation, our weekday coping plan. Burt played the central role in it. Toady pumped the pink can a day or two each week, Tuesday and Thursday, but Burt was always there. Always. Even if a holiday fell during the week, Burt and *Today* were there. And later, when Burt wasn't, it became much more disturbing than an unmade bed or leaving the house without breakfast. It was as if we'd arrived to find a cross bearing Walter Cronkite, the church burnt to the ground, or the avenues suddenly intersecting in line with each other, and Telegraph crossing at right angles. Burt was that much our guidepost.

On the first Friday he didn't show up, I started to know him better—though I wonder now, really, if I ever knew him at all.

I picked over the last piece of pizza, by now rather full. I'd eaten the beautiful turnip and the spinach, too, and had swirled a bit of lamb in its sauce.

"You know," Raci pointed her empty fork at me over two equally empty Pinot glasses, "I'm not sure Preston is right for Nettie."

"The Englishman?"

"Irish. She is so smart and so beautiful."

I nodded, agreeing with both.

"She's not as busty but every bit as lovely as, what was that woman's name?"

"Woman?" Of course, I knew exactly who Raci meant, but I did my best to play the forgetful man approaching sixty.

"Burt's woman."

I feinted, keeping away from talking about Gabby and Ella. "Do you mean Maggie?"

"Don't be silly. The busty one. The one Burt had a child with. The cellist."

Maggie's willow-like fragility couldn't stand in for Gabby's gorgeous face and remarkable figure. Raci might remember better, but in her company I had to try to dissemble while avoiding being obvious. "I'm not quite sure, Raci."

"Don't try to fool me. You told me she was a goddess."

I was caught. "Oh, Gabriella." In *Twelve*, I'd called her Linda. At a loss and afraid of tipping both my and Nettie's hand, I said simply, "Yes, she was beautiful."

"Quite fetching you thought." Raci tapped her tines on the table. "Well, Nettie shouldn't waste her good looks on Preston. What happened to her, anyway."

I tried again to deflect Raci's line of questions. "Maggie?"

"No, Els. The cellist."

Then I slipped, using her pet name, "You mean Gabby?"

"Oh, it's Gabby now? Yes."

Gabriella and I had been long-time friends in New York ever since I'd landed there. I'd first met Gabby in Oakland in early '85. Raci and I were still married then, and our eldest, Nettie, was only nine. Her one-time lover and recovery-program founder, Burt, introduced us. Gabby drew me in like a well aged Scotch, as she did most men. But I had a marriage I was trying to save and a problem I was trying to solve: crawling out of that bottle of whiskey. So it wasn't until after Raci's accident, a move three thousand miles east, and a couple of years away from my Oakland days, that Gabby's and my friendship gelled. Even though Nettie was a part of it all, Raci knew nothing of it. And now Gabby was dying, and I was trying to be there for my little New York family, still keeping Raci in the dark.

So, I had to lie to shield Nettie, whom Gabby had mothered through Raci's disaffection and absence. "I haven't the slightest idea, Raci."

"She must have raised the kid," she said.

"Indeed." Change "she" to "the two of you" and it would be be right, I thought.

Then Raci moved into a reiteration of her visit to Minneapolis. I'd heard Nettie's version already.

. . . We met in the bad-coffee cafe across 29th. I've said before that she was so beautiful I was petrified, a pillar of salt for my thoughts. Of course, Burt just acted like always—casual, charming, talkative, and full of smiles. The word "debonair" came to mind. I knew, though, he could see just as well as I could. I thought then that he was just more mature than my sophomoric self. I had no excuse for acting or thinking like a teenager. Burt just seemed less subject to the transforming effects of Linda's perfect poetry.

In contrast to me, Burt had grown up under both the kind and watchful eye of his grandmother and the hopeful eyes of the joyful Baptists. His part in the pageantry of his neighborhood seemed to have been that of the corner preacher. He was open, friendly, righteous, and skilled in the gospel of patience. And, though not for Burt himself, perhaps, he knew the path to salvation. I'll never be sure now, but from the course I watched him follow in the two years of our association, Burt reverenced physical amour rather than the other, heavenly, kind of love. More so, it was, I think, social attraction for Burt that became his general and predominant *affaire de coeur*, being more pervasive by its open, active nature than the other two kinds of love. He loved people. In any case, poetry had no part in any of his affections.

I had no ships to launch that day, or any time, but I sure as hell knew beauty when I saw it. Just as that other poet said, time was frozen, and all seemed true and beautiful at that instant. At the moment of our meeting, I came close to believing in God's creation. This was truth. That's all I needed to know.

Okay, we were in the crummy cafe across from

the prosthesis fittery, sitting under the painted window. Instead of strolling up the street to the waffle house, which served lattes and great drip coffee, which this particular morning housed most of the gang from the meeting, Burt took the less traveled road. Why he asked me to come across the way with him and the goddess, I did not know. I thought that perhaps he, too, was abashed by beauty. I was soon to find out.

I had seen her in the meeting, of course; she was Burt's guest speaker, whose voice intoned loveliness itself. The coffee bar was keeping me busy that day (my own guest appearance), so I remember only the melody but little detail of her share. I'm not telling it anyway, since her story was told inside a meeting. We protect anonymity.

After the final words, Muckey, Toady, and Hillside-Glenn (he was still with us at that time) filed down the stairs on their way to the waffle shop. I might have said, "I'll catch up with you." Burt had to count the cash and stow everything in the locker. His speaker lingered, waiting for him, I supposed. I'd just finished rinsing the pots and wiping the counter when they were ready to descend.

"Up for an adventure in coffee, Moe?"

Burt realized that I didn't quite get his drift, so he explained plainly, "Join us for a cup across the street." It did not sound like a question, more of a plea with a hint of command. In that way I got the idea that Burt didn't want to be alone with this woman, that he perhaps didn't dare be alone with her.

"Thanks, I'll be glad to, but 'adventure in coffee'?"

"You'll find out."

The effect of being near Linda was exactly the

opposite one usually experiences with people, beautiful or not. Pores, moles, stray hairs, and uneven features jump out in an intimate encounter, as if you were viewing one of those giant Chuck Close paintings.

I'd been forty feet across the room, behind the coffee counter, seeing Linda around the posts that held up the ceiling, but now was in her aura, shaking the softest, warmest hand I'd ever encountered, and from that vicinity Linda's beauty was shockingly perfect. It turned me to stone.

Her face, it seemed from every angle, was totally symmetrical, young and smooth without makeup marauding over it, and radiant in a plump-cheeked, attentive but slightly distant aspect, as if she were there but viewing all she saw from a step or two removed. Later, over the cafe table, while she was chatting with Burt, I began to think this slight remoteness came from the propinquity of her eyes, not crossed at all but nigh each other, a bit high over her straight-lined, sensitive nose. Linda's mouth was a remarkable mixture of firmly-outlined lips and soft lushness, both of which resonated with her breathy voice, as if by traveling over them her words absorbed both the sensual and direct qualities found there. Her features were long in keeping with her strong, tall stature, and everything about her face and body, too, from her blonde curls to the curves of her ample breasts, played musically in harmony with each other part. It all made sense, as she played in the string section at the symphony.

"It was no problem, really, Burt," she said, releasing words in sonorous phrases like the long, slow drawing of a bow. She accompanied her voice with the play of her shoulders and a dip of her head to one side, as if she were hugging her instrument between her legs and tipping her cheek to the scroll and pegs.

Burt replied with his slingshot-like grin, winding his neck up, his head turning with it, finally to swing back with the big smile saying, "Oh, yes it was, and I appreciate your coming. Your time is valuable."

"Practice time is precious, but overdoing it can be a mistake. I needed the break."

And while Burt mouthed some of his grandmother's affectionate and conciliatory words to Linda, improving the value of her visit to our needy and nervous group, I meditated on just how different from the general crowd upstairs was this melody of a woman. Unlike them, she practiced and prepared.

Of all the faces I remember from those years around the tables, few if any prepared or practiced anything other than obsession with cocktails. Upstairs, perhaps, it was the *ad hoc* nature of our attendance-our only requirement was to draw as honestly as possible from our recalled experiences—that itself voided the need to prepare and actually annulled any recitation of a practiced speech. There was yet to be, if we were good at revising our behavior, a time when we practiced or prepared: right now as cooks, we slung hash; as workers, we needed supervision and a time clock; as travelers, we lost our way frequently; as friends, we fell away. Most of us just wanted to be ourselves, left alone, and had only a spit of discipline to bend our unknowable will and uncontrollable cravings to tasks that required research or regimentation. That was my nature and the impulsive qualities of most of those hanging around Burt's door. Were

we to attempt anything approaching a symphonic
resonance, the cacophony of abrading noise would
have driven even the deaf from our midst.

So Linda, reflecting dedication to something
other than self, to engagement that required
cooperation, to talent that increased by training,
grew to me more beautiful and more frightening,
too. It might not have been the proximity of her
eyes to each other but her professional commitment
that put her at that small remove I had sensed.
Accomplishment augmented her physical allure in
a most terrifying way.

As for Burt, I could only guess. He waxed a
bit more loquacious than usual, a little on the
jittery side, and once or twice, it seemed, acted
the thespian, painting on an expression—interest,
surprise, affirmation—a couple of shades beyond
the intensity required for everyday conversation.

"What do you do with the kid, your daughter,
when you practice?" Here he lifted his reddish,
bushy eyebrows high on his forehead.

At the mention of her young one, Linda smiled—
gat-toothed like Burt—stunning me once again.
"Grandma is a great help in that way."

The utterance of that word, "grandma," cranked
Burt up. "The world cannot love grandmothers
enough to pay for all they do." He too smiled
broadly then shook his head sadly.

They talked on gaily, Burt nodding and bowing
too. Linda replied softly to his jabbering. They
got along quite well in a way that hinted at an
intimacy I couldn't explain, a closeness that
left me out. Was I there as a chaperone, showing
Linda that Burt had no undue intentions beyond a
thank-you coffee? At one point he reached out and
squeezed her hand lightly, then held on. Linda
did not withdraw it. My heart raced at the thought

of holding that hand. Burt continued gabbing. He
seemed flustered and was trying not to show it.

They talked on.

I lost myself in my thoughts, trying not to
stare too much at Linda's face or her breasts,
sipping in tiny draughts the horrid coffee, much
worse than meeting-fare, so that when she spoke
to me, I didn't hear her. When I realized she was
addressing me, I nearly toppled over.

I raised my gaze to my two companions from
the third teaspoon of sugar I'd been stirring
into my brew, trying to create something potable.
Burt was giving me a crooked, ironic smile under
raised, expectant eyebrows, as Linda looked
directly into my eyes, driving from my mind all
thought, all rumination, all capacity , autonomic
or otherwise, to respond, with the harmony of her
narrow gray-eyed gaze. "And what about you, Moe?"
she asked, for at least the second time.

Burt rescued me. "Moe's been looking back a
lot, maybe too much." He cracked a jagged laugh,
and, thanks to heaven, Linda turned her gaze back
to Burt. I was freed and could speak again.

"Yeah, I've got a thing about the past," I
said. Then I prattled on about being married—
some kind of defense against the enormity of
my attraction to her, a shield to hide behind
while I scampered away—about my three kids, about
how bad I'd been in the last year, my previous
incarnation, about my job, about anything that
led me away from the disastrous magnetism of
her harmony, the whisper of her respiration. Had
I not been completely out of my mind, I would
have told her I was unable to see further than
her alluring face, couldn't forge beyond aghast
worship of her comely radiance, couldn't decide
if I needed a sister or a lover. Fortunately, I

was too insane to be truthful. "I'm really just a regular guy." That was the best I could do.

The coffee turned my stomach, and I had to pee. And when I was on my way back from the pit they called the W/C, Linda was standing, leaning lightly into Burt, her bowing arm draped softly around his shoulder in a chaste and collegial hug (something I couldn't have stood). I approached with "a-hem," they separated, and Burt swept by me on his own trip to the john.

"I'm picking up my daughter at my mother's," Linda said. She glanced after Burt. "Let's wait outside," she said, taking me by the arm.

Out on the corner, she turned to me, and as if she had read every thought I'd let run through my head since climbing down the meeting room stairs, she gazed into my eyes, took my face in her oh-so-soft hands, whispered "Moe," and kissed me fully on the lips.

"Watch out for Burt, will you Moe? I know you look up to him, and that's fine, but he isn't everything you think he is. He reveres your ability and education." I must have looked as astonished as I felt both for the kiss and her request. It was as if she'd boxed my ears to instill the message, but had used her wonderful lips instead. "Really, Burt is just a boy in a man's body."

I bobbed and nodded my head.

"You don't know, do you? Burt and I were a number once. Burta, my daughter, is his."

"Oh." My fantasies of the last half hour fled before Linda's news.

"Burt truly can't deal with children. He is a child himself in his way, so our love could not . . ."

"Work out?"

"Yes, and though I adore him even now, I can't

38

watch over him or help."

"So, you want me to?"

"In a way. Toady is a great supporter and friend to Burt, but Burt thinks the world of you. Two friends are better than just one. I wanted you to know."

She then folded me in her arms like a fulfillment of dreams and softly said, "Be good, Moe. Watch out for Burt. Don't let him hurt himself." Then, Linda walked up the hill and was gone.

Inside, though Burt was counting coins at the register, I thought he'd watched my encounter with Linda outside.

I plunked down on the hard chair, disassembled in every part, deciding that if I needed a lover again, Linda was the one.

Burt sat down, churning more sugar into his coffee. He pursed his lips, wound up his neck, and swung back to me to say, "As my grandmother often said, 'Beauty is as beauty does.'"

In a rare moment of composure and control, I looked steadily at him, shaking my head slowly and said, "Not now, Burt, not now."

In silence, Burt and I finished the swill they call coffee there. For me it was an antidote for Linda's kiss-sealed plea and for her gorgeousness, neither of which I could consume in such a distilled form as hers no matter how many gallons of spirits I'd practiced drinking before.

Burt gave me the most wistful look I'd ever seen on anyone's face, as if to say not even the love of that woman would make him right, though all he said was, "Well, shall we go?"

We left the cafe, parted at the corner. I went to work, Burt to wherever he existed off-time. Though I kept my pact with her, watching over Burt as much as my poor abilities warranted, we two never mentioned Linda by name to one another again.

I thought then: some things are best left alone.

Noon

Drink up with me now and forget all about
The pressure of days, do what I say
And I'll make you okay and drive them away
The images stuck in your head

Elliott Smith, from "Between the Bars"

The glass shattered. Racine's third Pinot flushed across our little table, forcing me back, tipping the chair as I flew up to avoid the flood. Greg rushed in with black cloths. He knew what was needed by ear alone.

Raci gushed excuses like cheap wine. "How clumsy. I was just reaching for Els' hand. I'll pay for the glass."

Greg floated above the mess gracefully. "No need. It happens all the time. Relax. Let me wipe the table. Watch your skirt."

I picked up the chair. I was tempted to throw it. Nothing's better than five ample glasses of wine, well, four and a half, atop a cappuccino to create mayhem. My daughter had been right: "Mom is lighting-up." And Nettie might not know the extent of the damage. I'd seen it plenty and so had Greg. Nothing to do but forbear, be helpful, and back away when the coast was clear.

Then Raci started to cry.

"I'll clean up here," Greg said. "Fetch a cab and take her home." Neither of us could stand the tears.

I gathered Raci's things and guided her to the door, mentally cursing my bad judgment, wishing I had quashed her desire to be "where the magic happens." The alchemy and sorcery of alcohol always found the cracks in discretion and flowed freely through. As I helped Raci climb the seven stairs up to the sidewalk, I felt, after twenty-two years sober, that I had descended again to the first step on a return to *Today*.

The cabbie grinned when Raci slumped into the seat and raised an eyebrow at my demoralized state. "Liquid lunch? Where to?"

I wanted to reply, "Hell," but gave him the address. "Take the long way." I rolled down the window and thought about another boozy re-emergence that had ended just the same way.

. . . It all seemed to fit. The hundreds of explosions Tom had survived in boyhood may have rendered him impervious to harm from the outside. His study of war over long years and devotion to being the subject of faux machine-gunning may have proved helpful during recruitment. His lack of fear outsized him in military eyes.

The imprint of his mother's death-wish likely telegraphed through him. At five foot two his stature gave him something to prove to the United States Marines but also offered the Corps a special quality it wanted. Tom joined the service in 1968 and by the end of that year crawled down the mouth of his first Viet Cong tunnel.

None of us would know much about it, despite three Purple Hearts and a Medal of Honor—all of which, except in his attempts to write about it, he rejected. It was through that writing I came into his life again:

"Moe," he said in his grating voice over the phone, "it's me."

As it turned out, he was in Washington, DC, talking over bad long-distance lines and drunk besides, so even had I been awake, I might not have recognized his voice. It had been eight years.

"Me who?"

"MacIntyre."

"Tom?"

"The one and only, buddy. In the flesh, across the wire. Are you sick? You sound sick."

"It's four in the morning here. I'm not awake."

"Well, hit the floor, buddy, I'm coming your way. I've been up all night working on a big project. I need you to see it."

Back and forth over the next ten minutes, I finally made sense of what he was saying. He'd written his story, he said, and wanted me to see it, and as I learned later, to polish it for publication. I suppose I was the only English major he knew around Duluth. And my name was in the directory.

All I knew at the time was that he had "written" dead drunk all night, and likely had been soused for his past two years in civilian life. He would be nearby, staying with his recluse father in Cloquet, our hometown, which name, being French, rhymes with "good day". Tom had asked me to pick him up at the airport.

I hadn't seen him since his return in 1970, and we had not parted friends, exactly. In '66 we'd graduated, having overcome acrimony followed by terse competition and, finally, reconciliation. In eighth grade I'd smacked him across the face and sent him sprawling on the highway median. In retribution, I supposed at the time, he'd stolen a high school class office that I'd first envisioned, created, and occupied. Of course, knowing the right people, he did a better job than I had in junior year. Before graduation, though, we sewed up the rips in our friendship and tacitly agreed to tolerate each other-it was a small place. Still is. Then he joined the Marines.

When Tom called that night, I had nine weeks to finish my master's papers and pass my exam. I was supposed to be studying like a fiend, but I'd been touched by Tom's call and his insistence that I be the only person to see or work on his manuscript. Always, he knew the right people.

Two days later, I waited at the airport through three flights arriving from the East. Tom had been scratched from his first flight. He was on the passenger list but had not boarded the second. I guessed he was too drunk for either. Eight hours later, I watched the passengers file off the third. Still no Tom. He hadn't even made that final plane.

Six days later at eleven o'clock in the evening, without notice, he knocked on my door, and when I opened it, tripped over the threshold, dropping to the floor in a heap, where he promptly passed out. This was no longer play-acting. Tom had moved into the real world.

I didn't pay attention to the cabbie's route, but by the time Raci began to stir, we were suddenly before my brownstone.

She woke, startled by the absence of motion, I suppose, vaulted out of the cab, and hung over the rear fender while I paid the driver.

"Is she okay?" he asked. He watched Raci in his side mirror. "She's not going to spew on my cab is she?"

As if waiting for her cue, Raci heaved her "breakfast" and "lunch" over the trunk of the car. The driver slammed on the horn. "Jesus Christ!" He kept honking.

"Here's a ten. Get it washed," I said and slipped out to help Raci up the curb.

The taxi was long gone by the time we found the top stair. Raci apologized at each halting step, "Sorry, sorry, Els, I was really looking forward . . ."

"I know. Too much excitement."

"Sorry. I feel so bad."

Yes, remorse is terrible. So don't give it reason to root, don't give it room to burst forth. Still, I had only one humanitarian option. "Come upstairs, Raci. Get cleaned up. You'll feel better."

We negotiated the tiny elevator. She was a mess. Wine had spotted her skirt. Vomit splattered her coat front. She leaned on me all the way to the fifth floor then caught a low heel in the lift's gate track and stumbled. When I opened the apartment door, she tottered into the hall. I was ready and caught her before she hit the wall.

When Raci foundered once inside, I knew I was in the barrel for the rest of the day. My experience at *Today* and my friendship with Tom had schooled me to be kind to the afflicted.

. . . Tom had fallen in through my doorway. I dragged him up from the floor and with the help of Sharon, my first wife, dumped him in the bathtub we had draped with our raggediest blankets. I tossed his bag at the drain end and went back to bed.

"So this is your great friend Tom from high school?"

I wasn't happy either. "He's having a rough time in civilian life, I guess."

Sharon turned onto her side, facing me. "Maybe, but can he have it somewhere else? Wasn't he staying with his father in Cloquet?"

"Let me sober him up and find out if he has his manuscript with him. I'll send him home tomorrow while you're at work."

The sight of Tom wavering at and falling through my doorway did not match what I had read about him in the Pine Knot, our hometown paper, only two years before his reappearance:

McIntyre awarded Medal of Honor

SINGLE-HANDEDLY DESTROYED AN ENEMY BUNKER, RESCUED A WOUNDED COMRADE UNDER HEAVY FIRE, AND ATTACKED AND ALONE DESTROYED TWO MORE BUNKERS BEFORE BEING WOUNDED WHILE ATTACKING A FOURTH BUNKER.

NOON

When I got up to pee, I rolled Tom onto his side and propped the bag behind him. I went back in a minute to check and to slide the shower curtain around the tub. Sharon might have to use the toilet during the night. She could shower at the hospital before work.

Next morning we tiptoed around making breakfast, and at seven forty-five I saw Sharon off to the ER. Then I went in to shave.

I'd just soaped up and was bringing the razor to my cheek when Tom screamed and swung out on the shower curtain rod, pulling the whole thing down over him. All the while wrestling with his bag and taking the curtain to the floor, he yelled the word "kill" and something else in what sounded to me like Vietnamese.

I pressed myself against the wall. "Tom. Wake up. You're in Duluth. It's Moe. You're in my apartment."

The struggling under the curtain stilled. Then the whirling lump beneath the mangled rod and torn plastic curtain deflated as Tom sighed. He wormed his way out of the tangle and looked up at me, still lathered up and ready to scrape. "Shit," he said and grinned, then grimaced, clapping his hands against the stabbing pain in his head. "Ow. I'm dead." He fell back and rubbed his temples.

Tom came around slowly. Coffee and a little food seemed to help, though only time cures. After a curtain-less shower in last night's bed, he was able to string more than three words together. True to form they were, "Got a beer?" Then he asked, "Or schnapps, or a little something?"

I understood, believe me, but frowned anyway.

"Hey, hair of the dog. It'll clear my head."

"All I have is wine, Tom."

"That'll do."

Two glasses did the trick. He seemed fine then, and in the bathroom noisily rustled deep into his duffel bag. He brought out a manila folder bound with two thick, blue rubber bands. Tom slapped the bundle on the kitchen table. "This is it," he said. He smiled big. "Take a look."

Tom slipped the blue bands off, snapping one, and pushed the folder, half as thick as the Duluth phone book, over to my side of the table. It was ten o'clock already, and I hadn't cracked so much as a poem or an author's timeline. Tom beamed, pride dancing across his forehead.

"I've got an hour, but then I have to study."

"Okay, okay. Just take a peek."

The file was a mishmash of newspaper clippings, dog-eared pages torn from books, half sheets of lined paper scrawled over in around six colors of ink. A packet of photos of combat soldiers kneeling around a hole slid out from between pages of a *Newsweek* that announced "Tet Offensive!" across the cover. The snapshots spewed out on my lap. I paged through the folder as carefully as I could, but fragments and shreds of paper kept sliding to the floor. I spilled a few more pages and photos bending over to rescue the first. Tom watched.

When I had it all together again, I asked, "Where's the manuscript?"

Tom grabbed the file and scrabbled through, disorganizing the whole mess again. Paper slid across the table and most sheaves fell to the floor. "Shit," he moaned. "Shit, shit, shit." He stood suddenly, more papers fluttering down from his lap. He walked right over all his stuff on the linoleum and sprinted down the hall to the bathroom. I heard him unzipping and rummaging through his bag, saying, "Shit, shit, shit."

Noon

I went back there. Rumpled shirts, pants, and worn boots were strewn over the tub and floor. A sock was hanging halfway into the toilet. The bag was empty now, and Tom was bent over it, jamming his hands into pockets and shaking out every item of clothing. Just as suddenly as he'd quit the kitchen, he stopped searching. He rose to attention on his knees and slapped his back pocket. "Goddammit," he said as he slid two fingers inside and pulled out a twice folded wad of papers. "Eureka!"

Tom beamed at me. "Here it is." He held the papers out.

If I looked shocked, he didn't let on. I hesitated to take his manuscript, but Tom pushed it at me and shook the packet. "Hey, it won't explode."

Even double-sided, the eight sheets were hardly a couple thousand words, but at least they were written in one color of ink, though in a jittery, crapulous scrawl I found nearly impossible to parse.

I abandoned hopes of study, and the rest of the morning we spent examining Tom's script. There wasn't much of any use, and most of that was bad. Since I had to continually ask him to decipher a squiggle or shaky phrase, it took time. About midway through, Tom went to the fridge and poured another glass of wine. He offered me the bottle, but I held off. On page six, he went for another, and I joined him. I wasn't going to be studying anytime soon.

I transcribed as we went along in order to be able to read it later:

> The tunnels are a big part of my war experience. It was how the Cong fought. They were old. Left from wars with at least the French.

They hid and escape, guerrilla-style. I'd go in right
after them. Look for prisoners. They really stunk bad.

Our motto is *Non Gratum Anus Rodentum*:
Don't give a rat's ass. And I had to pull out
buddies those bastards killed more than once.

It was scattered. Changed tense mid-sentence.
He lost antecedents like mad. Set up comical
juxtapositions. Everything there smelled rife. The
cadence was jumpy and made it largely unreadable.
I took a second glass and opened a new bottle.

Raci was lighter than I remembered, and in her condition
I moved her, slowly, across the hall and shut the door. I
propped her against the wall, hanging her coat on the hook.
Once we shuffled our way to my bedroom, I suggested she
remove her shoes for comfort and her skirt for cleaning. I
sat her on the edge of my bed, and when the shoes and skirt
came off, lifted her legs up and tucked her in. Let her remove
the sweater if she wanted.

I drew the sheet to her chin and folded my Saks comforter
away from harm. Raci drifted off on her wine cloud. Looking
down on her on my pillows for the first time in twenty
years, I felt my long-idle affection rouse me above clouds
of aggravation. I reached down and brushed her hair to the
side, lightly stroking the fine forehead I'd always treasured.
Even drunk, Raci was captivating.

Over twenty years before, I had sat at her hospital bed,
looking down on this same face though then battered and
bruised by the accident. Back then I had felt caught between
the urges to attend and care for her–should she live–and a

raging desire to run, to wall myself off from shock, loss, and fear. Newly sober, suddenly a single parent, just then jobless with medical bills soon to mount, and in sole charge of burying our two little ones and comforting our distraught, surviving daughter, I convinced myself that I had nothing to give Raci. The allure of helping fellow drunks that had, just a week before, led me to LA did not extend itself over this crushing event. The people of *Today* could not help me with this. Though it felt like a dream, it was much too real. Raci's accident–Michael and Siiri perished with the impact–could not be cured by the platitudes I heard and repeated at *Today*. It would not be amended by corrective action and camaraderie. It was nothing I had ever dreamed of in my philosophy. So I ran. I abandoned her. At the time it felt like salvation.

I watched Raci's uplifted face, so young-looking even now, I vowed to stay the course. Now I could do something, I told myself. I could be responsible and caring. I had learned some things, had improved my life. I felt ready to make amends, however small and simple, for my long-past failure to care.

As a start, I took Raci's skirt and overcoat to the kitchen. I dabbed the wine spots with a clean sponge and sprayed them from the reverse. I thought the splashes might hide once the garment dried. The coat, a light canvas one from Carapace, cleaned up well with just a light soaping.

I hung both garments from curtain rods to dry in the sun at the window above my blood-money desk. Their ghosts reflected off the dark work surface.

. . . By the time we had finished the second bottle of wine that morning, I was loose enough to answer Tom's incessant questions. "What do you think?" He asked about once a minute. "You get what I mean?"

I had my own stuff to worry about, and Tom's writing, his experience in Nam, and his present psychological condition proved more daunting than trying to dodge the draft. Finally, I had no choice but to tell him.

"Listen, Tom, I know this is your first draft and everything, but . . .," he didn't let me finish.

He grabbed at the papers. I held on, and he yanked so hard the pages tore.

"You don't get it, do you?" He yelled at me. "You had to be there. And where *were* you?" Tom glared at me. "Oh, I know. You were marching down Superior Street holding a Eugene McCarthy banner or a 'stop the killing' sign. Weren't you? Well, weren't you?"

"All I'm saying is that it needs work."

"Yeah, you were sipping wine and smoking dope while I crawled backwards away from those rice-grubbers' booby traps, shitting my pants every time I slipped down a hole, thinking of nothing but snakes and spiders."

I held up my hand. "Tom, why didn't you write that?"

"What?"

"What you just said."

"I did."

"No, you didn't. You wrote about it."

"Go fuck yourself. What the hell you mean?"

"Relax. I'm not the enemy. Take a breath, and I'll tell you."

After a minute he had calmed down some. He turned curious.

"Bring your reader down the hole with you, man. Make him smell the shit. Scare the pants off him. Hell, make him wet himself. 'Boom! He's dead. Splattered on the walls.' That's what you need to do."

"Why didn't you say so?"

We were drunk. Tom was drunker. So I only said, "'Cause I'm an idiot."

He considered my confession, continuing to hold his half of the torn sheets.

"Will you let me write a few lines?" I said. Tom glowered with suspicion. "I'll use pencil." Finally, he gave me a nod.

I wrote on the bottom of the last torn sheet.

> The tunnel stunk. I gagged on the air. But *I* wouldn't be one of those dragged out, freaking, screaming. I swallowed my own puke. I crawled forward, feeling my way inch-by-inch.

> It was how the Cong fought, psychological. Any second, a snake might strike, a trip-wire could blow my legs off.

I don't want to say it was good, but it must have touched a chord in Tom, even drunk. Immediately, he started to bawl. Then he took it all, stuffed everything back in the folder, tied the snapped band, then bound it all a little more carefully with the other blue binder. He wiped his eyes with his sleeve, then stood, and without a word fled the kitchen for the second time that day.

Again, I followed him and watched from the doorway as he shoved his things, even the one sock dripping toilet water, into his duffel. He zipped the bag and shouldered the load.

"I guess you're leaving."

"Yeah. Your wife doesn't want me around anyway."

"No, you're wrong about that."

"Listen, Moe, thanks for your hospitality and

time." He was sounding his old sociable self again. "But my dad is waiting for me. I've been traveling a week." He'd sold his plane ticket and hitchhiked and boozed all the way from DC.

He pushed past me and clumped down the stairs and out the door.

So, there I was, drunk on wine, alone, an editorial and friendship failure. That night at dinner I swore to Sharon I'd never try to help a drunkard again.

She just screwed one side of her mouth up, speared her chicken with a fork, and drawing her knife slowly across, sliced a piece off, all the while looking at me.

I improved Tom's story. Over the years, usually in the kitchen, in apartments in three different towns, we worked on it. Sporadically, Tom followed my moves in Minnesota and in fits and starts put his story down on paper. Bit by bit, I made it understandable, all the time keeping it raw.

While Raci slept, I stood now over the desk Tom's work had bought for me and, hands in my pockets, shrugged an apology to my old friend. "I wish you were here, Tom." I felt the key and drew it forth, looking at it like something just found. Why not? I was in a revising mood now and couldn't really go out or make much noise. I unlocked the drawer and brought out *Twelve: lives with(out) drink.*

I re-read the section describing my first revisions on *Rats* and looked forward in the narrative to *Today* and the people there. I knew it needed something, or needed to lose something. My editor was urging me to "kill my darlings."

"You want to gut the story," I'd argued. "Who is William Faulkner to brag about out-takes?"

"Els, I'm not trying to cut your juicy passages. I simply want to spare your readers."

"I feel you want to push my characters to the curb."

I was winning through my whining.

"Take another look, Els. Take a reader's-eye view. Then we'll talk."

She had been after Hillside-Glenn and even Muckey D! I might be able to sacrifice something, but I couldn't throw those two under the editorial bus.

Lifting the manuscript from the drawer, though, I thought that perhaps I could beat my editor to the punch.

. . . *Today* gave us some stability. Five days a week, you could count on starting your day solidly. Could tell where you would start. After a couple of days off, you were glad to see *Today*'s faces, and the others were glad to see you. The weekends had to take care of themselves.

Saturdays and Sundays didn't give me much trouble since I was already back living with DeLorr and three kids. So that was the time we spent together, just like a normal family seemed to do, getting ready for the week coming up.

Right off there wasn't much enjoying each other at home. There was too much tiptoeing around dear old dad and his nerves to be much fun. So waiting for the good times to come was more of what we did those two days a week, that and trying to stay out of wrangles and the breaking of furniture.

Monday through Friday, we were "training" for real life to come. The weekends off away from the meeting spelled a special feeling of loss. Saturday felt hollow, not going to work, not seeing my boozer friends, seemed like teetering on the cusp of graduating some school or program, knowing your mates would be moving on without you.

Weekends—while being rest and relaxation for ordinary people—were a time for alcoholics to ruminate on what had improved over the last five days. To do the "mental" work. Having that time was, for the "normal," an important restorative. For the *Today* crowd, though, surrounded by family, the weekend was a strain, something to live through, empty, scary, and lonely without alky-pals. Then to the relief of the drunk and the family, the Monday sun would show its blessed face.

Besides Toady and Burt there were regulars who anchored our bottoms in the chairs and smoothed the feathers that had been ruffled over the weekend or that had been bent out of shape near-permanently in the darkness that preceded each of our entries through Burt's door. Most did nothing but show up, and that was enough. It was, usually, plenty for each just to keep coming, and it was ample for those who stayed and hoped the others would, too. After a while you could almost depend on the meeting, like something—besides trouble—that stayed the same.

In fact, the group who knotted up before Burt came rambling in, eyeing the assembly for whatever person he thought might do some talking that day, were the regulars: Len, Susan, Hillside-Glenn, and Muckey D, to name some I knew best early on. There were others than these, each lending a wisp of flavor to the stew we were brewing every weekday, an aroma to lighten you up and carry you on. When someone disappeared, it seemed that his scent lingered a while until it was pretty certain that he wasn't coming back very soon, or ever, but by that time a new spice released with the next boozer in the door and added to the steamy soup we cooked up. It was a hit or miss process, and sometimes in the recesses of memory you missed a bit of black pepper or a leaf of oregano but discovered the bite of cayenne or pungency of basil. It didn't mean you didn't want the oregano back, but you were going to slurp that broth just the same.

Still, regularly having the basic ingredients was a comfort. You'd wonder on Monday, look expectantly on Tuesday, hope and pray on Wednesday, but if the person you missed didn't show up by then, you just turned to those who were still there. Something you dared not wonder was what you yourself were adding, or if you'd be the next one to jump out of the stew pot and drain off somewhere dark and unpleasant. That never occurred to me, or maybe I wouldn't let myself think it.

None of us remember Burt asking Susan to take the guest chair or Len either, even when more than a year had passed by, and neither of them did much beside anchor things by sitting down. Like the table would float away unless Len laid his hand on it or without Susan's coffee cup to weight it down. But that they did for a long while: just sat, being there. And there shouldn't be the impression that those two were a couple. They weren't. Mostly none of us were, with the notable and temporary exception of Maggie and Burt, but that came later. And Toady had a woman, a wife I actually met, but, of course, she wasn't going to come to *Today*. Not in a million suns.

Len had been a sailor all of his life. Fifty years before, he'd shipped out of Glasgow and had never gone back. I'd met him my first time, sliding ashtrays down the picture-of-mahogany tables.

Ashtrays might have been all he could handle. And that wasn't unusual, especially, you'd think, for a guy who appeared only in profile. Maybe straight on he disappeared. His face was that narrow behind his huge hatchet of a nose. He was pink. Whitish-gray hair flowed like wide rivulets, held solidly in place with Lucky Tiger or some other hair oil, atop a short forehead, over white eyebrows, always seen in profile, so bushy you couldn't help staring at them—one at a time—burgeoning like silver junipers growing on an ocean cliff. His grin—seen only from the side—a marvelous, agreeable but sharkish beam, spread from his bare upper lip, cracking open toward a giant, flat ear like it would join the lobe at the back edge of his jaw. He smiled like he was tickled by a memory he couldn't contain any longer. It broke forth like an argent dawn running beneath Highland clouds. It must have been his years at sea that had sculpted the contour of his face. I see him now, looking just as short seated as standing when, always only one jacketed arm visible as if showing two would give him too much dimension, one hand patiently resting on the table past its coat cuff doing exactly nothing, firmly at ease. Len's voice rang clearly as a mountain lake, sure with a reluctant echo. He formed each syllable like a note waiting for a trill. None of us remembered what he said. None could forget how it sounded. Just keep coming, Len.

Susan did. And then she didn't. She was two years old with us when she disappeared. She and Len were like bookends, sitting across that empty space, a no-mans-land nine feet on a side into which I'd never seen anyone go, enclosed by the

surrounding square made by eight tables. Like
Len, Susan was seen from only one side, front-
on. From the side she disappeared into something
like a cotton-tassle mop someone had set up in
a corner to dry. She wore her hair long and
stringy, parted down the middle, and it hung to
her skinny shoulders all around, letting only her
lean face poke through at the front. I usually sat
on the same side as Len to look directly across
where Susan plunked down each morning. They were
opposite all right. I don't think Susan smiled at
all, but she showed teeth, long ones, straight
sided from gum to bite, each an isolated, narrow
rectangle, marching in file across her mouth,
keeping a gap between each of them. All were
aligned and straight, and most were discolored.

Every day, Susan wore a hooded sweatshirt that
hung off her bony shoulders down to her stick-
like thighs and at the sleeve, cuffs draped over
her skeletal hands. She walked in, straight and
narrow in her jeans and tennis shoes, got her
coffee, and went to her chair directly across
from Len. When Susan spoke, she sounded tired
and philosophical like she suffered a lot, mostly
alone. Her voice, though, was gentle, slight, and
kind-sounding, and she wasn't one to claim to
know a darn thing, even though she obviously did a
bunch of thinking all the time and philosophized
in a spiritual sort of way.

Most of these folk I knew only one hour a
day, Monday through Friday. Even if they stood,
waiting outside in the knot, not much important
was revealed and little to nothing intimate was
shared there. Inside, you didn't ask questions,
not during the meeting. For example, like us all,
Len was who he said he was. Susan revealed all
she wanted you to know, which equaled all you

needed to know. Have your opinions, draw your conclusions, even make judgments, but keep them to yourself.

One other member I recall being there the day both Burt and Toady were absent was Hillside-Glenn. He didn't go by that name originally—just Glenn—but since there had been two of the same name when he first arrived, whenever anyone mentioned him they added "hillside" since he lived in the Oakland Hills east of downtown. The other Glenn lived on the flats. When flat-land Glenn disappeared, we still used Hillside-Glenn to refer to the Glenn who stayed.

Hillside-Glenn was big and was contoured like those Russian nesting dolls, thick round head, no neck, barrel-chest, taut but rotund middle, wide hips, heavy thighs and short legs. He might have been six-four and looked like he'd grown too far, poking up through his hair making a wide, bald dome, or like the heft of his body had pulled everything down revealing the bare round-top.

I wouldn't say anything if he hadn't invited me to his house in the hills, but since he did, I can tell that his favorite thing right then, other than passing out pamphlets to newcomers, I guess, was sitting in his redwood hot tub listening to the birds nesting around his house. It was his way of soothing those famous nerves everyone at *Today* was always talking about. I hadn't known him well right away but started to chum with him after Burt saved him.

It happened fast, came out of nowhere as far as I was concerned. You don't forget sudden heroic acts, at least I haven't, and maybe that's because you feel so helpless, perhaps stupid or mean, but I remember this one like it was yesterday because of how impressively Burt acted.

NOON

Glenn always sat in the last chair by the window, right beside the little literature table. That was his responsible job: to fill the table before the meeting, arrange the pamphlets there, and put them away after the final words. It doesn't sound like much for a grown man to handle, of course, but some of us were not so lucky as Glenn and couldn't fulfill even one simple request to save our own lives. For Glenn, the literature table was something to hold on to when just listening to his heartbeat throughout the day was difficult. When simply existing got tough.

The morning Glenn went down there might have been twenty of us attending, and someone was reading at the time. I had my eyes on Burt who, as usual when others spoke, was listening, grinning hugely, and nodding encouragement. The penetrating blast of a moan wailed out behind me. Burt focused. He stopped nodding, sprang up, and strode around the corner of the table. No one else moved. The reader stopped. I looked behind me to Glenn, who had suddenly become an air-raid siren, blaring a warning, mouth wide open and foamy, body shaking all up and down its six-foot-four length. He was still in the chair but couldn't be for long for all the jerking and warping that was wracking his frame. The metal folding chairs bounced around fiercely beside Glenn and literature flew off the table all over the place.

Burt is tall but slight. I don't know how he did this: He was there, right in front of Hillside-Glenn in just two strides, and looking fierce as I'd ever seen anyone appear. He lanced out both arms, grabbing that huge earthquake of a man by the collar, lifted him like a sack of wrangling cats, and laid him down softly right on the floor.

"Clear this area." Then Burt rolled the big

man on to his side, Hillside-Glenn still shaking like mad. "Toady, bring me a wooden spoon from the coffee counter."

Burt delicately slid the spoon into Glenn's wide open mouth and flipped the big man's tongue, pressing it in place. He held his patient's head up and stroked it softly. It was over as fast as it started. Glenn quieted. He became at least a version of himself again. Burt tidied his patient up with his own handkerchief and talked to him in a calm voice. "Has this happened before?" It had. "Do you want medical assistance?" He didn't. "There's a cot in the office, you should lie quiet for a bit." Toady and Burt helped Glenn into the office, which was open by this time, and a couple of minutes later Burt came back alone.

While he was gone, we sat there in silence. Len picked up the pamphlets that had spilled all over the floor and straightened the chairs. When Burt came back, he sat down at the head of the table, nodded his raised eyebrows and smiled at the reader, "You were saying . . . ?" And the meeting resumed.

I felt relieved. Burt knew what to do to rescue a man from seizure. No one was hurt, and we were going to have our meeting, something that was important to us all. It seemed that if Burt could get us through Hillside-Glenn's scary event, he could bring us through the day, maybe the week, and perhaps our whole lives without more pain and destruction.

I suppose Burt's action was why I jumped in and took on his role when neither Burt nor Toady showed up one Friday a couple of weeks later. By then I'd realized how important it was to everyone else that the meeting be held, that unusual circumstances not block the path we were walking. For people in our condition, anything might set one off. No one was going to say, "Well, the room was locked, so I just went to the corner store for a half pint of Wild Turkey," because that's just excuse-making on someone else, but any of us just might do it. So, it's best not to provide an opportunity for mayhem if it can be avoided.

The day I took the lead, I hadn't questioned why the doors were open with no leader inside. People were just filing in when I arrived. Probably Burt and Toady had come in early to unlock, but there was no coffee brewing or literature out on Hillside-Glenn's little table. The group locker had its padlock firmly in place. The laminated copy of the opening reading was always left taped to the head table. Good.

The bunch of us who came up the stairs were waiting for something to happen, for someone to get things started, for Burt. We needed Burt, and if not him, we'd settle for Toady. But neither showed his face. Every time the door opened downstairs and one or two people tramped up that steep, narrow staircase, each one of us held his breath. It was three minutes to eight but it wasn't Burt. A few more came in. And pretty soon, with a minute to go, it was looking like a shutout, a bust, a no-meeting morning and I, for one, was feeling very nervous with the weekend coming up when I would be sequestered in the bosom of my loving family, something I needed a Friday antidote to survive.

The office wouldn't be staffed until 8:15, but this meeting was to start at eight. With that minute to go, Len started to shuffle his feet, and Susan looked like she couldn't move without her coffee. She sat still but kind of quivered, ready, I thought, to shriek. Hillside-Glenn just slumped in his chair, forearms on thighs, with his big hairy hands clasped between his knees. Maybe he was praying. He might have been despairing. I couldn't stand it.

I spilled over my edge of reticence. I sprang up, then walked as calmly as I could to the head table as if I had it planned all along. As if I had permission, had been chosen to lead this otherwise abandoned meeting. I sat down there. Len laid his hand on the table again and relaxed. Susan sighed, and H-Glenn straightened up and took notice. I read the plastic-coated card: "Good morning. This is the *Today* group of . . ." and off we went. And when I got to the volunteer reader's part, I nodded to Susan. I was seeing her in profile being off to one side of her. She looked grateful to do the reading, sitting straight up and attentive. She jumped on it, put on her horn-rimmed glasses, squinted past her stringy hair, and slowly read the twelve steps from the big posters on the wall.

About the time she got to the fourth step, in came Toady and Burt. Toady was picking his teeth and rubbing his belly like they had just been to breakfast, which they had, and he and Burt, looking like he hadn't eaten a thing, stood at the back of the room just inside the doorway. First, they looked at each other, then looked back at me, then at each other again, Burt nodding all the time like he was approving my application for a job or something. He crossed his arms over the long scarf that wrapped his heavily-veined neck and draped down over his corduroy blazer, smiling and almost bowing, up and down, all the while Susan read. Just before I resumed my part, ignoring me like I was in charge, Burt went to the coffee counter to get things cooking while Toady rustled around in the cabinet for Folgers, the literature, collection-baskets, and the old pink can. I heard Susan sigh again, continuing to read as the coffee began to trickle down.

From that time on, with no further vetting or discussion, I chaired the Friday meeting each week. Burt crossed his arms at the end when I came up to him, waggled his head, smiled, and said in his best gravelly voice, "You sure look good up there. My grandmother would be proud." I'd taken a leap forward in sobriety, though it felt at the time that I had tossed a life-saving buoy into the water then dived in to save myself. And, because that's the way things happened—they always evolved without change—no one said "boo." And by the following Wednesday, none of us could say who it was that used to be Mr. Friday. Like Burt always said, "We live in the now."

That was Burt's way of saying, "Don't let it go to your head." Running the meeting was an honor. They'd said, somewhere, that you had to be sober a year before getting the job. I wasn't near that threshold, but since it was an accident rather than a choice, my head didn't swell. One thing I did notice, though, was that the room looked different from the head table. Len was still in profile, now Susan, too, but my new responsibility changed the view.

I began to notice people more since I was facing everyone. Before, they were a voice behind me or the back of a talking head. Now, out front, they showed their faces. We called on volunteers, so the chair had to pick who went next, not that anyone would complain if they weren't called on. It was good to mix it up, so everyone got a chance. That was where the sign-in list, voluntary, of course, became important—a list Jude later used to defrock our minister/leader Burt. The list organized things for the chairperson, and for me it kept track of how we were doing. Twelve in attendance was all right, twenty good, and thirty-five outstanding, not that judging by numbers helped soothe the nerves. Usually, it was twenty or more. Of course, I knew they didn't come for me or for my guest speaker if I had one, but the greater the number the more robust the chatter. I always felt better seeing twenty or more faces out there in the crowd, and Friday helped that. "Prepare for the weekend" could have been Friday's motto, and that was what they all were doing.

One day a week sitting in front brought individuals more to my notice. Clarence, for instance, came to my attention: tall, light skinned, with vacant green eyes. He knew the lingo. He spoke the words. He drank a lot of coffee with six lumps of sugar per cup and ate a goodly number of cookies if we had any. He never put a dime in the basket. Even though he spoke up, none of us could understand what he was saying. It was as if the correct words were strung together in the wrong order or as if ideas were missing from the sentence he'd just uttered. He looked good most of the time, ate well all of the time, and never made literal sense.

Of course, everything is a lesson to you when you're trying to save your own life and get straightened out, and there was a precept or two to be learned from watching Clarence. Without digging too far down in the dictionary "forbearance," "charity," and "tolerance" come to mind. I know, it sounds a bit biblical.

Old Clarence didn't give anything; he didn't

have anything. He sucked up the goods for that very reason. His jabber was the very best he could do, and he let it fly as if he spoke it thoughtfully, commensurate with his acumen, and sincerely in harmony with his heart.

Who was I to judge?

When Clarence raised his hand, especially if no one else was doing so, I called on him and kept listening even though I couldn't get the gist of his story. Come regular and just listen (that's what Burt said). Clarence wasn't going to change, no matter what came at him or who was tossing it. I wouldn't alter him an iota, and he was so regular that his attendance gave us all lots of practice forbearing, chariting, and tolerating. That's how love worms its way into a heart. Like the old Chet Powers song says, "Smile on your brother . . ."

I always thought "try" was the best word in that chorus. I guess that's what Clarence would have said if he were a poet.

Another regular, an old guy, who had lived hard a long time, was maybe 65 but shrunk down so he looked much older, came, not every day but when he had a mind to, and whose name I never really heard through his garble, propped himself up against the coffee bar in back and would raise his hand first every day he was there. It didn't matter that he wouldn't write himself on the list. Well, you had to call on him, but all he'd do is report the number of days it had been since his last drink. It would be something like 11,482. That was it. That's all he'd say, but it made everyone think: first we had to do the calculation to get the years, then we had to admit this path we were on, if we followed it properly, might succeed at least in making us old. Anyway, each raises his voice after his own manner.

And that's the way it was, what you called, twenty years before, a mixed bag of accents, viewpoints, fashions (from leather to lace to leotards), sexes, and stories. Stories, accounts, myths, chronicles, fabrications, tales, reports, fables, yarns, white lies, big lies, and damn lies, I suppose though not too many, and epics. Everyone had them, and little by little, usually not all at once, you'd learn them. Those stories, told within the four walls of *Today*, you won't hear, not from me, unless you were there in person and had already listened. But once on the sidewalk, outside, under the awnings, when people did talk, what they said was maybe a little less honest, trussed up a bit, but sounded no less colorful. All that is tell-able, especially now when so many are dead or gone.

It was outside that I learned Muckey's story, something he never mentioned inside *Today*. Stories from there, you can tell. Muckey D's was one I knew well.

While working on the manuscript, I heard Raci rise and totter into the bathroom. Perhaps her renewed presence led me to cut old Clarence out of the story. He was more outlier than Tom had been in life, and though I was fond of Clarence and his character, too, I knew he would be cut in the end.

Raci had started the shower. I read over what I had done. It would be clear to my editor that I was at least attempting to keep the story clean. As self-indulgent as the whole thing seemed to me, I didn't believe my readers would know. In the readers' hands it would be fiction.

Perhaps Raci could judge. Immediately I closeted that

thought. But revisiting the story with someone like Raci in the house called to me. I couldn't keep a lid on the idea. If I could show her Muckey's story, the very next section, she might feel better. She had known him as Dwayne, and the tale did not really involve her, at least in the fictional version.

Steam flowed out the opened bathroom door. "Can I use your robe, Els?" Raci curled out from the doorway, smiling, her hair cascaded wavy and wet over a bare shoulder.

"It'll be big on you, but go ahead." She sounded clear-headed. I thrilled at her homey appearance.

She emerged in the bathrobe, tousling her hair with a towel. Raci came to the desk and settled in the leather side chair. She smiled. "You were right. I feel better." She said nothing about the pages open on the desk, nor did she renew her apologia.

"Could you eat something?"

"Something light would be good, but don't go to a lot of trouble, Els."

I turned the page on Clarence and looked, perhaps sheepishly, directly at her. I had to smile. As bad as our times had been, and as many years as we'd been apart, I loved her yet. Not deeply, perhaps, but in a solidly affectionate way. We'd had children and good times together.

"Good to see you smile, Els." She stroked my cheek.

"Thanks. Now, while I rustle up some nourishment, look at this story."

"In *Twelve*? Really?"

"Yes. I'm curious to know what you think." I did want to know, but this was also my olive branch to Raci, telling her my tender feelings for her had overcome my annoyance with her. Our marriage had always been that way.

She looked at the heading. "The story of Muckey D." She came close to a wink. "Fiction, of course."

"Well, the best of everything comes from life, then, doesn't it?" I went to the kitchen. I called down the hall, "Some whole wheat toast and scrambled eggs too much?" She was already reading but nodded.

. . . Muckey D hailed from a small town up in a Montana mining area near Butte. The mines were starting to play out in the late '50s, so there were a lot of men hanging on the streets with not much to keep them busy. His dad was one of them but was more enterprising than most, starting up Mr. D's Fresh Fruit store with his brother from California.

Muckey's mother died before he was sixteen and wasn't around to stop Dad from selling her folks' house in Garrison where Muckey had been raised. Muckey may as well have been in the grave himself for all Dad listened to him.

They took an apartment in Butte above the storefront of Mr. D's Fresh Fruit. When the business got going good, Muckey's dad and uncle took turns driving the old California Trail and State Route 15 to get the best crops crisp and clean up to Montana. Later, Dad left Muckey, then seventeen, in charge of the store, going off to pick cherries, peaches, or apricots. The brothers drove out to the orchards, picked like mad with men they'd hire, and hauled two huge loads back to sell. They'd choose 'only the best.' That was their motto. When Mr. D came back, he'd take over the restocked stand, leaving Muckey nothing much to do.

"I had a driver's license. The old *muckamuck* didn't trust me with the goddamn fruit truck, though. I was more like him than he knew. I could see opportunity. I was unloading trucks for him almost for free anyway, so I kept my eyes peeled for other work. Went looking for truckers to help, gotten paid or not. Didn't matter. Lots of times I worked for chicken feed, but that's how I got in at the goddamn Roxy and into Roxie, too."

Muckey told this story many times, and it was always exactly the same the whole way through as if he'd written it down and memorized it, Montanaese, cursing, bad grammar and all.

One time Muckey said, "They'd call me 'The Homer of Helena,' whoever that guy was."

Perhaps that was why he wouldn't let you interrupt him for anything, as if a pause would throw him off the track he'd laid. When he got to this point, when he mentioned the Roxy and Roxie, he'd more than pause. He'd stop dead every time. He would look off into the distance (even if you were in, say, a booth at a coffee house where there was no far horizon) kind of mournful—and no one could look sadder than Muckey D—and just before you were about to ask, he'd say, "One was a goddamn movie theater, the other my girl.

"Both were beautiful. Roxie was dark, darker than Burt here (he'd say that if Burt were around). Italian-dark. Huge glistening eyes (he'd peel his eyes as wide as he could at this point)that you could've swam in them if she'd let you. Brown eyes to send you to goddamn heaven. Dark-brown hair. Sweet-smelling that sniffing it was like pushing your nose into a full night of rose beds and snuffling in deep. Goddamn, I loved her hair. Hubbahubba. And soft. Everything about her was so soft. (Muckey rubbed and hugged himself here and always let go a long sigh that made you want to shake him to stop.) Soft cheeks. Soft little hands. Ultra-soft breasts. Even her feet were like little pillowy things." (He sighed again. "Give it up, Muckey," you'd want to say.)

Of course, he told us this long before any of us met the real Roxie. Once she did show up, though, she fulfilled the promise of Muckey D's words in more ways than appearance.

"I met the Roxy first. Out back in the alley. I'd been to the movies, sure, but this is where I started working the Roxy. Down the alley from the theater, I was lounging on my bed reading Mad Magazine. A truck rumbled by. Then another tractor-trailer pulled past my bedroom window at the back of our apartment above old Mr. D's Fresh Fruit. When the second passed, I was up. Down the stairs. Out the back door. I nearly got whacked by the goddamned third rig. All three semis stopped near the end of the block lined up at the back door of the Roxy.

"Well, I got a job unloading that morning. I got another installing, starting that afternoon. I got a third helping out in the theater as permanent as I wanted it to be. That next week, I was working nights at the theater and days, part-time and low pay, at D's.

"I guess the owner of the theater, Mr. Fredrickson, didn't know the loads were coming right then. He coulda' been ready with a crew. Well, he did have a son, Jep. Like old Mr. D that gave him a built-in crew. I filled that crew out to a T.

"Truck drivers brought anything they hauled to the tailgate. No goddamn further. I was glad of that. I was happy Mr. F wasn't prepared. What was in those trucks?"

Here, if he were standing, Muckey D would put his hands on his hips and tilt his head to one side, or if he were sitting, he'd spread his arms up in a "V" and tilt the head. I always wanted, after the first few tellings, to yell out "four hundred forty-six plush seats," but Muckey was a friend in sobriety. It was his story. After what seemed like a full minute's pause, he'd say, "Four-hundred and forty-six plush seats," though one time he said, "Six-hundred plush seats," which sounded too approximate to believe.

"And who brought every goddamn one down off the tailgate and lined them up in the alley? (He repeated his "V" or hip routine at this point.) Yeah, yours truly, Muckey.

"And all this time I was working just to be doing something. Mr. F, dressed in suit and tie like he was going to a big hiyu, leaned by the back doors of the theater watching. Smoking his eternal chain of cigarettes. He followed every move I made. He must have smoked a goddamn pack of Lucky Strikes, keeping his eye on me. Every cigarette he'd smoke he butted out in the sand of a standing ashtray just inside the open door. A minute later he flipped out a new one from the pack. He snapped open his Zippo lighter and flame it up. Goddamn, that man smoked.

"I don't know if he was waiting for me to break something or wondering if I'd slow down or quit halfway through. He never lifted a finger or gave me a hand. I just kept moving, sliding each seat nice and easy off the tailgate and nestle it careful like a sleeping baby beside the one I'd just set down. I had them all in rows with no aisle between along the backside of the building.

"I might be sore and could be poor the next morning, but I wasn't about to slow down or stop. Not with him watching. I worked for three hours unloading those trucks. Labored at a clip of two and a third seats a minute. So, I was done. All the trucks had pulled out. Old man Fredrickson said, 'Let me show you something, kid.'

"He brought me inside and turned on the lights. I'd never seen a theater fully lit. And what did he show me? ("Four hundred forty-six busted and worn-out seats," I wanted to scream. But I liked Muckey and waited him out.) "Four hundred, forty-six busted and worn-out seats: kicked, ripped, burnt, and beaten to sagging. In the dark you might not have noticed. But if you sat in one that tilted forward it'd spill you out on the goddamn floor.

"So Mr. F says, 'Can you handle a wrench, kid?'

"'Of course, I can. You got the wrench, I can work it.' Instead of a wrench which he'd never used in half-a-million years, he hands me three crisp ten dollar bills. 'Seven more like these if the new seats are in by the matinée tomorrow. That gives you a full day.'

"Hubbahubba, I got paid ten dollars an hour that morning. More than I earned in a week slaving for Mr. D. I knew I could earn the rest of the hundred if I worked hard. A *motengator* of a wad.

"Fredrickson assigned Jep to help me. He got the same pay as I got from my dad: somepin' you could stick in your ear. He was a year and a half younger'n me, but strong and smart. We ripped out the old seats in a pretty big hurry. Used a black pipe slipped over the end of the wrench. With a ton of torque and a few drops of penetrating oil. I'd gave a smart tap with a ball-peen hammer. Then the nuts come loose fairly easy. Too much force, you'd snap off the bolt. Then you'd have to drill the goddamn thing out. And how many of the one thousand seven hundred eighty-four bolts did we break off?" (Muckey says this with his hands on his hips.) "Three!" He holds up his thumb and two fingers.

"We didn't finish by matinée the next day. Had to knock off while all the kids and mothers came in to watch their cartoons. But before the seven o'clock show that night every seat in the house were fixed in place. That included the hundred fifty-six in the balcony. I've never been so bushed in my life. Leave the necking and groping upstairs for someone else. I went to bed.

"Fredrickson was true to his word and more. He forked over the seven tens and an extra twenty dollar bill. 'Get some sleep, Kid, clean up, and I mean squeaky clean, and be here before tomorrow's matinée.' With the money he was doling out, I didn't ask questions.

"He put me to work chucking the trash and sweeping up popcorn duff. Emptying ash trays was a big job in itself. He kept fillin' them himself. During the movie, I was up keeping the projectionist awake. And once he got to trust me, I spelled his kids at the candy counter. The pay wasn't that much better'n the fruit stand, but, hey, money was money back then. Finally, the big payoff arrived: Roxie came to her first movie there, and I was in love.

"Roxie Rodelli came from Drummond up the road only a few miles. I'd never seen her before. She came in with a blonde girlfriend I didn't even look at once. They come to see the most popular movie we'd had for a while: *Cat on a Hot Tin Roof*, with Paul Newman and Liz Taylor, hubbahubba. The Drummond girls were late and most of the seats were taken, so I had to help.

"You know how people are. They always leave a seat between them and the next group. Well, I had to get two bunches to squeeze toward the center of the row about midway down. I freed up two seats on the aisle where I could keep an eye on the most beautiful girl in the world. Later, Jep filched a bit of popcorn for me, and I brought the bag to Roxie. Knelt down in the aisle next to her, 'You left this at the counter, beautiful.' Roxie didn't question me, just said 'thank you' and smiled. 'See you on the way out, Buster.' I knew I was in.

"After the show, I met Roxie and her friend in the lobby. I still had to sweep and close up, so I said, 'Meet me at Jim's Diner across the street, and I'll buy you each a burger and fries.' They were going there anyway. 'Just tell Hank it's on me—Muckey.'

"Roxie was looking a whole lot better to me than Liz Taylor. I learned Roxie had an edge to her, something like Liz's character, Maggie, in the film. She was a bit hard and real devilish. I didn't mind that. At first.

"Don't we always make our own trouble? I sure did that night. Rolling all the way up to Drummond with these two babes, Roxie was right by my side on the Chevy's bench seat. Her blonde friend snoozed, riding shotgun.

"I got to bragging about the car that I'd bought with the hundred Mr. F paid me. I told Roxie about all the money I was making working two jobs. Then I yakked about how my dad ran loads up here from California.

"'I'd like to get to California,' Roxie said. She was real interested in getting out of Dodge. 'Drummond's a one-horse, dead-end town,' she said. 'And I'm not sticking around to raise somebody's babies on slag heaps and mining sloughs. California is more my style. Maybe Hollywood.'

"I told her they'd love her there. Big mouth! I wished I had kept my trap shut. You know how we are. Big shots. *Muckamucks*."

Muckey D never laid the blame on anyone
but himself. That was what he preached if he
sermonized on anything. That's one of the things
I liked about him: every rotten thing he'd done,
every bad turn his life took, each bar fight he'd
won or lost were all on him. No one else was at
fault. Though he censured no one, he knew very
well and would tell you plain out, too, the exact
point at which he'd taken a wrong turn in his
life. And his abiding love for Roxie Rodelli was
the condition that started him on his drunken,
downward path that finally landed him right where
I met him on the corner of 29th and Telegraph.
Probably every one of us knew about Roxie, but
strangely, because he yet revered her memory and
was notwithstanding in love with her, he never
talked about her upstairs, never in the meetings.
He'd only tell the story privately to two or
three people at a time. He'd told it plenty,
since everyone knew it by heart.

"Yeah, I was *the muckamuck* around Roxie. I told
her I'd show her California on one of the truck
runs. Told her I'd bring her there for good as
soon as I'd piled up enough coin to get a start.
What a loudmouth. If it seemed uncool to Roxie,
she kept it quiet. She just let me rave on. That
first night she was stroking my leg while I drove.
I had to say something to keep my mind off that.
Course I meant every word of it. I was serious
about this girl. And I figured she was serious
about me.

"About a month later, my dad laid it out to me.
'Listen Marty,' he used the name Mom had given me
so I knew he was serious. 'Two things: if you're
going to have Roxie here all the time, one, pay a
little rent, and two, stop making so much goddamn
sack-racket all night long. I need my sleep even

if you don't.' I thought I'd been pretty careful, sneaking her upstairs after the late show. But Dad was wise all along. Wiser than I knew.

"I was already working two goddamn jobs. Now I took on a third at Jim's, cleaning up at the end of the night. After the last show let out, I'd finish at the Roxy and sweep up Jim's after one o'clock. I wanted to save up as much as I could for our trip to Hollywood. I knew it would be spendy. Roxie and I had settled down a bit. I was working like a maniac and didn't have much time to snuggle with her. But I thought we were still as tight a couple as always. She worked some for Mr. D and then told me she had a part-time job somewhere across town in the evenings.

"We saw each other mostly in the wee hours, and I was so worn out from working, I neglected her. 'A couple more months of this and I'll have what we need, babe. We'll load up the Chevy and head south before the snow starts to fall.' If I had looked close at her right then, I might have known. But, no, I was so full of my own shit that I didn't even look. Funny I didn't bust my britches bragging all the time.

"On toward September that year, we were up at his house when Mr. F dangled his car keys over my hand and said, 'Take Jep here up to his catechism, would you? And stop by the theater to pick up the cash box. Bring both back when you're done.' Well, he didn't let just anybody drive that car. It was a favor to him, sure. It was an honor to me.

"We were halfway to the church when Jep said, 'Can I drive? Got my permit last week.' We were pretty good friends by then, so okay. He pulled out from the curb and headed for the highway. 'Hey, what about the church?' 'Fuck the church,' Jep said, and on we went. I understood. We joyrided for a while. 'Let's pick up the box so we don't forget, and I'll stop by my place for more smokes.' We were practicing smokestacks, just like his dad.

"Mr. D's was closed when we passed. 'That's weird,' I said. 'Pull around back. We'll stop here first.' When I got back downstairs without the smokes, Jep must have thought I'd seen a ghost or a murder. 'You all right, Muckey?' I spewed my guts right on the front fender. 'Let's get out of here,' was all I said. He roared down the alley. We forgot to get the cash box.

"'What happened?' Jep asked, and in about a minute when I felt my stomach settle some, I told him. 'I went up to my goddamn room for the smokes. Heard someone wrestling down the hall. I stood by the door to Dad's bedroom listening to lots of heavy breathing and grunting. Of course, I peeked in the open door. I wish I hadn't. There was Roxie, my Roxie on top of my goddamn, cutthroat father. Both naked as jaybirds, balling up a storm so much that they didn't even notice me. Jesus, my father's fucking my girlfriend. Stop the car.' This time I missed the fender."

Then Muckey would laugh though he looked quite sad, a little bit sick. I don't know if Muckey was torturing himself by telling about Roxie or if it helped him ease the shock and pain. One thing for sure was that it was his turning point.

"We took the car back to Mr. F, and I pleaded sick. Of course, it wasn't too long before he'd hear all about it, but I took off for two nights. I just drove around. I even slept in the Chevy. On the third night, I'd worked the Roxy and Jim's, too, and got up my courage to face the music over at the fruit stand.

"The apartment was empty. All the furniture was gone, including mine. They were nice enough to dump my clothes out in the middle of the floor of my room. Roxie hadn't forgotten my California-bundle. All the goddamn cash I had saved up was gone. Below, in the store, they'd packed and taken everything: fruit, cash register, scales, and signs. Both trucks were gone. I knew where they were headed. It would have been no good to chase them even if I'd had the gas money. I rolled and tossed around that night on the heap of my clothes in the middle of my empty room. In the morning I moved into a closet at the theater where old Mr. F said I could keep my crap. My boss let me sack out on a cot there for the next two months."

That was Muckey D's saga, or at least his version of the turning point of his life. He took the story from there up at *Today*, leaving out all the stuff about his dad and Roxie and everything, telling his "official" *Today* version. It wasn't embarrassment or his need to keep it private—every *Today* regular knew the story anyway. What it was, you see, Muckey D had an obsession about the girl, and an *idée fixe* of any kind, we all knew, was bad medicine for the nerves, and jangled nerves were poison pills for boozers, for oneself and for others. Maybe Muckey was wrong to keep the long version out of meetings—you are supposed to tell the truth, after all—but most of us understood that he didn't want to infect unsuspecting newcomers with his mania, at least as long as it still played havoc on his heart. Given that, Muckey was a good man.

Afternoon

The potential you'll be, that you'll never see
The promises you'll only make

Elliott Smith, from "Between the Bars"

Raci was still bent over the manuscript. "Salt and pepper on the eggs?"

She jerked her head up, startled. "Oh. Already?" She pushed the script away and ran her fingers through her hair. "I better style this mop first. Can you hold on a minute?"

She drew the robe around her, moving toward the bathroom.

I stopped her. "No hurry. Take the skirt; it's not perfect but ready. Hair dryer's under the sink." I broke the eggs into a bowl and moved the pan off the heat. "Five minutes." Though I was enjoying the ancient familiarity of having Raci with me, I wanted her out of my robe and clothed.

While Raci dressed, I set plates at the counter and poured her a small glass of tomato juice, then went to the desk.

I took a peek at her place in *Twelve*. In the margin she had check-marked "Muckey D never laid the blame on anyone but himself. That was what he preached," and had lain the pencil on the facing page.

The hair drier stopped screeching. I tiptoed back to the stove. "Should I brew some coffee?"

Her answer floated down the hall, "Oh, that would be nice."


```
    . . . Brew, v–tr: 1. to make ale or beer
from hops and malt by infusion, 2. boiling any
beverage, such as coffee or tea.
    We never thought much about any but these first
two since, next to distilling, brewing was the
nearest to our hearts. Calms the nerves. There
is, though, another definition germane to our
lives whether we thought about it or not: 3. to
concoct or devise. And most of us did so much of
that, maybe not all in the past either—we had had
to lie in our old alcoholic life and found it a
hard habit to break now that we were sober—that
```

rightly we could be termed brewers.

It was not all that odd but quite remarkable from the point of view of the knots gathered up five days a week in front of the artificial-limb store, that the verb brew is both transitive and intransitive, meaning in its passive form, *v-intr*: 4. to be imminent, to impend. This last idea fit most of the folk that were lucky enough to make it to Burt's door, including our master of ceremonies himself. Most were "about to _____," fill in the blank as you will. They were impending, not really being or doing but having the possibility of existing or acting, becoming something else. That's what most of us craved, we thought, to be someone else, someone new, anybody but the person we were. We wanted to be shut of the people we'd been before. All of us were concocting a new, sober character, as disappointing, we often found, as our previous incarnation. Who Burt wanted to be, I never knew. Anyone but himself, I guess. Maggie wanted a child with Burt. Toady wanted to be a bigwig in business. Muckey wanted Roxie. Jude, money and swagger.

The true difference for us all between drinking coffee and the meadhouse kind of brews is that we could recall our previous sip and our prior personae.

No surprise to anyone that our group would drink coffee as if it were water, no, as if it were booze. It wasn't uncommon to see any of us visit the coffee bar in the back of the room three or four times in an hour. That might not count the times the more ambitious coffee maker brought the pots around to the tables like a peddler of good tidings. The snap-in-the-holder cups were not large, so some of us had to be swilling eight to ten of those cups a day, drinking it before bed as well as just after rising. You'd think someone with a case of nerves might get worse from coffee jitters, but most derived an anodyne benefit, close to narcotic in some cases, even from the weak coffee brewed for meetings.

It was an easy switch to make. Beer to coffee. Brandy to caffeine. Gut-rot wine to *cafe con leche*. Cointreau to *au lait*. Chardonnay or Dom Perignon to java. Coffee is warm going down. Caffeine gives it a kick. Add sugar, six or eight cubes a cup for some, and the jolt becomes a high and an invitation to suck up the very last drop, all the more reason for twelve Webster entries, including -table, -break, -house, between "cofactor" and "coffer."

It wasn't *Today*, or Burt either, that sanctified coffee with ritual. That comes with anything human. The juju of repeated acts is well known, providing control over the emotions and assuaging most any neuropathy. We had plenty of both. The cult of coffee grew inseparable from our gatherings. It provided a sacrament to bless the soul.

The high priest or priestess, then, was the coffee maker, by which I don't mean the Bunn coffeemaker, but a person. It was a position like literature person, clean-up crew, chairperson, or meeting rep. An entry level position of great importance requires vetting if not application, though none of us were very big on interviews and *vitae* sheets. The qualifications varied from group to group, I'd learned, but the outcome needed to be the same in each case: the coffee needed to be ready shortly before the meeting began and had to flow freely up until a few minutes before it ended. No one refilled during the closing words.

Easy. Yes, for an ordinary person. In fact no normal person like either of my wives, DeLorr or Sharon, desired to be a coffee maker at *Today*. The sound individual had no special need for the discipline of rising early enough to be ahead of time, enjoyed less necessity to practice regularity and stick-to-it-iveness, like the jumpy basket cases we all were when we arrived. The ordinary person went to work in the morning, without stopping at our gathering.

Easy. Dispose of the old grounds. Place the filter in the basket. Add six measures of fresh Folgers. Put a pot below the drip spout. Push the button. Listen for the faint hiss of the Bunn. While the first pot is brewing, organize the sugar, coffee-white, stir sticks, paper napkins, and spoons, and, if there were any, donuts or cookies. Put these last out on paper plates. Pour without spilling, scalding, or over-filling.

Easy? Not so very much for the newly arrived. Usually the requirement for coffee maker was several, often three months of consistent attendance with concomitant sobriety, long enough to be known and to get to know other folks. But sometimes a month seemed long enough, depending on the need for help. And amongst us good help was hard to find.

I remember distinctly one person, besides Maggie, who usually worked Burt's counter for him, serving as coffee maker in the years I spent at *Today*. That's as it should be. The idea behind the process was service, not personal notice. To be of help to others without receiving compensation, working quietly behind the scenes sans thanks or kudos promised the elixir we, the agitated and anxious, sought upstairs. That is what Maggie and many anonymous members achieved. Maggie, though, was simply notable due to her grace and her connection to Burt. Service proved the cure to ego. Seeing as how in each of our cases there lived but one person in charge of getting us up those stairs in the first place (i.e. oneself), getting us outside of ourselves, serving others was what we wanted to do. We worked toward what Burt recommended: "You get better by staying out of your own way."

Self. It had a way of creeping in, and once reestablished began mixing the love-of-me potion that sometimes led to a tumble down the stairs, metaphorically or bodily. Either way the bruises were the same.

We saw it in Toady—the one coffee maker I remember well—not too long after I installed myself as the Friday chair.

In addition to his chairing two meetings a week, Toady took on the coffee-making job on Fridays.

"It's really a return to basics," he said. I couldn't see he needed to do that, since he was what we called "deep" in the program, had a wife and a very good job, a fancy car. But could I say no? I was new, and I needed a coffee maker. I was a baby in service and didn't know the danger signs. It wasn't until after Toady tripped coming up the stairs, so to speak, that I understood what had been going on. Inside.

Anyway, it started with the creamer. For most, the canister of white powder was good enough. It was the sugar they were after and the caffeine, so whatever off-white talc came out of the shaker holes as long as it colored the coffee to look like you'd added milk, it was all right with them. However, it wasn't all right with Toady. He had studiously avoided the stuff all along, drinking his brew black, and now that he was serving others, he made it clear that he didn't want to feed that "poison" to his people. Every Friday, then, we had half-and-half, which Toady brought himself, first a pint, then as we got used to the idea and started using more and more, a quart, sometimes two. Hey, he was providing. Who was I to object? For many it was their main source of nutrition.

That went on for a month or two, but then Toady was talking about other improvements. He ran a cleaner through the machine, some liquid that was supposed to remove the scale deposits that lent bad taste to the grounds as the water flowed in. He brought the glass pots home to run through his dishwasher. Ordinarily we rinsed them in the utility sink and let them air dry. That, Toady said, was not enough to keep his coffee's freshness uncontaminated. Squeaky-clean it had to be. Okay. He had come on Thursday night, collected the pots, and returned them Friday morning.

But once he'd purged the machine and cleansed the pots, adding a water filter to the system as well, Folgers didn't taste rich enough for Toady. He had to play the big shot in the coffee business.

Those were the days when coffee aficionados were multiplying like java-rabbits in the area. Peet's Coffee was setting higher standards for sipping the brew and jacking up both the stimulation within and the price tag on the outside of the bag of coffee. The coffee-gurus recommended buying beans and keeping them sealed until used. We were used to the two-pound can of Folgers, which Toady well knew and which was probably why he at first ground those beans at home and poured them into a Folgers can. Likely he closed his eyes and mixed half Folgers and half *Peets* at first, a sacrilege to the connoisseurs, and little by little eased the Friday people into his fold. He did this and carried his coffee can back and forth from home so the other four days of meetings wouldn't deplete the Friday supply.

It wasn't the transport of the special can that tripped him up. It wasn't even his insistence later on to grind beans just before the meeting. By that time we had special raw, crystal sugar, real heavy cream, homemade cookies to replace his initial change to Pepperidge Farm, set out on china platters, and warmed, ceramic cups for all. It was none of those. Or all.

I think it was either the outcry of Monday through Thursday coffee drinkers who'd tasted, perhaps become addicted to, Friday's brew, or the fact that when word got out, attendance shot up like all of Oakland was getting sober. Toady put on quite a spread.

We had gone from a modest, supportive, and caring group populated by a handful of unfortunate regulars to a pre-weekend celebration of buzz-heads, sugar freaks, and cookie monsters who jammed the room to overflowing and formed a line at the coffee bar all meeting long, keeping Toady very busy. To match the pace, he took on an assistant.

Of course, if something *had* to be done about the situation—and it needed to be done—*I* was to do it. It was *my* meeting. Mr. Newbie was forced to act.

For my money, Toady had been around. He'd been chairing meetings while I was spilling my triple shot glass of Cointreau over the vest of my three-piece suit, or dropping my gin and tonic in the middle of a circle of my business associates chatting about their accomplishments. You never saw businessmen step back so quickly. Anyway, I did not feel, let us say, qualified to curb Toady's behavior even though it was, as Burt said, my meeting. I talked as friendly with him as possible, one morning when he was cleaning up, polishing the Bunn, packing the china and *Peets*. I took a timid and tentative tone.

"Hey, Toady, how's the coffee business?"

"See for yourself. We are packing them in, aren't we?"

"I see, I see." I posted myself at the end of the bar so he couldn't get around me and escape.

"We're going to have to bring in an espresso maker, I think. I know a guy who wholesales them. I'm looking into it."

"Listen, Toady, some of the regulars are wondering . . ."

He sniffed trouble in the air, like we do when the other shoe is about to fall at home or work. He stopped wiping, polishing, and packing. He put both hands on the counter edge. "What, exactly, are they wondering? When good coffee will come Monday through Thursday?" He faced me and now crossed his arms over his ample chest. Then he got animated again. "I've been thinking of bringing in a fridge, too, so we can expand the service. I've got a friend in restaurant supply who'd install a dishwasher here at cost. A commercial-style machine, do up to thirty place settings at a time."

"Toady, Toady, listen to yourself," I said.

"Yeah, I hear me. I'm just trying to be of service. You know. Look how many people we're helping here." He was about to tell me the count which, of course, he'd been tracking because he had to plan ahead, making sure everyone got their coffee and cookies on Friday. "Isn't that what we're here to do?"

"Some people are asking for a business meeting," I said.

Now, business meetings are rare. We're supposed to have them about once a month, often for only five minutes, but usually not much needs discussing. The type of meeting I was talking about, though, speaks of controversy with some acrimony mixed in, and is called only when someone has a beef. Business among us frays the nerves. You see a lot of people skittering out from that kind of meeting, needing a smoke. A very long cigarette it must be, since they never return from it. When you have nut cases like us in the first place, imagine what happens when complaints must be aired. The fallout is why business meetings are so rare and so short.

Toady's jaw dropped, then jutted out. "What the fuck?"

"Look, Toady, this isn't *Today* at Peet's Coffee. It is a recovery meeting. Can you ease up on the fancy stuff. Just a cup of coffee is what most people want."

"So, you want membership to fall off? You want to drive people away?"

"No," I said. "And don't take this personally, but we're not supposed to be promoting, either."

"I'm promoting?"

"In a way, yes."

He grabbed his big box of stuff and pushed past me. "Well, see what happens when you serve gut-rot with talcum powder and artificial sweetener. You'll beg to have me back."

"Toady, you're taking this all wrong."

He was hurrying for the stairs, and I was afraid he'd roll all the way down with his load.

"Let me help you," I said.

"You've helped me plenty, Moe. Get yourself another coffee maker."

He humped downstairs, swiveled around to butt the door open, without as much as glancing up at me, opening my arms from the upper landing.

It was three months later he returned to *Today*. He looked like hell, had drunk off a lot of weight, but his nerves had settled down for him by that time.

The Friday crowd had thinned just as he predicted, but to me the regulars seemed to be happier, able to lay out their baggage around the tables without a gallery of onlookers washing down Toady's homemade peanut butter cookies with his stiff brew cut with real dairy cream. Somehow, not right off, but later on, Toady seemed more content too.

Coffee making can be hazardous. And though not much was said when Toady didn't show that next week and folks found Maggie behind the counter brewing good old Folgers and putting out day-old donuts cut in quarters to make them stretch, no one was surprised. Most had seen it coming. We were sad, but we all kept trudging, following our noses. The comical thing to watch was the reaction of those coming only for the coffee and cookies. One sip of the swill Maggie was given to brew brought a grimace to their faces and a backstep to their walk. Nobody spewed, but there were a lot of plastic cups standing half empty on the counter.

I felt terrible. I'd driven an old timer out of his job and out of the meeting. Burt tried to comfort me, saying that Toady had some ego things to work out, but he was clearly pained. Burt and Toady had come in at the same time. They were a sort of best friends. And when I asked Burt to let his pal know I meant no harm, he confessed he hadn't seen Toady all that week, that his wife had called him looking for her husband. Then I felt worse.

"Make the bed," Grandma said. You don't have to toss on king pillows, silk sheets, or have a golden fleece for a bedspread.

That's what Toady had done. He stirred up the coffee service into something fancy enough for pride, but, as Burt's grandmother said, "Pride knows no limit. It will blind you half-an-eye at a time, until you can't even see the bed much less make it." This isn't what I thought at the time, so much, seeing as I was working out some things of my own, but looking back from the time Burt hurt Maggie and then lost himself in LA, I saw obsessive pride mixed with a modicum of hurt and fear had everything to do with it.

I can't say what Toady gained from the experience, but when he returned, wasted and wan, he was different. He never lost his deep, resonant voice that, like no other, was able to assure the regulars that help was on the way, that the future was worth waiting if not working for, or that each of us had value, especially in serving others. Somewhere in the bass of his words there was now a sonorous message of experience and prodigality. Toady had descended more than the stairs to the street, going deep into the basement of despair, and, slipping between the bars, had come back less of a bigwig and more of a man.

None of us wanted to try that, but if we went down, Toady had shown us we'd be welcomed back just as we'd done when glad to see him return.

The day he limped up the stairs, we saw him coming three blocks down Main, keeping up with

Burt as best he could. Of course, Burt was waving his arms in the air, probably nodding up a storm, and very likely agreeing with everything Toady was telling him. When they came up to the crooked corner by the cafe, Burt was smiling, like to crack his jaw.

"Let's get the coffee on," he said. Burt turned the key, and up we went.

"You make the best coffee, Els."

I hid the shame she innocently inflicted. "It is practice." I lied about my ritual. "I don't really intend to."

She raised her cup with two hands. "Even so, it's soothing. Thank you."

Sleep, a shower, and, now food and coffee had done her good. "Would you like more of anything?"

"I'm fine."

I took her empty plate. "So, how did you like Muckey D's sad tale?"

She held up a finger. "I'm just about done. Wait until I finish." She took her coffee back over to the desk.

I cleaned up, feeling homey, content. I moved her coat, now dry, from the window to the hall rack. Coming back I watched Raci dropping her shoes, one then the other and curling up on the chair, basking in warm April sunshine. This was the Raci who'd been around for most of my story. Soon she'd be the only eyewitness to whom I could talk about those days.

. . . I hate it when I get philosophical. I don't strictly mean philosophy as in Plato or Aquinas or Kant, but the less heady kind of wonder about existence. You know, life.

Sometimes, though, you have to admit looking at life is unavoidable, maybe even important. I've spent moments checking this out when my life felt to me like I was riding a merry-go-round, not in the negative sense of being trapped in an overly repetitive cycle, but like looking at the world moving along outside the canopy of the carousel, vignettes of existence coming back around each time looking advanced a frame or two as people in the background strolled by, or stopped to watch, or turned their backs to buy cotton candy at the striped-canvas stand over there, or stooped over to pick up a dropped pacifier or dollar bill. Those thoughtful times, looking at life passing by, seemed to carry a rhythm with them, as if from the oscillation of the cam moving the pole of the pony I was riding up and down, a cadence that made life out there appear regular for all its sideways movement and vertical gyration, made existence seem continuous and stable, despite the whirling round of the ride. I experienced two times, though, that sent me and my carousel flying, both tagged by the end of a marriage.

Looking back to Sharon eyeing me while slicing her chicken the night after Tom left me drunk in my kitchen marked a day that jarred my stability. Sharon might as well have cut me out of her life that night, because eventually, she did. Her leaving knocked me off my horse, and I went tumbling down our apartment stairs out the door.

Before the worst hit, I managed to finish my degree at Duluth. With studies and teaching at an end, I met with Tom on and off again, "working" on *Tunnel Rats* and looking for jobs without much success in either. It was mid-year, and teaching was tight. As a result, I made the switch from academia to booze fairly easily, and working with

Tom, mostly drinking with very little editing, did not help.

Tom invented a game for us, likely imported from his Vietnam days.
"Give me a synonym for 'drunk,' Moe."
I said, "High."
"All right, mine is 'fuddled.' You see?"
"See what?"
"You have to counter mine with another. See?"
"Pickled."
"Good one. Blasted."
Tom jotted our words down in columns under our names.
"Okay, I'll keep track." He wrote on the back of a manuscript page:

TOM	MOE
drunk	high
fuddled	pickled
blasted	shnockered
soaked	bibulous
blotto	shot
half-shot	quarter-shot

"Hey! That's not fair."
"Not fair? You used 'half' and I use 'quarter.' Why not fair?"
"Okay, but no more of that." We continued.

TOM	MOE
on a spree	tight
on a bender	on a tear
top heavy	cockeyed
carbuncled	

"Carbuncled?"

"Yeah, it's an Aussie term."

"Okay, can I use French?"

"No. Only English, but any kind."

The list went on: top-heavy, stewed, half-gone, primed, afflicted, beery, winey, chock-a-block (another Aussie term), tipsy, peppered, boryeyed, muddled, jiggered, inebriated, blasted, tooted (up), juiced, hazy, moory (another), petrified, potted, bagged, hammered, petrified, ossified, having a skinful, sotted, soused, pixilated, more sail than ballast (south seas), tanked, dagg'd, polluted, crocked, merry, dipsy, sloppy, soaked, mellow oiled, dipsomaniacal (Tom objected), all mops and brooms (I objected), pie-eyed, muddled, stewed, bombed, and podgy.

I grew depressed.

Sharon had been kind at first. But eventually she had to threaten. Then she found one of our game lists in my pants pocket.

"Moe. Get out of the house. Find some work, anything. And stop hanging around with that tunnel rat."

As a result, likely with a suicidal vengeance buzzing in my head, I accepted a job with a life insurance company. I thought the income would placate my wife, which it did, but once my training period was over and when I had to start "producing," recalling easier, happier days as a student, my mood descended dangerously. Soon I was avoiding the office, hating the job though I was good at it, and found I couldn't stand to be with Tom, who scoffed and derided my new effort.

"You got to be kidding, Moe." He downed a shot and shook his head.

"I've got to do something with my life."

Tom pursed his lips and snorked his nose in distaste. "You're an insurance man like I'm a ballerina." He slapped his forehead.

I felt like I was begging. "It's not like I'm abandoning my writing."

"Sure, sure. What have you done in the last three months? Huh? Besides make notes on cocktail names? Sold policies and propped up a three-piece suit." Tom was right. I was miserable. Then it grew worse.

I lost my wife. Despite my bringing home some bacon, Sharon walked out. Imagine a newly divorced, hard-drinking English major pedaling financial planning and life insurance. Oh God, how I hated that business now. I couldn't do it sober. And while I was doing it, even though I was boozing, I couldn't work with Tom anymore. None of it fit. Then I lost the job. All that was the first tumble off my pony.

The next five years passed in a twirling blur. Somewhere along that lacy, looping line, I met and married DeLorr, who I hoped would save me from myself. I adopted her daughter Tilla as my own.Her father, an incarcerated drunk, consented. I wasn't yet sober, but I was certainly happier. I tried normal life once again: job, wife and daughter, writing, and in rapid succession, more kids. A couple years later, we left Duluth for Minneapolis, moving with a thermostat company that had hired me, then on a mind-boggling promotion to the West Coast to what soon became a new merry-go-round.

I controlled my drinking and had hidden it at home by feeding DeLorr excellent California wine even before we moved to the state. Try as I might, though, I was still no corporate man.

When I first arrived in Oakland, three years before meeting Burt and the gang, I viewed my existence optimistically, as a vivacious role in an exciting scene. But boozing was really my self-appointed work assignment on the West Coast.

The events at my new job, the turning of the wheel surrounding the corporate calliope, held the measured lilt of my ride stable for a time, anchored it in place at the fixed axis of gears attached below the office-wheel floor, whirling around day after day. People came and went, not rapidly but steadily enough to create a pleasant variety to the business life, and our common purpose and dependence on each other—at the office and, because we were strangers in California, at home, too—lent a permanence to the air of achievement, streaming through the hopes of employees riding the fanciful animals of their personae. It was not, ultimately, balanced or lasting.

It was nothing new that I'd far overreached my abilities or nature. My bosses thought I was a manager, managing. But I knew from my crying jags on the couch at home that things were bound to go south.

My dissatisfaction grew. My drinking became more and more inventive, and as my homelife began following the trajectory of my worklife, downward, I drank more and sought out better, more copacetic and soothing company. Her name was Robin. I was her boss's boss there at the company.

As our sorties to the Potrero Hill winebar multiplied, starting with lunch, soon adding an occasional afternoon sip when we could manipulate the schedule, I found myself lingering in the city for after work drinks instead of heading home to DeLorr and the kids, and discovered I was falling in love. Robin was, too.

Now I had a legitimate reason to want to go to

work. I spent a good deal of my time at the office with Robin strategizing about her department and about ways to see each other more. There were our lunch dates, afternoon tastings, and after work letting-our-hair-down drinking sessions, all at bars. Soon, when she invited me to her apartment, I began bedding her (in her husband's bed) once a week during the late afternoon.

Robin invited me on a weekend junket up the California coast that was to occur a couple of months later. I said I'd go though I had no idea how I could free myself from wife and kids. As the date grew closer, I grew nervous, irritable, drunker, and fought with DeLorr frequently.

Finally, I told DeLorr—we were in the laundry room where she seemed to spend much of her time folding diapers and sheets—that I needed time alone, that I'd be moving to an efficiency across the bay, closer to work. She didn't understand, of course. That was the problem. I needed someone who did.

That was the second time I was thrown, when my merry-go-round began to lift off its bearings to become a strange and wild ride. I thought I was straddling the horse, but I was really dragging the ground, one foot locked in the stirrup in full view of everyone but myself.

I could have known. I didn't want to. My sales manager uncovered one truth: "Looks like someone's searching for an apartment," he said picking up the want ads I'd left on the passenger seat. I figured, mistakenly, that a lie covered it.

Several weeks later my operations manager caught me in my office, telling me, "Hey, I've been there." He'd fallen for a beautiful saleswoman a couple of years back in his former branch, divorced his wife, and married his new love, eventually leaving Pittsburgh for the West Coast. "Can I give you some advice?"

I was shocked right out of my chair. "Hell no," I said. "I know exactly what to do!" And I did. I grabbed my coat and headed for the Potrero Hill wine bar. Once there, I called Robin over to cry on her shoulder. Word was out.

Crying and whining didn't work. In another month, I was busted, not fired, but demoted three steps. I lost my management job and was back to selling. The saving grace is that I now worked with Robin as an equal.

I wasn't selling the company product as much as I was cavorting and drinking on the company tab. My love affair at work that marked my second fall lasted only three months past the beginning of my sobriety. Once dry, to pick up the shattered pieces of my life, I moved back home to DeLorr and the kids and found *Today*.

So, three years after starting my big shot management job, I arrived at Burt's door, having taken to recovery meetings in the city just two months before.

I was thrashing around in life, trying to survive the upending of my world. All I was doing at that moment was watching the stream banks of life as I, in a river of booze, flowed by. I had no will to measure or account for what was going on. It was enough to stay above the liquid line, to live another day. I knew important events were happening around me, but it was only later, looking upstream into the past that I could admit when deeds or disasters began and what course my sad life took.

This was my muddled condition as I as hit bottom in the backwaters of *Today*. At that instant Burt and Toady ringed me with a life preserver. Susan and Len were bobbing along, heads above water, undifferentiated in the flow from the folks like Muckey D and Hillside-Glenn, until their acts committed them to beach, stand ashore, and one by one extend a hand to me.

Once saved from a beery drowning, I began to discover other important players at *Today*. Maggie joined and soon became important to Burt. Jude followed to quite the opposite effect. Jude impacted us all in a negative way. I knew Maggie within my first year, Jude a bit later. I had the sense that Maggie and Burt had met elsewhere and that he had brought her to *Today*, though later I revised my judgment and thought it more likely that Maggie cajoled her way there over Burt's resistance. Either way, when I saw her first, she was watching Burt very carefully, with interest. Jude came from another place entirely. He had and continued to spew destruction along his path and would have crushed more people at *Today* and may have done the meeting in entirely were it not for the unselfish works and deep love of my good friend, Muckey D.

"This is the first time I'd known the whole story." Raci was ready to talk.

"The whole story?"

She brought the manuscript over to the bar, looking carefully at the surface I'd wiped before setting it down. "Don't I know these people? Aren't they Dwayne and Ona?"

The djinni was out of the bottle, I knew, but I tried to forestall what I had guessed would be inevitable. "Ona?"

Raci wasn't going to have it, but she trod lightly. After all I *had* wanted her to read the story even before she'd arrived at my door.

"Yes, Ona, aka Roxie. Dwayne, whom you call Muckey D. I remember a rather disturbing lunch with them."

"Maggie's luncheon, I suppose. How could you tell?"

"For one, you mention Burt in the story." She thumbed through. You're quoting Muckey telling it. 'Roxie was dark, darker than Burt here (he'd say that if Burt were around), Italian-dark.' Want to see?" I didn't. "But why change Dwayne's and Ona's names if you don't change Burt's?" She asked a ringing question.

I was caught. Probably, I'd wanted to be caught. "To protect anonymity. I fictionalize names of those still alive."

Raci sat still, running her fingers over the page she'd turned to. If she was not weighing her next question, she was trying to remember something. It was neither. It was calculation: "Was it really that bad, Els?"

I thought she'd ask about the other names, including DeLorr's. Instead she'd hit me broadside. "That bad?"

She started paging back in the book. She'd reached her page: "'Right off there wasn't much enjoying each other at home. There was too much tiptoeing around dear old dad and his nerves to be much fun.' If I've got it right," she twisted her middle finger around her pointer, "DeLorr and I are just like that." Raci's eyes met mine. "Was it really that bad?"

My own truth flashed at that instant. Yes, Raci had come to see "where the magic happens" but my reluctance to have her had been insincere. I had wanted to test *her* magic—that which I remembered from years ago—in the flesh. I had been living with my disembodied *Twelve* characters rooted in past times so much that I could only feign disinterest in a member of the living, breathing cast. And Raci, despite her tragedy and our enmity, was very much alive.

Raci couldn't stop, and I could not stand in her way. She read, "'For the *Today* crowd, though, the weekend was a strain, surrounded by family, something to live through.'"

105

Her hand left the page, went to her mouth.

Please don't cry, I thought.

"I know it got that way later, Els, but at that time I had hope. You'd come home, you'd quit drinking." She shook her head. She bowed her face toward her heart. Her hair fell like grief over her eyes. In a minute, Raci raised her head, shook off despair, and smiled at me, expectant, optimistic. "But at least DeLorr is alive!"

I reached over the counter and took her hand. "We were both trying to be just who we were or maybe just who we hoped we'd become." It was a sentence I'd stricken from *Twelve* just weeks before. Apparently, it had stuck with me. I owed Raci something. "And, yes, DeLorr is still alive."

She squeezed. "And, yes, Moe is still with us, too."

I couldn't stand it. I let go Raci's hand. She pouted.

I tried to soothe her disappointment. "And Toady lives, too. I never knew his real name. I loved him and his *petit nom*. I had to use it."

Raci brightened with my words. "And Maggie? I really liked her."

I didn't want to wax glum. "Let's find out later. I still want to hear about Muckey D's sad tale."

It had been clear to me that Raci had not cared for Dwayne, had not liked Ona either. Her feelings might color her reading of the story, but perhaps I could work around that. And something else I wanted to know gnawed at me: "Incidentally, when did you read about 'dear old dad?'"

Whenever Raci was guilty of something, she flicked her tongue up to the right edge of her mouth paralleling its trajectory with her eyes. I hadn't seen that, of course, for twenty years and more, but I recognized it in an instant. She crimped her lips together and, then, smiled and shrugged her shoulders. "While you were showering this morning." Raci opened her hands as if to explain. "I thought that maybe you'd left it out for me." She gave me her I'm-guilty look again.

She'd hidden it, of course. "You weren't that sure." I worked at sounding playful.

"After I saw the dedication, I thought it would be okay."

So, she'd known. Immediately I reassessed her bad behavior at lunch. Obviously, the script opened a spring of emotion that had welled up fresh. I nodded.

"It's okay." I took up and patted her hand. "What about Muckey?"

Racine Davis had always been beautiful. Yet, as foolish as it sounds to say, it was her mind that had drawn me to love her. If Raci was quick of tongue, it was because her thoughts formed sharp and fast. She was literate and insightful. Despite everything else, the avalanche of pain and guilt, I found that her lithe intelligence hadn't changed.

"The piece is entertaining. It's certain that Muckey will figure in the Burt plot. I see foreshadowing of Burt and Maggie in the choice of *Cat*. That's a nice touch. I suppose I'm spoiling it because I know Roxie shows up again, but I'm hoping you're opening a redemption theme there."

Now I touched my lips and looked down. I had to shake my head, amazed and awed.

"Am I wrong?" She struck an alarm.

I looked up, straight into her eyes, "Not at all. You are too right even if it stands on prior knowledge. You astound me."

"So, then, this Roxie/Muckey romance contrasts the Burt/Maggie story. But, maybe, in reverse. Faithful man, scattered woman?"

"It's already implicit?"

She smiled. "It is. Certainly." She fondled the manuscript pages. "But I'm wondering about the Moe/DeLorr story, Els."

"If it ends badly, you mean?"

Had I not blunted my mind with twenty years of soaking

up suds followed by two decades of self-delusion, I might have seen this coming. Then again, under a distilled cloud of denial, perhaps I had led us to this talk. Raci took it up briskly:

"I've no doubt it does close on a down-note. It's fiction, after all." Then she flashed a sharkish grin. "But in any good story much happens outside of what is on the page." She let me off for the present with that.

"What else should we look at?" Raci was just warming up.

"Don't you have a plane to catch?"

She tongued her lips, "Yes, but not until tomorrow."

Right then I wondered if her hotel was fictional. Where else would her luggage be? Without surprising either of us I said, "So, let's play it by ear."

"On to Maggie?"

I wanted to steer away from love themes for now, to calm down. "There's one part about Tom I'd like you to read to me. I'm wondering how it sounds. Game?"

She pushed the manuscript of *Twelve: lives with(out) drink* to me. "Yes, find my place."

. . . I'd been single again nearly a year, had been dating Delorr, who, thank heaven, had flown with Tilla to visit her parents in Oregon when Tom popped up again. To say it was unexpected was to say it was Tom. To say he didn't meld well with my romantic life was beyond redundant. The same about his boozing. Of course, he was drunk. It was already noon.

I'd come home from my thermostat sales job, the one that was to eventually bring me west, to rest and fix lunch. That afternoon, I was to drive over to Wisconsin to survey a bank building for my company. The bell rang almost immediately after I arrived. I checked before opening the door just to make sure it wasn't the perpetually incessant Mormons I'd let in a year before when I first moved in. It was Tom. I wonder if I would have let him in had he not seen me peeking, but, then, I supposed he'd watched me enter.

"Moe, it's me, Tom," he said to the window curtain. "I've got something to show you."

I opened the door. "You haven't joined the Mormons have you?"

He shook his head, "Hell, they don't even drink coffee! You going to let me in?"

I led him to the kitchen, always our favorite place no matter where I lived. "I'm fixing a sandwich. Want one?" He sat at the table and slapped down a huge book.

"Not hungry."

"Well, I am, and I have to leave by one. Work."

"This won't take long," he said. Tom smiled and patted the book. "Moe! I published it!"

"*Tunnel Rats*?" I couldn't believe it had grown so huge or that he could have gotten it ready in less than a year.

Tom flipped open the tome and thumbed through the first few pages. "Well, part of it anyway. They included it in this anthology, *Veterans' Stories of War*." His finger drew down the page, a table of contents, to "Vietnam" and then paused at his own name. "Here it is: 'The Sack of Ben Suc' by Thomas C. McIntyre, USMC."

I put my sandwich on a plate and rounded the table to look. It was a vanity press book, which answered both my questions but raised a new one. "How much did you pay for this?"

Tom slapped the facing page, crestfallen at first, then angry. "What do you mean? The book was free. I entered a contest."

I took my place and started on my meal. "Was

there an entry fee? Just asking, Tom."

He smelled a rat, but his excitement propelled him. "Yeah. But they selected my story from thousands of entries. This is legit."

"Let me see." He found the page and turned the book to me. "How much?"

"Just two-fifty. My dad lent me the money."

I couldn't tell him that I was glad they hadn't taken him for more.

"Of course, each added copy is seventy-five, but you don't have to buy more than three." I held up my hand, trying not to calculate, only to read. Just under five hundred dollars. Pirates!

"This one is yours, Moe, to keep."

"Tom. Please. Let me read." I hoped to temper but not quell his enthusiasm. Tom was still my friend. "And, well, thanks. Thank you for the book."

I read the first paragraph. I found two typos and a misused verb. I scanned forward. The material was not only new to me, not having encountered anything like it in Tom's manuscript, but as I skipped through the piece, about four or five thousand words long, I suddenly realized that Tom hadn't even been in Vietnam at the time of the action he described, January 1967.

I flipped back to the title pages and located the editor's name. His statement covered his butt: "What you read here is exactly, word for word, the testimony of the soldiers who fought these battles. The editorial board collected and supervised the ordering of the veterans' stories without interfering in their telling." Tom came around my side.

"What are you studying there? The story's further back."

I sat back, pointed to the disclaimer, and

while Tom read it, said, "I wish you'd given me at least a chance to proofread it."

"So, what's this gobbledygook? They wanted the vets to sound authentic. Isn't that what you've always been preaching?"

I looked up at him. No way did I want to hurt him, nor did I want to argue. Either might send him out the door in a huff. "Tom," I swiveled my chair and canted it to the wall. I reached a hand to his shoulder, "of all the guys I've known over all these years, you've been the closest to being my best friend." I poured all the sincerity I had into those words and worked to keep anything snide stuffed inside. "I, I'm caught in a bind here."

"What kind of bind?" He was getting tense.

"I am your friend, right?" He nodded. "I've worked as your editor, right?" Again, Tom assented. "I just wonder if I can be both and tell the truth, too." He looked dumbly at me. I asked him to sit down.

Was I being unfair, not having read it all? I wondered at the time if my reaction was just my own hurt feelings. Still, I plowed on.

"I have some questions about this, and I have a few things to say, too. Can we talk it through?" Tom looked suspicious but nodded. I proceeded as tactfully as I could. "I do think you've done a good thing here, Tom. I haven't read it all, but I think it's fine." He had his hand on the book and was smiling. "What I would have done, given a chance, is copy editing and proofing, so that the text would have been error free and always clear."

"Isn't that their job? The guys who put it out? The boobs I paid?" He was beginning to understand my views.

I pointed to the disclaimer. "*I* think it is their job, but they squirmed out of any responsibility, right here. They disowned any burden in this statement. Each soldier-writer owns his mistakes."

"That's not so bad, is it?"

I bit my lip and frowned. "No, it isn't, even if you're planning to publish other stuff."

"Of course I am."

I sucked in a big breath and dove in. "Then stepping forward on the right foot is important. Most in the publishing business will overlook a false step like this." I said it and instantly tried to soften it. "One, but not likely two."

Tom didn't blow, much to my relief. "This is a false step?"

"I think you've published a first draft instead of a finished piece." I looked into his eyes. He was working it out. "It isn't so much a wrong move as not putting your best stuff out there." Tom sat still, thoughtful, maybe not relaxed but quiet.

"Yeah, it isn't my best. True. But I wanted to get it out there by the deadline. What's wrong with that?"

I wouldn't take the gloves off, not yet, but right then I didn't have time to pussyfoot around too much. "Nothing, really, but consider . . ."

"What? Tell me."

"Okay, there are a lot of errors: typos, misspellings, wrong tenses and just plain missed meanings." He was staying with me. "Then you paid to have it published."

"No, Moe, I won a contest."

"And the prize was what?"

"Well," Tom was thinking, finally, getting it, "publishing, I guess."

"It's called 'vanity press' by most people."

Now he was angry.

"You think this is vanity?"

With open hands I pushed the fierce air back at him. "No, not for you. But others, many others, will think so. That hurts me as much as it can damage you."

Tom was stunned by my words. "This can hurt you?"

"When *Tunnel Rats* comes out, if I am still your editor, people will associate 'Ben Suc' with it."

Tom shook his head. "So what? Isn't that good?"

"They are two different things."

He did not follow.

"'Ben Suc' is either essay or fiction. *Tunnel Rats* is memoir."

"What do you mean fiction? It happened."

"Yes, but you weren't there. So you aren't writing memoir which actually makes the editors of *Veterans' Stories* culpable. They didn't even check dates."

Tom hung his head. Then he perked up and said, "I knew guys who were there. It was just before I landed in-country." I was again looking at the piece.

> Lucky and Tom were at point. We held back. There was gonna be tough VC fire, we'd been brieft. The trail was surly booby trapped so we were off it. Suddenly, the village was there. No VC. No firefight.

"So are Lucky and Tom the guys you knew?"

"Yeah, more or less."

I sighted Tom down a rifle barrel. "Well? More? Or less?"

"Less, I guess. Does it matter? Moe, I'm telling a story, something that really happened. So what

if I stretched things here or there? Who cares?"
I read a few lines down:

> "They melted into the jungel," I told Lucky.
> "Screw the VC. We're gonna torch this place."

"No one cares, but who is 'I' who's telling
Lucky?
"Me."
"Tom?"
"Yeah, me."
I tapped the page with my finger. "Just a second
ago you were part of 'we,' and Tom was with Lucky.
Now, you're Tom."
"You picky-ass bastard!" Tom was on his feet.
I held up my hands and shook my head. "Stay
with it McIntyre." I mustered some command. Tom
sat down. "It is picky, but that's what you pay
for, Tom, a finicky, anal-retentive bitch." He
laughed. Self deprecation usually worked on Tom.
"You got anything to drink?" The tension was
getting to him.
I wasn't about to replay our Sharon's-kitchen
drunk. Tom needed to face facts. "No. How about
water?"
I poured him a glass. "There's some good here.
First of all, the writing is good. It brings
the reader there." Tom sipped his water. He
practically beamed. "I like the dialogue. And the
story does seem real. All that's good. In one way
I'm glad it's fiction or whatever it is."
"Why's that?" Tom was glued to my critique.
"It reads a bit like *Tunnel Rats,* but it's
outside the storyline of that book. It's not an
excerpt. So, if you want to, we can take up the
memoir as a totally separate piece."
Tom was not ready for that. He'd come to

celebrate and garner praise—who wouldn't want
those, certainly I would—but suddenly I was
confronting him with difficulty: work, discipline,
and the unknown. Maybe he could read my own
anxiety and, likely, my insincerity. I'd been
watching the clock for the last half hour. I had
to get on with my building survey.

Tom stood again. He took out a pen, turned to
the first page in "The Sack of Ben Suc" and wrote
something across the top of the page. He closed
the book and handed it to me. "I know you've got
to hit the road, Moe, but this is for you. Keep
it."

He smiled weakly at me and we hugged. I
couldn't think of anything to say. I didn't want
to apologize.

He slapped my arms, looked into my face,
knotting his brow and mouth. He nodded. "Let's
keep in touch."

During Raci's reading I alternated between listening
with my eyes closed and watching her through narrow slits.
Whenever *Tunnel Rats* was mentioned, I checked her voice
and sometimes her expression. Raci read well. I did not detect
a telling catch in her voice, did not see a sour expression pass
over her face. I felt relieved.

"Thank you, Raci. How did it sound to you?"

She showed me her expressionless, thinking facade, the
one she'd always used to cover her lies. "It's natural. The
dialogue sounds, well, authentic."

"Suggestions?" I wanted to get her talking.

"'You got anything to drink?'"

I must have looked horrified.

She laughed. "No, not for me. 'You got anything to drink?
The tension was getting to him.' I wonder if you should say

'Tom looked for a tension reliever,' or something."

"Sure. I suppose Moe couldn't really evaluate Tom's reaction." Was she playing with me? What did I really want from her? She watched me, alert now with a hint of a frown.

"So, *Tunnel Rats* was something in the works with you two before, during, and after our marriage?"

There it was. After twenty years was she going to claim part of my royalties? I dissembled.

"In a global way, I suppose. Nothing firm. It was really afterwards."

Raci was tough. "But firm enough to define a style."

If I hadn't been ready to answer her, why had I given her the manuscript? Why had I asked her opinion? I wanted, perhaps, to appear open, unafraid. But I wasn't sure at that moment. So I lied: "For starters, that meeting, the one you just read, did not happen. That part is fiction."

"You're lying, Els."

Panic bit at the fringes of my story. I had to spin a yarn with a calm and straight face.

"Not at all. Remember when I got Tom out of jail?"

"In Minneapolis. Yes."

"That was the first time I'd seen him since you and I met. Don't you remember?"

"Seems so."

"Was so." I felt like a kid arguing, insisting on boldfaced untruths. "This part is a bridge over a wide river of absence. I hardly saw Tom for five years."

Raci shut the manuscript. "Don't fret, Els. I'm not after your book money, or blood money. It hardly matters now anyway. Wasn't I the one who left?"

She put it as a question. Did that mean she no longer accepted my version of her leaving? Had she finally remembered something long forgotten after the accident? How was I to answer that question?

116

I had claimed abandonment. I believed Raci *had* left. Then I found out five years later she'd headed out for a surprise New Year's visit to her parent's Oregon home. Nettie had remembered after reuniting with her mother. No one else knew. The night she left, before getting out of the state, Raci collided with a red light runner.

Now, I answered her, "I'm not sure anymore."

She bit her thumb and looked away.

Don't cry. "I didn't know what to think, Raci. And, I admit, I didn't give you much choice." She straightened up, folded her arms beneath her breasts, and drew a deep breath.

"Don't cry, sweetheart." I tried to choke them off, but the words just flew out.

Raci shook her head. "Those tears are all spent, Els. I can't mourn forever. Don't worry, I'm not after your book." She flashed a crooked smile. "What else do you have? How about Maggie?"

"I'd like to talk about Maggie, but let me read you Jude's entrance to *Today*. There is some mention of Maggie in it, but let's leave her loveliness for later."

I read.

```
    . . . Looking back, it seems like an oddly-
plotted novel with two characters so alike
entering in succession but playing parts so
widely disparate. Jude, for enthusiasm, matched
Maggie exactly. Each came in for the relief our
meeting promised: camaraderie, understanding,
gentle guidance, regularity. But Jude proved
public and businesslike, organized, driven. He
was on the fast track for salvation, though he
was so animated and friendly that I never caught
the full drift of his self-centered intention.
Again, if you thought about it (but who did?),
```

anyone so insistent on "completing the program," as he said, was not likely to stick around to help others or leave without turning over a few trash barrels on his way out. Back then if I had those thoughts, I ignored them. Had I acknowledged my judgments about Jude, I might also have applied them to Maggie who, very much in her delicate way, upset some barrels of her own while passing through.

Still, people came and went frequently. Their getting involved proved all right, though getting attached could spell hazard. Often the only damage done was to the comer-and-goer. Occasionally, though, the wake of a passage was strewn with debris. When Jude flew in and in time swooped out the door, wreckage rained. It is fair to say, though, that it took both Jude and Maggie to make a mess of Burt, though Burt himself lent a helping hand.

Jude was young, medium-built, and athletic. He looked like he'd never brooked an ounce of fat on his frame. He could have been a runner had he not been so impatient, but if he was associated, physically or psychologically, with any sport it was skiing. He was built for it: not overly tall, spry and muscled amply, attentive, and daring. And he had the money for it, so he was a skier.

The history that led him to join us had mountains, cliffs, and upward winding roads running through it, coupled with fast cars and empty bottles. His money was never attractive to me, but his excitement won me over. It was the kind of hubris that led one to tip thin, narrow boards down a thousand-foot descent over slippery terrain marked with objects as immovable as fir trees. He was not careful, especially of others. He did not see beyond his own purpose. He was not tactful. Nor was Jude kind. So why did I like him?

On a day when we both had the time for breakfast after the meeting (an early lunch for me), Jude told the table filled with the better-heeled regulars he tended toward, but which also included Muckey and Hillside-Glenn, about his fabulous weekend with family at Sea Ranch, probably the priciest, most remote real estate development on the north coast of California.

"My God, it was beautiful there. So peaceful walking near the ocean, then settling at the fireplace after dinner." Jude often laid it on thick with that nonchalance of which the wealthy who associate only with the rich are singularly capable.

Muckey buried his hostile reactions in his waffle. Hillside-Glenn smiled sweetly. I obviously betrayed my thoughts: Some friend you turned out to be. You extended an invitation a month ago, then sneaked off in the night!

By that time I had been acting as Jude's sponsor for a couple of months, which meant we were in daily contact with each other, even over the weekends. I hadn't expected to join his family or anything, but his bragging scraped the scabs of false invitation.

Jude caught my drift and looked genuinely pained, almost distraught. "Shit, I remember now. I'd invited you. I'm so sorry."

Well with Muckey and Glenn there, I wasn't about to admit to feeling anything although I apparently looked disturbed. "No, no, my mother-in-law paid us a visit. I was obligated anyway."

"Hey, next time. No doubt about it."

Of course, my doubt was now as thick as his daddy's bankbook, and I wasn't lining up for another bruising either. I'm too delicate for that. The next time, there was not even an invitation. I took what Jude delivered—nothing.

Burt had always coaxed us to take what comes. He'd turn his head over a shoulder then swing it right back saying, "Oh, yeah, it's all about baby steps." Then he'd purse his lips, crinkle his brow, and burst into his big smile. "My grandmother taught me that." He loved to mention his grandmother. She'd raised him. She might have been the only one ever to love Burt. He'd never mentioned his parents.

So, on the authority of Burt's grandmother, I let Jude's rudeness go. Joining in his family fun wasn't actually my idea of a weekend retreat, anyway. His *faux pas*, though, should have warned me of what was likely to come from Jude. He was smooth, but he was high-and-mighty, too. It would be months, yet when he acted, his deeds would be unmistakably in his style, as if he lived on a rarefied plane of ethical existence the rest of us wouldn't understand.

I wasn't looking downstream in those days to piece any of this together—I was clinging to a boulder upriver of a roaring waterfall, hoping for a miracle like a sudden, severe drought. Taking a guiding role in Jude's meeting-life didn't tell me that something important had happened, though it had. We'd joined in the river of sobriety flowing downstream toward I knew not what, just moving together. And as likely as was Jude to succeed in whatever he wanted, heedless of whom he stepped over to do it, he was a stand-in for all of our cravings that could lead us astray as soon as the tide changed direction. The waters were already shifting.

Len was sliding ashtrays around, and Susan was

swaying side to side in her chair, centering her attention on the plastic coffee cup snapped into its yellow hard-plastic frame as if it were some *drishti* around which she formed her thoughts and her life. It was summer, a Thursday two weeks after Toady had packed up his coffee caravan and hit the road. So we needed a chairperson for that meeting and for Tuesday, too. No one objected when I suggested Jude take over.

He asked me to share my story, his first guest chair, which was likely why I remember what everyone was doing while I sat in front with nothing to get ready, nothing to think about but my own sad tale. Jude was in back with Burt, getting briefed on coffee making in case he couldn't get a volunteer to take over the job right away. In those days, Burt would make sure things were going well at the beginning of the meeting and would sometimes disappear into the office once it opened at 8:15. Other times he went down the stairs, coming back at the end of the meeting to lock things up and count the cash, though, as Jude was to point out later, he didn't do a lot of accounting.

All the daily chairpeople had a key to the front door but not to the locker containing the literature, collection baskets, and coffee fixings. Burt's absence made it difficult, then, to run the meeting. Not having a key had never bothered me—Burt had always showed up—but Jude began moaning about it after two or three weeks. It was Burt's meeting, and, though the members were supposedly self-governing as a body, he ran things as he saw fit. At the time, group politics were far from my mind, as I was thinking only of my own wracked state which I was to report on today, in just a few minutes, trying mightily to keep it upbeat. Leave the rabble-rousing to Jude.

It's all right to give a snapshot of my own tale. Seeing as how I am the sole owner of the story, no one is likely to object.

The most recent event was that I'd drunk my way out of my West Coast management job, thank God. I'd found that in big business where you're dealing with the Rockefellers and other people who own skyscrapers and businesses that manufacture tanks and rockets, there are not many who will listen to your personal problems. Mine, I'd always thought, were demanding wives whose middle names seemed to be "Bickering," as unloving as two Medusas to a stranger. . .

Raci rose up. "Do you have to say it that way? And you're dumping me in with Sharon!"

I should have read over this part, I realized too late. "Raci, I'm sorry. Actually, it only shows what a chump Moe 1s. It's obvious *he* was the villain."

"Well, it hurts. You didn't really think that, did you?"

"Raci, it's not my memoir. And no, I did not think that. It was a difficult time."

Now she cried. I moved to comfort her, but she pushed me off. "Then, it only got worse, didn't it?"

"Raci, don't. It wasn't your fault." I didn't want even to approach the place her emotions led. I embraced her.

"I ruined everything."

She wept. She shook terribly, even when I held her. This was what I had dreaded most about her visit. It was the thing we had never faced. I hugged her to me a long time.

"Raci, *I* ruined our marriage. No one blames you." And that was true. Not only had I been unfaithful and a drunk, I had had a choice and decided to abandon her. Afterwards, I couldn't face it and ran to New York, taking Nettie with me.

Now Raci was drying her eyes. "Well, Els, I do. I blame myself every single day."

I drew her to me again. "No, no, no. Don't, Honey. I love you."

She pulled away softly, blew her nose. "Thank you, Els." Raci smiled weakly.

"I'll change Moe's thoughts, his statements. They don't have to be such wreaking words."

She straightened her self and nodded. "If you want to. It would be fine. Finish reading this part. Then, I'd like to go for a walk before sunset."

"All right," I said. "How about this . . ." I wrote as I talked:

"'. . . there are not too many people to listen to your personal problems. Mine, I'd always thought, were wives I couldn't understand, who wouldn't fulfill my incessant need to be loved and admired.'"

The part following I read over: ". . . and in my current marriage, a growing passel of kids that, through no intentional fault of theirs, drained the family coffers and showered less and less love on dear old dad the drunker and drunker he got." In Raci's presence I wanted no more mention of lost children.

. . . To get going for the day, I'd been drinking two large mugs of high-test coffee each morning, and after consuming wine at lunch and cup after cup of coffee all day long, I found it necessary to stop at the store to pick up the nightly bottle for dinner.

Wine aids the digestion, you know.

After a while, I bought two, one for dinner prep and one for the table. Then, after the kids went to bed, I topped off the wine with a highball or two. It was the nerves, you see. My ganglia were twisted strands so taut that were I to let one snap, the whole megillah of family life and lies would unravel like a tightly-wound scroll bounding down a mountainside. Somewhere down below the inebriate surface, I knew, just as I later knew about Burt's past with Linda, that I was doing exactly what I didn't want to do, that I was engaging a life for which I was unready, unfit, and unappreciative.

Some of that was before I took a promotion to the coast, a place that seemed like the answer, like paradise, but was, at least for a boozer like me, just a broken-off piece of land separated from the stable continent by fractures and wandering fissures, which, unannounced, was to plunge into the Aleutian trench sooner or later. I did not fail to realize the poetry in the place. It was a metaphor for my own life, which seemed broken-to-pieces, soon to be swept into a gaping dustbin when the earth shook again. It did shake, too, rumbling through the middle of my house.

At the meeting, we all clung to stability, hoping we could hold on long enough to catch our breath before the next shaker. All except Jude. He leapt over faults and, he thought, conquered mountains.

The coffee briefing with Burt now over, Jude collared one of the newer regulars and got him to try out the job behind the bar. Jude, I found as I watched him ply his management skills, left a "volunteer" no way out. This was his fast-track method in everything. Jude wasn't shy about asking for help and could give you six benefits for agreeing before you could think of one reason you shouldn't. He was encouraging, that was for sure, especially when he was roping you in. Once you agreed, you were in, and Jude was gone, leaving you to struggle as best you could. Jude's rule for you: Good luck, you don't need my assistance.

I recognized inherent corporate management techniques, something my bosses had tried to instill in me, probably imbued in Jude's childhood during the dinner parties his father hosted. Where he got his confidence was less a puzzle than why he believed so firmly in that legacy of those inherited principles. They hadn't helped him through the last few years. After all, "humility," not "righteousness," was our by-word for recovery. Still, the energy he poured forth convinced us that he knew what he was doing, and he *was* right in the short run. But Jude turned out to be myopic. Over the years since, I've decided he should have done things differently.

The coffee gig settled, Jude paraded to the head chair a few minutes late and without apology for the tardiness, he began the meeting, eventually giving me a much-too-nice introduction and the nod to begin my share.

As usual I started my history with the morning I woke hearing a voice that my girlfriend sleeping right next to me did not perceive: a question asked loud enough to wake me from a Cointreau-infused sleep:

"Moe," a voice said, "why are you ruining your life?"

"That's a loaded question," I thought, but I wasn't awake enough to argue. The conclusion implicit in the query was undeniable, even to my fogged brain: I'd just been demoted. I was staying with my girlfriend while my three kids were across town living with my estranged wife.

AFTERNOON

I was drinking wine, brandy, and orange liqueur by the bottle, starting before lunch, and had admitted to myself that it was all downhill from this point. It had been tough, but I had earned each iota of disappointment all by myself.

The best I could do upon hearing that question so early upon waking was to wonder if I sobered up enough, maybe stopped drinking for a couple of days or so, would abstinence clear my mind enough to tell me what to do about it all? On impulse I decided on the spot to quit for a while. At first for a day, then, later, three days without a drink.

The three days passed. I needed a week, I decided. During that week, I learned that alcohol takes a month to drain from the body. Okay, a month then. During that month, I learned from the cross-town version of our meeting here—I hadn't come to *Today* as of yet—that it took three months to detoxify.

By that time, my wine-purveyor girlfriend had laid it on the line: "No more sex until you make up your mind." She was referring to my clear-headed idea to move back in with wife and children where I belonged.

Suddenly, life seemed to be getting simpler. In the clearing fog I was beginning to think I'd rather move back, that I couldn't stand the guilt anymore without my booze.

I worked toward my conclusion since Jude had started late, telling the assembled souls that by that time I'd found out that one year sober was supposedly a turning point. I would shoot for that, and knew it would be easier to do back at the family ranch.

I finished my story, concluding sincerely.

Life was better now and, though not perfect, it progressed nicely in a more salubrious and felicitous direction. Of course, I used different words in the company of *Today*, 'healthy' and 'happy,' but that was my story.

Jude passed the basket. It was a good take. He ended the meeting in the usual way. It was just afterward that he asked me to stand as his sponsor.

His request said as much about me as about Jude. My corporate job experience, the masters degree I'd earned, my engagement with the world of work now that I was dry, all indicated to him that we were alike. Jude didn't just want to sober up, he wanted to clean up his life, as he thought I had, to be able to live like his dad, a successful businessman, flying a private jet, living in a big house on the hill (where he could throw dinner parties, though not for the likes of the denizens of *Today*), and enjoying the fruits of having a beautiful, perhaps moneyed wife. The one thing Jude could never get though—a big deal no matter how much he minimized it—was to regain his best friend whom he'd left wrapped around a mountain pine on a skiing adventure. Somewhere in the recesses of his consciousness, he must have known that.

It was during this time that, after a fashion, Jude and I became friends. We met for coffee, had a meeting or two at his house the next town over, and sat together at meetings. I invited him to meet my family and once, my last salvo to friendship, to Hillside-Glenn's for a dip in the big redwood soaking tub. That sort of thing. In time it became clear that Jude wasn't the kind of pal to introduce me to *his* outside friends or to *his* family. We never took in a movie or a game of any kind. Looking back on those days now, I'd say we were program friends. Buddies at *Today*. We had one thing tying us together: spirits.

This was also a time during which a great deal was happening. Glenn took his dive. I was changing jobs again. Maggie and Burt were getting closer, which meant that Burt spent more time with her and needed added help at the meeting to fill in for his, well, inattention. Toady'd left.

It was a fast time. Hard to keep track of all the tragedy and comings and goings. All you could do was occupy the chair an hour each morning and hope for miracles. That's exactly what I did and thought that Jude did, too. Muckey took to making coffee. Jude was too uppish for Muckey who, being at the back of the room, kept a distance from the "preppy prince," as he called Jude. Sometimes he said, "preppy prick," just for variety. I didn't try to smooth it over between them.

I had a duty to each and was caught between them. I kept to the basics as much as I could, waiting, as was my wont, for something to happen.

I laid the manuscript on the bar.

Raci rose immediately. "I don't like Jude already. And I never liked Gael. Now, I need that walk more than ever. Fresh air!" She stormed down the hall, leaving me relieved she'd focused her upset on Jude—and on Gael, his non-fiction name—rather than on Moe's kids, girlfriend, or estranged wife. Raci came back with her coat draped over her shoulders.

I checked my coffee supplies. "Let's walk over to McNulty's. I need a few things, and you could, perhaps, pick out some gift-tea for your Irish friends."

She'd calmed down. "Is that the famous importer Nettie raves about?" Nettie did like the store, and I had sent her twenty pounds of beans over the years since she'd moved to Minneapolis. Naturally, Raci would have tried their flavored coffees.

The day outside had grown warm for April. "Let's drag the coats along anyway," I said, "We might need them after sunset." Raci and I turned toward 6th Avenue and strolled. She threaded her arm through mine. We held hands. It felt natural. I was beginning to feel the relief I'd hoped for when we'd agreed to meet.

A few people just getting off work passed us. "We don't look to these people like a long-divorced pair, Raci, do we?" She noticed them for the first time and laughed, a kind of private laugh you hear bursting from couples engrossed in their own world.

"Maybe they think we're just late-middle-aged lovers on their way to an afternoon delight." She laughed again, pressed closer, and smiled up to my face. I couldn't help but echo her movements. I too laughed.

"All right, then," Raci said, "now tell me how you first met Maggie." Raci squeezed my hand. She had waited for long enough to hear about Maggie, whom she had met once, and, finally, I felt comfortable talking about her. I could talk and stroll, looking forward without seeming to evade Raci's gaze. I chatted as we strolled down West 11th Street toward 6th Avenue, drawing much from what I'd written of Maggie in *Twelve*.

"Maggie came to me at a meeting saying, 'So you're Elmoe.' As if she had heard all about me somewhere and had been dying to meet me. She was all excited, a bit flustered it seemed, and skittish."

"I remember her being flighty," Raci said.

"She was, and tall, too."

"I don't remember that, but then I only saw her steps down

in the kitchen and seated at the table."

"She had me by half a head and stooped a little, I thought, to reach my level, but, doing that she seemed to tower even more."

"Maggie was thin. Thin and very white."

"Yes. And she moussed her black hair. Around that pallid face it intensified in contrast."

Raci swept a hand over her bob. "Black and curly. You like that style?"

"The classic dark Irish? Not so much."

"I noticed her eyes. Sharp blue markings on brown irises. And she didn't wear make-up."

I thought about the Maggie I'd first met. At meetings she always donned long sleeves and wore slacks. Both seemed roomy. They'd accentuated her delicate frame in graceful drapery. Her movements were cautious, somewhat tentative. Her hands thin and bony, fragile-looking, though smooth in motion. "You could tell that Maggie had always been frail."

"I wondered when we went to her luncheon. She looked too delicate, and that's why she wore flat-heeled shoes, I bet. "

"Maybe. I thought it was to cut down her height." Maggie hadn't been the only slightly built woman at our meetings, but there existed another dimension in her. A special willowy slenderness, a hollowness of sorts that the others entirely lacked. "Maggie seemed birdlike: tentative, excitable, a bit scattered, hesitant seeming."

"To me she seemed graceful and gracious."

"Are we talking about the same woman?"

"Yes, from different points of view."

We both laughed. "When I first met Maggie, she flew at me." Effusive and smiling, she joyed in sharing a thought, a moment, a commonality. Her serious edge was buried deep. She'd cavort on the outside.

We stood at the stoplight. Raci looked up at me. "Did she

ever come on to you?"

"Now why would you ask that?"

Raci swung our arms—we were still holding hands—and caressed mine with her free one. "Oh I guess I'm a little jealous. You admired her."

"No, she never threw a pass. She was all about Burt. That was what made her sparkle." I could see Maggie standing in front of the half-open shutters in the morning light upstairs where I'd met her that first time, swaying a bit, talking with Burt. He fixed rapt attention on her.

"I had the impression you knew her before she took up with Burt."

"True. They weren't a couple at first. And yes, we had chatted, like people do waiting for the meeting."

Raci smiled curiously looking up at me. "And so?"

"So nothing." I pointed. "We've got the light. Come on."

We walked across the Avenue of the Americas.

"We were some of the few quitters." I told Raci. "So we waited together away from the smoke. Under the awnings, anxious for the music to start. Not every day but a few times."

"So non-smoking buddies?"

"I guess. Really, I had not truly *seen* her until Burt's sunshine flooded her with light. His focus on Maggie made everything about her wonderful."

"Love does that, Els. It gives us warmth and excitement and soothes at the same time."

I squeezed her hand. "Love lent a sparkle to Maggie's eyes. That's sure." Burt had a way of focusing on one, but his gaze applied to Maggie was more a gluing. I'd never seen the like in him before. "Burt had a sudden fetish, and it made him self-conscious. He turned tensely aware, as if he stepped on stage before he was sure of his lines."

"That's not good."

"No, it wasn't." I had never heard him at a loss for words

131

before. "That's how I decided Burt was in love."

"That was the problem, wasn't it?"

"Yes, and I knew it. Linda had warned me. Eventually, I confronted him."

"You did?"

"Sure. I was worried. 'Burt, take it easy. This woman is real.'"

"Of course, you could guess his reaction without knowing much about him. 'I know what I'm doing. Don't worry about me.'"

"I pushed him harder."

"Really? That doesn't sound like you, Els."

"Yeah, really." I butted Raci's shoulder.

"And what did you say?"

I was off the *Twelve* script, making it up as I went. "Say? Well, obviously, I asked, 'Does Maggie know about your daughter?'"

"And Burt? He just stammered, right?"

"Not really. Burt put his hands on his narrow hips, 'Oh, my little detective is at work.'"

"Right, Els. Very unlikely."

"I swear it."

"And he'd told Maggie nothing."

"You're right, but Burt assured me that Maggie loved him and that made it all okay."

"Denial!"

"Yes, he wanted to be fixed. He didn't, couldn't know. He was unable to see that part of himself."

"Just what you were warned about."

I was in deep now, having to juggle names and stories. "Yes, that given the chance, Burt could only hurt Maggie, like he had Linda and her daughter—I nearly said Ella— Roburta."

Raci poked my ribs with her elbow. "Well, what in the world happened to Grandma's 'Baby steps?' I guess they didn't apply to Burt." Raci looked down the avenue toward

132

the library clock tower,

"Right." I seemed to be losing the high ground here and had to be more forceful. "I looked him in the eye. 'Don't hurt her, Burt.'" We'd crossed and walked a block while I was telling her all this.

She stopped me at the library steps. "Go on, Els. You did not."

I turned to Raci. I tried to gauge her feelings about my version. "What makes that so hard to believe?" She shook her head.

Suddenly Raci grew ecstatic, "Look. Tulips." She grasped the tine of the ornamental iron fence. "Can we go in?"

We were at the Jefferson Market Park, adjacent to the library. I was relieved. "Why not?"

At the gate a volunteer in overalls leaning on a rake said, "Please. Come enjoy the tulips before they droop from the heat. The best bench is in the shade of the library right at the pond." She pointed her earth-stained open hand.

Raci and I sauntered to the bench and sat. "We're surrounded by tulips, Els." She grasped my arm with both hands and rose to kiss my cheek. "Oh, I'm sorry. I shouldn't have."

Her kiss, after over twenty years, flooded me like sunshine after rain. "No, no, it's all right." I awkwardly kissed her forehead.

Raci looked around. "And how quiet it is here," she said, trilling like a wren. We listened to the trickle of water tickling the flat stones at the other end of the pool. And as if to remind us both we were in the city, from the far tower-end of the former courthouse, the library clock bell struck, five pudgy brass strokes. They marched around us, circling in the air along both sides of the building. "Magic," Raci said. She wiggled closer on the seat and grasped my arm again. She did not kiss me then.

Raci and I settled into the silence left by the bell, taking in the brilliance of the flowers and the sharp green of the shining lawn.

The docent approached. "I'll give you the tour, if you'd like."

"I'm content to sit. You go."

Raci stood. "I'd love that."

I watched those two move to the tulip beds on the other end of the pond, two women chatting like high school friends. I had been on that tour many times, usually with Gabby. We'd taken the girls there frequently on hot summer days, especially in the early years. Nettie and Ella loved to kneel at the little waterfall watching for imaginary minnows amongst the lily pads.

I was struck by longing. Nettie was now in Minnesota. It was looking like a permanent relocation. Ella I saw frequently, but it was more and more around Gabby's illness and, now, the hospice. And Gabby? I would miss her most. We shared nearly everything, raised our girls as sisters, and shared our careers. Gabby's symphony had become a hit. She rose with it, becoming as well known in music circles as I was among novelists. All that was coming to an end. Girls grown. Gabby going. And I?

I looked across the park. Raci crouched over a flowerbed, her hand caressing a plant. The docent stood stiffly above, pointing. They were adrift in the April afternoon warmth.

I wanted to tell Raci about Gabby. About the years in New York. About raising Nettie—I had never thought I could do it alone—giving her back the little sister she had lost. I wanted Raci to meet and to like Ella. After a trying but promising half day with Raci, I longed to draw her back into my life. My real life. It was the why of *Twelve*. It was the reason I'd invited her home. It was also the reason I was afraid.

The shade of the building and newly leafed trees soothed

my earlier irritation. It seemed to me that Raci and I were alone here, landed on a quiet atoll protected from a squalling sea.

"Els, where are you?"

"Oh. I drifted off, I think. How was the tour?"

"Just fine. I love that woman! What a gem." She sat next to me. You were deep in thought! I nearly had to kiss you awake! Thinking about Maggie?"

How could I tell her? I couldn't.

Raci prodded me. "So you *were* attracted to Maggie."

I took my time answering. Looking up through the elms, I banished visions of Gabby, of Nettie and Ella. I was glad of Raci's question. Maggie was one I could talk about.

"I'll admit to being open to Maggie." I slipped my arm over the back of the bench and squared to Raci. "I fell in love, but not as a lover. It was something like warming up to a favorite aunt, a woman at once loving and protective, but strangely unattainable in a familiar way."

"And what did she see in you?"

"Oh, I expect my wounded state attracted her. I was another stray she'd picked up along the street. Burt wrongly thought that she was the lost one in need. I suppose we were all dazzled by her presence."

"You seemed awed by her. I remember."

"It was the candidness of her artless efforts. She'd built a world around her even as she sailed down our stream of alcohol recovery."

"Always a poet at heart, aren't you, Els."

"Yes, and a bad one at that."

"Reminiscent of Moe, I think." Raci's cajoling and her hectoring felt familiar and comforting.

"I was the only one who saw how transitory her presence among us was. How unlikely a match they were. How painful Maggie's openness was to her."

"That's the work of a novelist, Els." She smiled.

"Thank you." I touched her shoulder. "She didn't realize what their affair was likely to cost. We all were trying to hang on for better days. The thought of failure, even if you've been warned is not something you are likely to dwell on." I moved my hands to my knees. "Let's walk." I pushed up and offered my hand. We circled the garden. Raci gave me a vicarious tour.

"At the beginning of their affair, I became part of Maggie's circle at the meeting. It wasn't exactly clear at first what was going on with her and Burt. I took what I saw pretty much at face value. Initially, they acted like friends, that was all. Everyone liked Maggie a lot. Why should Burt be different?" We left the garden and walked down Christopher Street.

"Well, he was different to Maggie"

"One Friday morning, I was early getting things set up."

"Getting out of the house, I suppose."

Oh, Raci! I let the comment slide. "Maggie was making coffee that day. She suddenly stopped, standing stock still. Then she smiled, privately, to herself."

"I can see it," Raci said.

"I'd been keeping an eye on the coffee business to make sure it went right and, besides her looking quite perky that morning, I'd noticed an unusual shininess about her as she worked. When she paused simply to smile, I knew something was coming."

"Aha! I know what's coming."

"It wasn't a pass."

"Not what I said."

"She motioned me into the dish room behind the coffee counter, even though there was nobody else in the room, saying she had something private to tell me."

Raci joined in. "Happiness has that positronic quality about it that makes you want to share."

136

That had been true for Maggie. Was that what *I* was feeling?

"Yes. I joined Maggie in the kitchen, put a hip against the sink, folded my arms. 'You're all sunshine and smiles. What's up, Maggie?'"

"Let me guess," Raci said, "'I'm in love.'"

"Precisely. I wasn't surprised. She was acting exactly like that."

"Did you give your blessing?"

"Well, at that moment a voice sounded in my mind, 'Watch out. Watch out for Burt.'"

"Love had no great results for him."

"No, it didn't. I said nothing to Maggie. I was there to listen, not to warn. I said, 'You look like it. Who's the lucky one?' As if I didn't know. She folded her hands over her heart like she was about to pray and said, 'Burt and I are in love.'"

"Then you said, 'Congratulations!'"

"No. Before I could congratulate or console her, Burt just then arrived. He came around back of the coffee counter. For all his faults, Burt was high on the perceptive scale. He could tell right away what was up. Yet he acted his jovial self, wound up that sinewy neck, swung his face back toward us, and tilted his head, beaming his knowing smile."

"I know," said Raci, "he quoted his grandmother."

Raci *was* bright. "'*Can't have a bit of fun,*' like Granny always said, '*but you just have to tell someone.*'"

"He shook his head in mock disgust. He'd said it to Maggie in such a tenderhearted, loving way that I could tell that he was pleased."

"Sure, despite the fact that it led to a terrible mess."

"He'd blushed his freckly cheeks to death in embarrassment but seemed content with Maggie's enthusiasm."

"They must have felt relieved the secret was out."

"I suppose so, but Burt also seemed concerned. Maybe his previous affairs had gone on the rocks *because* they became public."

"So you were in the preacher's position, counted upon to give a blessing."

"I said, 'Your secret is safe with me, and it couldn't happen to a more wonderful couple.' I meant it too."

"But you didn't go as far as saying that love conquers all."

"Raci, I'd been around enough to know better. It is love, but there is a commitment that comes with admission."

"Oh, Els, you are too cynical."

She made me smile. "Perhaps. But I kept my word. I was quiet about it all. I watched them. Anyway, that was when Maggie and Burt became a couple.

"We're here." I pointed to McNulty's door, 109 Christoper Street. "Smell the coffee?" We went up the steps and inside.

"Good afternoon, George. How's the coffee today?"

George bowed in his Chinese fashion. "The Columbian is fine, Mr. Mattila. What would you like?"

I ordered and introduced Raci, trying to keep things simple. "This is my wife, Racine Davis."

"Congratulations," George said.

"Ex-wife," Raci corrected.

Always unruffled, George continued, "Congratulations."

"Ms. Davis would like some tea to take to Ireland."

I let George give Raci the cook's tour and watched his assistant bag my order, while I breathed in the scents of the shop. When they came back, George to the counter, Raci to my side I said, "Let me pay for the tea, too." Raci started to object. "My treat," I said.

Back on the street Raci thanked me. "The tea smells delicious. I'm glad to have seen the shop, finally, after Nettie telling me about it. And hearing George."

I smiled. "Quite a surprise, isn't it?"

Raci knew what I was talking about. "You expect pidgin."

I'd thought that every time I bought coffee.

"But you get a deep-throated Brooklynese, and very well-educated to boot," she said. "Nettie never mentioned it, but then, she kept New York between herself and you."

Our daughter *had* kept her life with each of us as separate as the East and West Coasts. I knew nothing of the goings-on in California, and, as far as I'd known, Nettie never mentioned her New York connection with Gabby and Burta. They were *our* secret.

"I've gotten used to George. It's my own bias from Oakland, but I wouldn't expect his voice in San Francisco or even here in Chinatown."

We laughed wickedly. Raci and I were having fun.

"So what happened when Burt and Maggie came out of the closet?"

"Oh, they kept on in the public eye of the regulars as two friends. A love affair between members is their business and best kept outside our fraternity."

The inevitable problems of couples could only distract alcoholics from their primary purpose: to stay sober. A torrid love affair usually spelled trouble for at least one if not both of the participants. There had been married couples at *Today*, but that wasn't the kind of love Burt and Maggie had. Theirs was the burning kind that goes out of control when a wind blows the wrong way. And wind picks up quickly and shifts fast. Especially amongst reforming drinkers.

"I was part of the inner circle, so I knew most of what was going on. It all seemed fine."

"Doesn't it usually, at first?"

"Burt hadn't changed, other than showing up in the morning with Maggie instead of Toady, who at that time still hadn't resurfaced. He was 'whereabouts unknown.' Burt waltzed around as usual, smiling, agreeing with most everyone in his gracious way, and quoting the hell out of his grandmother's wisdom. I was happy to play the third wheel from time to time. It put me closer to Burt. And I was getting to know Maggie better as well."

"Didn't you ask yourself, 'How such a fragile person as she was could bring such destruction?'" Raci wanted to know.

"That question was still off in the future."

"But you might have known the answer was in her bones."

Dusk

People you've been before that you
Don't want around anymore
That push and shove and won't bend to your will
I'll keep them still

Elliott Smith, from "Between the Bars"

The late afternoon air was growing cool, the sun moving west toward Minnesota where we two had started out years before. "Short way or scenic?"

Raci buttoned her coat. "I'm up for more." We walked each carrying a handle of the bag, swinging it between us. I'd bought eight pounds of coffee.

That morning I had discouraged Raci from warming to the neighborhood. Now I found myself showing her its high points, which meant nature or what passes for it in New York. "Let's watch the boats on the Hudson."

I led Raci to the 45th Street Pier.

"That's New Jersey?"

"In all its glory."

Raci took it in. "I didn't realize there were so many skyscrapers over there."

"Land is much less expensive," I said.

"What's the clock tower there?" She pointed to the restored Lackawanna station tower. I filled her in.

"They just completed the work last year, no, two years ago."

The light sparkled on the river, and even though it was breezy we stayed to watch the 4:00 pm from Hoboken push through the chop toward Manhattan. "Brisk enough for me," Raci said after the ferry passed.

We walked up to 11th street, cutting between the bank and playground to Bleeker Street, then past St. Vincent's Triangle and back to my street. The air did me good. Raci seemed happy, thoughtful. At my building, before we climbed to the stoop, she stopped. We set the bag down. Raci leaned into me turning her ear to my heart in a nestling hug. "Thank you, Els. For being so kind and thoughtful."

I gathered her into my arms, nuzzling my chin into her hair. Now it smelled more sharply, like nutmeg. "You're the reason I'm still single after so long." I rubbed her shoulder.

She pushed free and looked into my face. "I always loved you. I'm so sorry."

"If the crash hadn't happened, we'd be together yet."

Raci picked up the bag handles. She climbed the steps.

It seemed the elevator took forever to descend. We crowded inside, the bag between us. I took Raci's face in my hands, caressing her cheeks for a moment with my thumbs, then I kissed her on the lips. "I am sorry, too. I wish I could have done better, but I was crazy just trying to stay afloat."

We reached my floor. I fumbled with my keys. "It was life, Els. It was long ago. I think I understand." I let her in, and she strode straight to the kitchen. I knew now that we would talk about the accident, but neither of us was ready yet. Slowly, I hung my coat in the hall.

"Shall I unload the bag?" She called from the kitchen.

"Yes." I shuffled in there. "Coffee? You shouldn't open the tea yet." I searched for something to say. I picked up the manuscript. "Want to finish reading Maggie?"

Raci stared at me, then left the bags on the island. She came round, looking from me to the book I held. She dropped her coat on a stool, took the book in one hand and centered the other palm on my chest. Looking me in the eyes she said, "Not just yet," and gently pushed me back down the hall and then into the bedroom, where she laid the book down.

"That's for later," she said. She undid a button.

"You sure about this?"

"Very."

. . . We were walking over to The Raquette where Burt said he'd meet us, Maggie and me, taking our time since besides opening up every day on time, Burt didn't care to keep a rigorous schedule of appointments or anything, even with Maggie. I stopped in that half-a-block stroll for the fifth time or so, letting Maggie catch up a step or two and finally had to ask, "Are you okay?"

I'd asked twice already, but this time I added, "Are you hurt?"

Maggie looked like she was about to cry—what did I say?—but she took those three steps to even our progress, grasped my arm lightly, tentatively, maybe even tenderly, holding me in place. She looked me in the eye when she talked.

"I am hurting, but I'm not hurt," she said.

Now what kind of sense did that make? I just waited, hoping she'd explain.

Maggie gently guided me forward by the elbow so I would stay with her no matter how slowly she strolled. It was one of those controlled saunters that people take when they're talking about something serious, you know, stopping every few feet or so to face each other. I allowed her to lead me.

"I've been hurting like this since I was thirteen, and actually before that, but before that time I didn't know why or that there was something wrong with me."

"There's something wrong with you?" I couldn't believe it, but some of her manner even before this assured me I was wrong.

She sidled to the fern-covered fence and stopped. "I guess I'd developed a high tolerance for pain; I just didn't know anything else growing up. But after I'd gone through puberty, the pain increased. Finally, it got so bad, I couldn't stand it. I knew something was off. The doctors were shocked, too. After their tests they told me I had suffered brittle bone disease since I was born." She was definitely tearing up right then. I was, too.

Like a goof, of course, I blurted my ignorance, "What the hell is that?"

DUSK

Maggie was kind. She patted my arm, gave me a practiced I-understand-you-healthy-people look, and took a long breath to begin. I suppose she had explained it to a lot of people. "My bones break easily. They're thinner than in most other women. It's like a genetic osteoporosis."

I knew nothing about that, either, but kept the old *boca* zipped, just waiting for her to explain.

And she told me all about it. She'd broken a forearm, three fingers (hers were thin and delicate-looking for sure), and once, when she'd been drinking, her right femur. That last incident had landed her in the hospital and forced her to sober up.

"I was killing my pain with gin," she said. "I didn't care. I was so depressed that I wanted to die."

Physical pain wasn't something I could identify with. My pain was always social or emotional or psychic, I guess. But she was convincing me.

"I was hanging at the Egbert Sousé, you know the place named after the W. C. Field's character. It wasn't rough or anything, but I'd never told any of the regulars about my bones, either, so when one of the guys at the table plunked down in my lap, he snapped my leg in two. It wasn't his fault really, but I screamed like a banshee and passed out. That was the worst pain I'd felt up to then."

Now she had me fully in tears. I wanted to squeeze her but held off. "Maggie, I'm so sorry."

"Yeah, it was a bummer."

"Are you over it? I mean the disease?"

Maggie seemed better now, talking about it, you know. "No, I'll never be over it, but I learned that I don't have to kill the pain with booze. I can learn to live with it again, as brief as my life might be."

Now I took her, very softly, by the arm. "You're going to last, longer than me, at least."

She shook her head, looked over at The Raquette to check, I supposed, for Burt who wasn't out the door yet, and then told me: "We don't live very long lives unless we're extremely careful, and that's not me, I'm afraid."

"We?"

"OIs. The people who suffer Osteogenesis Imperfecta, my disease."

"You will too live long." I insisted like a kid confronted by life itself. I didn't want to believe what she was telling me. She was too gentle, too lively, too enchanting to be in this fix.

But Maggie didn't look hopeful. "I'm already losing my hearing and have mild asthma, so I don't think I'm a lucky one."

I doubted, but Maggie seemed certain.

"Burt know all this?"

Now she moved toward the club. I let go of her, growing a lot more careful about touching her arm or anything. She went a couple of steps. Burt still wasn't out. When she turned around to me again, she was really crying, bawling right there on the street. I wanted to hug her, hold her, but I wouldn't risk cracking a rib.

"I don't know how to tell him. I'm afraid," she said.

It was the non-interventionist character of Burt's program, at least as I followed it, that made me comfortable being upstairs five of seven days a week, and I couldn't see myself getting in between Burt and Maggie. On the other hand, I had the feeling that she had spilled all this at my feet for a reason. She needed to tell Burt. That I knew, and she did, too. So for the first time in a year I felt pushed to make myself go against my grain and get into other people's business. I knew it already. What I didn't know was that it wouldn't be the last time, in particular with things to do with Burt.

"You think he'll dump you, huh?" Bad word, "dump," but fitting, and she took it well. She stood erect and wiped her tears.

"You know how sensitive he is. I don't want to hurt him."

Though it seemed to me that young women always frivolously claimed "I don't want to hurt him," I was already in too deep to argue the point. Burt would be hurt, of course, but it would be worse for him if he accidentally broke a couple of arms or hips and was then told about her OI. I was getting her drift.

"I suppose you want me to help you."

Her gaze spread over my face like a hopeful prayer. "Would you, Moe?"

I'm a pushover for a lady, a featherweight if she's needy. What makes me think I should bumble around helping is beyond me since I'm also out of touch with reality, mostly. I'm always defending and bailing out the girl, unless we're married. This time was no different.

I wasn't about to become their therapist, so I made a deal with Maggie. "I'll give you an opening to tell him. The rest has to be up to you and Burt to work out." She moved in to give me a smooch, but seeing Burt skipping down the steps at The Raquette, I stepped away. "Burt's out. Let's go to the waffle shop."

Once we sat down, a silence fell over the three of us. Burt, I knew, sensed something was up. He didn't let on, but by the way he tapped the Formica tabletop and swiveled his head around a lot, I could tell he was on edge.

People You've Been Before

The waffle shop was nearly empty. Thank God no one from *Today* was there yucking it up. We would have the requisite privacy. The white-enameled walls set with black-and-white prints in thin black frames made voices echo off the checkerboard linoleum floor a bit, so I'd suggested one of the red leather booths by the front window. The high tufted backs and pleated cushions would hold our voices inside the booth.

I'm no social engineer, but as soon as Maggie slid into the booth, I went in after her so Burt would be facing us across the table. I planned to leave as quickly as I could when my mission was accomplished. I'd set things up right.

They ordered waffles and milk. I guess Maggie drank a lot of it for the bones.

"Just a coffee to go," I said to the waitress. I wanted to be able to exit pronto, more to give them a chance to talk than to avoid discomfort and embarrassment. Burt wasn't the kind to make a scene, at least that's what I thought then, but no chances taken, no troubles found. "Yeah, with cream," I told the waitress.

I got the coffee right away and talked fast before their orders came. It was easier than I thought. I must have drawn on my public speaking days, covering the bases without hesitation.

"Hey, Burt. I want you to know something."

He pleated his forehead, widened his eyes, and not unkindly brought me into focus without saying a word.

"This is something I just found out, and I think you need to hear it."

Now he spoke. "Let it out, Mo-by," he said using his pet name for me.

I stalled over a sip or two of my coffee. I looked at Maggie to see if she was ready. She looked all right. "Actually, Maggie has something to tell you. It's nothing bad, though it isn't that great either. I'm just here to help a bit."

The important thing then was for me to shut up and look for the right opportunity to make an exit. That came almost right away.

"Darling," Maggie said, "you need to know something. I have a disease." She right away realized she'd put it wrong. "No, not that kind of disease, something more serious."

I don't think that they were aware I'd taken my coffee and gone. They might have forgotten that I had even been with them that morning. I moved carefully away, around a few of the tables, and out the door.

I looked at them through the Kuleto's decal on the door glass and picture window. They were leaning in to each other, talking and holding hands over the table, looking as if they were about to make love. I took the long way back to my car so as not to walk in front of them outside. Ten minutes later, I passed by Kuleto's again, driving to work, and Burt had switched sides, sitting now alongside Maggie, and still holding hands.

I had the sense of Raci next to me, warming under the covers but quiet. The surprise at our lovemaking receded like a caress up my spine into a sleepy invitation to escape. She had my little halogen lamp on, was turning pages, reading.

I drifted. Raci was reading "Maggie," I thought, and falling away, I struggled to think of what else was there? Moe's background. A filler of sorts, less important. Tom popping up in Minneapolis. Hillside-Glenn.

"Raci," my swirling mind uttered. I cuddled to her turning aside from the light toward what through the steam rising from his hot tub became thoughts of Hillside-Glenn bathing under sunshine filtered through redwoods. It was an important juncture in *Twelve*, one I was still revising. Often, half sleep brought me narrative solutions. So, I let myself drift there. I peered at the scene. Saw the characters assembling there. Then, as if squinting at words I had written, I saw some I wished I'd written. Then imagined I had.

. . . Muckey and I were friends. That was not rare at *Today*, but it wasn't common either. For me it was downright unheard-of and a bit uncomfortable having a friend there because upstairs I'd be spilling my guts, telling all my fears, evil and regrettable deeds, and admitting to my insecurities, but outside I'd be a well-educated, positive-talking comer, and at the time a family man to boot. It might have been the wide variance between my up- and downstairs persona that bothered me. Anyway, since Muckey didn't care about all that, we were friends.

He had many. Muckey was a chatterbox at and away from the tables up at Burt's, and people loved to hear him tell stories of life in the mining towns of Montana and of his adventures in Hollywood once he chased Roxie down there. His fables attracted friends.

Hillside-Glenn was one of those. Those two met frequently for breakfast after the meeting (I was usually off to work), and Glenn had Muckey up to the house for dinner more than a couple of times. Glenn, though a good cook, I'd heard, was always more interested in getting people to come up and hang out at his redwood hot tub than in feeding them supper and introducing them to his wife. More than anything else, tubbing, as he called it, was his favorite thing to do: sit in the big, deep wooden soaker he'd built by hand amongst a small grove of redwood trees downslope from his house in the hills above town. Though the trees were few in number, the trunks themselves were gigantic and the canopy high, high up.

Muckey didn't like water all that much and hot-tubbing was not really his style, being from cold-water Montana, so when Glenn finally insisted on him giving it a fair trial, Muckey asked me to go along for company.

"Goddamn," Muckey said, "the more the soakier, Moe." Glenn seemed flattered. At the time I was acting as Jude's sponsor, and maybe to point up my politeness in contrast to his own uninviting, crass behavior, I asked to bring Jude along. Actually, Jude drove his Mercedes coupe up there while I walked the half mile from home along the skyline.

I dipped downhill from strolling the hilltop road and came to Glenn's stucco two-story, which must have been his Italian wife's choice and true love, as it was more Mediterranean than the deep-woods, cottage-y effect Glenn seemed to like. So, the house was hers, I guessed, and the hot tub under the shade of *sempervirens* was his. Not a bad compromise, though it was not that good for Glenn as it turned out.

Like most of us, his snootfuls had piled a heavy weight on his marriage and either had to stop or be done around a woman other than his wife. Maybe that was why Glenn's spouse roamed around in the house and he rambled in the yard. Ultimately, it was health issues, as they say, that really caused Glenn to halt his assault on his liver. He'd told us several times at breakfast:

"I was sitting in the tub doing absolutely nothing, and my heart started racing in my chest like a fat water-strider trying to catch a mosquito or something. I tried breathing slowly and deeply, but the ticker wouldn't stop pumping at full speed, like three times a second. Then I got so dizzy I could barely get to the railings to hoist myself up the steps to the deck. I was weak, short of breath, and the damn thing hurt like a cracked rib.

"I figured, well this is it, but somehow I flopped onto the deck and grabbed the bell rope dangling over the deck bench. Ordinarily I used it to signal the house in case I wanted a sandwich or needed something. This time I rang the hell out of the thing. The missus looked out the kitchen window and saw me sprawled across the deck in my full splendor. She knew right away what to do.

"The doctor said, 'You've got to leave off the booze and cigars, too, unless you want us to fish you out dead from your own pond.'"

I didn't think they'd said it exactly that way, but Glenn liked his drama as much as anyone else. Likely they recommended meetings for him while he was hospitalized. And once he was out he came down the block to 29th and Telegraph, possibly to save money on the institutional meetings. They patched his heart up and sent him off with plenty of pills and advice. Later I thought it was odd they didn't prescribe bathing in the house rather than in the woodsy fresh air, but likely they had prohibited it. We've all seen the warning signs at spas cautioning the pregnant and those with weak hearts. But lectures as a general rule didn't mean a thing to anyone like Glenn or his new friends down at *Today*. He would listen but only to what he wanted to hear. It was too bad, really.

Glenn's experience was fairly typical. Heart attacks happen all the time to the drunken. I don't know if booze puts more stress on the pumper or if it hides the symptoms until it can hide them no more. His response, too, was usual. Glenn paid partway-attention to the advice. He stopped drinking, cut back on cigars (the harder to quit), and dipped in the tub, usually when his wife was not there to nag or report to the cardiologist. Since she was home as a rule, I suppose he wanted our company so he could indulge in more frequent soaking. We were willing to give it a try just to please Glenn.

One provision he'd added to the tub was a knotted safety rope that coiled down into the water, the end of which bobbed on the surface tied to a redwood float. Glenn wouldn't want one of those plastic buoys in his all-natural tub.

When I arrived that day, Jude's convertible was parked in the driveway, top down as usual. I let myself in, as instructed, at the side gate, a rounded-top door through a mini-roofed stucco buttress that swooped down from the second story. Nice architectural touch. Past the side of the house you'd follow a stairway tight to the house, tiled in Portuguese decos, then past a patio of the same tile to exit, entering another world entirely, through a rough-hewn redwood gate, onto ancient-timber steps flowing in a graceful S-shape down to the hot tub deck far below the house. Glenn was one of those handy homeowners who took interest and great pride in improving his property.

A redwood deck surrounded the ten-foot diameter tub built part way into the hillside. The platform ran round the tub something like a quarter moon, narrower at the far side—the tub being eccentrically placed in it—and wide at the staircase side. Glenn had rigged a shower vestibule on one side of a redwood trunk and had constructed covered benches, something like bus stop enclosures, that you could use while drying yourself or for changing. The bench beneath the little roof lifted up, revealing a chest full of towels and robes. Nice. A squat alcove, too, topped by a cedar-shingle roof fitted between two giant redwood trunks sheltered Glenn's refrigerator, stocked with juices and sodas now, but in days of yore, holding beer and wine. I bet Glenn had enjoyed a lot of good times down there before the medics came.

I was last to arrive. Muckey and Jude were in the tub, their robes hung on pegs near the tub entry. Glenn had just hung his robe on the tree-rack and was headed for the shower. He turned, fully nude, opening his arms for a hug to welcome me down, showing off the zipper the surgeons had installed on his chest. He noticed me staring and said, "How do you like the job? Could be a tattoo." He fingered the scar. He quickly released the naked embrace, thank God. "Welcome to Esalen-above-the-Bay," he said. "Take off your clothes and stay a while."

Glenn's retreat may not have inspired the deeper spiritual possibilities of Esalen, but it sure was soothing to booze-hounds in renewal. The setting couldn't have been improved: looking beyond a gap in the redwood grove out over lower treetops that followed the contour of descending hills, the bay and ocean beyond expanded infinitely, a sight as calming as the steaming waters flowing through the tub. The prickly-smelling tannin emitted by the tub itself and dripping off the surrounding trees from the likes of which it had been made infused a feeling as heavenly as a slowly-sipped shot of the finest oak-aged scotch whiskey. In the morning, which was the time we'd arrived, the last wisps of fog twined with the steam rising off the tub, ballooning over us bathers like a vaporous canopy held down by the overhanging redwood fronds. The tub was wide, ringed by a subsurface bench, and was deep enough for one to slip well below the surface for total immersion. Glenn called that dip the Baptist's Plunge, a doorway into another world.

The place was steeped in magic. The enchantment lightened the spirit and loosened the tongue, too. We talked. Muckey retold his Roxy and Roxie story, though everyone there had heard it at least twice, and promised to give us a glimpse into his days at the Hollywood bungalow, right after he got himself a Coke from Glenn's refrigerator. But by the time he settled his bottle into one of our host's handy deck holes made for the purpose, the conversation had moved past him and onto Jude, who was telling a skiing story.

Muckey let the Preppy Prince's story flow. It was that kind of Saturday morning. Interrupting Jude's story once, he asked, "You ever ski Mammoth?"

Jude threw him a hollow-eyed glance as if he suspected something unkind and stopped his talk.

"Hey, just asking."

Jude looked around the ring we formed, each sitting exactly in one of the four quadrants of the tub as if we wanted our skinny-dipped bodies as far out of reach as possible. He seemed to be appraising the trustworthiness of the men sitting in the tub. Apparently satisfied he said, "You're going to hear this eventually anyway, so I might as well start it here."

The mood turned serious as if a cloud above the redwoods had dampened the sun. The pump kicked in, churning the water slightly, and seemed to give Jude the impetus he needed to tell the story.

"Yes, I've skied Mammoth many times. My dad used to fly us into June Lake Airport on Fridays, and the whole family skied until Sunday afternoon." I started to drift off in my own thoughts, something like: yes, daddy and his airplane, what a wonderful life. Something in Jude's voice, though, pushed those thoughts to the side of the runway.

"Once I got my license, though, I wanted to drive. Gave me more time to imbibe with my friends and chase women along the way." He cast a sly smile around the ring. "It's a long trip, but I'd cut school to give us an extra day to drive, though the truth is, the way I was driving at the time, we didn't need to leave early. Still we did.

"Dad had given me a 1974 Chevy. An early birthday present. The Blazer four-speed convertible. It was a 307 engine and rolled up and down mountain roads in four-wheel drive like you were driving on a Nevada freeway. The car wasn't new, a couple of years old, but Dad hadn't done much with it. Coming fresh from the garage he stored it in, the thing looked and acted brand new. God, that automobile could move. I'd taken a couple trips that winter to Squaw and twice to Homewood, staying on the California side since I only had a permit, but when I turned sixteen I copped my provisional license and started driving all over the place, including to Mammoth.

"Nineteen seventy-six, late April, we rolled out of town with the top down and the way-back loaded with a case of beer and three bottles of wine all tucked under our ski gear. I had a Johnny Walker hand warmer in my vest pocket. The weather was balmy, topped out around 75 in the valley that day. Of course it was cooler in the mountains, but we just bundled up and kept driving topless.

"I don't know how much of the beer we'd had or how many pulls on my flask, but approaching Pine

159

DUSK

Crest on 108 I was uncorking a bottle of my dad's BV Cabernet Sauvignon. God what a stomach I must have had then. Asbestos-lined.

"Then it started to snow, really snow, but I just kept rolling, even when, in a couple of minutes, we were taking on drifts in the back seats and storage. 'Pull over and put the top up, Jude,' Bill, the guy in the back, shouted over the music. He was getting the worst of it back there. 'Sure, where though?' I said. The road down from Sonora Pass is narrow with oncoming traffic. Even though I didn't think he could see any better than I could, when he yelled, 'Right here,' I pulled over.

"We immediately discovered that what he thought was a pullout was a drop-off. Braking to somewhere around fifty, we went off the road, tipped and flipped, then rolled down the embankment, turning over three times, and slammed into two big pines, landing by some miracle on all four wheels. The roll bar saved me and Julie, my high school sweetheart, but Bill was gone. He'd left the car on the first flip. Fucker wasn't even buckled in.

"The rescue crew found him twenty yards away wrapped around a stump. Dead." He looked around at us again, as slowly as the rising of the steam. "That's how I killed my best friend."

I wanted to leave. The spirits that calmed and relaxed me were conjured away by Jude's disclosure. And that's what it was, less a confession than a declaration, something he had not told inside a meeting, publicly, with no possibility of response (something that just had to be accepted), but a story meant to bring retort, sympathy, or absolution from us, told to a social gathering ill-equipped by protocol to deal with it effectively. Jude had dropped an H-bomb. The tub pump stopped abruptly. We had nothing to say. Glenn slid his portly frame off the ledge and sunk down to his second baptism. Muckey, who might have been feeling a bit upstaged (though his story was a hoot rather than a hammer), sipped his Coke.

I stared open-mouthed at my so-called sponsee. "Why didn't you tell me this when we worked steps together?"

Just then Glenn resurfaced, looking not at all redeemed. The tension across the surface of the pool was so taut that something had to give.

Glenn spoke up. "Maybe that's something you should share with Burt."

"Hey, Glenn, if I want your input, I'll ask for it," Jude said. "I wouldn't share shit with that cardboard saint if my life depended on it."

I had never before seen Hillside-Glen angry. His face flushed and his eyes practically popped out of their sockets. "You little prick! You're talking about a man who saved my life, not to mention my soul. You're too good for him, is that it?"

Jude didn't hesitate. "Fuck you, fat boy. Burt is a phony, and you and everybody else know it. I wouldn't tell him what day it is, much less my private stories."

At Jude's attack, Glenn lost color. If he'd been mad, now he seemed injured, punched in the gut.

Muckey jumped in. "Whoa there, both of you. Simmer down, Glenn. Stay calm. And you, Jude, we're not in a meeting here, but we are still program people. Stick with the steps, brother." I was nodding support, I believe.

Jude mumbled, "Sorry," then more audibly, "I've got to go."

What a chump I'd been to sponsor a guy like this. I was in it now, though—it's all about accepting, about learning to live with what you've done, with whose lives you've wrecked, and about going the distance with people. When Jude pulled himself up the ladder, dried and dressed, I followed, donning a robe. I was pissed but said, "I'll walk you to your car."

It was a pretty quiet climb up to Jude's convertible, and all the while I wracked my brain for something to say, for something that Burt might say in this situation, a phrase or saying that fit. I had no grandmother to quote, only the book which tells us if we don't fully admit our crimes, we'll drink again.

"You know, Jude, keeping this to yourself risks a relapse. You've got to come clean."

I didn't really believe in God or, perhaps, forgiveness either, and had no other wellspring of wisdom to share. Comforting words seemed inappropriate. "Something like this can sink you to a new bottom. Wake up, Jude."

Then it hit me. These are just feelings. Burt would say, "Feelings are like nights. They come and they go." His grandmother told him just to wait, and sure enough his feelings would change. I'd tested this out plenty. Maybe it was the only thing that had got me through to this point.

At the car I put my hand on Jude's shoulder. Then I pulled him into a hug. "Listen, Jude, nothing is going to change what happened back then or with Glenn either, but how you feel about it will change. Give it the time it needs."

Apparently that was going to be enough for Jude. "It *was* his own fault anyway." He climbed into the Mercedes. "I'll see you Monday morning. Don't worry about me."

"Well, I will, so call me tomorrow. We'll talk."

Jude looked past the open doorway toward the hot tub. "What's Muckey yelling about down there?"

Just then the bell started ringing like mad

from down below. It sounded like murder.

"What the hell is going on?" I said. I ran for the patio steps. "Come on."

Jude was right behind me, I thought, but halfway down I looked up and saw him turning around toward the gate. "Jude, we need you, I yelled." He looked back but pushed through. I kept going, running toward Muckey's wailing voice. I thought I heard Jude's Mercedes start.

At the last steps to the deck I stopped. Muckey wasn't there. Glenn was gone too. "Hey, where are you guys? You fooling with me?"

Just then, Muckey surfaced in the tub.

"Ha, ha. Big joke."

"Help me Moe, goddamn it!" Muckey screeched. I saw Hillside-Glenn's arm around Muckey's neck. Muckey, looping a hand across Glenn's shoulder, grabbed for the rope with the other but both men went under again.

Off with the robe, I jumped down the last steps to the deck. I braced myself on the tub ladder and reached for Muckey's hand that still grasped the last knot on the safety rope. I pulled hard and up he came. This time without Glenn.

"He's drowning. Help."

It took the two of us to get Glenn above water and tied under his arms with the rope, but there was no way even the two of us could heave a man of his size onto the deck. Glenn was looking bad. We both yelled ourselves hoarse for Jude to come down, but he never did. Once Glenn, or maybe it was just Glenn's body, was secure above water, I got out and rang the bell like a crazy man. Then, still naked, I ran up to the house. It was open, no one home, and I called the 911 rescue squad. I looked out the front windows for Jude, but despite having heard Muckey's calls as clearly as I had, he'd left.

DUSK

What had happened? As soon as Jude and I topped the stairs beyond the patio, Glenn went into seizures. "He started shaking and smacked his head on the goddamn tub rim," Muckey said. "Then he went down, stirring the water like a blender. You saw what it was like at the meeting when Burt grabbed him."

Muckey had tried to handle the big man, to bring him up to the surface, but Glenn had grabbed his arm and, without knowing what he was doing, I suppose, dragged Muckey under with him. "I kicked out to get him to loosen and when he did, I swam to the ladder to call for you guys."

In the meantime, Glenn's gyrating had stopped, and Muckey went down after him again. "Glenn was hard to find, and I had a hell of a time turning him right-side up. Finally, I used the goddamn safety rope Glenn was all tangled in to bring us up. That was all before you came.

The ambulance guys told us: "You were not likely to revive your friend. Even if you'd gotten him on the deck. He'd sucked in water immediately and likely suffered a heart attack at the same time."

"That goddamn Jude. He acts like God's own *muckamuck* but isn't worth a shit on a slag heap," Muckey put it.

"Yeah, Jude brought on bad karma. He laid it on and sped off."

Muckey looked miserable, sitting on the bench, his robe over his bare shoulders. "I can't help but see him roaring down the hill. Running from his host who's goddamn drowning. And you know what he's thinking?"

"No, what, Muckey?"

"Of the nearest and dearest to his heart: himself!"

Muckey was angry, and he was right, But that kind of thinking will pop the top of a cool one.

So, I didn't let myself dwell there.

The next Thursday, Muckey and I went to Glenn's memorial, met his wife and grown daughter. We paid our respects. Even though no one else from the group went, Glenn's wife sent a letter of thanks to *Today*, for all the months the group had helped her husband be a better, happier person. Letters like that were unusual around there. It was good for everyone at the meeting when Burt read it outloud. Glenn had been happy with us.

Jude got up and left when Burt started reading.

The "Preppy Prince" did not disappear. He stuck around at *Today*, making me and everyone else uncomfortable. He did hint privately that he'd disgraced himself by driving off, but skillfuly "delegated" blame to Muckyey and me for not saving Glenn, just as he had with his fatal crash in the mountains. Corporate life taught him that.

"Oh my God," he told me, "I should have been there for you guys." That was the kind of guy he was.

"Oh my God," brought me fully awake. Yeah, oh my God was right. I was envisioning Jude, growing angry when here I was lying next to Raci—she was sitting upright in bed bending over the manuscript. I reached a hand and stroked her bare back. She didn't move.

"Did you have a nightmare?" she asked.

"No. I was just thinking about *Today* and Burt and all.

"I'm just finishing your, I mean Moe's chapter," she said.

It was just as well. Most of the reaction I attributed to Moe during Glenn's death scene was indeed fiction. When Jude erupted, when Hillside-Glenn defended Burt's reputation, and when Muckey intervened, I had remained silent. I'd never coached, prompted, or comforted Jude, either. It was not something I wanted to admit to Raci, or maybe even to myself.

So I let her read and wished for the fiction to be true.

DUSK

. . . My story is about Burt, about the brief
time I knew him. It is also about Tom and how he
crossed and dotted my life, like t's and i's. It's
not really about me. Still, it gets complicated,
at least in my addled brain, unless I keep in
mind what I did, what had happened to me, and how
I felt about it. I'll try to keep my part short,
down to the essentials just so you can see what
I mean. The source of stories is sometimes as
important as the tales themselves, and might be
more revealing than the why of them being told.
You can decide for yourselves. My story starts
long before Burt, even before I first met Tom.

Sometime between Christmas 1953 and the next
two nativities, a quiet and intimate evening
gathering, comprised of my mother and two older
brothers, lit by the lights of our Yuletide tree,
was interrupted by banging at our front door. My
father was not at home, and the chaos outside
startled us all. Me, it scared. At five I had
never known anyone entering from the front door.
We came and went by the kitchen door all year
round. Our visitors and relatives used the same
route. The intensity and location of the noise
pierced the warm safety of our circle. Mother had
been reading, I think, a story having to do with
the holiday.

The front door leading from the enclosed porch
flew open in a rush of frigid December air. My very
drunken father—I've concluded this since, though
at the time I couldn't begin to guess what was
wrong with him—despite his stomping in the porch
dragged in a mound of snow behind him, along with
an overly jolly Santa Claus who cascaded more snow
melt liberally from his fur-lined cap down to his
high black boots. The room filled with the odor of
steamy, putrid, overripe cherries—actually, as I

myself later discovered, Jim Beam's brandy, mixed with the rankness of sodden wool clothing in need of laundering.

"Look who I found outside!" My father boomed.

The giant Santa howled, "Ho, ho, ho. Merry Christmas."

Mother, already in the midst of containing the flood of melting snow, pushed Santa and his elf back the way they'd come, using a broom as much a barrier to further advance as an implement to sweep snow back outside.

"You're getting everything soaked. Get out in the porch and brush off."

Jolly old Saint Nick complied, but the rejection of my father's brilliant Christmas gift to his children cooled his rollicking joy and heated his ever-ready ire. "Some welcome. What the hell is wrong with you?"

As much on cue as I was to be all my life, mostly mouthing the wrong lines, I burst into tears at a legendary Santa who had immediately become much too real and at my dad's fierce reaction to Mother's caution. A five year-old's mind can take only so much without tearing back to his expressive, infantine state. It was not a primal scream, but close and inconsolably deep.

"You're scaring the boys!" Mother yelled.

Not to be defeated, Father pushed her aside, grabbed old Mr. Claus and said, "Come here, Moe. Meet Santa."

I cowered behind the couch. The two inebriates advanced unsteadily, whereupon St. Nick caught his coattails on a branch and his foot on a chair, falling sideways fully into the Christmas tree, grasping for a hold, but instead bringing my father, too, down into what became the mess of tinsel, bent branches, and shards of smashed bulbs and splintered ornaments. The tree lights went out.

DUSK

My mother screamed. Both the fallen drunks wallowed in the debris of crushed presents and broken limbs, muttering, "Jesus Christ" over and over again.

That is all I saw. Wailing, I joined my brothers in the bedroom—they'd been sagacious enough to see trouble coming from afar—and together we listened to jolly-old apologies and the consequent uproar of fighting which ended in the slamming of the front door and the sounds of Mother crying mixed with broom swishes and blubbered curses.

My five year-old, photographic mind had developed the immediate mental negative of the scene: jagged bubble lights, snapped pine twigs, and the star of Bethlehem dashed to the floor, burnt out, and black. A memory it did never forget.

So, you swear, as soon as you are able to comprehend the immediate causes though hardly the baffling, latent, and adult circumstances surrounding the behavior, never, never, never to imitate that kind of act before your own children.

The ardor of such prepubescent promises sustaining over the years an onslaught of worldly confusion grows thin and forgetful as one matures. The subject of that oath, boozing, was never temptation as such but eventually became to me an invitation to simplify, to shut out, to escape confounding life, at least for a little while. I barely left middle school before I was bellying up to any convenient bar that would admit me, mostly private ones in friends' homes. Though along the way as I picked up a wife, then a different wife with a child, then two more kids, and so on, I considered myself smarter than my father because I hadn't brought down the family tree.

Still, the energy, brilliance, and enthusiasm of youth are over time no match for a life without restraint, thoughtfulness, or compassion, especially the last. Never having been exposed to these latter three, I felt free to excuse damage and destruction I caused much as my father could blame the toppling of the tree on my mother's obstinate orderliness. Besides, subjection to the drudgery of thinking ahead and caring for others flew in the face of my tacit mantra: An unexciting life is not worth living.

I didn't set out to be a drunk, but like all boozers found myself surrounded by liquor. The variety of basic libations proclaim the prolific dissemination of drink: mead, wine, chardonnay, brandy, scotch, pinot noir, bourbon, triple sec, whiskey, vodka, malbec, gin, C_2H_6O, rum, tequila, schnapps, ouzo, rakia, grappa, absinthe, potin, sake, vermouth, cabernet sauvignon, gamay, merlot, not to mention beers: ales, pilsners, ambers, and malts.

I was to try nearly all those and some I've failed to name here, still maintaining a generous clearance from the tree. Never mind that by this time I was both ruing and celebrating my first divorce, a real heartbreaker which I hoped would be a salvation as well. We'd drunk together. Instead, without her, I drank for two.

On New Year's Eve nearly twenty years before my voice-from-the-blue enlightenment, I and my six Beefeaters-and-tonic, and a quart of that very same gin joined a raucous party that had been even busier than had we three (bottle, six drinks, and me). Standing in the circle of friends jibbering nonsense to each other, Earl, the host, held his arms aloft for attention. "Ladies and curs," he said over the din, "it is time to play Mixologist, the friendly game of bartenders!" He acquainted us with the rules, so called, and began by naming a mixed drink, "the martini." The player to his left in the circle then took his turn and so on around the circle. One was supposed to, after his turn, take a swig from whatever libation he then held.

The first rounds stayed with the tried and true admixtures made famous time and again by movie stars: martini, boxcar, Black Russian, tonic (gin), sazerac, Tom and Jerry, sidecar, boilermaker. Sweet drinks followed: brandy Alexander or Manhattan, brandy sour, gimlet, fizz (gin), Tom or John Collins, Mickey Slim, and Mickey Finn.

"Ah, ah, ah. That's not a bar drink!" Earl bellowed.

The contestant, a large bearded man, then offered, "Shirley Temple (loaded)."

We went on: tonic (vodka), piña colada, tequila sunrise, Bloody Mary, cosmopolitan, Harvey Wallbanger, screwdriver, White Russian, seven and seven, mimosa, mulled wine, bushwacker, and grasshopper.

It wasn't long before new ones of dubious repute were mentioned: New Orleans hand grenade, *adios* motherfucker, sex on the beach, virgin sex on the beach, sperm, blow job.

Earl quipped on that one. "The drink or the favor?" Drunken laughter followed.

The woman to Earl's left said, "French kiss," and the round became raucously provocative: pink panties, wet pussy, dirty Shirley (really loaded), porn star, pink panty dropper, Asian cum shot (gained general groans), sex appeal (a cheer followed), tie me to a bedpost, fruit tingle, screaming orgasm, blue balls.

The circle was running out of the salacious: dirty bong water, cactus cooler, day at the beach, Tokyo tea, lady cello, Skittles, coco loco, touchdown, devil's breath, nutty Irishman, funky cold Medina, call a cab, sea breeze, fat frog.

Now Earl, attempting to cross the finish line, rattled off a blitz: dirty banana, blackjack, Spanish coffee, Don Pedro, a Gilligan's Island, Bahama breeze, Malibu Bay breeze, orange crush, grape ape.

The lady to the left was not to be outdone. She turned to him, thrust and circled her plevis and offered, "'The sloe comfortable screw,' which is," she said, "southern comfort, added to sloe gin, topped by orange juice and Galliano or other liqueur like chartreuse or strega then decorated by a cherry all served in a Tom Collins glass (a water glass to some)."

Earl quipped, "How can one say no?" Then he anointed the floor with his highball, a tall whiskey sour, I believe, like this: "Who is the King Bartender?" he was asking, swinging his arms and swaying from his ankles upward. The glass hurtled, of its own accord, he later claimed, to the kitchen floor, bursting into the incipient silence that grew total in one second.

Horror on the faces of the drunken is a terrible sight; multiplied by eight it is a devastation. I'm sure, as I did, that, besides Earl who laughed hysterically, all of us around him thought "How could you be so drunk at seven-thirty in the evening?" And, perhaps it was just my own thought: "I'll never get that bad."

And then, I did.

Nearly twenty years later, at the initial mixer of a corporate gala, amidst colleagues barely known to me, my wineglass dropped to the floor, and it was nice enough to shatter over the Oxfords of our circle of six. A disembodied Earl immediately whispered in my ear: "Welcome to the club." When I looked up, I was alone.

DUSK

Some of this has as much as a six thousand-year history, though I doubt the Harvey Wallbanger was popular in Babylon. If it had been, it would have been governed by a lesser known Code of Hammurabi. Unfortunately for many, the code did not punish wine merchants in the same way as faulty architects. If you fell down inebriated, never to rise again, your bartender would shake his head, but if the house fell on you, the architect would lose his. Likely, Hammurabi liked his mead. In any case, though the distillers, wine-makers, and brewers file off into the fogs of receding time, they stay, yet, very much with us.

To be fair, not all of us in the good old USA contribute to over consumption according to the Washington Post.[*] Half of us imbibe less than a drink a week, forty percent of us not even one. I have moved from the top ten percent to the bottom ten percent of my countrymen and women, from the class that downs ten or more drinks a day, 73.85 per week, to the class formerly called teetotalers.

As a result, I have time to work. I have some ability to think. I have Cheerios instead of cheers for breakfast and rather seldom spill my milk.

My latter-day spanking came from my competitors in business. I'd come west for the job, never mind the lessons in incompetence. It seemed all right. No one, including me, really knew what my problems were. Like the rest of Burt's devotees— there upstairs before I'd converted—I thought I was safe viewing the world from the inside of a bottle. After all, once the hep oil was gone what

---

[*]   *The Washington Post*/Wonk Blog, September 25, 2014

172

other use was there for the container? Perhaps I was brought to my rival's favorite bar, or maybe it was an unhappy coincidence, but we competing managers met.

"Let me buy you a drink," he said to me. And I was never so glad to have made a friend.

"Sure." And he ordered my favorite before I could name the brand.

What came could have been named "a slap in the face" were there such a concoction. He paid for my favorite Cointreau straight up: a triple shot which told me that not only was my trademark drink widely known (and snickered at), but so was my prodigious consumption. Even so, standing there humiliated and horrified, I couldn't set the sticky glass down, until, that is, it was empty.

I could not hide. It would not be long before my boss would buy me my last triple, a triple play which retired my side. I was tagged out, sliding and on my way to Burt's dugout, hearing voices all the way.

If I'm sounding jocund about it all, consider the alternative. There is little aid in the misery of abject depression. Having piled up three lifetimes of destruction and horror in less than a third of one, a drunk like me must adopt the sanguine as his solace or perish under tonnage of hedonic debris. The hurt I inflicted on those close to me, in direct proportion to nearness, assured me I was a self-made man. One none could love.

What amazed me, once I finally sobered up, was as unlovable as I felt, those around me did, truly, love me, again in proportion to proximity. Love is not a solid commodity but more a stream that varies its flow, changes direction, and the hypersensitive reformed one, newly stripped of his medication, perceives at times that a flood of

affection is threatening to drown him and wash
him away.

As she read, I fingered the fused vertebrae and the surgeons' signatures all along Raci's spine. She did not stir a bit. "You're as wonderful as ever," I said.

Raci closed the manuscript, turning and setting it on the table. I watched her spine, wincing on my pillow, as she twisted. Apparently, she had no pain. She turned, looking down at me.

"I never thought we'd do that again." Raci was crying. "The last time was just before that Christmas."

It had been a day before Tom showed up. I remembered well. "I loved you so then," I said, hanging onto the first words long enough to add, "and I still do."

Her tears dropped over my chest. She cried harder. "Not without hating me, too."

"Raci, I do not."

"How could you not? I as good as murdered those kids, Els. Our kids."

It was out now. I took her hands away from her face, turning and gently pulling her to the pillow and to me. "Hush. You had an accident." I hugged her to me and let her cry.

It had been horrifying. I quaked with it yet, but now after twenty years, maybe we could talk past the hurt. This woman shaking in my arms, agonizing, had left me.

At least that was what I thought at the time. She'd packed the suitcases, a big food box, and games and toys for the kids, driving toward her parents house in Oregon. She didn't make it. A drunk ran a light, smashing Racine's body and slaying our two young children.

Nettie had been unhurt but deeply depressed. She wouldn't visit her mother in the hospital. I tried not to drink. I was, indeed, stone cold sober, though in shock, when my lawyer asked me, "Do you want to let this go through?"

"What go through?" In a fog, because she had left me, I'd filed for separation.

"Your divorce. Do you want it to go through?"

Raci was unconscious for two months. She woke to learn that Michael and Siiri had died in the crash. And that she was to be divorced. Of course, she fell apart.

Even sedated, she herself couldn't bear to face Nettie. The feeling was mutual. Both were devastated.

I understood. Nettie did not, but Raci was too deep in physical and spiritual pain to care.

I was raising Nettie alone then. I was angrier than I'd ever been, and was just barely holding on myself. "Yes, I told the lawyer, let the divorce go through." At that moment, I did not want what was left of Raci.

I'd like to say it was Nettie's hurt that galled me and goaded me on. My own hurt only intensified the pain. Couples, even those on solid footing, often do not survive the death of a child, much less two. Anyway, that was what I told myself then. I always regretted it.

Now, holding her against my chest, I wanted to comfort her. "I have forgiven you. That began when you and Nettie reunited." That had been in Nettie's tenth grade, after nearly four years of silence. "I thought you couldn't forgive me. . . for ending things."

Raci stopped crying. She studied my face. "It was hard, yes, but I have left all that behind. I forgive you Els. I understand."

Perhaps *she* did. *I* had never been able to explain my actions. Now was no time to try.

I took her hand, slipped atop her gingerly. We made love, lubricated by tears, in the most tender, thoughtful way, each to prove our forgiveness of each other.

Afterwards, this time, it was Raci who slept.

DUSK

. . . "I'm in jail."

Why Tom called me was more a mystery than how he knew I was in Minneapolis then.

I would have called a lawyer, my father, or if I were Tom, my sister, who lived in Saint Paul, but that's not the way Tom McIntyre operated. He'd been drunk, I figured, for all the years since I'd seen him stomp down my stairs in Duluth.

He had not called or written me in all that time, but I'd heard about the cars he'd crashed and rolled, including one that burned. About his toppling into St. Anthony's Falls at two in the morning and being rescued by other solstice celebrants. About the jobs he lost. But Tom wouldn't want to fess up to any of his own people, even though the blind themselves could see he was a hopeless boozer.

As for me, I knew that I drank too much. My bosses and coworkers seemingly encouraged it, but no one had pierced the looking-good armor I lacquered with morning coffee and high-striding energy, and after hours, mellowed with grass. I wasn't admitting anything either. My private life was closed. I supposed Tom felt no different.

"Hey, if you can pick me up, they'll let me out," Tom said.

I'd moved to town three months before, with my new wife, DeLorr, and her daughter, Tilla. DeLorr was four months pregnant with Siiri. I was starting over in the big town. So, as far as my old friend, my wife wasn't a problem. Sharon would have taken my car keys rather than see Tom again. DeLorr hadn't even heard of him.

"I've got a friend in trouble," I told her. "This will take an hour."

The sheriff's deputy had picked Tom up going the wrong way on a one-way street. Tom had told the cop that he always took that shortcut home from his club after closing at two a.m. No one was ever on the street anyway. The deputy didn't like Tom's story. Instead, the officer added to Mr. McIntyre's wrong-way violation a list of offenses: operating a motor vehicle while under the influence, driving without a license, reckless driving, and failure to stop. These joined a list already grown fairly long since Tom moved south six years before. Still, they were willing to let him out so he could work the next morning if a sober customer picked him up. How Tom had worked that miracle is known only by God himself— the jail must have been full up. Perhaps all the deputies were Vietnam vets. I wasn't exactly detoxed, but I seemed sober to the fuzz.

I grabbed a fifteen-minute parking spot at the jail and went in, it seemed, through six gates. I also waited two hours before I saw Tom. I signed him out and promised to take him home. He shouldered what looked to be the same duffel bag he'd had seven years before and waltzed out onto 4th Street. I held the door for him like he was a dignitary. I had no love for the all those sheriffs myself.

The first thing out of Tom's mouth was, "Shit. You got a parking ticket."

Had we been a minute later my car would have been hauled off. As it was I had to pay the tow truck driver cash.

"Don't worry, Moe, I'm good for it. I'm just broke tonight."

He was broke and was locked out of his apartment, too. Two things that had slipped his mind when he called me. Imagine a landlady wanting rent.

I had to bring him home to meet DeLorr, who would soon be getting to know my old friend. Her impression that morning at four o'clock differed little from Sharon's seven years before.

177

DUSK

On the way to my house that night, predawn morning actually, Tom broke his news. "I've got it with me."

"What? What have you got?"

"*Tunnel Rats*, the whole damn book. Well most of it, anyway."

"*Tunnel Rats*. Your manuscript?"

He hitched his shoulder up and flipped me a hateful grimace. "No, not a manuscript, a book." He indicated a thickness, holding up his index finger away from his thumb. "What do you think I've been doing for seven years?"

My own thoughts now made me laugh. "Honestly? I thought you'd been drinking."

He clamped and thinned his lips, shaking his head in disgust. "I was hoping you'd read it. I took your advice. It's all different now."

Act enthusiastic. That's it, be a friend. "Wow. I'm happy for you."

My new job—the one that would carry me west in two years—and my marriage were taking all my time. I hadn't read a book, even the ones I wanted to get to, in five years. Literature and reading were seeming more and more like things of the past, but Tom's attitude told me he wouldn't want to hear that. "Yeah, I'll take a look. Be glad to."

He said, "Great," and right then and there as I drove home, he fell asleep.

I parked at our kitchen door which I'd left unlocked, and since I couldn't rouse Tom, left him dead to the world in the front seat.

I caught a couple of hours myself, and when I came to the kitchen for breakfast, there he was chatting it up with DeLorr and Tilla like he'd known them all his life.

"Hey, Moe. Thanks for the rescue last night.

Can you give me a lift to the club?" Tom never hesitated to ask for help.

DeLorr gave me that what-should-a-wife-know look, and I said, "Actually, I'm giving Tilla a ride to school, going the other way."

"I can take a bus, don't worry. They won't fire me." Then he squinted his eyes to slits and stretching out his lips tautly upward when he remembered he was broke. "Can you lend me a ten?"

DeLorr turned her burgeoning belly to the stove. She was getting acquainted with the McIntyre bravado.

"I'll give you a ride," I said.

I rushed Tilla to get ready, stuffed her lunch into her backpack, and called my office. The three of us left DeLorr at the kitchen door waving, not to me or Tom, but to Tilla. "See you at three, Honey."

We were down the short drive and gone, so I didn't see DeLorr reappear in the driveway waving Tom's manuscript. He didn't tell me on the ride that he'd left it. That was the McIntyre way.

There was nothing for it. That night I slept fitfully. I woke at three in the morning, went to the den, and reluctantly opened *Tunnel Rats*. Then I couldn't put it down. Tom had followed my advice. He'd certainly worked on it, if not for years, then for a good long time.

> My first time down a hole, I sneezed. The Viet Cong heard. The air raked my nostrils with acid tines. I dropped my flashlight and flapped my nose shut to stop the second choo. My ears were like to blow. Expecting to die, I pissed my pants.

> The VC hear everything down there. They'll blast your ass off if you so much as fart. They can smell you, too, so I never washed with soap.

DUSK

They didn't, that time. I copped the light and turned it on the floor first then on the walls like Donny taught me to do, inching ahead on my belly.

"Any time you see or feel somethin' funny, you stop. Dead stop," Donny had said.

I had been topside when Donny himself didn't think two tiny holes heart-height on the walls were anything. "All clear," he'd whispered on the wire. He advanced. Then VC poked spears through those holes either side right through Donny. He blasted the m-f-ers through the wall pumping all nine out of his Smithy. Shot himself once.

But Donny was dead. Poison tips. The spears crossed right at his heart.

I was the one went down to retrieve him. I'd seen the last of wet pants long before. This time I spewed breakfast when I saw him hanging from those bamboo rods. But after that, I was too angry to be scared.

I'd turned twenty-one that week.

Tom went on, telling it like it was. He brought me down the hole with him, smelling the VC, feeling for tripwires, looking for little holes in the walls. After an hour, I was shaky and cold. I had to go back to bed, but I was afraid to move. I shuffled along, watching for snakes and wires on the hallway floor. His story was that effective.

I'd finished reading by the end of the week, growing ever so glad I had dodged the draft. At five foot eleven inches, I'd been too tall for tunnel duty, but there was no doubt ever in my

```
mind that I was destined to die in war. The best
thing for me was to avoid the whole thing. Tom's
book was as close as I wanted to get.
    I called his club to tell Tom I'd finished
Tunnel Rats. "Mr. McIntyre is no longer with us,"
the receptionist said. He knew nothing else, or
wouldn't tell. I didn't know where his locked-out
apartment was and couldn't find out. No one had
heard from him, not even his sister.
    I put Tunnel Rats on the shelf to wait for its
creator, and when we packed up for California, Rats
went with us. We, the book and I, waited a good long
time for the author. But years meant little to Tom.
Like drunken sprees, they just passed out of mind.
```

I felt Raci stirring. My thoughts around Tom's visit were interspersed with feelings about making love to Raci. They were even more complicated than responses I'd had to other friends or lovers. I sensed hope for better times springing up. Even doubled, our intimacy was insufficient to plaster over decades of guilt and grief on each side. Would it be a start? The promise and hope we'd shared back in Minneapolis might be impossible now.

Raci rolled toward me. She laid a hand on my chest but didn't open her eyes. To herself, it seemed, she smiled. Sweetness now only accented sorrow. Loving sharpens guilt and remorse. Her eyelids fluttered, then softly opened. "Hmmm. That was very nice."

Whether she commented on her nap or our embraces, I couldn't decide. "You slept." Raci turned her face to mine and studied a while.

"You look thoughtful. What have you been dreaming up?" She stroked my cheek.

My thoughts were too rough to tell her, too volatile. "I've

been remembering our days in Minneapolis. Around the time I rescued Tom from jail."

"Oh, yes. I was carrying Siiri." Her voice held not the slightest tremor. She snuggled her hips to mine. "Those were good days, Els."

"I think I was drinking a bit. Likely too much."

"Don't worry. Even when I quit for the pregnancy, I didn't notice. I was so in love."

Maybe a remorse or male-post-release response shied me away from talk of love. I wasn't ready to go there. I veered again toward stories of Tom. "Did you know that Tom showed up at *Today* one time?"

She may have felt disappointment, but Raci went with the direction I set, at least for the moment. "It's been a long time. I have no recollection of that."

I dove for cover with the story. "It was Veteran's Day."

. . . Oddly for a Tuesday, the coffee bar was buzzing fifteen minutes before the meeting was to start. Fortunately I'd come early and could give Len a hand. Toady was doing the leadership honors up front.

Veteran's Day was one of those special events that called to people to come in out of the cold of their lives even if for just one day. If any single species of firewater moth flitted at the candle of booze, it was disaffected Vietnam veterans. The room was full of them, all men. In 1987, if they wore any kind of uniform or insignia it was a bandanna tied at the forehead, round the neck, or dangling out of the back pocket of Levi's. The California November had turned crisp, so black leather vests over USMC or Army t-shirts completed the outfit. They were loud. They were raucous. And tense, uneasy jollity pervaded the room.

I was pouring. Men were still streaming in. As a haven for the downtrodden, *Today*'s reputation was high and wide at that time. We were out of cup holders and were using the eight ounce Styrofoam cups. No one complained. We had plenty of packaged cookies. The guys were generous, filling the tip jar with ones. Someone even put in a fiver. We needed more pots. I went behind to wash out a seldom-used one in the back room sink when at the counter I heard Tom McIntyre's voice: a small man's baritone, scuffed to near hoarseness, holding forth with a dancing rebellious sound.

There was no doubt it was him. I quickly wiped the pot, came out from the back, setting it below the Bunn's cone, pushing the brew button. These tasks took not a minute, but Tom was gone from the counter. In that crowd his tunnel rat stature was hidden in the forest of strapping vets most of ample girth and tall. As I continued to work, I heard his laugh up front in the crowd. Even when I slipped around the counter to unfold more chairs—it was now wall to wall people—I couldn't see exactly where he'd gone. I'd do what I was good at, wait. When the meeting began, everyone would sit down.

Toady started the meeting, "Welcome home." I knew he'd been in the Navy in '68, and his opening brought down the house. They cheered as if they were at a USO show in Saigon. Then Tom spoke up. It wasn't really part of the meeting, so I'm repeating it, "Hey, I've *been* home." He gave the "been" a plantation patois twist and "home" a repugnant huff. The room went silent. And there was many a head nodding. He hadn't said, "And there was no there, there," but he may as well have. The vets in the room were a special slice of survivor who had returned home from hell only to find themselves in purgatory.

That taught Toady a lesson. Anyway, he backed up and restarted the meeting in the usual way. He had asked one of the early arrivals to share his story. All I can say is that they were veteran experiences, and everyone was paying attention like they were listening for VC to sneak up on them. No one moved for ten minutes.

The Vietnam vets had taken over the meeting. No one else would get a chance to share, but that seemed all right with the regulars. Listening was something we could do. Many of us had dodged or been unfit for service. This one day was theirs. It was their Thanksgiving and Christmas together.

When the veteran-chairperson casually glanced in Tom's direction, Tom stood up and immediately started in. What he said isn't a part of this record, but what I felt and thought certainly is.

I was listening from behind the coffee counter. Tom was holding forth on the other end of the room. I could hear well but couldn't spot him around the posts and people. Even standing, Tom didn't rise above the big guys sitting between us.

His story told me it was him. First horror, then anger, then resentment (the boozer's death wish), crept over me. I had been overjoyed when I'd first heard his voice. But now what he was saying, though not filled with outright lies, certainly didn't jibe with what I knew. He continued his first line of argument: being home was a torturous limbo. When he explained about his lost manuscript, which he claimed was stolen from his pack, I wanted to shout out, "I did not filch your book." He didn't name names. After all, why would he name someone he thought was back in

PEOPLE YOU'VE BEEN BEFORE

Minnesota? But by his description, I was the guy. I hadn't wanted the manuscript. I saved it for him. The story was a small part of his share, but I couldn't hear the rest. Now I wish I had, but my ears shut out everything he said in a roar of recrimination.

When the meeting ended, I positioned myself outside the upstairs door. Every last person there would see me before he turned down the stairs. I wanted to set Tom straight. I wanted to grab him, shake the hell out of him, and hug him. I wanted to smack his lying mouth and to kiss it too. Going all the way back to our childhood, he was the one closest. He was the one most like me.

The crowd was slow to disperse. The buzz of chatter filled the room and spilled into the hallway where I waited to seize Tom. I'm not much of a fighter, and I was shaking all over. I felt cold. Some *Today* regulars and then a few vets came out. Toady and Burt left. I said goodbye to Len and Susan. Maggie and Muckey weren't there that day. Finally, Tom emerged. He was half turned to a companion of about his same stature, talking a mile a minute, looking over and away from me.

"Tom," I said, "it's me, Moe." I felt a rush of relief just having said his name.

Tom looked and glared. I don't think he could believe his own eyes. Men were pushing from behind him. "Hey, get moving, Ratso." Tom stood firm.

"This is my meeting, Tom. I come here every day." Why I felt I had to explain my presence, I'm not sure, but he acted like I had violated his privacy, his rights.

All he did was stare. Then like he'd encountered a VC in a tunnel, he whirled and backed down the stairs faster than I thought possible.

"Hey, Tom. I want to talk with you."

His companion intervened. "Back off, mate,

on this day Ratso doesn't talk to civvies." He
followed Tom, bouncing down with his back to me.
  I yelled out, "Tom, for Christ's sake."
  At the bottom of the steps Tom looked up and
repeated the tunnel rats' motto: "*Non gratum anus
rodentum*. I don't give a rat's ass." The guy with
him laughed loudly. Tom went out the door. A
crowd of veterans followed him.

"You took things so seriously at that meeting," Raci said.

"I did. That program saved my life, or at least saved me more misery."

Before I could recoup the comment, Raci softened it for me. "There was plenty of it to go around, drunk or sober."

"Drinking made it worse. And for Burt and the rest."

"Even sober, everything was tense for you people."

"You people?"

"Yeah, alcoholics. Remember the luncheon? It couldn't have been more tightly strung."

Raci had been to Maggie's pre-Thanksgiving luncheon that year. "I don't remember another time. So unusual."

I filled in: "Those affairs weren't unheard of, even among the regulars at *Today*, though they never passed for 'normal' gatherings. Most members had social lives, though many had worn out welcomes at parties of that kind." That day drunken histories were out, and that was enough to make even this slightly formal occasion tense or at least uncomfortable. "Its the nerves, you know. Unsoothed, the synapses keep one jumpy."

"Burt was certainly on edge," Raci said.

"You know what was so unusual about this event wasn't just that it was by invitation—Maggie had handed me a card, envelope and all, outside the meeting—but that it was a couples' gathering."

"It was a weird mix of insiders and outsiders."

"Well, most of Maggie's guests were rooted in *Today*. But her inclusion of women from outside the group made conversation very awkward."

"You couldn't rely on your famous days-drunk stories."

"We called them drunk-a-logues. The fits and starts of polite talk and the confused shuffling of places really put an edge on. For me at least."

"For God's sake, Els, it was a Sunday brunch. One with strangers. When has that been comfortable?"

"The jitters didn't last."

"Ha, they completely blew out the windows and doors. Burt made sure with his devilish lewdness," Raci said.

"Well, no one but Maggie would have risked that kind of event. No one else was so open to drawing in such a dangerous melange.

"Let's see, five *Today* members (Burt, Toady, Dwayne, whom I called Muckey, and Maggie) and non-members: you, Toady's Cheryl, and Ona up from Hollywood."

"Oh sure. Roxie Rodelli of Drummond, Montana, aka Ona. How did that happen?"

"Maggie was lukewarm on Dwayne, but she had met and adored Ona at *Today*. Dwayne's old flame was practicing sober living in LA and had reconnected in some odd gestalt with Mr. D, Jr. So Maggie had to invite both."

"Did you know they had found each other?"

"Dwayne wasn't about to blab to the *Today* crowd. At first, he didn't even say anything to me. But over the week previous to the invitation, Dwayne had brought Ona to the meeting. She was staying in town over that weekend before heading back down south again."

"I remember her at the lunch saying, 'I'll never leave Hollywood. It's my home!'"

"She actually lived in Culver City and bused it to a job

DUSK

Dwayne had found her in Venice Beach. Even after bumping down there ruined, broke, and cast off the senior Mr. D's fruit truck, the dazzle of Hollywood hadn't left her."

Raci laughed. "Isn't love picturesque?"

. . . Three months prior to Maggie's luncheon, Muckey'd disappeared from *Today* with a word to no one. Roxie'd made a collect call to him, and without hesitation, he had rescued her from a dope-house in downtown LA. Muckey got her on her feet, housed, employed, and surrounded by good people all within that month. When he returned to our little club, he was pretty quiet. Some thought he'd fallen off the water wagon. Worry and suspicion about that increased when he began slipping out of town—what we didn't know—to visit his old flame every other weekend afterward. Muckey, though, was sober. I just had that trusty feeling about him, even though he was in desperate love, which is usually a danger signal.

The beach restaurant Roxie worked had shut for fumigation all that week, so he brought her north for a break and, maybe, to keep an eye on her, too. At *Today* Maggie, who'd never been told Muckey's Montana story, had taken to Roxie right away.

On the occasion of Maggie's party, I was happy I'd kept my spouse-bashing to a minimum at *Today*. It's one thing to confide in a friend regarding one's marital bliss, and it's another kind of cocktail when spilled out over the meeting tables. That embarrassing flood tends to drip on and stain your pants. Besides, no matter how evil a cast I threw over DeLorr's and my marriage, I knew most of the difficulty was mine. Of course I seldom mentioned that fact to DeLorr herself. As close to arrogance as that might be, I still had some self-respect. Anyway, DeLorr had stayed with me, probably for the sake of the kids. And she didn't kick and scream—she'd done that plenty over the years—about missing half a soccer game to make it to Maggie's on time.

So there we were. Six of us, Muckey D. and Roxie, Toady and Cheryl, and DeLorr and I seated at the dining table set up in a wide entry open to the apartment's common areas, looking two steps down into the kitchen and lower, beyond into the living room to a picture window view of the city below. We were daintily sipping water, getting acquainted, and watching Maggie, who'd comment from time to time over her shoulder, fussing with her chicken dish at the oven.

Toady's wife, Cheryl, a dazzling dresser, came in a sleek pantsuit starred with just the right number of sequins to accentuate her lines and to complement Toady's dapper black shirt and golden tie. It was hard for us all not to tower over Toady, and you have to give Cheryl credit for wearing flashy but low heels. In bare feet she had him by a head. Still, an ebony couple well dressed in black are dashing anywhere.

Toady had taken up guitar again after his return and was singing in a band now. As enthusiastic about this job as the corporate one he'd lost while on his spree, he was telling us about his new combo that was giving a free concert that evening. Roxie asked what the band played. Other than those two talking, we were all being too polite, munching on veggies and nodding approval at everything. We were likely wondering where Burt was, but no one had asked.

And if I had wondered, which I had not, whose idea this pre-Thanksgiving lunch gathering was, one look at Burt as he suddenly appeared from the inner

sanctum of an adjoining room would have dispelled
any guess in his favor. An inmate, completely
nude from the ankles up, entering in only very
tight shoes before an audience of grumpy parole
officers would have looked less uncomfortable than
Burt did at that moment. If the party had been his
idea, he obviously regretted it now.

Burt lived in the private world of his mind
and was so surrounded and bathed by that world
that even though he was continually surprised by
intrusions like this party coming from outside,
he completely ignored them. Burt right then was
a man, whistling and scrubbing in a shower whose
curtain is slid to the side revealing nakedness
to the world. He stood exposed, conspicuous in
his meriney skin, next to either the light or
dark complected, but danced on, sudsing as if
the whole world were his spa. This was Burt's
constant condition of being. Something right now,
though, was surely off.

At *Today*, he would look normal even in his
present distress. There, his kind of nakedness was
on par with that of others. But here in Maggie's
apartment, in formal social company, even though
we thought he counted us friends, his disregard
for appearances and conventions immediately took
on a dangerous rake.

Raci seemed to be reading the text from my mind. She
quoted Burt: "'As my grandmother used to say, *There's nothing
so lovely as a well-set table.*'"

"I remember, he leaned way over Ona who was sitting
beside you. He sounded like a cartoon wolf, 'And you look
lovely enough to eat.'"

"I thought, 'God help us.'"

"So you noticed that Burt couldn't keep his eyes off her?"

"It was glaringly clear. That and that he ignored Maggie

completely. I wondered if he was trying to upset her."

Raci pushed back. "You thought no such thing!"

"Did so! I also can see Toady halting, mouth open, in mid-promotion of his band, 'We've got Lionel Richie and Stevie's Skeleto . . .' He just stared at Burt."

"Didn't we all? But not you."

"Did so. And when Dwayne started to rise, Burt just said, 'Relax, friend, no harm in admiring the lady, is there?'"

"I was horrified, Els. I didn't know Burt at all, and he was not acting like the man you'd described. He shocked me and so did Maggie. She seemed too calm."

Raci went on. "When Burt swung down in the chair next to Ona, I thought Dwayne would explode. Burt all but draped himself over her."

"That's when Maggie came in. 'Burt! Behave yourself.' Maggie had stepped up from the kitchen, a two-pronged serving fork in one hand and a plate of olives and peppers in the other. 'You're sitting there next to Moe.' She pulled the chair out with her foot and pointed the fork at him. 'Have a seat, Mister.'"

Raci tried not to laugh. "They weren't on best terms. What did he say? 'My grandmother told me to find a woman just like herself,' was it, I think. He nodded at Maggie, 'You've got it Granny.' Then he plunked down."

"Maggie handed me those appetizers. 'Munch on these while I finish in the kitchen.' But she meant 'watch Burt.' Everyone, it seemed, wanted me to watch Burt."

"Maggie went back to the stove."

"It was no wonder why Burt was so taken with Ona." I thumbed through the manuscript.

     . . . But Burt didn't stop ogling Roxie.
     And well he might, though with better manners.

DUSK

Just as Muckey had said, Roxie Rodelli was an Italian beauty. Despite the hard usage and a long run on smack, she looked stunning, even in her jeans and sweater. As thin as she'd become on the dope, her dark skin glowed, her thick, wavy hair framed a smooth high forehead, and luxuriant eyebrows crowned large brown eyes. Muckey had described a beauty, but he hadn't done her justice. Roxie Rodelli's Roman nose was perfect, straight and in proportion to her face, and her smartly lined lips seemed to smile slyly each moment as if to say, '*baccime* and enter heaven.' Sometimes a chin disrupts the harmony of a face, man or woman, but when Roxie turned hers up at you she radiated strength enough but not from a dangerous looking point. I thought a dimple hovered somewhere there. Yes, Roxie was remarkable, petite but breasty, thin now, but straight enough to send out a glow. She wore beauty like a silk gown, shimmering in its own form.

Burt was right to look. He'd heard Muckey's tales of Roxie. Except in this setting Burt acted plainly wrong.

"Now, tell me Miss Rodelli, it is Miss, isn't it?" Burt did not wait. His eyes strafed the outline of her body. "Tell me, how is it I haven't seen you on screen yet. You've got the talent."

I wondered what Grandmother would have said to his line of questioning and about his salacious stare.

"I've known a director or two down there, used to skin pop with 'em in the Brown Derby's can. Maybe I can hook you up."

Nobody was talking. No one but a Burt not one of us had seen before, whom none of us knew.

DeLorr elbowed me, saying in effect, so this is

the famous Burt C I've heard so much about? For all her faults, DeLorr was a straight arrow, and her glare prodded me to intervene, to save some face. After all, we hadn't even finished the *hors d'oeuvres* yet.

"Hey, Burt," I said, "have a jalapeño." As an afterthought I added, "And practice your pickup lines in private." It hadn't come out right. But there it was.

Fortunately, Maggie was back just as Burt swung his head around to bark at me. She tapped his shoulder with the tines of that big fork and leaned to his ear to whisper. Then she caressed the other shoulder lightly, lingering at his ear and kissed his neck. Burt got up and followed her into the kitchen.

Roxie said, "I've broken jerks' arms over less, but he's the host, isn't he?" She didn't know about Maggie's disease, I bet.

Muckey sat still and muttered, "Goddamn."

Burt came back with a bowl of buttered parsley potatoes in one hand and a platter of chicken in the other. Maggie followed with greens and a salad.

"Damn," Muckey said, "I'm hungry as a heated grizzly."

I don't know where he got that from, but it was the right thing to say at that time. We laughed. Burt, too.

Maggie had culinary talent. Our nerves and our growling stomachs toasted the advent of food, and we moved right to it. Besides years swilling the booze, eating showcased our best talent. DeLorr had a good appetite for food, not drink so much, and I joined the heaping plate club to relieve my social distress. And the conversation snapped back, too.

```
"You're playing Stevie Wonder?" I asked.
"Yeah, 'Skeletons'," Toady said. "You know
'Messin' with your conscience.'"
```

Raci remembered, "Ona sang, and most of us joined in the lyrics."

"Then, Burt knocked his water glass over and jumped up. His chair slammed down behind me. He swore."

"Maggie sprang up halfway, then grimaced, and sat down again right away."

"I grabbed my napkin to mop as much as it would sop up, but Ona was there from the other side of the table, daubing Burt's coat and pants. She finished by wiping the chair with my napkin, and reseated him. 'I do this at least twice a day at the restaurant.'"

"'Powerful lyrics!' That was Dwayne. He didn't seem happy at the table service, but kept it to that one snide remark."

"That's when it all became clear. Cheryl put her hand on Maggie's arm, 'Are you all right, girl?' And I couldn't tell if Maggie was about to smile or cry."

"She looked like she'd cry. 'This is as good a time as there will ever be to tell you . . .'"

Raci struck out. "That ass Burt. He growled. I mean like a bear. But Maggie shook him off. I'll never forget it: 'I wanted to wait until dessert, but I'll say it. I'm expecting.' Then she did smile. And then she cried."

Now Raci herself looked to cry.

I tried some off-kilter comedy: "Of course, the women went to her instantly, lavishing praise and comfort, softness and joy."

Raci countered my direction: "And the men sat dumb as doorknobs."

"In the past we'd have popped a cork to express ourselves."

Raci had staunched her tears. "Of course old Burt raised his empty water glass, more like a master of ceremonies than a father, 'Here's to Maggie's baby. Congratulations, girl.' And all the men followed Burt's lead, except you. At least you had the good sense to say, 'Congratulations, Maggie . . . and Burt.'"

I felt the heat of Raci's ire, still burning after all those years.

. . . We clinked our glasses. Then Burt stacked our plates and headed for the kitchen, mumbling something about pie. But after clattering the dishes in the sink, he kept going, disappearing stage left where he'd first entered. He was gone a long time.

After the women hugged Maggie and chatted about a baby shower, Burt's absence was generally noticed. Maggie started to get up. "You just stay right there," Cheryl told her. "I'll serve the pie. Is coffee made?" And the posse of women took over from there.

We were spooning whipped cream onto slices of Maggie's homemade pumpkin pie and celebrating with coffee when Burt reappeared. In his absence we'd learned Maggie was three months along, hoped for a boy, and that she was prepared to raise the child herself. We'd had quite a conversation. But it fell to the floor like Burt's chair when he joined us again.

"Still having a baby-jubilee, I see. Well, I'd like some pie." He lifted his fork and started right in, not just on the pie, but chatting with and leering at Roxie. I swear he was angling his leg toward her under the table too, but if Burt reached her at all, she didn't let on. The only times he mentioned the pregnancy he called it "Maggie's baby."

The men drifted outside, ushered out by the women's talk of babies. We tried to talk about anything else.

What made that hard, you should know, is that what we have in common, besides the alcoholic's incomprehensible demoralization, is its cause, plain old booze. None of us wanted to talk about giving birth, but neither did we want to chat about alcohol addiction. Ordinarily, we would not even mention hospital or "farm" recovery programs or, certainly, discuss technicalities or details of such. The particulars, we found, were traps or stumbling blocks. For us it was plain old abstinence. And if it is that you practice, what does it give you to talk about? Nothing.

So, it wasn't too long, maybe about the time it took Toady to suck down an Old Gold, before he said, "Well, I got to get to our warmup session. We play at seven."

Muckey was giving Roxie a lift to the airport, and I had kids to pick up at the soccer coach's house. We went inside. I think the ladies were planning the shower or something, but left off when Burt, closing the deck door, came in last.

"On the way home I said, 'What the hell is wrong with that Burt?'"

"And I, 'In a word? Booze.'"

"You knew that was bullshit, Els. Just an excuse. Plenty of drinkers—you for one—have children. And they acknowledge them, too. 'Maggie's baby.' What a crock."

"Before we left the deck, I at least confronted the SOB."

"You did not," Raci said.

I never defended my *Today* friends, not to Raci. I didn't want to argue now that we'd been getting along. And I wouldn't insist on what I'd said to Burt—it *had* been twenty years. I believed, though, that I'd at least *wanted* to confront him with the warnings I'd been given, the words Gabby had uttered outside the bad-coffee cafe: "Burt is a child himself." Actually, I wasn't sure how much I'd said to Burt at Maggie's party. I wasn't sure what I'd said to Raci, either. Still, I couldn't admit to having said nothing.

"How do you know, Raci? I certainly did."

"Just like you said, 'Practice your pickup lines in private'? Remember, Els, I was there!" She glared at me in disbelief. "Besides, on the way home, you admitted you'd said nothing."

Something was eating at Raci. I considered the situation at Maggie's party. Just twelve months prior, I'd moved back home to be with my kids. And, of course, with Raci, too. So in the interest of domestic harmony as well as truth, I usually had agreed with her. I had said, "Burt is full of it, I know." I wouldn't confess I'd said nothing else. But why was that bugging Raci?

Had I known how it would all turn out, including coming to know much more about Gabby and Ella than I ever told anyone besides Nettie, I could have saved myself a lot of pain and trouble. But I've always been better at waiting to see than at reading the coming attractions on the proverbial wall. Foresight was not my talent. I had just kept going to meetings, driving to work, and coming home on time. I still did.

It was necessary to feather my marital nest with a few white lies, never mind the outcome. My marriage served as a refuge, though at the time I gave louder and more credit to my sanctuary at *Today* than to being a couple. Our union, except for sheer accident, could have lasted a long time past the years Raci and I had just been reviewing, long enough to see the kids grow and prosper. It didn't, and the event we'd just re-witnessed between Maggie and Burt marked the beginning of our destruction: the lapse of *Today* despite my vain attempts to save it; the end of our marriage; family truncation. Maggie's party marked the beginning of loneliness and loathing. Was that pricking Raci's ire?

The truth was that like beating a rug over a clothesline, Maggie's luncheon eventually pummeled off us dust motes that attended *Today*. Burt, just as Gabby predicted, had disowned his child, clepping it, "Maggie's baby." Maggie herself seemed to disappear at those words. And completely, though in agonizing stages, the event ground *Today*'s founder to dust. It all went, along with all his gleeful evangelizing, his kind helping, his long-time livelihood, and, finally, his very life.

Without telling Raci, years ago or right there in my New York bedroom, I wished I had spoken as I claimed.

Raci got out of bed and again threw on my robe. "Why didn't you say something? Why didn't you do more?"

I didn't dare ask. What did she mean? About Burt? About us? What was it? I held one of the pillows on my chest, crossing my arms over it, using it like a shield against her words. I kept quiet.

"Well?" Raci knotted the robe. "You write it like it was a huge gag. And even though Burt was only as big a cad as you sometimes, you should have kicked that man's ass. I suppose those who jump ship at the first sign of a storm have to stick together."

Raci was throwing me in with Burt. It wasn't in a nice way, either.

"Why don't you just go *now*? You've left me helpless before!"

That was it! She had *not* forgiven me. Perhaps for the act, but not for the behavior. Not for abandoning her.

Raci turned on a bare heel. She marched out. The bathroom door slammed, and I heard water running.

Yes, why hadn't I? Why didn't I say something? Do

something? Why didn't I stand up to Burt? To Jude? To Tom? To anyone? To my own depression and fears?

Was Raci just back to her old judgmental self? Was I wrong even before I had made a move? I had to ask myself why. Like most of my questioning, I looked for the answers in what I had written.

. . . Monday, I had been looking out for Burt, and for Maggie too, starting already in the early morning following Maggie's announcement. Burt was in evidence at *Today* but not in attendance. He seemed to have slipped in very early to rustle up literature, coffee fixings, the pink can, and baskets for the collection. It was all there, sitting behind the counter waiting for the chairperson to put it to use. Whether by arrangement or not, Toady took Burt's place at the table and ran the Monday and, next day, Tuesday meetings. Wednesday had a regular leader but still no Burt. He must have come in to re-stow everything and lock up the pink can and the cash collection, but nobody had seen him. Nobody had seen Maggie, either.

I didn't ask around. I waited until Thursday, which was Maggie's coffee duty day, sure she would come then. But when I trudged up the stairs it was Len crouched behind the coffee counter fumbling around. That was a shock in itself. I was the third person to enter the room. Jude was at the front table, setting up and setting out literature, which Hillside-Glenn used to do.

Maggie had been Jude's coffee maker for a couple of months. I'd hoped to see her together there with Burt. Often they'd come in early arm in arm. And since Maggie hadn't been to a meeting since before her brunch, I felt sure she'd make this one. Service keeps you sober, you know. Not today. No Maggie. And Len was in trouble.

Coffee was streaming down from the Bunn cone, spitting and sizzling on the empty pot warmer. It sent up a cloud of brown steam. Len, swearing like the sailor he was, worked a broom behind the counter. Up front, Jude ignored the whole fiasco.

I trotted behind the counter, jumped over the broom, and hit the off button on the Bunn. I grabbed a pot and a rag from the dish drainer in the utility room behind, wiped the warmer, and put the empty under the cone. Len had shattered a pot and forgot everything else.

"Let me help you, Len." I didn't have time to ask Jude what the hell he thought he was doing, or remind him that Len had no business making coffee. It was good enough he could drink a cup without spilling. He was best at sitting in profile and at sliding ashtrays along the tables. Len wasn't up to complexity. I was certain that Jude's instructions that morning had been both casual and vague.

People were now tromping up the stairs. Let Len save face. "I'll make another pot when this is finished," I said. The Bunn is very fast. "You put out the sugar, whitener, and cups. I'll do the pouring." Len sighed in relief, in profile of course, and dumped the pan of shards and plastic pot collar into the trash. He was shaken by the experience, that was clear, and I hoped it didn't drive him to drink. I thought I might have a word with Jude afterward. For now, I was the assistant to the emergency-relief coffee maker. I made coffee, helped Len serve, and, for that time, forgot about Maggie and Burt.

The meeting ran its course. It went smoothly. Jude ended it in the usual manner, and I said to

Len, "I've got some time this morning, let me clean up. You've done a great job."

Len looked haggard. He rasped out a "Thank you." He nodded, his hatchet face bobbing slightly, and fled the scene. I've not seen him since that morning, another man down on Jude's watch.

Jude set the donations basket and can on the counter I was wiping, rattling the can to see how much change was in it. "I'm taking these with me. I want someone to know."

"Why not leave them for Burt?" I said.

Jude put on his best corporate faux-reluctant expression, the one I recognized all too well that meant "I'm about to tell you something confidential and unkind, because it is necessary." He counted the bills from the basket as he spoke. "I don't know if you've noticed lately, but Burt has been a bit shaky."

"I haven't seen him since last week." It was tempting to tease Jude with news of Maggie's brunch, but I wasn't about to harness his own bad manners. Even without Maggie's baby announcement on Sunday, I would have felt protective of her privacy. There were reasons she hadn't invited Jude, and not because he wouldn't find a date. Anyway, I left it at "last week."

Jude folded the bills taken from the basket. He tucked them in his shirt pocket. "Well, I have seen Burt." His stern expression reminded me of the judge years ago who was telling me then, "You've started something very bad in Duluth." The look was inhumane. Before Judge Jude, of course, I played the defense attorney, not the accused.

"Listen," he said, "yesterday I was manning the hot-line across the hall. I had the service window open just a crack, when I saw Burt slip by. I slid the rippled glass aside and watched."

"Okay, okay. Burt came in and cleaned up after *Today*. So what?"

"Yeah, he cleaned up, all right. Put the coffee cans and literature away, and stuffed all the basket cash in his pockets. Emptied the change can, which was darn near full. I don't know exactly what he took, but he also stood at the locker counting bills from the cash box. Looked like a couple hundred."

Now it was my turn to cross-examine Jude. "So, from a slit in the windows, across the hall, and through the meeting room doorway and around a locker door that swings out your way, you saw Burt pocketing money?"

"I know what I saw," he said.

"And why shouldn't he take care of the funds? Maybe he was going to the bank."

Jude blew a laugh at the ceiling. "Bank? Yeah, the Sheep's Fleece Bank. We don't have an account, Moe."

I hadn't known. The thought had never occurred to me. Since I'd jilted the juice, I'd tried my best to follow that old path of least resistance. You know, ask me no questions, and I'll tell you no lies. I put a dollar or two in the basket each day and felt it was the least I could pay for what I had gained. Jude, though, made it his affair to know the business of others.

He tapped his pocket. "I'll bring this tomorrow morning." He held up the bills. "Fifteen dollars." He jiggled the can, opened the lid, and said, "Eight or ten quarters there." He held it out for me to look. I stepped back.

"Don't get me involved."

"Fine," Jude said, "but I'm going to do some investigating here." He slid the can into his backpack. Then Jude gave me a knowing glance, a sideways kind of raised eyebrow look, which on him looked sinister, devilish. "Did you hear Maggie is in the hospital?"

I hadn't. "What?"

"Just up the hill. I don't know the details." He swung the bag onto his back. "See you in the morning." Brushing the bell at the door, jingling, he was gone. I hadn't even mentioned the jam he'd dragged Len into. To Jude that would be a meaningless detail.

I felt like I had once again dropped my wine glass to the floor. Everyone had disappeared. There I was in the middle of a bare, empty room, alone with confusion and my burning desire to hide.

I went to work. At least I pretended to. By this time in my career I was climbing down the corporate ladder. No one would miss me at the office, and what if they had? There have been times when work was, or seemed like, a salvation. It got me out of the house. I earned a few bucks. Nowadays, though, my heart wasn't in it. This day, I just drove around, passing by the buildings of a few of my accounts. But I didn't stop in. I took a client lunch, without the client, down by the bay, just watching the ships sail through the Golden Gate and into the harbor. I didn't feel hungry, and the ships dieseling under the bridge jammed with pilots truly working depressed me. I thought about going to another meeting and dropped by Telegraph and 29th. I parked up the hill from the bad-coffee cafe. The three o'clock meeting would have already started. I walked by the prostheses hanging in the barred window, a forearm and hand, a couple of legs. I stood aside for a drunk who was bumbling along the storefront, steadying himself with the bars.

I couldn't face going upstairs. I retraced my

way and stepped over the drunk, now sitting on the sidewalk propped against the building. I went round the corner toward my company car. Jude's mention of Maggie came back. I looked up the hill, and climbed toward the hospitals at the top.

Three separate hospitals crowned the hill, surrounded by clinics and labs. I found Maggie on my third try. She was at the smallest, an old private hospital that sat in the center of planted terraces leading up from baroque gates and filigreed wrought iron fences. I told the receptionist I was family, our mothers were sisters. The business suit helped. Had Susan or Len tried to see her, or Burt for that matter, they'd have been turned away.

"Please," the nurse who showed me Maggie's room said, "if she wakes, don't mention the baby."

"Oh no, no, I won't."

"She doesn't know yet she's lost it. She's sedated, you know."

"Yes, yes, I know."

She opened the door of the indicated room. "Five minutes. She is likely sleeping."

Before I lost the opportunity, I asked, "How serious is this? I mean . . ."

"Her pelvis is broken and three vertebrae cracked. We won't know until she's out of surgery tomorrow."

More shattered bones, more surgery, more pain. Maggie had known all that lay ahead. She'd told me. But it had come so much sooner than she thought it would. Or maybe she saw it approaching near.

The draped body I saw was not Maggie. A corpse-like figure reclined under the hospital blanket. It was a fleshless skeleton that lay between arms so much thinner than those I'd before thought bony, that had replaced the woman I knew. The skin over her face seemed stretched so taut as to be nearly transparent. Her lips had disappeared into the pallor of her complexion. Closed sunken eyes and sallow cheeks had taken over her sweet, vibrant looks. Maggie's expression was one of a skin-curtained, pained, and tortured skull.

I couldn't stay. If I had wanted to hide that morning after Jude's antics, I wanted to run now. The stillness of death gripped my throat. I had to leave.

But as soon as I turned in that silent, terrifying room, I heard my name.

"Moe. Stay." Maggie whispered the words. "I missed my service," she said.

Eyes open, she looked more alive but still far away.

"Len took over. I helped. I've come looking for you."

Maggie fluttered her plastic-braceleted hand. She crooked just two fingers. "Come," she croaked. Her dry voice only hinted at the old flush of life with which she'd always spoken.

I touched those spindly fingers, then lightly stroked a finger across her forehead. Her eyes were glassy but alive.

She drew out the sound into "thane" and after more effort "cue." Whatever she meant, the touch, my coming, filling in at coffee, or all of it, I pressed her with my eyes. "You're welcome." I wanted a drink. No, a bottle."You shouldn't talk, just rest."

Her eyes struggled. She focused past pain, past the glaze of dope. "Made up, Moe." I leaned close, over the bed bars. "I went wild." Her voice was faint. "Made love." A wisp of a smile fled across her mouth. "Kept Burt happy."

Maggie closed her eyes. Her words had drained her. She was spent. Again she sank beneath her vital shell.

The nurse touched my shoulder. In the hall she said, "She spoke."

"Yes."

"Those are her first words to anyone. That's good. Thank you for coming."

You're going to think ill of me, I know. But you can't think worse than I did of myself, and not because I had had so much practice over the years. Amid all that others were suffering, Maggie broken and bereft, Burt sneaking around, hiding from friends, Len, draining right along with the Bunn, who did I think of? I felt sorry for me. I wanted to get into a bottle, seal it from the inside with a cork, and let my troubles float away. That was something I knew how to do and had nearly done when we lost Hillside-Glenn.

Less than a week before this day, all had been dandy. I was tolerating work and being tolerated. Same at home. I loved *Today*, Burt and Maggie, all the dope-heads and ex-drinkers. I felt secure in the wisdom of Burt's program that we practiced. When trouble came to others, like Glenn, though, life grew complicated. That I don't deal with well. Blame it on nerves.

Wires had crossed in my mind. Sparks, fire, and charred insulation followed. The party at Maggie's had been a mistake. We'd mixed too much reality into recovery, and it sent me spiraling off. The fact that I was not alone, that Maggie suffered more, was no cure. In my eyes it made my mewing little distress worse.

I've said before that my best talent was an ability to wait. I'm naturally good at impulse, surely, but I'd learned to abide. A day, an hour, a minute, even a few seconds made all the difference. Waiting and a developed habit saved me that day. When I reached my car, instead of roaring down the block to the liquor store that two blocks down Ferny had been beckoning, I sat for less than a minute in the car. It was five o'clock. Time to knock off work and go home. Habit. And that's what I did. I went home.

"You look like shit, Moe. Did you get fired?" DeLorr looked alarmed. She'd been afraid I'd lose my job and that we'd slip behind financially. My employment had been as steady as hers, but my nearly nine months out of the house had drained the old bank account down to the red line.

"No. Not yet." I couldn't be optimistic.

She put her hands on her hips. "What then?"

I started with the point she'd have most sympathy for. "Maggie's in the hospital. Broken spine and pelvis. The baby is gone."

That brought on a rare burst of softness from my wife. We commiserated. Then she recovered her hatchet edge and started in on Burt. I told her about that morning with Jude. She didn't know Len, so I said nothing about him.

I hoped DeLorr would tell me to steer clear of the obvious trouble coming. That would have been more in keeping with my capacity to deal with life, my own being difficult enough. I suppose this is what you get from radiating the look of confident competence. Those around you believe it better than you can yourself.

"Listen, Moe, go in early tomorrow and confront him." DeLorr thought Burt had brutalized Maggie. She wanted justice. I wasn't brave enough to stand in her way, so I told her I would, even though I knew I'd never stand up to Burt either. I'd come home out of habit. Though I'd had hopes for comfort, now I was being sent out on what could be a suicide mission. Anyone who has been drunk for a couple of years or more knows you can't fight fate. Glenn had found out: fate is always bad.

The next morning, I pulled up at 29th and Telegraph a half hour early. The meeting would start in an hour and a quarter. The street door was already unlocked. I opened it quietly and started up the flight of stairs. Why I was stepping so carefully, I didn't know. Then I did know. A row was going on up there. Thanks, DeLorr.

Burt and Jude were yelling. I listened from below.

"That is my money!" Burt yelled.

"The hell it is. This belongs to the group," Jude said.

"You're stealing it!"

"I am not. Moe knows I have it."

Obviously, try as I might, I couldn't get out of this. Even without me present, Jude had dragged me right in.

"You guys are stealing!" Burt screamed now.

I stomped up the last few steps and swung open the door forcefully. The bell jangled fiercely. That quieted them down. I entered and held up my hands.

"Listen to me, both of you. Burt, you know me better than this. Jude, I told you I wouldn't be involved." They both glowered.

"Now, I've got a meeting coming in," I said. "Jude, hand over the money." I extended my hand. He did as he said he would and gave me the cash. "Now, come back for the meeting if you want, but leave now."

As soon as he complied, I handed the money to Burt, who jammed it into his coat pocket and made toward the door. I sensed DeLorr pushing me toward a cliff.

"Wait, Burt." He paused. I couldn't face DeLorr again without asking. "What happened to Maggie?"

To me, Burt looked like he was reaching for a lie. I intercepted him.

"I saw her at the hospital yesterday. She talked a little."

That snapped Burt back from falsehood and from this other persona—an enraged, debilitated ghoul—I had seen for the first time today.

"As my grandmother would say," he began, then stopped. "Look, if you think I did that to Maggie intentionally, you're wrong." His voice rose toward the screaming one I'd heard from the stairway.

I raised my hand to stop him. "No, I didn't think that, Burt. Maggie said you two had made up, made love. It was she who got wild."

Burt slumped against the wooden lockers. His freckles burned red over his paling skin. I took his shoulders—the only time I had ever touched my friend. He steadied.

"We were both happy. We went at it too hard."

"Is that how it happened?" I could see it. Returning, reaffirming, and joining in joyful repentance. They'd come together through their troubles, loved, moved, perhaps, to orgasm, then relapsed in the breaking of brittle bones.

"She should never have tried for a baby." He stood against the lockers, shaken and shaking. Burt cried. I moved to him again, but he pushed my arm away and fled.

Before I noticed it, he was gone. _Today_'s locker stood open, Burt's key dangling from the padlock on a noose of responsibility. I swung the door shut, slapped the hasp closed, and slipped the shackle through. I snapped the lock shut. I pocketed the key. That is how I inherited yet another job through Burt's absence. I became, for a short time, the keeper of *Today*'s keys.

Jude wasted no time. Bright and early Monday morning he was at *Today*, ready to tear open the locker, and not to get the literature and coffee supplies. I was a minute behind him, able to stay the righteous indignation he felt gave him permission to pry.

As I walked in Jude was brandishing a small tool used for pulling nails, a cat's paw. "I'm going to open this thing right now," he said.

Jude was headstrong, but I was his sponsor. He was supposed to listen to me. "Wait a little, Jude, Burt should be along any minute." I didn't tell him I had the padlock key in my pocket. I'd no inkling Burt wouldn't show up to open the meeting. He'd arrived in time faithfully since before I landed there thirteen months ago. I couldn't imagine the meeting without him.

And there is the rub. And the trap, too. You go along thinking that stability lies within a certain sameness. You think friends stay friends. You believe marriage is for a long time, if not forever. Aging only means getting better, deeper, richer, like good furniture.

Not on your life. Everything was changing fast, people diverging from our path, disappearing; all was in flux. All had been changing forever, and I was more at sea than even Len had ever been. So, if you want stability, you must account for change in your plan. I thought of Len who I suspected had left the meeting though I hadn't confirmed that yet.

Len was my best metaphor for stability. He'd developed sea legs. No matter the pitch or roll, he stayed upright, even though at last he had hurled overboard, as I found out, doing emergency-relief coffee duty. But that incident wasn't a lurch or a wave either. That time Len experienced what sailors aboard small freighters do: the sea troughs-out from the bottom of the vessel, and there's your ship in midair for a second, until it splats again down in an ocean. Even an old salt feels the suck of the leaving wave and the vacuum that sends the ship into the air above a receding sea. At that moment he lets fly his breakfast. Day to day, though, Len stayed afloat. And I had been learning from him in my own heavy weather. I stood, gripping the railing, riding the ocean on the flex of my knees all the while.

So, Jude and I waited. It was the longest ten minutes I'd spent since I'd taken the Friday meeting for the first time. Jude paced around the room. Around is the right description, too. Around and around and around in a big square-cornered circle. I slipped into the back kitchen and washed pots which no matter how much they'd been rinsed were always filmy and unhealthy-looking. I gave three of them a good scrubbing.

"All right," Jude said, halting his wandering, "that's enough."

I poked my head around the doorway just as he was about to attack the hasp. "Hey, look here!" I held up the key.

"Where'd that come from?"

Friends aren't forever, but even friends like Jude were worth keeping if possible. So I lied. "It was back here in the kitchen."

What Jude was after were the sign-up sheets, bound in a Mead composition book, actually five books kept together with a big rubber band. Each had a hundred sheets on which the members listed their names each day. The chairperson noted the day and date, the speaker if there was one, and at the bottom of each page, of most interest to Jude, the amount of money collected in the basket. The record went back to the very beginning of *Today*. Those comp books formed the beginning of Jude's investigation.

When Burt failed to show up, I kept the key and demanded that Jude return the books to the locker by the end of the meeting. He could work on them in the meantime, but they didn't belong anywhere else but the archive. I was a bit curious about the financial matters, too, but felt protective of Burt. The kind of vigilante path Jude was following didn't seem right. I wasn't the one to stand in Jude's way, but I did want to talk to the other *Today* chairpersons before much else happened.

The next morning, Toady came in to set up, and I opened the locker. I told him about the key and about what Jude was doing.

"Well, I'm glad you grabbed the key. Maybe it's time for an accounting," Toady said. "Burt's disappeared."

Members came and went, that was true. Our founder's leaving, though, was something altogether different. It was monumental. Dropping out of sight in our experience at *Today* could only mean one thing, and I couldn't believe it of Burt. "Are you sure? How do you know?"

Toady would be the one to know, but I wanted to be positive. Despair hung over my shoulders like a lead vest in the x-ray department. At that time I felt that Burt had saved my life. He was my sponsor, my mentor, my guru. If he'd fallen off the boat, I was meant to drown. Toady understood.

"Look, Moe, every one of us has his lapses.

I'm evidence of that. It doesn't mean that the survivors should go down on the same ship." Toady put his hands on my shoulders and looked into my eyes. "Burt saved me too, but I am not going to slip into the booze because he's off on a bender. Neither will you."

He had steadied my rocking boat. Toady understood. "What we need to do while he's gone," Toady said, "is to continue the good work Burt was doing here. He'll be back."

"Where is he?"

Toady didn't hesitate. "He's left town."

"How do you know?"

"When Burt didn't show up for our usual breakfast on Saturday at the waffle shop, I knocked on his door. His place is around the corner a block down, you know."

"He wasn't there? So what?"

"No he wasn't. And the door was ajar. His coat closet was empty. A lot of his clothes were gone from the dresser, others he'd left tossed on the bed. He's gone, Moe."

I wanted to know where.

"I'd bet on LA. He's spent some time down there over the years. It's where he'd go." Toady put his stubby index finger to his lips. "Hey, Jude."

Both Toady and I clammed up. People at *Today* would know soon enough about Burt, but neither of us wanted to make Jude one of the first.

"I wanted to get started on the audit I'm doing," Jude said. He'd dragged in his Macintosh computer. He set the machine down and went to the locker, taking out the books.

"Just leave the top one for me, would you, Jude?" Toady was very polite. His request fed me the tacit approval I wanted. With Burt on the lam, Toady, Jude, and I were the triumvirate of *Today*.

DUSK

Jude took the four ledgers from the archive and sat with his computer on the literature table that he moved to the rear of the room. Toady's new coffee maker came in, and we were on the happy trail to recovery.

What Jude accomplished in one day was making a ledger of the collections from the beginning. He had the daily cash charted and totaled over the four years since *Today*'s beginning. He included the coffee fund when noted. The pink can take was never recorded.

By the end of the next day's meeting, Jude had an initial report ready for me to see.

"We've got 221 weeks since the beginning. Average take was seventy-six dollars and fifteen cents a week. The total, not including Monday through today, is nearly seventeen thousand dollars."

It sounded like a lot. "Are you sure it's that much?" I said.

Jude frowned at me. "Hey, numbers don't lie, and that doesn't include around fifteen dollars a week of the coffee fund. I extrapolated that from the occasions it was recorded. That's another three thousand."

"Where did it all go? Coffee, supplies, literature?" I said.

"Exactly my question. I'm working on a profile now. I want to call a business meeting tomorrow."

"You can't do that." I was floored, totally aghast. "Jude, tomorrow is Thanksgiving."

"I don't care if it's . . . Thanksgiving?" He gritted his teeth. "Shit. I'm out of town, then."

"What about your meeting?" Not only did we meet on holidays, it was essential that we be there, especially for the big three, Thanksgiving,

Christmas, and New Year's.

"Can you take it, Moe? You'll be here, won't you?"

I would be there. "All right. I'll take it."

"Great!" He made an about-face and marched into Beryl's office just across the hall from the meeting room. She oversaw the whole district, kept the rent paid, and had scads of records, though most of them were based on what meeting leaders like Burt turned in to her.

This was depressing. I had wanted to leave my corporate life, and here it was, in the persona of Jude, following me. Finances, spreadsheets, computers, and managers out for blood. On top of it all were the holidays, Hillside-Glenn's nagging absence, Maggie's troubles, and Burt's disappearance. And I had started to worry about Len, too. I knew what to do, but I decided to wait instead. Muckey D and I went to breakfast together. That usually cheered me up.

But Muckey was moaning. "It wasn't such a great start for Roxie. The meetings were okay, but Maggie's goddamned party bummed her out. You know, Burt's attentions and all. She won't be coming up for a while. Maybe at Christmas." It didn't seem like the right time to tell him that Burt had split. Muckey was chomping at the bit to visit Roxie again.

"Are you going south for the weekend?" I said.

"I can't afford it now."

"Could you speak at *Today* on Thanksgiving? I'm filling in for Jude."

Is the Preppy Prince off to seaside or whatever? "Why not."

"Yeah, it will give you something to do while you and Roxie are apart."

That put him on again. "That girl, I'll tell ya. She is fine." We ordered Belgian waffles to celebrate beauty. It was all Muckey could talk about.

"She is a very nice person, too," I said. My mood was lifting. It always felt good to compliment a friend.

Muckey went on and on. Yes, Roxie was wonderful, soft, kind, interesting, an acting prodigy, I suppose, but no woman, or man for that matter, was as great as Muckey made his jilt-prone lady friend out to be. I let him drone away.

Through the front window of Kuleto's, I kept my eyes on The Raquette, not truly thinking I'd see Burt emerge from the double door any moment, but somehow expecting that I'd see him there, under the golden eagle. Had he canceled his membership before he left? I decided not. That wasn't the kind of thing someone in relapse would think of.

"You see something over there?" Muckey said. He'd noticed I wasn't listening.

"Oh, I was just keeping an eye out for Burt."

Muckey wasn't pleased. "That guy I can goddamn do without." He swore. "Hey, by the way, where is that dude? I haven't seen the jerk since he was playing footsie with Roxie."

It's one thing to keep mum. It's deception when you're asked directly. I couldn't predict what Muckey's reaction would be. I chose a middle path: tell some of it, leave out the speculation. "Toady said he's out there."

Muckey shook his head like a rattle. "Did I hear that right? He's gone out?"

"He hasn't been opening up all this week. I've been doing that."

"I'll be damned. I suppose the whole thing with Maggie and his baby sent him over the edge."

Muckey sounded quite sympathetic; he'd been there. "Where'd he go?"

"If I knew, I'd tell you." It wasn't exactly a lie, but I didn't want to mention LA or anyplace near Hollywood. "Toady might have an idea." Had I been certain—and how could I be?—I would have told him, as unsteadying as it may have been.

Muckey turned to his waffle, which had just arrived. "I need a break from Burt. Still, I hope he'll be all right. Some never make it back. Hell, some never make it in."

He buttered his food and lifted the syrup over the waffle. "I dedicate this Belgian waffle to the memory of the best goddamn literature person ever, Hillside-goddamn-Glenn."

I seconded his dedication.

Muckey went on to talk about Roxie's entry into the ranks of the sober and clean. She hadn't been his first rescue, but she was the one he loved most.

Midway through his second square of waffle, Muckey returned to the subject of Burt. "Is that why Jude is bringing a goddamn computer to the meeting? Because of Burt?"

Muckey wasn't the only one who felt uncomfortable with the clicking and clacking during the meeting. We were a fairly tolerant bunch, but no one had ever seen a computer in a meeting before. Some had never seen a computer at all.

"Jude is doing an audit."

"About time, I'd say. There's a lot of cash coming through those doors every day. And what happens to it is anybody's guess. I suppose some of it goes to the rent, some to the national office like you're supposed to do."

"Mr. Corporate America is the one to find out," I said.

"You and Jude on the outs?"

I tried to be fair after my wisecrack but found it hard. "Since Hillside-Glenn went under, I've cooled some. And now this audit."

Muckey talked with his mouth full. A little syrup dribbled out one side. "Yeah, and not too many of us have thrown our best friend at a tree." He mopped his chin.

Yes, even among our ragtag outfit Jude was a hard case, but hard cases deserved a chance, too. Still, Jude made a great many people nervous. As you know, nerves are a dangerous thing to pluck at where alcoholics are concerned.

I had inside information directly from Jude, actually un-information in the form of an omission, one so surprising as to shock me, but I wouldn't divulge that under any circumstances. Suffice it to say here, I didn't think Jude felt remorse for his actions around his friend's death. It wasn't exactly blame the victim, but not too far off.

"Well, Muckey, some of us have done worse."

He chewed and swung his head side to side over his plate. "Yeah," he mumbled through the waffle, "maybe. Not many, though."

"Hey, let me buy," I said. "You're my speaker tomorrow."

Muckey nodded and looked surprised, too. "Thanksgiving's tomorrow?"

We all needed a calendar.

Evening

Drink up, baby, look at the stars
I'll kiss you again, between the bars
Where I'm seeing you there, with your hands in the air
Waiting to finally be caught

Elliott Smith, from "Between the Bars"

And when looking for the answers in that which I'd written, what had I found? Mostly that Moe was a chump, "following the path of least resistance." Raci knew Moe better than I knew Moe or myself. How many times had I said, "Don't get me involved." Even now, afraid of a woman I'd twenty years since divorced, I stood in the middle of a bare, empty hallway, alone with confusion and my burning desire to hide. My mousy knocking resounded on the bathroom door—the running water had stopped ages ago. I cowered timidly before the noise as it bounced up and down the hall and echoed inside the bathroom.

"Raci," I murmured to the door, "can we talk?"

What was I going to say? Could I count on Raci to remember Jude's investigation? Had I told her I'd said, "Hand over the money."? Could she hear that now?

I plucked up my meager courage, felt as bold as I ever had, or tried to sound like it, "I've got an appointment to make, Racine Davis. Come out of my bathroom." I'd told Ella I would visit Gabby in hospice but it wasn't truly scheduled. Increasingly, though, since Raci blew up at me, I wanted to get out. Even in her condition, Gabby always made *me* feel better. I knocked again.

She said something this time. "So you want to run now? To hide?"

"This is something I have to do. I'm sorry."

"You feel sorry all right. For yourself." She knew how to turn the knife once it hit bone. She was also correct.

"Are you going to open this door?" I tried to pound. It was feeble.

"All right. Give me a couple of minutes. Blame it on the nerves! Why don't you go and read or something? I'll be out."

Bile, bile, toilet trouble, Raci's angry, locked in bubble. The rhyme made me smile despite rising ire. "Of course, dear. Take your time."

I went to the bedroom and dressed. She still was not out,

EVENING

so I again picked up *Twelve* and read. Gabby, my beautiful but unfortunate friend I'd named Linda, appeared in the chapter I selected. I always loved to read about her.

. . . It likely goes back to the story of the first bounteous harvest shared by whites with the natives. I'm sure the gang at *Today* felt about as uneasy as the Pilgrims did, strangers in a strange land. Like them we were in a new country—sober days and teetotaler nights—that looked mighty different than their merry old England only slightly more inviting, having worn out the welcome mat there, just as we had where we came from. Not that the Wampanoags were any more fierce than our families who watched for signs of imbibing or other trouble from us, but those two groups certainly knew the territory better and had us outnumbered. In any case, most of us preferred celebrating Thanksgiving with our own kind at *Today* rather than with family, though many like the twenty or so surviving Pilgrims at Plymouth, were expected to sit down with Aunt Lucy and Uncle Hank, our Mashpee Wampanoags so to speak, even if they had already given thanks upstairs at *Today*.

I was covering for Mr. Thursday, Jude, who was likely eating with rich relatives at a fancy restaurant up the coast. No resentment, just a fact. And being the substitute was an advantage. I was let to leave the house early since I'd done my due diligence by baking pumpkin pies the night before. All I had to do, then, on the home front was to show up toward noon to greet DeLorr's family and to pretend to be happy about it all.

Holidays are the hardest times for most of us above the artificial arm and leg shop. We're always

224

nervous, but around those special, traditional celebrations, quakiness and dreams set in, easily sliding into neurosis or worse. All of us are on high alert against boozing during these times, and some of us even include Independence Day and Halloween in our list of fidgety festivals. I usually substitute sugar for alcohol during the latter one. But do I have to tell you about holidays? Even if you enjoy decorating, singing, opening up to joy, you still can see how some feel, well, on an emotional edge at those times.

Walking down 29th, I was carrying a pumpkin pie. I rounded the corner. Like I say, we are all touched by occasions. Still, I made a triple take at the window, seeing the prosthesis shop had decorated for Thanksgiving and maybe a bit for Christmas, too. The window was lined by twinkling lights in six colors, garnished by plastic pine sprigs here and there. In the center of the plate glass, they'd set a table around a huge rubber turkey surrounded by resin trimmings and piles of artificial mashed potatoes that dripped perpetually with glossy gravy. The proprietors hadn't taken anything out of view, of course, so off to each side the arms, legs, walkers, and canes were crowded together as if staying to witness the celebration. At the table sat a lone mannequin, a napkin tied at its neck, holding a fork over its plate, the other arm being truncated at the elbow. The fork rested in the grasp of a mechanical claw. "Invite your disabled to dinner," a placard in front of the turkey said.

The vendor's efforts did not cheer me up any. In the window I saw my reflection, as if standing at the table holding a fresh baked pumpkin pie, mouth agape, about to say "Happy Thanksgiving" to the dismembered android at the table. I couldn't help feeling something for the dummy in the window all alone. For years, it felt, I'd been as odd and isolated as this half-armed, no-handed figure in an artificial limb store. Not to dwell on the dismal, but you get the idea. I shook my head. I had to laugh. What else could I do?

"Pretty cool," someone up the block at the meeting door said. I laughed again. It was Muckey with a handful of others, waiting for things to start. No one else would have much appreciated the grim metaphor of that window. We all likely thought that if the mannequin had a choice, he would have followed everyone else upstairs when I unlocked the door. As it was, I looked down from the top of the stairs to see if that had happened.

Actually, I was still looking for Burt. I was still looking for Maggie, too. And though Len wasn't a main cog in our operation and hadn't been gone long enough to haunt me, I suppose I was looking for him as well. The usual chatter sounded in the stairwell, and I heard a few names mentioned. The early in the crowd wondered who would show on a holiday, but I didn't hear Burt mentioned once. Likely Muckey had informed the knot of *Today*-ers waiting at the door that he was AWOL.

Upstairs, I opened the locker as unceremoniously as possible. No one besides Toady and Jude, yesterday, had seen anyone but Burt holding the key. You never knew who was teetering on the brink there, and with Burt gone anyone could begin to lean the wrong way. So, I tried to act nonchalant even though the situation was far from normal. I stacked the coffee, ashtrays, and literature on the counter and was about to move to the front of the room to get Muckey settled at his speaker's post when, light as a butterfly, someone behind me touched my shoulder and followed that with a whisper of warm breath at my ear.

"Excuse me, Moe," she said.

I'd expected Maggie. I turned. It was Linda, our cellist, looking every bit as beautiful as she had the only other time I'd met her. And very much closer.

"Linda." We hugged. Now, when this occurred three months prior at the terrible-coffee café, I nearly passed out for joy. Maybe it was being in the meeting room where a whole lot of hugging went on, or perhaps I had crossed another threshold along the way. But I hugged her hugely though nimbly and was the first to let go. "Happy Thanksgiving."

"Same to you, Moe. Do you think Burt is coming? I was hoping to see him."

Not that I thought Linda came to see me, but I had to hide the letdown behind the sadness at Burt's absconding. "I don't think so, Linda." I took her hand. "He's been out of sight since last Friday, and Toady, at least, believes he's left town. Maybe gone to LA." I cast a glance around for Muckey. He was chatting with Susan. He hadn't heard me. I touched my finger to my lips. "That's speculation I shouldn't repeat."

Linda looked worried. She squeezed my hand. "He'll be back. He's been out before." She may have been comforting me, or herself. I don't know, but I would not mention the circumstances of his leaving. Linda had never met Maggie, as far as I knew.

"He's gone before?" A touch of disillusionment hovered on my question.

"About every three years or so, Burt zings off, it seems," Linda said. She touched my arm with her free hand. I wanted to be her cello string. I wavered at her touch. "Don't worry. You'll carry on."

It seemed to me like one of those Biblical appearances where an angel of the Lord arrives with joyous news. I felt good that she took an interest and thought I could fill in. I was encouraged. The uneasiness I had felt at the window-of-the-rubber-turkey eased. Yes, I thought, I can carry on. "I've got to get this meeting started. You staying?"

Linda was staying. We loosed our holds on each other. Now I regretted having Muckey instead of Linda as my speaker. I wanted to hear her story. However, service called, and with Linda's inspiration I went about my duties with a smile.

The meeting went well. Muckey was at his finest. He told the story I'd heard before about saving Roxie. He didn't use her name, of course, and simply made the point that by helping others we help ourselves. I thought he sounded quite saintly, actually. His rescue of Roxie formed the peak of his perfection and his joy. He raised spirits of the right kind for a Thanksgiving morning. And I did get to hear Linda's story after all, though since it was told in anonymity, I can't be revealing anything here.

The room was full, and people kept filing in throughout, carrying seasonal goodies to be shared during the marathon meeting that began a half-hour after *Today*. That meeting would run from ten o'clock through the next morning, serving as a sanctuary for the disaffected, unconnected, escaped-from-family, and anyone else who wanted to stay on the happy road to destiny. So by the end of *Today*, the room was packed, squeezed more by the tables set up at the rear of the room and by members arranging and rearranging dishes full of food that covered the tables.

I thought of the golem in the window downstairs. Watching the tables being set during the *Today* meeting warmed me. Here I was inside a celebration looking out. Usually, I'd felt outside, separate, estranged, looking in. I wondered what table Burt sat at now. Maggie couldn't be sitting at table at all this year. And maybe because a very short man, though quite stout, came in during the meeting, Tom came to mind. Perhaps he'd be carving a bird with other veterans. That would be good. Was he sober? That Thursday, I did not know, but I'd find out soon enough.

I locked up for *Today* after carefully counting and noting the amounts from the baskets and the coffee jar. Food was still arriving. The room was roaring with laughter. In the middle of the jollity, I saw Muckey talking with Toady. I went over to thank Muckey for a great share and to do damage control if needed.

"Hey, Moe, you didn't tell me old Burt went to LA." He stood defiant with his arms crossed. I had been right to come over.

Toady wanted to intervene, but I took the lead. "It's an unconfirmed rumor as far as I'm concerned. Unless you know something I don't."

Muckey was like rock. Toady knew something, that was clear.

"What is it, Toady?"

"I got a call. I should say Cheryl did." Toady was shifting from one foot to another, a nervous version of his happy hop. "It was person-to-person, collect, from Burt Carter."

"Toady here wasn't home, so Cheryl didn't connect," Muckey said. "But the call came from goddamned Hollywood! You could have told me, Moe."

He didn't give me time to explain. My speaker's

mood had fallen from the heights of helpfulness to the darkest depths of despair, and he pushed past me. "I've got a coach to catch," he said and fled down the stairs.

"Let him go," Toady said. "He exaggerated."

"What about?"

"The call came from LA, for sure, but we don't know it originated in Hollywood. Muckey is jumping to conclusions."

"Did you call back?"

"No. Cheryl said Burt sounded strange, and there was a ruckus in the background. Typical collect call. Besides, they don't give you a number."

"So what do you think?"

"I think Burt is running, and yeah, that usually means to a woman."

I had wanted to chat with Linda, but now I didn't even feel like talking more with Toady. Typical holiday. It wasn't yet ten o'clock, and I'd run the gamut of emotions already. I left my pie on one of the tables and followed Muckey's path down to the street. I'd lost any appetite I'd had. Fowl for breakfast isn't my favorite. I'd already been chewing the same rubber turkey leg long enough.

Raci slipped into the bedroom. She gathered up her clothes, tossed my robe on the bed, and trotted down the hall to dress in the living room. I sat on the bed, hugging the manuscript.

I waited a bit and called out, "Are you decent?" I rose and stepped into the hall. "Are you ready?"

"Are *you* ready?" Raci called out, appearing in the doorway. She tossed a huge book over to me. "You are such a liar!"

I dropped *Twelve* to the floor and caught the heavy book like a football. The manuscript splayed its pages over the hardwood floor. I set down the book Raci had thrown to me, and I squatted, retrieving my disheveled work. The book was *Veterans' Stories of War*, the anthology Tom had given me.

"Coward!" Raci boomed out again. "Liar and coward!" She marched down the hall and poked my shoulder. I lost balance and went sprawling down in the midst of *Twelve*. I kicked out, sending sheets in all directions. Raci stood on the sheaves now, towering over me, rifling a finger, "You lied to me, Els. What else is new? Shit, this book . ." she kicked it toward me off the toe of her shoe, "sat right in front of us in the bookcase, and you denied its existence."

I stayed on the floor.

"So, which part is fiction, Els? Do you know anymore? The sweetness we shared this afternoon? Was that part of the fiction?"

Raci was just warming up. I could see the signs. I tried to stand up. She stepped toward me. I fell back.

"You believe I'm angry about your leaving me, abandoning me, but that's not it at all. It's your denial. You refuse to stand up for anything, anything but for yourself." She stepped back and turned her head. She swung back to me. "You dragged me into your sappy book. Why?"

"I just wanted you to read the story," I said weakly. Then I countered her attack, " What did *you* want? Just to see? No, I don't think so. And you sneaked around the book even before I invited you into it, didn't you." She took another step away. I stood. "So who is being disingenuous here? Who is wrong. Whose agenda is so damned moral and right? Yours or mine?"

She wasn't about to back down. "Afraid of a woman? Worried she'll take you to court to claim her part of that tunnel rat's book?" Raci smiled slyly. "Or half of all those books. How would you like that?"

"Don't tell me you wouldn't like a piece of my 'writing

action'. You always have, haven't you?"

I'd backed to the wall at the end of the hall knowing I'd riled her up. I knew Raci wasn't done.

"Always, a bunch of lies and excuses. Fiction! Ha! Bullshit! You don't know what fiction is. How can you when you don't know what truth is?"

I was now flattened against the wall. "Raci, I didn't lie when I said I loved you. I still do."

That quelled some of her fury. She came closer again.

"Okay, Els, I came here with expectations, quite frankly. I've always loved you despite what you've done to me." She shook her head. "I was hoping that we could at least abide by the truth."

I should have said nothing, but asked, "What is holding us back?"

Raci's voice shook. "You keep hiding behind some sort of fictional persona. What in the devil is worth hiding at this stage of the game? And lies, lies, lies. Grow up Els and tell the truth."

I wasn't about to spill my life out to Raci. "Listen, Raci . . ."

"No! You listen, whoever you are. Do you even know? Who are you, really? Elmoe Mattila? Maybe the famous Tom McIntyre, or Moe whatever-his-initial-is? The specter of the Rat's Ass? Are any of these real? Or like me and DeLorr, just your imaginary playmates. Was there really a Tom?" Raci tapped her forehead. "No one was home at his house as far as I ever saw. Just like you. Are you the ghost of the McIntyre who froze to death, having willed yourself the springboard of a writing career? Shit. You're the one who's been crawling through tunnels. Come on, Els, straighten up and say it like it is for once."

I didn't wait to listen. Good. I didn't really have anything to say without telling her about Gabby and Ella. And I couldn't do that.

232

She stormed back down the hall and flopped down, fuming, on the couch under the windows. I watched from the entry. She crossed her arms under her breasts and bent her head. I swept up the pages of *Twelve* and Tom's anthology, arranging them on the hall stand.

I *was* a coward and a liar. No, I had never confronted Burt despite what I claimed, a postulate Raci did not believe anyway. I didn't really stand up to Jude, not about killing his friend, nor about running while Hillside-Glenn drowned, not about the injustice of his going after Burt. My ex-wife was right, but maybe, just maybe my lies and, likely, my spineless reluctance fed my writing, my "fiction." Well, it had worked before.

I took my coat from the rack and slipped into it, calling from the apartment door, "I told you I have an appointment. That's the truth." She didn't reply. "You're welcome to stay. I'm getting Chinese takeout on the way back. We'll share." Silence. "Let's talk when I get back. Please, take some time." Still nothing. So, leaving the keyed deadbolt open, I left, clicking the door latch quietly.

That had been too much and too close. If I were in denial, I didn't want to know about it. I unwound and distanced myself, taking the stairs five flights down.

. . . "Don't get close," Tom wrote. "You go down alone. You stay that way. Even back home. You're always solo."

I sat bundled under two wool blankets and my heavy sheepskin throw, keeping one hand below the covers, the other holding his book, Tom's manuscript, steady under the lamp beam. I had an electric heater going but felt frozen. Everyone else was sleeping. I couldn't turn on the furnace without waking them all. I didn't want to have to explain.

EVENING

What was I doing up at two-thirty in the chill of the first December morning of the year? I barely knew myself.

Half an hour before, I'd been enjoying a warm Pacific breeze flowing through my hair, standing on what I dreamed—not yet having been there—was the beach at Malibu. With me were Burt, dressed only in Hawaiian-patterned swim trunks, and Maggie, loose, long-armed, her paisley gown rippling, surging around her in wind that had unfurled her hair. Together on the beach, those two shone, a glorious, glowing aura. Burt turned to Maggie, saying "Watch this," running backwards into the waves, stretching his arms out to her as he went, then disappearing under a huge breaker. Maggie cried out. She reached across the tide line, impossibly trying to grab his arm.

"No, Maggie!" I screamed. "It's too rough for you." I seized her hand, restraining her. She pulled, yelled, and tugged harder toward Burt. In this dream her arm separated from her shoulder with a horrible tearing sound, and when she looked back at me, her face was confused, forlorn. Then she entirely disintegrated. All that was left of her was a pile of bones all akimbo. Her beach dress curled into the air and sailed, tumbling over itself down the beach. I fell to my knees before the heap of impossibly thin ribs and femurs that had, an instant before, been Maggie. In my hand I clutched only a dried, bleached skeleton's forearm that fragmented and fell, leaving like crushed saltines only crumbs of her hand in my grasp. That woke me.

"You okay?" DeLorr said. I must have yelled.

"Yes. I just have to go to the bathroom." I was sweating and once out of bed chilled immediately. I took a robe from the closet, slipping quickly out of our room. A good part of me clung to the dream, to Maggie, to Burt, wanting to save them, to save myself. The so-called reality of my life: job, wife, kids, house on the hill, all embodied in DeLorr once again asleep in our bed, appeared in the dead of night less important than my sober, or not so sober, friends at *Today*. Even as sleep sloughed off me into the cold of the hallway on my way to the toilet, that shimmering beach, the goldenness of friendship welled up in my chest, promising both the love and the redemption that I craved. Even the impossibility of saving anyone, even myself, held no weight despite that aurulent vision. And that, I think, led me in the next few minutes to my small study and back to the sole totem to fraternity I had in the house, Tom's book, which had been shelved, once we'd moved to California, between William Faulkner and a sales training manual.

Free of the dream, I knew that Maggie was broken and gone. Likely, Burt was too. But Tom, my longest-time friend, I felt, was still there with me despite our Veteran's Day falling out. And now that he had, ever-so-brief as it had been, touched down at *Today*, I could hope he would return. He seemed, in the sea of loss and disaffection I'd been wallowing in lately, a fortuitous island of hope. He had written the book. If he didn't show up again, Tom still lived in his writing. And however unintentional was the leaving of his manuscript with me,—my purported theft—I accepted possession as providence.

Huddling for warmth, I paged through his volume looking for comfort and renewal, looking, I suppose, for the boy I'd known when we were fast friends. And, perhaps because I had seen him last in company of other veterans, his friend

who'd pushed me back, I found a description of
soldierly camaraderie in Tom's story.

The rumors flew. Constant. The weirder the more we
believed. Everyone thought there'd be an eclipse. We
talked about the Cong coming out of the tunnels in the
dark, thinking it was night. Then we'd blast their balls.
We hoped it was true.

Of course, it wasn't. It was, but not for us. The
Russians saw the eclipse. For us the sun burned clear
and hot all day long. By the time the Russkies were in
the umbra, it was already night outside Saigon.

False or not, the rumor in the skies threw us on our
backs. We were looking for the stars.

"Don't freak when the sun goes out," Perth-ass had
jibed. He was always saying stuff. All the Aussies joked
constantly.

"Sure, sure, P-a," I said, "like I don't know what's
happening? I, for one, went to high school."

He bitched. But I'd made the point. It was P-a who'd
looked at the sun over his shoulder all day long. And
when night fell, he took out his binocs. "Well, anyway,
look at this."

He knew the southern sky. Proved to me it was
prettier than the northern dome. We lay on a platform
over a rise by the river and studied the Southern Cross,
the Jewel Box, and Carina, passing the glasses back
and forth. It was terrific. Most of the time in Nam it's
cloudy. But March is clear. That sky dazzled me. We lay
there for hours.

Then, Perth-ass rolled toward me onto his side and
handed me the binocs. "Hey, Mate, I love you."

"Don't get weird on me, P-a."

He patted my chest. "No, no. I don't want to poke ya, Mate, I'll just never forget ya."

Afterwards, I wished I'd said something else, but at the time I just mumbled, "Yeah, me neither."

Next day, forty yards ahead of me, P-a in the lead grunted down what we thought was a command tunnel. "Corner right, mate," he said over his shoulder. In a minute three shots banged my ears. Then three more. Then nothing. P-a was either reloading or dead.

Finally, I decided on dead. Now *I* had to do some killing. And I would. With gusto.

Inside, the two Cong were dragging P-a up an incline. It was slow going. P-a had cleared my way. I moved fast, caught them right off. I tossed my light at them. Fools stopped. I slashed one's throat as he reached for the flashlight. Then I stabbed the other in the chest. I tied them together and stood them up. Cong-shields. Light-weight. I dragged that bitch-bundle up the tunnel a hundred yards before I saw the others. They flashed us and didn't shoot. I blazed away.

I killed one for every shot P-a had fired. I gouged the fuckers' eyes, put 'em in my pocket. Then I went to P-a and carried him out on my back, crawling.

Every time, I tell the newest volunteers, "Don't get close. You go down alone. You stay that way. Even back home. You're always solo."

I didn't cry for Tom, then. I shivered. I loved him, even as a killer. I understood what P-a had felt. I knew what Tom saw afterward. "You're always solo," rang true at 3:30 in the morning on a winter Monday. Even through the horror of what he wrote, I was closer that morning to Tom, to Burt, to Maggie, to Linda and the rest than I had ever been before. I couldn't define it, but I knew that I was thick with them as long as I lived.

I said it in that little, cold room, well before the first dawn of December, "Hey, Mate, I love you."

I could lose and live. I didn't have to be a mess. Even atop a pile of bones, of eyeless bodies, of artificial limbs, I could float, and not on a river of booze. Right then, I did not doubt it.

I put Tom's book back on the shelf, turned off the space heater, and trundled back down the hall, back into bed with DeLorr.

She made a sound and stirred. "You all right?"

I snuggled in close to her. "I'm fine."

The wellbeing I'd felt that long-ago night was something I wished for now, and with the same woman. Raci blew up. She'd done it plenty during our marriage. But she'd also settled down. I expected that would happen in my absence.

As for me, connecting with Tom's story did not bring me peace, but maybe my visit with Gabby would.

I was on my way to her hospice associated with the hospital that had treated her Parkinson's, the Langone Orthopedic people. She was still talking though she could hardly lift her hand. I'd lied about Gabby that morning. Raci didn't need to know, especially that Nettie was party to the relationship. Now, after our day together, my deceit felt dirty, unnecessary. I'd just wanted to keep things simple for everyone.

The twenty-minute walk gave me time to think, to consider my wrongs, my sins I suppose, especially as they affected Raci. As a husband, I had been trouble. After sobering up,

I was at first unbearable and afterward totally diverted from our love. Then it ended with shocking suddenness.

Now, just when I began hoping again, I felt the decay of my denial. I had written Moe with *all* the kids. He hadn't abandoned *his* wife. But my two *were* dead. I *had* left Raci. I *was* keeping secrets. Worse yet, I felt like I was ditching Gabby, who was soon to die, for a healthy and beautiful Raci. The fact was, I couldn't help myself. I felt as venal and false as Gael, Jude of *Twelve*, killing his friend, then Hillside-Glenn, and, in consequence, Burt, too. I was no better.

I just prayed I wasn't leaving Raci to drown.

Raci's visit revived a soft spot in my heart for her, a place that hadn't rotted, that hadn't shrunken to nothing. Taking strength from that discovery, despite my fears and remorse, I had allowed myself, for the first time in over twenty years, to feel hopeful for the future, hopeful for saving, maybe correcting, the past. Perhaps, at last, I could admit the truth. Even though I'd fought with Raci, I nearly skipped up the steps of the hospice.

"Hey, Papa Els." It was Ella, standing in the hallway by her mother's room.

I embraced her. "I'm glad you're still here. It got late, sweetheart."

"As grandma used to say, 'Better a day sober, than an hour late,' even if it doesn't make sense." She smiled her father's gat-toothed grin and batted her eye lashes. Grandma in this case was Gabby's mother.

"How is she today?" I hated to ask. It put the onus on Ella.

She looked toward the door, which was closed. "She didn't have a great day, but you'll cheer her up."

I pinched her cheek. "Yeah, I'm a barrel of laughs. How long you been here?"

"Just since four. I stopped by this morning on the way to

work, too. She hasn't been alone." Ella cocked her head at me. "So, how was your reunion?" Ella and Gabby knew all about Raci coming to town.

I hadn't thought I'd have to explain. I had to think.

"Come on, out with it." Ella knew I was composing. "Give me the skinny."

"It is complicated. We're up and down. Actually, Raci is still at my apartment. I needed a break, and that's for sure."

Ella looked over her shoulder then turned a sly look back at me. "So the lunch hour grew into a whole day." Ella's close ties with Nettie and an innate salacious streak prodded her curiosity. "She staying the night?" Ella dug a finger into my ribs.

"I don't know." I jumped away. "If she can be civil, I suppose."

"Well, I have a date, Papa Els, so I'm out of here. But come in while I say goodbye to Mom."

Gabby seemed asleep. Ella went around the bed and kissed her softly on the cheek. "I've got to go, Mom, but I brought in the night nurse to visit for a while." Gabby opened those narrow set eyes, gazing into her daughter's face, asking with a look, "Night nurse?"

"Els. He's here now."

I moved in over Ella's shoulder and smiled down at the woman of my dreams. "You look wonderful, Gabby." A wisp of a smile fluttered on her lips. I bent down carefully and kissed them.

"Okay, you lovebirds, I have a date." Ella elbowed past me. "Stay out of the bed, buster." She blew a kiss to both of us on her way out.

I took the bedside chair and held Gabby's hand. It trembled and felt cold. We sat like that in silence, listening to each other breathe. "Ella's good, Els," Gabby lisped. I nodded. "Tell me. Today."

240

She would want to hear. I left out the love-making and abbreviated the tale for Gabby's sake, but told her most of what went on: about the lunch, the wine-drunk, looking through *Twelve*, our walk to the pier, how I'd been feeling, the fight.

"Make up?" Gabby looked sad. I knew what she wanted: someone to care for me.

I chewed on my lip and hesitated.

She squeezed my hand oh so lightly, tremulously. "Truth."

"Not yet. Raci is still at my apartment."

Though she didn't have strength left to talk long, Gabby could still look me in the eye and carry all the meaning she needed to convey. She held me in her crosshairs. Single words were enough. "Go."

I returned the squeeze. "In a while."

We moved to silence, which, after all the years we'd shared in New York, watching Ella grow, watching carefully for signs in her of Burt, and purposefully entwining her life with her "big sister," Nettie, was enough. After long minutes, Gabby's whisper broke the quiet. "Regrets?"

"Don't talk like that, Gabby." I knew she was slipping away, intentionally, releasing me.

She persisted in a look.

"My only regret is never having made love to you."

I thought she smiled. It was faint. "Did," she murmured, "years." She wasn't done and focused me, hand and eyes. "Ella's life."

"I only did what was right," I said. "She was so much like him."

"Second Siiri." She pressed my hand. "Friends, always."

Gabby lapsed into sleep. I stayed, wondering how she could say so much in so few words, when I spewed thousands which meant next to nothing.

Gabriella assured me of my goodness, especially at the

times I felt lousy, a vain and impoverished man. Recently she'd murmured the litany of people I'd supposedly helped: "Ella," always at the top of her list, "Nettie," "me," each time stopping for breath, "Dwayne and Ona," "my lover, Burt," "Maggie," whom she'd never met, "all those long ago." She named many we knew in Manhattan, newer friends, a good many sober, some already gone.

That I could feel so close to Gabby who was leaving us so soon, and only tenuous with someone I thought I still loved even after a two-decade absence, perplexed me. Perhaps I couldn't make it back to Raci. There was too much fiction in the way. I could stand to lose Gabby, though it would hurt, because we'd kept everything clear and honest from the first. The unsettled past with Raci, cut off so abruptly, though, had to resolve, I decided, before I could go on.

I felt lightheaded and jittery, walking back to the apartment, exactly as I'd felt when Burt's house came crashing down next to my own in a domino-neighborhood that was bound to collapse.

. . . Monday morning. Jude wasted no time running with all the information he'd gathered. True to his business training, he leaked a bit of his findings to the chairpeople before he called for a business meeting. Of course, I was one of those.

"Hey, Moe," Jude said, motioning me to the hallway outside the meeting room. It felt dirty, but I went with it anyway. "The books are worse than I thought."

I couldn't pretend not to know what he was talking about, but I played as dumb as I dared. "Really? How so?" He didn't need much encouragement to spill his news.

"There's at least twenty thousand dollars unaccounted for over the last four years, and not a dime was ever paid to Beryl for rent, and not a dollar was ever sent to the national office."

I didn't want to argue, but if he was looking for blood, I didn't want to play into it. "Well, literature, food, and coffee supplies must have cost a bunch over that time." I shrugged my shoulders and tried to look quizzical.

"Nope. No coffee or food receipts either. The only expenditure recorded over that time totals less than two hundred dollars worth of literature purchases. Less than fifty dollars a year!"

Jude put on his incredulous face. Then he looked incensed. It was lucky Burt wasn't around. Had he a rope, Jude would have tried to lynch the guy.

It crossed my mind that before a board of directors Jude would have pooh-poohed such an amount either as welcomed excess profit or inconsequential expenses. But here, he played it up as grand larceny, something he would not brook. And we shouldn't either, I suppose.

When he told me he was calling for a business meeting, I tried to stall him. "Hey," I said, "Christmas is coming up. I think a better time would be after the new year. Maybe Burt will be back."

Jude jumped on me. "No way. I'm not waiting for him to do his wind-up doll routine. He can't smile this one down. We've got to recharter, and Burt is out. Here." He pushed a sheaf of paper into my hand. It was an accounting, a two-page group charter he'd written up, and an announcement of the business meeting.

"Have you talked to Toady?"

"You're the first, Moe. I need your support." When he put his hand on my shoulder, I didn't pull away.

EVENING

"Support for what is the question," I said. I visualized Burt swinging from the awnings out front.

"Just come to the meeting. Get as many members as you can, will you? That's all I ask."

I saw him talking to Toady after the meeting. He posted his announcements all over the place before he left. He'd chosen Friday for the business meeting. "Great," I said to Toady the next day, "now it'll look like I'm behind all this.

Toady smiled and hopped from one foot to another a couple of times, saying "It's not hard to see what's coming from a guy like Jude." He reached to the floor and scooped up a discarded Styrofoam cup and with a crooked hop two-pointed it into the trash. "Listen, Moe, we're going to discuss it, recharter for the future, and nothing else. When Burt comes back, he'll deal with whatever it is in his own way. Don't worry about him."

Toady didn't console me. After my beach dream of Maggie and Burt, I felt I'd loosed a monster when I sponsored Jude, who was tearing the flesh of my mentor, my one-time savior. I owed Burt a great deal. No, I didn't want to cover up any wrongdoing, but there was not a person at *Today* who hadn't done wrong, certainly including Jude. Our hope was to strive to grow more understanding and compassionate. Jude's investigation felt like anything but that. I was nervous.

Friday was a big meeting. Always toward heavy holidays participation grows. I didn't have that much experience, just over one year, but I've confirmed that opinion over the time since. Two words say it all: *la famiglia*. Not just the family, but *the* family. Not only mom and dad, though that can be enough to make anyone nervous, but all the weird and hurtful stuff that Aunt Agnes, perhaps, or Uncle Harry did or said over the years. Or gibes from siblings, the insults or slights of in-laws. For instance, one of my aunts, having cornered me alone in the kitchen on a Christmas eve, remarked, "The party really begins when we start crawling around on our hands and knees." I was twelve. She winked at me over her whiskey glass. Then she laughed and whirled the ice cubes around. I can hear the cacophony yet.

For the crowd at *Today*, having a family was almost just as difficult as not having a family. I don't know who had it worse. Was it harder to face a disappointed mother in the flesh or in the memory. More often than not our own words, spoken in ire, lust, or plain drunkenness, were what haunted us. Then there were dropped and broken glasses of wine, beer, gin, you name it, on top of slamming doors, yelling and screaming, stupid accusations, insolence, taunts, and vulgarities, not to mention those little confidential whispers wondering what was wrong with Willy or George, or the same observed from the other end of the banquet table directed, you were sure, at you. Yes, what *was* wrong with you? And I wouldn't argue too hard that the loneliness of those without family was any worse than the alienation of those with. Ah, *la famiglia e buona*.

In any case, the room at *Today* tended toward full. Only half stayed for the business meeting, but that gave Jude a good audience of twenty-some to play to.

Jude was an experienced diplomat, but his findings had turned him vicious. I was glad that Toady was there to rein him in a bit. Each person in the room owed Burt something. As it turned out, he had lent money, likely from the baskets, to several of them. But dollars were not the currency of their debt to the man. Burt led us all through difficult times, the very lowest of the lows, brought us up from the blues, coached us through breakups and breakdowns. I had the vision of Burt as our pastor, of our meeting as a corner church, just like the one across our crooked intersection. And like many of those others around town, our pastor lived directly and only on the generosity of the parishioners. To my mind, though I'm not the straightest financial arrow in the quiver, Burt had what was next to a right of support. We all knew darn well that he had no job, was a student if anything, and though not averse to work, did not pursue it, either.

I guess Jude wanted the money back, but as I'd been told, "Once you open the bottle, the money you paid for it is gone." I wish I had thought to say that at the meeting. As it was, my thanks went to Toady, who steered the discussion to the future of the meeting, away from a coming-down on Burt's transgressions.

"Yes, we can tighten up the procedures," Toady said. "I don't want to undo any of the good that *Today* has done."

And that's exactly what we did. We vowed by charter to pay our rent monthly, send ten percent to the New York office, and keep track of our spending on coffee and literature. We unanimously elected Jude as the overall treasurer, seeing how good he was with figures. You have to be careful about what you ask for, but he accepted.

For the year I had been at *Today* I had not been so glad to see a weekend begin as I was that Friday. Once I realized at the end of the business meeting that I could relax, I found my neck stiff and aching. It had been that way since

PEOPLE YOU'VE BEEN BEFORE

Sunday night. I knew why; reading in a cold room alone is bad medicine no matter what kindness comes of it. In another three hours I might be able to look over my shoulder, but I wasn't done with tension just yet.

Jude left right away. I heard his convertible peel out—yeah he was the only guy I'd ever known to lay rubber with a Mercedes—and figured, rightly, that I wouldn't see him until the next Thursday. The last member to go raised a farewell salute and left Toady and me together.

"Whew!" Toady said, "I'm glad that's over."

We agreed on it. I lingered. It seemed he had more to say.

Toady pulled on his belt loops in a vain attempt to raise his jeans from below that froggy belly of his. They slumped right back down. "I've heard from Burt," he said. "I didn't want to broadcast it, but he called me, collect again, on Wednesday. Let's get a waffle. I'll tell you all the news."

Burt was in LA. He was in a bad way, too. The call had been a plea for money.

"He sounded pretty far out there," Toady said. "Drifty, long on pauses, about as high as you can get and still carry on a conversation. Of a sort." That was not, he told me, the time to send money.

"You have to wait until the demoralization sets in heavy."

Toady had experience on both sides of it. After leaving with his coffee supplies months back, he had spent every dime he had, every penny his wife had, on Chivas Regal, at first, then Johnny Walker Red, and then, Wild Turkey, and, finally, on to Ten High before he made his call. That call had been to Burt, and it hadn't been his first.

"When you're calling for money, you aren't ready, yet," Toady said.

"Was he drunk?"

Toady sighed and admitted the truth as he knew it. "Burt was a drinker. But that came later. First, he was an addict."

"He's on drugs?"

"Heroin, likely."

"Shit." At Maggie's I thought he was joking. The only addicts I'd ever heard about were seamen up in Duluth who brought the stuff in from Asian voyages. They were on the docks. I'd never been near. "That's bad."

Toady agreed. "It's not good." He popped a bit of waffle in his mouth. Seemed like he was giving himself time to think. When he'd swallowed that bit like some sort of tasty fly, he gave me a cold gaze. "He mentioned Roxie."

"Shit. He's down there with her?" I thought of Muckey, whom I hadn't seen since Thanksgiving Day. "That's bad."

"Yeah, not good for anyone, especially Roxie. I think she was there. Probably as high as Burt or worse."

"I wonder if that's where Muckey is?"

"Might be. I didn't ask. Burt went down, he says, to visit Miss Malone."

"Who?"

"Maggie, Moe. Most of us do have two names."

"What? Maggie's down there, too?" This was too much for me.

"According to Burt she's at UCLA Medical Center. Some special unit for bone doctors. It wasn't too clear."

"Her family is from Orange, she told me. That's down there. What a mess."

"I hope Muckey doesn't find them," Toady said.

"He might, but for all his stories, Muckey is pretty meek. He won't make trouble. But it might send him on a bender."

Toady gulped down a wad of waffle. His eyes bulged.

"Thanks for the update, Toady. It's a lot to swallow, but I've got the weekend to digest it all. I don't know what to do."

"Do nothing, Moe. Stay close to meetings, is all. There is nothing to do until the time is right."

Toady wasn't really a friend. He was Burt's pal, not mine, but he was a good sort and wise in our program. He seemed to be taking on some of his friend's work while Burt was out of commission. I was glad to have Toady around, a steadying influence. "Before all this started, people just left, and I never heard from them again. I think I liked that better."

Toady jerked around in his seat, something like a seated hop. "This is what 'deep in the program' means, Moe," he spoke slowly and in measure. "You take a chance. You get close. You risk injury." Toady settled on the Naugahyde and looked me in the eye. "You're getting 'deep,' Moe."

"Yeah, well, I hope I'm not buried alive or drown in the pond."

"*Chugarum*," Toady said. Then he laughed.

I left the waffle shop feeling better, though not as relieved as I'd been right after the business meeting. I felt like I'd suffered garroting. I'd rather be ignorant and wonder than be in the know and have to worry. I was feeling that old nervousness and was certainly too jangled to go to work. Anyway, it was Friday, and I had some Christmas shopping I could do. Why not take the

EVENING

afternoon off?

I crossed Main, walking on the church side of Ferny where I'd parked early. When I could see my car just past the step van that had taken the spot in front of me, I saw the ticket on the rider's side windshield. "Shit." I grabbed it out of the wiper and nearly crumpled it in the street.

"Shit is right! Another ticket." A little guy who'd been hidden behind the van, sitting on the bumper stood up. It was Tom.

. . . What is it that they say? Something about a bad penny or thinking of someone and they show up? Well, Tom had been on my mind that week, and I had thought of him often since his Veteran's Day breeze-through at *Today*. Still I was more than surprised, rather shocked. Remember, I'd confessed my love for him in the wee hours only a few days back. And now, here he was, standing before me, no, leaning there over the hood of my car.

"You better not toss that. Your license number is on it!" He pointed to the orange, crumpled ticket in my fist.

I smoothed the ticket out and folded it into my pocket. "Are your ears burning, Tom? I've been thinking about you."

"Yeah? Well, I figured. Probably not good thoughts, either."

I moved as close as I dared, within arm's length. I didn't want to scare either of us off. "Actually, Tom, they were warm memories. I've missed you."

"I didn't want to come back upstairs after the way I left. Hey, when you're in vet company, especially on Veteran's Day, you're back in the service. Don't pay any mind to P-a. My mate. He

250

was as off base as I was."

Tom was truly sorry. His voice was softer than I'd heard, maybe since Cub Scouts. "I got that. No hard feelings." I hesitated to bring it up but said, "That was P-a? I thought he was dead."

Tom looked at me, confused. Then he caught on. "Oh, the book? No, that was Perry Asbroth, from Perth, in the flesh. It wasn't the P-a in the story, at least the dying part." He must have realized the stargazing scene was on my mind along with the following day's slaughter.

Maybe I should explain. "I couldn't sleep the other night. I read." I could feel Tom holding his breath, like waiting for a tripped wire to do its evil. "It's powerful, Tom. Better than anything I've ever done." I meant what I said.

Tom's body eased, but he looked away and shuffled his feet. We were treading on heavily-mined terrain.

Let him think about what I said, what it meant to him. Now I wanted us to ease up, avoid tough stuff. "You got some time? I'm about to do some Christmas shopping. I've got the day off."

That brightened him up. "All right! I should get my dad something." He pushed off the car, walked, a bit unsteadily, to the hedges guarding the church grounds, and fished up a duffel bag from behind them. It was new, I noticed.

I opened the trunk. "Toss it in the back." Tom dragged the bag over to the car, stowed it, and took his seat beside me. "Hey, like old times."

"Yeah, like old times."

I drove. We avoided book-talk and anything about our last meeting. Tom had been staying across the bay with some veteran friends. He didn't tell me too much about them, but I got the impression he'd burned a bridge or two over there and had packed up. He was on his way to Minnesota to spend Christmas with his father.

Old Doc McIntyre was on his last legs.

"Your dad must be ninety."

"Ninety-four," Tom said. "He's alone in the old house, still." The old man wouldn't leave the house and, though not still in practice, he'd kept his license up, and his colleagues protected him. "He's got a nurse and a housekeeper coming in every day."

"What's the house like? Is he keeping it up?"

Tom shook his head. "He's lived there alone for thirty years. I don't think he's thrown anything out in all that time. Even newspapers. He sleeps in the dining room." The last time Tom had been there to supervise the exterior painting, the stacks of documents and newspapers filled the halls and lined pathways through the living room. The sun porch was packed to the ceiling.

"Depressing," I said.

Tom looked out the window. "He's like that mannequin in your downstairs window. He's been waiting to die for thirty-some years."

I made a stab at the upbeat. "I'm headed for a toy store. I think there's a chocolate shop in the block. Gift store." Tom nodded but said nothing.

When I pulled to the curb and reached for the door handle, Tom didn't move. He was thinking. "What's up, Tom. You all right?"

"Listen, Moe," he said in that particular tone of voice he used when he wanted something. I could have filled in the blank of his pause easily. He was out of funds. He was waiting for his father to wire him cash and send him a plane ticket. "My old pals have had it with me, too. So, I'm looking for a place to stay. Just a couple of days."

Apparently, the ticket and telegram were headed to my address. I was put upon, but I didn't care. The sentiments his writing had raised in me still burned heartily. DeLorr was another matter, but I could make it good with her. "Sure, Tom, through what, Monday?"

"I should be on my way that next morning." He still did not move to leave the car. I reached for my wallet.

"Can I front you twenty?"

"Can you spare fifty?"

Tom. Always Tom.

We cruised around stopping here and there. I took him to a corner lunch spot famous for pie and treated him on the company tab. Business. He wolfed down a poorboy and a salad. He wondered out loud if I was having dessert.

"Absolutely. Their pie is tasty. I like their apple best."

I was happy to help Tom. I assumed he'd taken a turn and might be sober. He looked fairly healthy and clean, still a little dauber down, but not depressed even though he was headed back to the Minnesotan refrigerator.

My business career was nearing its end, I knew, and I needed something else to get into to keep up appearances if not to feed the family coffers. I'd been wondering if Tom might consent to me editing his book. It had strong potential, I thought, and once it was cleaned up a bit, it would be marketable. Vietnam was still a story, and his subject had a waiting audience. I broached the subject while we savored the apple pies.

"What are you planning on doing with your book, Tom?"

He put his fork down. "What do you mean?"

Evening

His tone made me regret having asked, but I plowed ahead. "I think it should be published."

Tom cleaned the pie filling off his teeth, moving his tongue here and there, mouth shut, looking off at the ceiling and nodding his head a bit as if figuring what to say. Finally, he leveled his gaze at me, and at that moment I came to believe he was capable of killing.

"There's always something to pay, isn't there, Moe, and you don't get out of this world alive." He looked at his pie and shook his head decidedly. "As soon as you put a foot forward, they're sending you down. Using you. Putting you in the front line."

"I didn't mean it that way, Tom."

"Oh? You don't want to spruce up my story a little and sell it to the highest bidder? Grab a bit of the pie and run?" He stabbed the crust with his fork. "Suck up a little of the glory on another man's back?"

"That's not how it works." He was freaking out on me.

Tom rapped the table with the butt of his fork sending crust and sticky apple slices to the floor, "I know how it works, friend."

I thought about the duffel in the trunk, about the fifty I'd given him, about Tom snoring on the couch in my office, keeping DeLorr awake, about his ticket arriving at my house. I was stuck and couldn't let this blow up right now. I had to wait it out, to choose the path of least resistance. I gave him the friendliest look I could muster. "I was wrong, Tom. It's your story. You do what you want with it."

"Goddamn right, Moe." He went on mumbling, "It's longer now. I've added stuff to what you still have."

"So you still think I stole it?"

Tom looked surprised, "When did I ever say that?"

We finished our dessert in silence. Tom took a gulp of coffee and sloshed it around his mouth like Listerine. He chewed on his lower lip. "Look, Moe, I'm off base again. You've got talent and want to use it. I can't blame you for that."

"Thanks, Tom, but it's only an idea. Your writing moved me."

He swallowed hard. "Let me think about it."

I paid, and before we left, I called to let DeLorr know that Tom was coming home with me. Just for a couple of days, I told her.

"Moe," she said over the phone, "we're buying the tree tonight! What about that?"

"I'll get home early, and we'll go as soon as the kids come home from school." That seemed to satisfy her. DeLorr could be all right.

Tom and I entered through the lower level door, and I showed him the bathroom he would use and the office. DeLorr had already spread out sheets and a blanket on the couch and had stacked some towels and a pillow on a chair. I left Tom to settle in and went up to the kitchen to see DeLorr and explain it all. It would be best if I briefed her on Tom's short fuse. I didn't want any trouble.

As it turned out, Tom was a wonderful guest. He helped with cooking and cleanup, kept his quarters tidy, and was very handy with setting up the Christmas tree.

At the tree farm, Tom kept my two year-old son, Michael, busy, running in and out of the rows of pine and spruce while the rest of us deliberated on which variety and which tree to cut. He took an end of the blue spruce we'd selected, toting it to the car. We used Boy Scout knots he still remembered to cinch it securely on the roof.

Michael had taken to Tom immediately, maybe because of his size, and they became close in no time. "Unka Tom," Michael called him right off.

The weekend was almost idyllic. Remember, Saturday and Sunday hadn't been my favorite days, but with a friend in the house, I was feeling less put-upon, less responsible for everything being peachy. Not that I didn't get on with my toddler, but I felt relief that Michael had in Tom a new playmate who seemed quite all right with the boy's demands. It was a holiday for us both.

That night we stood the tree in its stand out on the deck and gave it a good spraying. Saturday, Tom and I lugged it inside. The girls brought out the ornaments and trimmings, and we snaked the lights around the living room rug to check for duds. I put the ladder up, and Tom and I wound the strings of lights, starting with the bubble lights, survivors I'd saved from my parents' collection, around and down the branches. I stood on the ladder, clipping the lights to branches as Tom stretched the cord out and around the tree. DeLorr heated cider and made sandwiches for lunch. I lit kindling around a log in the fireplace. Afterward, the kids and Tom hung the ornaments while DeLorr and I critiqued the placement and corrected as we saw fit. We talked about taking everyone to the movies for all their good work. It had been a great day.

Toward mid-afternoon, Tom's wire arrived. Western Union was open until five.

"We'll give you a ride down," I said. "You can come to the movie with us."

"Thanks, I'm pooped. I'll probably go on Monday. I'm taking a nap." He waved as he went downstairs.

People You've Been Before

We had to keep Michael from following. DeLorr lay down with him upstairs.

Later, we tiptoed past the office door on the way to the car and slipped out to our movie.

We didn't see Tom for a day and a half, and when he returned, he was not alone.

At one end of the couch, DeLorr was reading to our younger girl under a cone of lamplight. Michael was asleep on my lap. We'd been watching the bubble lights percolate in the flicker of firelight. The contentment of a Sunday evening in the Christmas season soothed even my usually jangled nerves. Michael snored softly. I smiled to myself. DeLorr's voice lulled me toward sleep. A soft December rain pattered against the windows.

I heard voices. I woke at a clatter out on the deck told me I was awake. If raccoons could swear, I'd have believed it was animals.

"Christ, P-a," Tom's voice shouted, "watch y'rself." More rumbling and fuss ushered their footfalls across the deck. They were singing now:

> *O Tannenbaum, o Tannenbaum,*
> *wie treu sind deine Blätter!*
> *Du grünst nicht nur*
> *zur. . .*

They stumbled on the German and broke into English:

> . . . summertime,
> No, also in winter when it snows.
> O Christmas tree . . .

They banged on the door, then, finding it

unlocked, entered. "Ho, ho, ho, Merry Christmas," they hollered in a sour harmony. And trooped through the entry into the living room, dripping-wet, sloshing small puddles along with every step. The two dwarfish characters wore soaked Santa hats and P-a dragged along a sodden red cloak.

"Ho, ho, ho," he intoned in a deep voice. Michael woke crying.

"Oh, Mikey-boy," Tom said, "don't cry, it's Santa Claus! Here Santa, ask the boy what he wants for Christmas." Michael howled at Tom's and P-a's approach, certain that something was very wrong even though he couldn't know what.

"Maybe he wants another song, Mate," said Santa. "An American one!" P-a started prancing around, twirling the cape, doing pirouettes.

> Dashing through the snow
> In a one-horse open sleigh

Tom joined in both singing and prancing,

> O'r the fields we go

They capered around each other, joined hands, and whirled savagely. And on the line "laughing all the way," P-a let loose and Tom flew fully, directly into our Christmas tree, which crashed against the sliding doors of the back deck and bounced off, falling directly over jolly old Saint Nick who'd tried to save himself and the tree from disaster. Now my girl, Tilla, burst into tears. DeLorr screamed. Michael, now fully awake, cried.

Tom picked himself off the floor, stood wobbling on widespread feet, trying, it seemed, to figure out what had just happened. P-a rolled out from under the tree, sopping wet from its spilled reservoir.

"Look what you've done," Tom boomed.

"Ta hell. It 'as you let go."

"Yer a Satan-Santa." Tom approached P-a.

"Fuck ya, Mate," he said and punched Tom square in the nose.

The two went down in a scrabbling ball, wrestling in the pine water and broken lights and ornaments, cursing each other, flailing madly. The kids screamed uncontrollably. DeLorr yelled, "Do something, Moe." Then addressing the roiling ball of tunnel rats, "Now, you stop it!" She took Michael up and pulled the girl along to the bedroom. Both were still howling.

"Tom, for Christ's sake stop!"

Then DeLorr was back with a broom, furiously smacking whoever was on top at the moment, until they stopped. Neither seemed to understand why they were being beaten.

Tom recovered first, looked around. "Who did this?" And as if to answer his own idiotic question he said, "Don't worry, we'll clean it all up."

DeLorr prodded Tom with the tip of the broom handle, right in his chest. "Oh, no you won't, mister. But you will get your stuff and clear out right now."

I tried to protest, but DeLorr beat me to it, "I don't give a rat's ass what you think, Moe. This is the last time your drunkard friends darken my door. Watch out, or you'll be next."

Tom was already down the stairs getting his duffel bag. P-a picked himself up, grabbed the soaking wet cape, and sidled past, wide of the broom, mumbling, "Sorry, ma'am, so sorry."

So much for serenity.

So much for a quiet weekend with the family.

EVENING

So much for friendship, and for nerves, too.

So much for Tom. He'd already left by the lower door, closing it noisily. I heard him hail P-a once outside, finding each other again in the dark and the rain.

DeLorr had plenty to say. It was a regular one-way argument, she taking both sides as I without reply mopped, swept, and reassembled what was left of the tree and its decorations.

One antique bubble light survived, like me, a double refugee of Christmases past and present, one that ushered me into a cruel adult world, the other that confirmed in adulthood that I didn't have to drink to be a drunk.

I stayed home that Monday. I didn't even go to *Today*. I took one trip to the village at the bottom of our hill to buy replacement ornaments and lights. When I returned, there was Tom, sitting on his duffel bag out by the mailboxes. When I stopped, he rose to his feet, a rumpled and humbled mess.

"I didn't want to trespass," he said. "The mailman came half an hour ago. Thought I'd wait."

Of course, he wanted the letter from his dad which, thank the spirits of Christmas, was there along with some bills for me. I handed him the envelope.

"Thanks, man. Really, sorry for the ruckus. It was my fault."

"It was, yes, Tom. My wife is about to throw me out." I looked at the sorry mess that was Tom. "I'm sorry, too," I said.

It was an opportunity, but neither of us could bring ourselves to embrace. True forgiveness takes time no matter what affections you hold.

"So, you're off to Minnesota?"

"Yeah. And I've got just enough cash for transport and to eat along the way. I'll send you your fifty when I can get it from Dad."

At least he hadn't asked me for more. "So long, Tom."

"I owe you, Moe. I won't forget it."

He shouldered his bag and limped off down the street. I watched him go round the curve. I got back in the car. No thought of his manuscript passed my mind then. That afternoon, stripping the office davenport, I noticed it was gone from its place. Just another opportunity spilled out and splintered on the floor. Why would any of us expect something else?

I'd walked to Shu Han Ju on the corner of 6th Avenue and West 11th Street. Christmas lights that Li Ho, the owner, had put up several decades ago mocked my recollection of Tom's visit.

"April already, and all set for Christmas, Li," I greeted him.

"Eat here? Or take out?"

In the years I'd been going to Shu Han Ju, I had never eaten in the restaurant, or, for that matter done much beside joke, say hello, or order and pay. "Mu Shu Pork," Raci's favorite always, "with six pancakes, Cashew chicken, and house fried rice."

"Very hungry," Li Ho said.

"I have a guest."

Li laughed and in Mandarin yelled into the kitchen.

"Ten minute." It was always ten. I sat near the windows to wait for the order.

"No deliver?"

"I'll wait this time. Thanks, Li."

EVENING

. . . In the same week that Tom left, Muckey came back, nearly broke, downcast, with the faded remains of a pretty good black eye, but dry. I wondered if I'd been right about him. He had discovered firsthand about Roxie and Burt. I tried to visualize the scene.

"How does the other guy look?" I said.

"You'll hear the whole goddamned thing in due time." He touched the eye, shook his head, and pursed his lips. "I've been through this with her before." I wondered if he might be referring to the bruised eye, his rescue of Roxie just four months prior, or the original jilting incident by his father years back. All came to my mind. Muckey did have a long history of love for Roxie, most of it painful.

We were walking Telegraph. It seemed easier for Muckey to talk while in motion. "It was terrible, Moe." He looked up into the clouds that were billowing in off the ocean. "I didn't see her, but she was worse off than the last time. At least then she had a suitcase full of clothes and a lamp with a shade on it."

"Where did you find her? What happened? She lose her job?"

Muckey held up his hand but kept walking. "I've got to tell this from the beginning, Moe. Hold the questions." Muckey's mode of storytelling kept his audience in suspense, while he told the whole story from beginning to end. If it hadn't been for the good training in listening I'd gained over the previous year, I might not have had the patience to hear it. If I wanted to know anything at all, I had to follow along while Muckey played up to something, leading me somewhere. Mostly I wanted to know about Maggie. I had an idea Muckey could tell me about her. I cooled my jets and let him take to the skies with his story.

People You've Been Before

"So I took off after the meeting on Thanksgiving. And, no, I didn't goddamn tell you. I didn't tell anyone if you want to know. I already stowed my bag in the bus locker. Had my ticket, too, before I talked to Toady and you after the meeting. If Burt was down there or not, if he was with Roxie or not, there really wasn't any time to be jawboning about it. Anyone with sense would have told me to stay at home, anyway. So, I just left.

"Let me tell you, Moe. The travelers sitting on the Greyhound at Thanksgiving are super depressed. But I felt up. I figured on finding Roxie and bringing her here. You know, she liked it up here. All that crap about Hollywood! Old, worn-out dreams. They die hard. Still, no call for pessimism.

"I wish the other people on the bus had been the same. Mostly they were mopey and bummed out. A lot of Mexican guys with us would rather have been working for cash that day rather than spending their *dinero* on a bus ride to Bakersfield or LA. Plus, my Spanish isn't that good. What did I have to say anyway? 'Yeah, I'm on my way to save a soul. Gonna gather up a wayward *klootch*. Have ta punch a guy in the nose.' No one wanted to hear my sad story. Not even me. I try to keep upbeat.

"I caught up on the sleep I'd been missing and in between naps figured on how I could work this thing if I could ever find her. The only leads I had were from the café where I'd found her a job and a couple of meetings we used to go to when she started out. Maybe she was still working. She'd *have* to have gone 'round to pick up her last check, anyway. And someone at the meetings might have heard about her. If neither panned out, I figured to get lucky.

"My pal JJ picked me up at the depot and took me to a big Thanksgiving dinner meeting in Valley Village. The food smelled great. Looked like a goddamned banquet. But it wasn't Roxie's crowd—bunch of *muckamucks* for sure. No one would have heard a single word on her. But I was well-fed, yeah, for the last time in two weeks it turned out. The rest was burgers and fries back in Hollywood."

I knew it would do no good, but I tried to prod Muckey to get to the point. "So, when did you get a lead?"

He looked at me, surprised almost that I still walked there with him. "*Tap'er light*, Moe," he said, "I'm getting to that."

Muckey D could be a strange sort. Of course, who wasn't in our bunch? I mean that if you took a survey, which you would certainly never do, about Muckey's chances of staying off the booze, I don't think many would have thought he could or would because they were listening to his yakking rather than watching his moves. What would I have said on such an opinion poll? Knowing me, as I had come to do during that year with *Today*, I likely would have gone with the majority. Muckey seemed erratic and dangerous to himself. But if I ignored the conventional wisdom codified in a few simple phrases—"easy does it" was one—and paid attention to Muckey's acts, I might have gone the other way. I'm supposed to be, as an editor, above the norm on metaphors, but I'll say that I truly believe that the guy had a heart of gold, kind through and through. And he told a good story, too.

"So I got a break just as I was leaving the Valley party. I remembered at Maggie's lunch Burt saying something about knowing directors or producers or something. Aren't they the same thing? Anyway, JJ had early on introduced me to some *grand poomba* Hollywood type. One of the coolest cats there. That was before I could eat anything. Food was all that was on my mind. Then later out on the porch Burt's director thing comes back to me and, presto, here this guy walks up again to say goodbye.

"He was cool, very cool. You know the kind of guy who always seems like he's lounging behind a goddamn movie camera. It's like he's in motion but standing at ease to view it all. You know, goddamn open shirt—*plumb spendy*—a sweater, ditto, swung over his shoulders, nice slacks. Italian shoes that made you want to go home and polish yours. You know, salt-and-pepper beard, freshly styled hair. He talked so casual, so relaxed and such. You know . . ."

I had to stop him. "Muckey, yes, I know."

"All right! So I said, 'Martin, (believe it or not, my own name) let me take a long shot: you don't happen to know a Burt C. from up north do you? He used to run around in Hollywood.'"

"'Light-skinned freckly guy? Big wide grin? A neck like one of those wind-up talking dolls? Yeah, I knew him, and I just saw him, too.'

"I must have looked starstruck. He laughed. I stuttered, 'Was Roxie with him?' Then I felt sorely dumb.

"'All over him, more like. Those two are headed for trouble. He wanted me to see her act, but I don't take to hop-heads. They were both sky high.' He stopped, realizing, I suppose, I knew her.

"'Any idea where I could catch up with them?'

"Martin told me about a crummy hotel on a back lot off Melrose. 'I should have tossed this but, here . . .' He gave me a map scratched out on a scrap from his wallet. 'Your Burt didn't know his own address. Like I say, I . . .'

"I finished the sentence for him 'don't take to hop-heads.'

"'Yeah. But good luck.' Now, for sure, he knew the score. He could tell by my hangdog look that I loved Roxie.

"Hey, Moe, I just can't help it."

We were getting pretty far downtown by this time, and I suggested some coffee. Muckey wanted to keep going.

"I've got some business down here. Coffee can wait."

Mr. Obsession had applied his grip. Muckey never turned down a cup. That told me he had something buzzing in that zigzagging brain of his. I needed to go along but had to watch out, too.

"Now I knew they were somewhere off the strip. I didn't have the exact address, just that map of some *coulee* off Melrose. That didn't work for me. I had to backtrack to get my leads. Next day I bused it down to Venice Beach to check the restaurant. Isaiah, the manager who gave Roxie the job in the first place, came out of the kitchen. He was none too pleased with me.

"'You told me she was off the stuff. Man, she screwed us up. Kept saying she'd be in and then didn't show. You know how hard I had to work to get a last-second stand-in? Fucked up!' He screamed at me. 'Then she shows up for her check. That's okay, but she had no idea how many days she'd worked. I told her three, and then we had a major row.'

"'*Um ver,* sorry, sorry. Believe me, I wish it didn't happened.'

"'And that bozo she came with!' He was really wound up now. 'I wanted to wring his scrawny neck. I told him so, too.'

"'Icy (that's what they called him), chill! *Tap*

'er *light*. I had no idea. No control. I'm here to find her. I'm gonna bring her back north with me. You won't be bothered again.'

"He'd gotten her address for taxes, I guess. "'If you see that freak she hangs with now, tell him he owes me a soup spoon. He filched one that last day. Probably cooking his shit in it.'

"I hopped the bus right back to Hollywood. Didn't even walk the beach.

"The 'hotel' wasn't a hotel but a warehouse behind a plumbing shop that showed tubs and toilets and sinks in the window. The sign over the back building door said 'HVAC/Sheet Metal'. All the windows wore bars but had no glass to show. A guy by the door was sitting on a heavy packing crate, elbows on knees, looking at the pavement. He could have been a sumo wrestler. Looked Samoan.

"When I came up he stayed put. Then he raised one meaty hand out to block the way. 'Where you headed, pal?'

"'I'm looking for some friends.'

"He smiled nicely but didn't move. 'So's everybody. No one's home, but who?'

"'Icy down at the restaurant told me Roxie stayed here. Maybe with Burt.'

"'No one's home.'

"'Mind if I look?'

"Next thing I know, I'm on the goddamned ground. For a big man, he moved fast. I guess I'd crossed an invisible line. Some sort of trip wire. That's how I got the shiner.

"'Look man, nothing personal, but I got a job here. If you want to see someone, go out onto the walk there and wait for them to come. Better yet, stop in at the café while you're at it and get some ice for that eye. Tell 'em Pea Soupo sent you.'

He was actually a pretty nice guy. "They knew him at the café. Another Samoan. 'Well, looks like you met Pea Soupo, pal.' Seemed like everyone around was pals.

" 'Yeah, he said you had extra ice.' He'd already put a couple handfuls in a plastic bag.

" 'Wrap it in this bar rag. It's clean. Coffee?'

" 'Sure,' I said. 'Maybe you know Roxie. Stays in the back, there.'

" 'Who told you that?'

" 'Icy down on . . .'

" 'Venice Beach. We know him. She's been around. In and out, so to speak.' He watched me, a huge grin striping his jowls. I stirred the sugar in and took a sip, trying not to choke and all the time holding the bar rag on my eye. 'What's your interest?' he asked."

Muckey broke off and, continuing to walk pretty fast, turned to me. "You know, Moe, all those people down there are pretty well-spoken no matter what we say about them up here. Intelligent. And they show some humanity. So I told him the short version of the story, starting in Montana at The Roxy up through her visit and all.

" 'Okay. Listen," Soupo's friend said, "She's just more Norwegian wood to us, but I loved my wife once, too.'

" 'You know her, then?'

" 'Pea Soupo booted them. Kept their bags. So they'll be back when they find some bread. Might be in Compton. She used to room down there. But I'd wait around.' I didn't tell him I knew the place in Compton. I had rented it for her in September.

" '*Masi*, thanks' I didn't know his name. 'I'm Muckey.'

" 'You're welcome. Fetu,' he said, and squeezed

my hand like a goddamn wet dishrag.

"Fetu had a cousin upstairs across the street who put me up. I had to pay $14 a day! Just to sleep on the floor, but the window looked right straight down the alley to the warehouse. So I called JJ to let him know. 'I'll give it a couple days,' I told him, 'then I'll go down to Compton to snoop around.'"

"Fetu threw in a good breakfast at the café. My set-up served as an islander's bed and breakfast. I helped out busing dishes and swabbing the floor. The work kept me busy while I kept my good eye on the alley. One eye. That's all I had. The other swelled shut for three days. So I either worked with Fetu or sat at his cousin's front window. I didn't want to be out on the street. One eye or not, I didn't want to miss Roxie if she came for her stuff.

"Three days it took. Forty-two dollars and my money running low. Then goddamned Burt showed up. Early evening, a quiet time down there. Dark already. Here he comes like usual, swinging his arms big, yakking up a storm, laughing, and nodding as if Toady or someone walked right next to him. But there wasn't nobody. He was alone. Still he kept on wracking that neck of his from one side to the other and smiling like a madman.

"I heard him first, then saw him a down the corner still. He sashayed right through the light and hopped up the curb just before a truck, honking like a train, could hit him. Just made it. But he paid no mind to nothing but his talking. When he came just shy of the alley, right in front of upended pink- and turquoise-colored tubs lined up in the plumbers' window, he stopped short. Stopped everything and shut up.

"Burt put half a head, just an eye, really,

at the corner to see who guarded the door. There was always someone there. Right then it was Manu, giving Pea Soupo a break for his supper at the café. Burt slipped around the corner into the alley, keeping close to the wall, and sidled down to the trash bins behind the plumbing shop. He stood there for a good five minutes, then whipped around the dumpster. 'Hey, Manu. Where's Pea Soupo?'

"'Right behind you, Burt.' My cold-cocking friend put a paw on Burt's shoulder. I nearly closed my eye. I didn't want to see what he'd do to Burt. 'Got your baggage check?' Soupo said. The voices echoed hugely in the alley.

"'Like my grandmother used to say, *Never go shopping without a nickel*.' Burt looked back at Soupo and grinned big. He looked really small next to Soupo.

"They went in past Manu. I tramped down the stairs across the street and slipped into the café. Fetu grinned at me. 'Looks like you'll be moving on, Muckey.'

"'No, I'll be back, I'm sure. At least to get my stuff.' I went to the toilet at the back.

"I watched from the can window that they always propped open a bit. It gave a good view of Manu sitting on the box. Burt came out first. Carrying two suitcases. Some ancient brown leather one, probably his grandmother's—scads of stickers plastered on it—and Roxie's little red cardboard case she had left Montana with years ago. Now it was pretty beaten up. 'Okay, Mr. Soup, we are all square.' Burt seemed to be taking chances, but Samoans practice restraint and action, both. Each got its place.

"Pea Soupo lumbered down the alley to the café door without a word. Still in the can, I watched

PEOPLE YOU'VE BEEN BEFORE

Burt. The best thing to do was to follow him, and
weighed down with two cases, it would be easy to
do. But he didn't leave. He hung out behind the
plumbing shop. First, he opened grandma's case.
He unstrapped it, running the big old zipper all
the way open. Then he dug around inside. Bound it
up again. He unsnapped Roxie's little red one.
With the case open, he put Roxie's clothes out
on the pavement and searched through what she'd
left inside. He slipped a small Baggie into his
pocket, shut the case, and threw it in the open
dumpster. Then he started down the alley.

"'Hey, man, don't leave that stuff there," Manu
said, setting himself for action.

"'Oh, yeah, my grandmother trained me better
than that.' Burt said. Set down his bag, swept
up Roxie's things. I had given her some of them.
Then he goddamned dumped everything on top of the
suitcase he'd tossed away. 'Better?'

"Manu shot a glance in my direction. He knew I
was there. With a word, he'd spring. But I didn't
want Burt. I wanted Roxie. I had to follow him.

"When he sauntered around the corner, I spoke
to Manu. 'It's worth five if you gather her stuff.
I gotta go.' Manu stood. I saw him futzing with
her stuff in the dumpster. I loved those guys.

"On my way out, I told Pea Soupo about it just
in case I'd broken protocol and whipped out the
door to see where Burt had gone. '*Masi*, Soupo!'

Burt had crossed the street. Standing at the
bus stop. I hustled down to the next corner where
I could watch and catch the same line. I pulled
my cap down over the good eye, threw up my hood.
Did my hunchback imitation. If he went to the
back of the bus, it would be easy. Even if he saw
me, my disguise—my big bulby eye—would hide me.

"He got on the 210, the same bus I'd taken three

271

days ago. Maybe they were down on the beach. But Burt stayed on when we hit Venice Boulevard. And on and on and on. I didn't count the stops, but it seemed like goddamned fifty. Anyway Burt sat at the back of the bus laughing and talking. Mainly with no one. I didn't have to keep checking for him anyway. I could hear he was still on. I sat a ways toward the front on the far side of a huge old lady. She surrounded herself with bags and *duff*. Finally, Burt pulls the bell and he gets out. I took the front door and turned away from him right off. See, I'm playing detective, now. I walk up the street, it's East Manchester. Duck into a doorway to look back.

"Burt sat on his suitcase. Waving his transfer around and, of course, talking a blue streak. So, I head a block down to the next stop and keep my eye on what Burt does. When I get on the next bus, he's at the back again. Another giant woman sat waiting for me with almost half a seat beside her. I squeeze in to hide next to her. We all ride for a while. Burt gets up. I jump off, too. This time I go around the corner. Something like McKinley Avenue. I watch what Burt does.

"He didn't see me. Burt saunters up the corner, crosses Manchester. He goes to 729, a brick two-story. Got a bicycle shop down below in the storefront.

"Now I wished I had brought my stuff. At least a jacket. With the sun long gone, it was goddamned cold. I have no idea how long I'd have to wait. I still didn't want to tip my hand. Not until I actually found Roxie. It could be a long and cold night."

Right at that moment, as if Muckey had been timing his approach, he stopped telling the story and stepped into the Greyhound Bus Depot, apparently where he'd been headed. At the ticket counter he asked for two round trips to LA. "You're comin' with me, aren't you Moe?"

So that was it. He lured me to the bus depot, hoping I'd accompany him to save Roxie. I shook my head. "It's nearly Christmas, Muckey. I can't just take off. I've still got a job, a family, and, honestly, both are on the rocks. One more problem and my boss and wife are likely to throw me out. And if I missed Christmas, she would."

Muckey looked about to cry. His pathetic, droopy visage hung lower and lower. It seemed he'd collapse in a puddle of misery. Still he managed one more plea, "I need help on this one, Moe. I can bring her home if you will come."

Here was an opportunity to do good service, the kind I'd avoided so far. "All right, Muckey. But it has to be *after* Christmas. Just another week or so."

Two weeks later, I had to say "please don't ask me to your next intervention," for Roxie's was enough for me. I suppose they are necessary for hard cases like her drugging, but if I'd walked in on a little circle of family, friends, and "helping" professionals wanting to assist me by facing reality and getting me off the booze, I wouldn't have heard the door slamming behind me. I'd have been out just that quick. Roxie? She was another matter.

They had her. Yes. But she'd also been had. There was nothing left. The trick was to get her to see that and keep her sane. We, a dozen or so of us, were sitting in a circle in the middle of the institution's commons area, when Roxie buried her head in that red, cardboard suitcase Muckey had brought back to her. Then I knew that she was beginning to see the handwriting. I don't know about JJ or Muckey, though I had to put out an arm to keep Muckey in his chair, but the rest of the circle just stayed in their seats waiting for the dam to break, like they had been at that point with their patients before. They knew why Roxie had been holding out. She thought she could recover her stash from Pea Soupo. No dice. Burt had shot that chance.

So, they had her, and good. And it was good. Finally, she could throw away those crutches, grow healthy, start telling the truth, and make something real, maybe something lasting, in her life. Muckey had always known *what* he wanted. Perhaps Roxie would discover her own "what." No more phantoms, impossible dreams, or wild adventures. They are hard to give up but worse to ride on down.

I was just glad to be beyond that rehab center and couldn't blame Roxie for not wanting to stay.

But stay she would. Muckey would be near to watch over her. We all knew that.

I'd learned way too much about Burt since Muckey came up to ask for my help. Roxie's intervention put a bit of spine in my determination. I'd been wobbly and nervous ever since Jude had started his investigation. The way Burt had treated Maggie and, now, Roxie, didn't help his case. Muckey's story about Burt in LA and, finally, Roxie's breakdown there in the intervention meeting changed my view of the man.

How I could stay upright without Burt's help and encouragement worried me. I split the old Burt I'd canonized from the new, satanic Burt I'd discovered in LA. I had to move from the apostolic to wary friendliness, or maybe to a distanced, simmering understanding as far as Burt concerned me. I had to, just to survive. Burt showed me a way to save myself, and now that meant I'd have to give up my illusions about the master-savior himself. That balance and my friends in Hollywood, especially kind-hearted Muckey, would stabilize the nerves, as long as nothing else happened.

And when I got back? Well, Toady was still around, as far as I knew.

There was something else in LA, though.

"Moe," Muckey said, "Roxie give this to me for ya."

"What's that?"

"She wouldn't say exactly but it's about the gathering yesterday. The intervention. Old suspenders—the doctor in charge, he meant—encouraged her to write it out. Said it would help."

"Why is she giving it to me?"

"Moe, everybody knows you help writers. Like that Tom fellow you know."

"Really?"

"'Course."

"So?"

"I think she wants you to see it. Fix it up. Put it out there."

My eyes started to water. I took the sheaf of papers, a proof that struggling as I was in my self-centered, myopic life, that I had reached out and helped another godforsaken soul, Roxie Rodelli.

"Thanks, Muckey. I'll be careful with this. I'll show Roxie what I've done with it when you bring her back to Oakland again. I meant it though it did not happen. The story was too good to touch anyway. I just kept it exactly as it was set down in Roxie's handwriting:

Twelve. I counted seven counselors or group leaders or therapists, whatever. One was my roommate. Me and the other four, down from *Today*.

He started. The skinny one with a big, straight mustache that looked like a caterpillar crawling below his nose when he talked. He wore suspender trousers and a plain white shirt. His tee shirt showed above the vee.

"You know all these people, but I don't, so let's hear who they are. We're all together here. You know why we're here."

I knew why. Me. It weren't my first rodeo.

Each ticked off her name, or his, mostly it was her, lots of titles and doctors and stuff. I knew them all. I met them last spring, lived with them a month. Now, after Muckey and them found me in the alley, I might get to know them better. I don't really know.

Then Muckey when it was his turn moved his chair with a tinny scraping sound and knocked over something behind him. "Martin. Martin Deutcher. Friend and alcoholic." Always the same. A bug-eyed, honest and lean guy, my Muckey. I guess I loved him. I think he had two tee shirts, one for wearing and one for wash. Always clean. He wore the red one.

"Jaime Jalisco, acquaintance. Alcoholic." JJ wore all black. His pants and hat were leather. He biked everywhere; I knew that much.

The last I knew only like a dream. It been another life, from a dinner with Maggie and from the night they found me, Muckey and JJ and him.

"Moe M. acquaintance, friend, member of *Today*." That was his way of saying alcoholic, but no one corrected him.

The twelfth was me. A goddamn dozen.

Everyone was looking my way. I must have looked cockeyed and weird. For two days I had washed my face one-handed, without even looking in the mirror. All I knew was that my nose hurt and one cheek was sore. My hands ached too, scraped, stepped-on. Only one pinky broken. I felt like throwing up, not just then, but all the time. I'd been off just eight days.

"Yeah. Roxie Rodelli. Alcoholic. Addict, I guess. If that's what you want to call me."

The caterpillar wriggled, said, "We call you Roxie, Roxie. What you call yourself is why we're here."

"Look Roxie," said Low—she had been there last time, a patient group leader. She bent across her lap, elbows on knees, and opened a palm to me, "we want to put out what we've seen, what we know. I don't know how you feel, but I do know what has happened to you, from the outside." She put out the other arm like she was serving a tray of food to me. "Can we do that?"

I guess I nodded or something 'cause they started in. In-take report. How I looked. Blood pressure and a bunch of numbers and medical terms I didn't really know, and then more numbers. Behavior was a big one. Lots of screaming. I'd punched a few people, even with my broken pinky. Lots of yelling. Someone described my face and hands. One mentioned rape. I didn't agree with that one. Maybe I didn't remember. It wasn't me, but whoever they were describing came from a world of hurt. Could have been, maybe should have been dead. It wasn't me.

I broke in. "Yeah," I said, "but I don't belong here. I've been here, and it didn't do any good."

Old caterpillar-suspenders turned to the guys. "Can you tell Roxie about your search?"

JJ went first. "Well, it started about three weeks ago. Muckey called me and wanted to come down. It was at Thanksgiving."

"I got here on Thanksgiving day," Muckey said.

"I took him to dinner at Radford Hall. And we got a lead from another Martin S."

Muckey took over then. "The director Burt knew, but I had to go down and talk with Icy to know where you'd gone."

He went on and on. I felt sorry for the guy. I'd made a lot of trouble for him, and expense, but, then again, I never asked him to come looking for me, at least this time. Really, all I wanted right then was to get out of that place with its circle of tinny chairs and inmates wandering around in hospital gowns and robes. They were all banging away at me there in that circle, but I just wanted to get fed and go visit Pea Soupo. He had something of mine.

Then Suspenders said something that turned my head.

"Tell Roxie about the suitcase, would you, Martin?"

I didn't see him hiding anything, but Muckey acted nervous. He reached behind his chair. He brought out my suitcase.

"Shit! You kiper. You stole that. That's mine." I stormed right over there and grabbed it out of his stinking hand. Gave him a kick at the shin which I missed. Then I fell on my butt in the middle of the group. I don't care.

I opened my goddamn case right there in front of everyone, too, tossed the clothes out on the floor. It was clean anyway since it was some sort of hospital or something. It don't matter who saw my underwear or anything. My little packet, a pouch hidden in a small, secret zipper pocket called me home. I wanted it. It was mine. But under the emptied clothes, in my hidden compartment I groped a big, fat zero. My heart pounded in my head. My stash was gone!

"You bastard," I was looking at Muckey. "You stripped me naked!" If the orderlies hadn't come right over, I woulda been on him. They held me and took me back to the chair no matter how I squirmed and bucked. My finger twanged something fierce.

"What is missing, Roxie? What so upsets you?" This was Low.

"I don't care. I don't care. You got my stash. I want it back. That's stealing." I could taste the fix. I'd have eaten it or shoved it up my nose or anywhere.

Low looked at me. "If you can listen, I

believe Martin will tell you about it."

She was calm. That burned my throat.

Then tears came. I heard me wailing. I crumpled from my chair. I cried for my fix like a child stoled from me. Now my heart bashed my ribs. Like jutting out a lower jaw like a boxer in a big heat.

No breath could squeeze between, but out it flew all a sudden like when the dam broke afore Anaconda slough in a roar of dirty slime. Air and tears and snot and blow flew. I heard myself snarking and snapping over my empty suitcase. Sobs drown' me under my loss, my bag. I sucked up my snivel, on all fours like a convulsion-dog. I hanged my head over that open suitcase. Wanting and shaking and craving. I sorrowed my lost friend, my only friend.

Low knelt beside me, a hand on my spine. "Listen, Roxie, I believe Muckey can set this straight."

I thought, "Bullshit." But that he did. One thing that man can do is tell a story and make you believe it. He had all the pieces exactly right: Fetu's breakfasts, Soupo, the alley, Manu sitting on his box, the plumbers, the dumpsters, and Burt whistling away and talking to himself while he rifled my suitcase and tossed it in the dumpster. Right in the broad light of afternoon.

Muckey couldn't ever tell what he didn't know: how Burt and me—mostly me—had raised the ransom for the bags. Muckey pegged Burt for the ripoff. I knew it was true.

Shit, that meriney bastard told me Pea Soupo had sold the suitcase a week before. Liar. Coward and liar. He had the shit all to himself to share with that floozy he thought I didn't know about. She'd trip you and beat you to the floor. "Goddamn you, Burt. I'm gonna kill you."

Muckey broke in. He was always forgiving and kind, "Roxie, you're better off without him and without the dope, too. Let's get you well and back on the happy road. You know that Burt couldn't help himself."

I could run off from him—I had done it many times—but could never argue with Muckey. I wish I had stayed in his bed over the fruit market. But I'm too much like Burt. I couldn't help myself, either. Low gave me a box of Kleenex. They all waited while I cleaned up and afterwards repacked my duds. Then they told more about how they'd found me.

Muckey said, "I'd rather Moe to tell it. He came down to help me. I already knew I couldn't do it alone."

So Moe tells about Muckey going back for help, and how when they came again they watched the place on McKinley until Burt left. The folks at the bike shop hadn't seen me for a week.

"They said you went back to Hollywood, maybe working the street. There was another woman upstairs with Burt."

"Don't you say it, Muckey," I yelled, "'Fuckin' Burt can't help himself!'"

Moe just kept on his report. "It didn't take even two hours to find you. There's always someone who knows."

"Yeah, like the fuckin' john who fucked me and beat me up. Christ, in an alley!" I started bawling again. Why root like pigs through all that shit? They had me. 'Incomprehensible demoralization' was me. I didn't want to go any lower. I got no lower to go.

Li Ho was calling me. "Mu Shu Pork, Cashew Chicken, house fried rice. $27.50"

I reached for my wallet. "Six pancakes?"

Li stopped at the cash register. "$28.75." He yelled into the kitchen, gave me my change and said, "Five minute for pancake."

Under the twinkling lights over the counter, I sat thinking onward, past that long-gone Christmas week. Past hearing Roxie's rocky voice at the intervention, in her story, to the soft tones of Maggie's words when I saw her the next day.

. . . Westwood was still decked out for Christmas and in a glory I hadn't seen outside my childhood imagination. Though I couldn't visit Maggie until ten, I'd come by bus early.

There was nothing much else to do at JJ's but sleep, and, sharing the living room with Muckey, sleeping in had become a rare luxury. Muckey's buddy was a great host, but I was glad this would be my final day under his roof.

Years ago, Mom took a turn on Ben Franklin's axiom and stated flatly, "Smells like fish here." That's when her relatives, our hosts, showed her, and us, her kids, the door. Well, there might have been a fish kill at the beach after Roxie's intervention because the ocean breezes filled JJ's living room with something rife. I wasn't about to play Mom's role. After my visit with Maggie, I'd take the Greyhound home, back to rain and fresher winds.

So a morning sipping coffee on Broxton, admiring the Westwood Village Theater, was a treat to myself. Sure, I felt guilty sunning myself while my family slogged through the rain up north and while Roxie struggled toward her own clean air. But taking the sun fed my soul, or so I planned to tell my family.

I understood how Roxie had fallen for the Hollywood line. LA could grow into a headache, but that pounding in the brain takes a time to root. My first impression had been favorable; actually, sunshine swept me up stucco walls to tiled roofs then set me down again in sidewalk cafés. In December, no less. And not one artificial limb store to be seen. LA's woods, West- more than Holly-, invoked dreams.

Of course I was privileged in a way. JJ lived in the hills just off Mulholland Drive, caretaking for some bigwigs, and I stayed, well, in the neighborhood so to speak, except when the three of us intervened with Roxie. Yeah, I liked LA, the hills, Hollywood, and this born-to-be-quaint village. But it made me uneasy, too. I'd already screwed up in a big way and in a much smaller place. This was the town that had swallowed Roxie and Burt, too, not once, but twice. If I stayed to the sunny side and kept my visit short, I might be all right, but in just three days I'd grown wary of the way the sun soothed my nerves. That's the kind of soothing that makes me jittery.

I stretched out my coffee sips, wandered off,

going the wrong way, sat at another sun-drenched place, and ordered my second cup to while away the time. I felt as if I should be in a meeting or something, but Muckey, JJ, and I had attended plenty over the last three days.

Something told me, though, I'd be taxed seeing Maggie, but in a way a meeting wasn't going to help. My visit was for her, I thought, not for me. So I sunned and caffeinated and waited for time to pass. That I was good at.

What I had no talent for, though, waited up the hill on the seventh floor of the UCLA hospital. Fortunately, I had little inkling, if I made it in at all, of what I'd find there. I'd been allowed to leave a message for Maggie but had no idea if she'd received it.

At the medical center I ran the gauntlet of station nurses who posed questions that I answered truthfully, and by fits and starts, after a telephone call or two upstairs, the staff allowed me to pass. All seemed to me overly protective, but, then, I had sworn to safeguard the anonymity of my friends up another stair though that meant, usually, harboring only the details they volunteered themselves. Mostly, I didn't even know their family names. Anyone willing to include their own given name in our ranks was free to come up. I saw no harm in that. I guess hospitals act no differently: they admit you if you're sick. Though Maggie and I suffered the same illness, she suffered another that seemed less important to me than it did to the hospital staff. Another difference, they had an elevator.

When I alighted and turned down the seventh floor corridor, looking at the room numbers above each door, a tall, thickly-built man stood from his chair, one of two there in the hallway, and ducked into a room beside those seats. The number told me it was Maggie's room. In an instant, before I could even touch the door, the same man flung it open and stepped out.

I moved to his right. He did, too. I switched to the left, and he followed. The door had swung shut during our dance. Then he smiled and laughed. He extended his hand.

"Michael Malone, Moe," then watched amused as I fought to understand. "I'm Margret's father." Even after the vetting I'd survived downstairs, I now grew more confused. "I'm sorry, I should say Maggie's dad, that's how you know her."

I must have seemed a fool, openmouthed, frowning to catch on, then saying, "Oh, you're Maggie's dad." I *was* an idiot: of course I had her name, written down, but never had uttered it.

He laughed again, then halted. "When they called from the lobby, I asked Margret's, I mean Maggie's nurse to allow you up. It's mostly family who sees her now."

"I hope it's all right, my coming."

"Maggie wants to see you. We received your message, and I'm glad you called. I'm glad you came." He stopped again. "Can we sit here a minute and talk?" He indicated the two chairs beside the door.

"Sit. Talk. Yes, sure. Of course." I was still chittering like a coot. Several nerves tore up and down my spine as if racing to hit my brain and body in advance of the other. One hit the flee alarm, another the freeze, but each pushed my clown button repeatedly. Mr. Malone took my elbow kindly and guided me to a chair. The corporeal jangling of my being calmed enough for me to settle on the chair and into my surest and most usual response: guilt. It was clear, I had done something wrong here and was going to have to pay. "I'm sorry," I began, but he raised his hand.

"Listen, Moe, my daughter thinks the world of you," he said over my repeated apologies. "Of all the people she's told us about from her life up north, you're the one we wanted to meet. Maggie's mother couldn't be here, but she wanted me to thank you."

I was still confused, but quieted at mention of her mother. "Thank me?"

Now he turned to put his hand on my shoulder in a way I had always wished my own father would have done. "You are the exemplar for Maggie. You helped her more than anyone."

This was the thing, one of them that day, I had no talent to accept. Singling me out for attention convulses my nature. "No, no, I'm only one of the crowd. I'm nothing special."

He put his hand to his chin, crooking the index finger over his lips suppressing his grin. As he shook his head a corner of his mouth lifted a knowing smile. "That's exactly what Maggie told us, Moe. You don't realize how strongly you affect others. She liked your modesty best."

"We're friends."

"Yes, you're the kind of friend she needed, especially compared to that bullshitting Burt. He used her. Perhaps has killed her. Maybe he did."

His vehemence and sudden accusation staunched any reply I could make. Even with Burt on the lam, now without Roxie, I still wasn't ready to dismiss him in the way Maggie's father did. When a guy saves your life, or looks like he did, you view him more sympathetically. At one time he had been Saint Burt to me. So, even with evidence mounting to damn him, it would be months before I would shed completely, once and for all, even my now-dinted vision of Burt C. That finality Burt *in person* would insure.

And now I was confused about Maggie, too. She couldn't have died. Could she? Her dad said she wanted to see me. Was that in the past? Was she gone?

Now Malone apologized.

"I'm sorry, Moe. I knew this day would come. I've known it for years, but that doesn't make it any easier to take. If not for Burt, another would have taken his place. Margret was vulnerable. She wanted life, a full life, and that is not meant to be."

Of course, I didn't want to hear all this. Burt had behaved badly like most of us at *Today*. We didn't expect much else, really, and when it happened, we accepted. Still, Maggie's father was right. Even before Maggie told me about her disease, I had sensed her fragility. When she confided in me, I listened. That's all, just listened. "She didn't expect a lot," I said, "but I know she wanted more."

Malone looked off down the hall. "Rightly or not," he said, "she wanted that child, something to leave behind for her mother and me."

He was talking again like Maggie was dead or close to it. "She told me it was dangerous," I muttered.

"She hoped against hope, Moe. That was her spirit."

Despite myself, I searched his face. "Is she all right? You're making me . . ."

Malone looked at Maggie's door and put his hand back on my shoulder, "She's fine, Moe. I'm distraught. I'm her father, after all." He stopped, thinking. "I thank you for being such a good friend to Margret. Please, go in now and see her. I'm sorry to have detained you."

I protested, of course.

"I've said more than I need to say. Please." He extended his arm toward the door we sat by. "She's in there. Go. I'm going to the lounge. See you soon. Margret shouldn't visit very long."

All this, just being in LA, saving Roxie, jumping through hoops today for the medical folk, and listening to Maggie's behaggard father made me wonder if I should have chanced the trip. Up until this time in my life I had been working to save no one but myself, concerned mostly with surviving long enough to prosper, and not doing too well at it as a matter of fact. Now I had seconds to prepare to see Maggie, who from all I had seen and heard was likely on her deathbed. I hadn't exactly bargained on that.

I pushed through the door and stopped in a little hall off the toilet room, letting the door swing shut behind me. I wasn't sure I could go further and must have stood there wondering seconds too long. Maggie spoke.

"Moe, is that you?"

Her voice sounded strong. "Yes, it's me." I stepped into the room proper.

Maggie reclined, propped up with pillows, on her hospital bed, atop the sheets and a ribbed white coverlet. She'd dressed in a long-sleeved, red pullover sweater and sleek black pants. She crooked one leg along the bed keeping her shoe off the covers while the other she draped over the edge of a bar lowered below the top of the mattress. She dangled her other black pump from the toes of her lowered leg. She smoothed a fine golden chain at her chest, playing momentarily, with thin, bony fingers, over the medallion hanging there. "Thank God for your coming, Moe. I thought

I'd go insane. My family is driving me mad."

She didn't laugh but smiled faintly, relaxing now against pillows behind her against the tall bed head. The movements, both the smile and the leaning of her body, were tiny, barely perceptible, but seemed full of effort.

"Maybe we should get out of here," I said, I suppose trying to carry on her mild humor, "I already talked with Papa." I took another step toward her to give her a kiss, but a tiny movement, maybe in that hand fondling the medallion or from her shoulders made me stop.

Again she smiled feebly, a bit of blue flashed past the brown of her eyes. "Another time, Moe. I hope Michael didn't lay his trip on too thickly."

"Michael? Oh, your father. Well, he's worried. I don't know why, because you look great." She thanked me, and it was true. Unusual for Maggie, she'd applied makeup. She looked healthy and beautiful for all her stillness.

"Tell me all about everyone, Toady, Muckey, Susan, Jude, and, of course I want to hear about Burt. Is he all right? Did *Today* make it through the Christmas marathons?"

For the last year I had practiced hard telling the truth, something I'd had to learn, especially talking to myself, so Maggie's questions, her desire to hear about Burt in particular called on the naked truth, which when it came down to it, I could not bring myself to tell. She might find out herself and could call me a liar then, but too much had changed in too shocking a way to merit anything but falsehood. I had to spare Maggie the reality. So like a confronted Peter, I lied to save my skin even at the cost of my soul. I wasn't going to hurt Maggie. Let her get stronger before that happened.

EVENING

"Well, yes, the Christmas marathon went well. I led the three a.m. to five morning meeting on Christmas day. We had seven, and not one elf, either." If you're going to lie, make it entertaining. "Jude is Jude, you know. Always counting shekels and heads. He's doing fine. Susan's the same, hasn't gained a pound. Toady's hopping around as usual."

I started with the easy ones. Maggie didn't know what Jude was up to, and Susan and Toady were always pretty much the same.

"What of Muckey? Is he still dating Roxie?"

"Oh yes. In fact he wanted me to come with him on this visit. And I'd heard you came down to the Med Center, so I said yes. I'm going back later today. Leave the happy couple to themselves." I'd warmed up now and thought I could spin a yarn about Burt. "Are you angry with Burt?"

Maggie seemed pained, that was for sure, but I couldn't tell if it was physical or emotional. She didn't answer right away. I waited.

"Moe, you don't know how much I miss him. No, I'm not angry. Hurt, yes, but mostly sad. Even though it didn't work out—they always told me I couldn't have children—at least for a while I had something of Burt and me living inside. I will always love him, and I'm going back as soon as I can to be with him. Is he all right, Moe?"

To be an effective liar you have to pass along some truth, so I said, "I think Burt is hurting." That much was true. So I embellished it. "I believe he wanted that baby as much as you did," a boldfaced lie I felt I had to soften. "He just couldn't deal with fatherhood very well." I tried, then, to be hopeful, "Maybe you guys could adopt someday."

Maggie grew smaller in her red sweater against

all those pillows. She seem to wither, confronted with the future.

"Yes, maybe," she said, "but you're right. Burt doesn't see himself raising kids. He's so independent. I love that man."

What could I say? I didn't have to say anything. As weak now as Maggie seemed, she took over, "Come closer, Moe, let me touch your face."

I still wanted to kiss her but didn't feel invited, so I came close. She reached out her medallion hand. I realized she had been hanging it from the chain as much as playing with the fob. She moved oh so slowly and just brushed my cheek before letting her arm fall to her lap. She sighed. "I'm tired. Thank you for coming."

I touched her hair, still full and moussed as always, and smiled down on her. "Call me when you hit town."

"I will. Good-bye, Moe. Tell Burt I love him."

When I left all those people in Los Angeles, years back, and returned on the long bus trip home, I'd felt blue each mile of the trip. Somehow I had expected back then to glow with a sense of purpose in a new life, having been for a change helpful and a good friend, but a productive new start was not to be, not for a long while.

I should have sensed, though I could not have known, that my house in Oakland was empty. No one would be coming to pick me up. Only the New Year's marathon meetings where *Today* was held up the street from the bus depot would get me through what was a return drenched in loneliness. My ultimate arrival home, with a predawn ride from Toady, brought me up the hill to the house. Two days before Raci had gone. She'd taken most of hers and the children's clothes and personals, leaving the refrigerator and all else empty. She left not even a note.

A package from Minnesota atop the office couch draped with old sheets and a couple of blankets, where Tom had slept was my only greeting. Everything and everybody else, I discovered that early New Year's Day morning were gone. There was one message on the machine—it was not as I had hoped from Raci—from Michael Malone telling me to call. Nothing else.

This night walking The Village to visit Gabby stirred that haunting time to the surface just as seeing Maggie at UCLA Center had punctuated the memory's beginning.

So, now, hugging the warmth of Li Ho's take-out and approaching home once again from what seemed a very long journey, thinking Raci would be there, I sensed a wobble in my life, in my confidence, in my hope. Suddenly, I feared, as never before, what I'd find there, at a time of life when resilience is thin and rare, when the future holds the promise of few joys made more precious by their rarity.

To slow my progress and stay this new terror, I took the stairs, resting for breath on each floor, breaking a sweat on the fourth, up to the fifth landing, where I stood panting and stared at my door, behind which I sensed a silence I didn't want to face again, but anyway reached my keys out to the lock, uncertain how I would feel at my very next step.

Night

Drink up, baby, stay up all night
With the things you could do, you won't but you might
The potential you'll be, that you'll never see
The promises you'll only make

Elliott Smith, from "Between the Bars"

. . . There's one way to say it: rain. Winter in Northern California means rain, sheets of it, somewhere manufactured and sent swirling south from the Alaskan archipelago sweeping along the Pacific coast drenching land, forests, and human spirits. Show me a liar and he'll tell us he likes rain. The Pollyanna reminds us that we need the rain. Granted, but so much and all at once? And on a holiday? Well, it was all I found, stepping off the bus back home, nothing other, and nobody else. I felt I had been left, been forgotten.

Cold rain had pelted and slowed the Greyhound milk-route bus from Watsonville on north without letup, bringing on a preternatural night. On arrival, the downpour sluiced off the depot awning and veered in below the canopy on gusty winds, wetting us each one as we scrambled to retrieve our bags from the belly of the bus. It soaked my back and calves and ankles, spattering up off the pavement like clear marbles bouncing off hardpan.

That last morning of the year, I'd bathed in sunshine. Now, I longed for Minnesota winter snow. That at least fell and stayed put, could be shaken or stamped off. Had I been asked again, at that moment, to survive alley searches, brave more addiction interventions, sleep four nights on JJ's floor, and suffer through hospice visits, I'd have bought a return ticket right then. This wet, lonely, cold, windy, and tiresome weather meant home, but not quite yet.

I called DeLorr for a ride.

I counted: Twelve rings. Finally, "Well, it's about time," DeLorr said, welcoming me in her way. I preferred soaking in the storm to the icy water she showered on me.

"The bus stopped everywhere between Oxnard and San Francisco. Anyway, it was cheaper than the express." My glossing of the expenses did not play.

"Don't call a cab. I'll pick you up in thirty minutes."

From the spouse's point of view, DeLorr was right, misunderstanding but correct in her own light. Running after the wayward on the family pocketbook, on family time, proved only slightly better than feeding paper money across the bar or liquor store counter. The latest events had drawn me away from home. To DeLorr saving a soul, even one she'd met, sounded suspect and avoidable. It smelled of fish. Happy New Year and welcome home.

"Happy New Years," a man outside the front door said. "Could you spare a dollar?"

It was New Year's Eve. "Sorry, I can't." He looked familiar, likely from *Today*. "Though I know where you can get a bite and a cup of coffee, just up the street."

"Where's that?"

"Twenty-ninth and Telegraph. There're meetings upstairs all night long."

"Those stiffs?" He said. "I wouldn't go up there to die."

I shrugged, deciding to give up on the guy, and went back inside. Without the evidence proffered by my new friend begging by the door, I could have forgotten how many do die without a chance of going up those stairs. My only real asset so far in sobriety was that I didn't die before meeting Burt. Could I help anyone besides myself?

So, feeling unworthy, I went outside again and gave my pal his dollar, saying, "Say hello to the stiffs up the street."

"I hope you appreciate this, Moe," DeLorr greeted me. "Tilla is down with a fever. I told Ellen she had to stay home in case I needed the car. I'm none too popular right now."

"Where was she going?"

"Out. Au pair's night off. You know what day it is?"

"Wednesday."

"Ha, ha. But that reminds me, your buddy, Jude, called. He insisted I take a message."

"What now?"

"He wants you to take over for him."

"Tomorrow?"

"Yes and no, permanently. He took a job in Atlanta."

This sounded just like Jude. He created a mess and blew town. "I'll call him."

DeLorr glanced at me and shook her head. "No need. He's already gone. He called from Georgia. You and your potted friends."

Yes, just like Jude. We could all be drowning, and he'd find something pressing him to run off. He also got DeLorr involved. That wasn't right. "What else?"

"Some guy named Malone called."

That worried me. "What did he want?"

"You, of course. He left his number. And that package in the back seat came from Minnesota yesterday."

There was no return address, only the date stamp from the Duluth post office. Perhaps a late Christmas present. It was sent book rate.

"Thanks, DeLorr. The trip was successful, I guess."

"Meaning?"

"Roxie is in treatment. Muckey is watching over her."

"And Burt?"

"Still out there."

"Maggie?"

"Malone is her dad. No news is good news. I should call him tomorrow."

At home, I sent DeLorr to bed. The four days

without help had worn her out. I stayed up
with Tilla, feeding her juice and keeping her
covered. Michael snored next door. Siiri dreamed
soundlessly. Ellen, our German au pair was taking
the car down to her friend's party.

"*Zurück vor eins.*"

"Be sure you are. Be good."

"*Na sicher.*"

I'd had the same exchange with my parents.
There is nothing you can do. Everyone is on their
own.

I opened the package. It was a present of
sorts. Tom had sent me his manuscript, again. His
note explained:

> Sorry, Moe, for all the trouble. And about
> blowing up at the cafe. I know you can make
> this a better book. Go for it. And if anything
> happens to me, make sure my bitch of a sister
> doesn't touch it.

> It's your book now.

Tom, apparently, had a jolly Christmas with the
family. He'd told me once his sister's middle name
was Enmity. "And she married Mr. Antipathy, too,"
he'd said. Love-loss. Love in that house? After
his mother's suicide, the very air inside chilled
a soul. Tom, born to parents already elderly and
very busy, had been alone since childhood.

Just when you think someone is so far gone that
he isn't listening to anything other than what
goes on in his head, he sends you his book or a
memento you shared. Tom was such a one, tortured
by his own life, unable to make it better unless

he threw it away. Needless to say, the fifty dollars was not mentioned or included. That was fine by me.

I opened the book. Tom had added a handwritten dedication: I wasn't quite sure about the order of his words

> For my father, my friends P-a and Moe, and for the motherfucking Viet Cong who taught me to hate their guts. This is their story.

I wasn't quite sure about the order of his words, whether to include myself in the hated or to feel loved. How he felt about P-a and his own father was important to understanding, but one thing was clear to me: The dedication at least needed some editing.

This time Raci left a note, of sorts. Cold comfort.

The apartment was dark. I called out for Raci. She was gone. I found myself trying to catch my breath from a stomach-punch, standing in the hall holding Raci's favorite Chinese dish and mine, neither of which would be eaten that night. We would find Li Ho's cooking in the fridge two weeks later, all the worse for wear. For now, I set the bag atop Tom's veterans' anthology on the stand, turned on the hall light, and closed the apartment door.

I'd lived there fifteen years by myself and never felt so solitary. Idiotically, I called out again, just to force the silence away. In the kitchen Raci had placed the manuscript on the center of the bar. It was open to the dedication on which she had scrawled: "Now, this needs some editing!" She crossed out her name printed in the center of the page.

The rest of her notes I found by the bookmarks she'd inserted. Raci had read "Moe returns from LA," I suppose out of curiosity, but what she found there must have sent her from anger to hurt to outrage. She'd circled "At home, I sent DeLorr to bed. . . I stayed up with Tilla, feeding her juice and keeping her covered. Michael snored next door. Siiri dreamed soundlessly," and wrote "pathetic coward!" over the words. Seeing her children's names there stabbed her. Below was spelled out in big red letters: F-I-C-T-I-O-N.

I turned from the book. It made me sick to think of it now that Raci had seen it all, but I could not then, or before when I was writing it, bear to close those children out of the story even though I'd buried them years ago while Racine lay in a coma. So they had stayed on in *Twelve* past Moe's return from LA.

All during that day, I now understood, I had *wanted* Raci to know. I wanted her to read what I'd put down. I stupidly had hoped she'd approve of keeping them, and herself, alive to me, to the both of us. But that attempt was futile. Likely it looked only as if I'd sought to cover up my abandoning of Raci.

She had been right: "Fiction! You don't know what fiction is. How can you, when you don't know what truth is?" Her words still echoed in that apartment.

Standing over the book I suddenly hated, I muttered, "Raci, maybe fiction, whatever it is, is all I have left." I turned the page.

. . . The only person in the room when I arrived for the 8:15 *Today* group was Linda. As tired as I was with travel, sick kids, and the homecoming, she took my breath away still.

"Happy New Year, Linda," I said. She was my breath of fresh air.

"And to you, Moe."

Just then a girl's voice came from the little kitchen behind the coffee counter, "Mommy, I can't reach it."

Linda moved toward the voice, looking at me, explaining, "Roburta is with me. You know, it's a holiday and Grandma's sick." She disappeared into the kitchen, talking with the girl.

I got busy with the literature and the coffee stuff, and cleaning up after the marathon meetings of the night before, which left an amazing variety of half-eaten desserts and food morsels behind. I picked through it and tossed what I suspected of contagion. I listened to Linda in the kitchen helping her daughter wash her hands.

During holiday marathons, regular meetings continued; this would have been Jude's day, Thursday, which just happened to be January 1. When *Today* was about to end that day, someone from the sign-up list would show up to resume the marathon. Those meetings had continued through New Year's Eve and would end at midnight that evening, shepherding the sober flock through the biggest drinking holiday of the year. I had learned recently that Halloween was a close second. I thought I'd stick around for at least one of the marathons. Insurance, you see.

While I was in LA with Muckey, saving Roxie, Jude had turned *Today*'s locker into a counting house. Posted on the inside of the door were directions on how to proceed:

- Count cash on hand
- Verify the coffee fund
- Note and mark the level of change in the literature jar
- Track and add to the balances money collected (Both coffee donations and the basket)

NIGHT

- Count attendance at each meeting and note
- Deposit funds each Friday

Deposit slips for our new bank account were inside the cash box. Checks, he noted, we locked in the office safe. Oh, Jude. Friday, he knew, was my day. Of course, someone else, not the fair-haired boy himself, needed to run to the bank. Thanks, buddy, and *bon voyage*.

I had little time to fret about Jude. A general cast of annoyance would have to do, and even that would dissipate in the next minutes as Jude's coffee maker, the Thursday faithful, and marathoners trudged up the stairs. I collared the first veteran of *Today* to tell her story. I set up at the secretary's table and paged through the meeting notebook. At the top of each and every page Jude had stamped: "attendance ___," "coffee collection $ __.__," "7th Tradition collection __.__." I had to hand it to him, he took the time to organize. Later I'd find the stamp and ink pad in the locker. Even though he had flown, I, for one, would make a habit of following his plan. Consistently.

The room filled. I made welcome and announcements and began the meeting. This had grown to be part of my life, a comfort. I wondered, though, had it become a mere habit? I let the meeting drone on, having dispensed my opening role, and thought about the question.

Had my attendance at *Today* become habit, cousin to addiction? Had my life itself shed the urgency of meaning and become one of continuous servitude to manner? Perhaps the words I repeated each meeting no longer carried the meaning they once had: a promise of freedom from liquor-induced dementia. They had instead grown only to be echoes of a long-ago dissipated whisper of betterment, now traveling in a wheel rut of routine. On returning from enervating adventures in LA, all these fears came into focus. Everything seemed changed: supporters gone, heroes fallen, loveliness languished.

The speaker tapped my shoulder. She ended my musing. My turn in the ritual at hand had come again. I spoke the words required automatically, as if inborn to me. We ended the meeting in our usual mantra, unanimously.

I turned to Jude's accounting. Twenty-five people attended, four and a half dollars, mostly in quarters, spilled from the coffee-donation bowl, and the 7th tradition basket yielded forty-eight, including one five and a ten. The holiday crowd had been generous. I stowed the money in the locker, would deposit it the next day when banks reopened. People were loitering, waiting for the marathon meeting to start. It was Linda now who touched my arm.

"If you have time for coffee, I'd like to talk," she said.

That would be better than staying for another meeting. "Sure. Where?"

"Let's go next door."

I was all hers, but said, "Don't you find the coffee there rather bad?"

"Yes, but that's why no one goes there. We can talk, privately." She looked down at her child. "Roburta won't mind."

If I had been barely breathing, standing so close to beauty itself at that moment, what I saw and realized next stoppered my wind altogether.

"Moe, this is my daughter, Burta."

For the first time, even though she had been in the room since I'd arrived that morning, I looked at this freckle-faced girl. And as I did, she wound up her neck in a familiar way, snapped back with a very wide smile, saying, "Grandma tells me to stay in bed when I'm sick," and looked at me with narrowly set but perfectly Burt-like eyes trimmed by long reddish lashes brushing over amber-and-green-rayed irises.

"Shall we go?" Linda guided my elbow, turning me around, and with Burta skipping right along, we headed toward the staircase. My head was swimming, my mind raced.

Linda settled Roburta at a table in the light of the front picture window. She joined her briefly, turning the pages of a favorite book to find the place, speaking to her softly, and ordered the girl a hot chocolate. Then she joined me. We were having Cokes.

"The chocolate is decent. Packaged, but good," she said.

"She seems content."

"You have a daughter about Burta's age, seven, don't you, Moe?"

"Yes, she's just nine. Tilla we call her."

Linda turned her full gaze on me; she smiled. "I have to apologize, Moe."

"To me? What for?"

She hesitated, then said, "The kiss."

Of course I knew which kiss she was talking about, the one I could still feel on my lips, but I said nothing.

"I wanted to make Burt jealous."

"Not of me. Why would he be?"

"Anyway, I apologize, though I enjoyed it, too."

I restrained a full confession. "As did I."

She held and squeezed my hand. "Good." Linda glanced over at the girl, who was engrossed in her book. "I think you can see him in her."

"Yes, very much. I had no idea."

Linda's eyes seemed to broaden; she looked serious. "Burt and I go back a long way. We got sober together. And Roburta was his greatest gift to me, better even than my music. That, too, he restored." She patted my hand, let it go, bringing hers over her lips. "You may know already that Burt doesn't do well with children."

I didn't know about Linda, but Maggie's baby, her lost baby, was on my mind. "I hadn't thought too much about it," I lied. She let it be.

"Well, a mother, if she must, will choose her children over anything, even the love of her life, but I wanted them both." She smiled and seemed to regret the confession. Her eyes narrowed again. "You were in LA."

"Yes, I loved it down there."

She didn't let me expand my enthusiasm. "Did you see him? Burt?"

Now the purpose of the interview seemed clear. "No. We went down for Roxie." I said her name reluctantly.

She nodded. "Yes, his latest obsession. That and crank. What did you hear? Please. Tell me."

I told Linda what I knew, that Burt was addicted, lived in Compton, had let Roxie go. I said nothing about the suitcase caper. "I don't know much, really."

"He's alive, though."

"Yes, that is true."

She sipped her Coke and took another look at Burta. "I want to ask you to do something, Moe."

"Anything." I meant it. For her beauty anything, but more than that for her suffering.

"Burt will return. He always has. This time, though, I'll be gone."

"Why?"

I didn't want more leaving, but here came more.

"I've accepted a chair in a new symphony in

307

New York. Though it's not as good an orchestra yet, this is advancement. The bustle will suit my mother. Lots of reasons, Moe."

She would move on with her life, yes. "What do you want of me?"

"I just want Burt to know. And from someone he trusts. He likes you."

"Well, he did, I suppose."

"Yes, he's told me. And he wouldn't have brought you here that day, unless he trusted you."

I thought about that day here in the very-bad-coffee cafe. This was my chance to know something. "Why did he bring me? He obviously wanted you alone."

Without revealing her gat-toothed sweetness, her lips turned up in a smile. "No, you were here to protect him."

"From you?"

"Yes, Moe, from me. I loved him ten years ago, I loved him when I met you, and I love him now. He needed protection."

"And that's why you kissed me."

"Exactly. Moe, please, tell him. Tell him I've left."

I threw up my hands. "I guess I can do that. If I see him."

Linda turned to her daughter, "Finish up, Burta. It's time to go." Then to me she said, "You'll see him. You'll bring him back. And you'll tell him."

She nodded, then reached over the table, and clasping my face in her hands, kissed me once more, fully on the lips.

The two weeks following my return from LA were the worst of my life, perhaps, maybe second only to the month after I'd returned home from my girlfriend's apartment in the city to resume life with DeLorr and my kids. Even then, though, I had never felt so alone. Although I did not know it, these weeks were soon to be third in a lineup of miserable times. But I'll save that telling for its own time.

In my time since rejoining the family, I had found, happily, a new home at *Today*, accepted a mentor/savior in Burt, developed new friends like Muckey, Maggie, Hillside-Glenn, Jude, and founded associations with Susan, Len, and Toady, all in the service of staying steady, upright, and dry. Over that time I'd slipped into a pleasant-enough ritual of meetings punctuated with reforming myself at home, at the office, and in the conduct of my life in general.

Then all began to unravel. Glenn drowned. Toady bounced out of *Today* and back in. Jude's classy shine tarnished like copper in a rain. Tom came and went all in a day. Maggie broke. Burt ran to Roxie. Muckey followed. Burt then cast her off. Then Tom came, crashed, and went again. Now Linda, who I knew intimately in one way, deeply in another, but mostly not at all, had made a career move. Even Len, who'd anchored one side of the tables at meetings, sailed off, I hoped, to another, safer harbor. Nothing was permanent. Now, there was more.

After I returned from Roxie's intervention, two calls, one I returned to LA, the other from Minneapolis wrenched this downward spiral into a nosedive. After several tries, I reached Malone the afternoon of the first a just hours after meeting with Linda.

As I'd been taking in the Pacific coast from the windows of the Greyhound just south of Pismo Beach, four hours after I'd seen her, Maggie died. Her father had little to say about her last moments. Now, I realized he'd sheltered me from

309

the truth when we met—if I had been attentive, I would have caught his drift—but now the news shocked me. I had convinced myself that Maggie was on the mend. I grew furious with Burt. Without saying so to Maggie's father on the phone, I now agreed with Malone: Burt had as good as killed her. He was no better, likely worse, than Jude.

I had no one to tell. Everyone was gone. DeLorr would hardly care, I thought. I left the house without a word and headed straight back to the marathon meetings, a lifesaver for me on this four-day weekend. I believed the liquor stores were closed, another godsend.

As in each choppy sea I'd navigated even before Len left *Today*, I took up the slack on every towline and had loaded on board too much responsibility for a man in my condition. Now, I sat in my rocking boat with no one but a crew of ghosts, adrift on the waters of *Today*.

That lifeboat provided some relief. And after bathing in my personal six-hour marathon meeting, when I returned home DeLorr further buoyed my spirits. She'd genuinely worried about me.

"You left the house so suddenly." That had scared her. "And then you were gone all afternoon and half the evening. I worried you were drinking."

I told her about Maggie, about my visit at the hospital and the report of her death. "I couldn't have felt worse. I needed some time, a meeting."

She touched my face, a tender gesture rare for her, and said, "I understand, Honey. People dying so young. It's not right."

"No, it is not right."

So I was not alone after all, not as alone as I'd felt. And I had another meeting to attend, to run, the next morning. That's when the second call came. Minneapolis called early.

"I thought you'd like to make plans for the New

Year, so I'm calling from home," my headquarters boss said. The opportunity I had been hoping for, but not wishing on too hard, had fallen through. My support at the company had evaporated. And with no surprise but with some relief (not any that DeLorr would share), HQ informed me, I was to lose my job in San Francisco though the company was obliged to keep a low level spot open in Minnesota. Did I want that?

In one category only I had been a winner: leading with the chin. Earlier that year I could not have been clearer about my feelings regarding the business if I'd stood on a desk in the middle of the office shouting, "Fire me, I dare you."

I hated the job. It had washed me off a liquid cliff. Drink had been the only way I knew to soothe my distress. Still, if I weren't the last to know, I'd be surprised, so far in denial I'd fallen. Now, nearly a year past my initial fall from grace as a manager, I was helped to make my own conscious choice. I just could not brook the business world anymore, but rather than standing up to be punched back down again, I improved somewhat by, as they say, exploring my options, discovering now that none were so desirable, and agreed to, after my boss's call, on the least offensive one, leaving the company with severance pay. Somehow my quasi-voluntary act made it seem all right.

DeLorr's fear and consternation outpaced the sympathy she'd shown me the previous evening. Although tempered somewhat by the severance check my boss promised, it grew stern again when I informed her I would turn to editing and teaching, my own natural though less lucrative bent.

"I'm going to prepare Tom's book for publication. I've already talked about it with some interested people."

Her sharp look sliced my bravado-balloon. "So,

Tom's paying you? I hope he starts with that fifty he owes us. I could buy some groceries."

"No, he isn't. But don't worry, I'll get paid."

She took another swipe of the blade, "I worry, Moe. Believe me, I worry." She then fell silent. For weeks.

Over the year I had stayed sober, I answered adversity with increased responsibility. I'd taken on the Friday meeting. Sponsored Jude. Worked at friendship. I even involved my family in some of *Today's* doings. I'd worried over Tom, and rescued my family from him when he fell. I'd trekked to Hollywood on a mercy mission. Stood by Jude even in his attack on Burt. And now found myself jobless, essentially on my own at home, floundering in meetings, and editing a book, authored by a less than steady writer whose subject was less a mystery than totally alien to me. By all rights and probabilities, I should have been drunk. But something kept me from it.

Maybe after all the so-called bossing I had had to do: the meetings I called, hiring, firing, reorganizing, encouraging, and promoting, all for the sake of profit and the well-being of the company, acting more like a mercenary than a manager, I felt more at home with a book. I had a task to make *Tunnel Rats* better, to bring it out greater than what it already was, with a story that needed nothing further than to be told. That there would be hell to pay for any of it did not seem to be my problem. DeLorr's take-home and my severance would be payment enough. As they always do, though, bliss and simplicity turned in upon themselves and tangled.

Tom's manuscript had changed since I'd last looked at it. Maybe the story hadn't been finished, but perhaps Tom, as he'd hinted, thought it should be bigger. It was certainly longer. I read the sections he'd added first, an easy task as the sheets were new, white, and crisp, lacking the crumples and coffee stains.

> We waited. The bulldozers were going in. While they scraped away the jungle in the Iron Triangle, we played mumblety-peg with bayonets.

> P-a batted one 'over the fence' just as a tripwire blew. VC. We hit the ground and let loose toward the blast. The whole platoon was pumping away.

That was Tom. But in the section following the one-way firefight, I read something that certainly wasn't Tom, except for the final sentence.

> Vo Thi Mo was hardly a surprise candidate for officer status since her father had been a Viet Minh fighting the French using an old World War II rifle.[*] She was a fucking shoe-in.

The sentences were too long. The point of view felt journalistic. Nothing looked firsthand, except the final sentence. And reading more, I recognized the source.

I'd picked up some of the lately published material relevant to Tom's story, just to gain perspective I didn't share with Vietnam vets. I'd read *Charlie Company* and several others, including one centered on tunnel warfare, *The Tunnels of Cu Chi*. In minutes I found Tom's source in *Tunnels*. He must have been drunk to lift it, nearly verbatim, from the book written by two

[*] TOM MANGOLD AND JOHN PENYCATE, *THE TUNNELS OF CU CHI* (NEW YORK: PRESIDIO PRESS/BALLANTINE BOOKS, 2005), PG. 230

reporters. Even blotto, Tom should have known it was plagiarism. And it went on, and on, for pages and pages. I had to find Tom. I had to stop him.

I started with his father. Tom's sister answered.

"Oh, you. I'll put him on if I can get him to the phone."

It took a while and some wrangling on the Minnesota end of the line before Tom picked up the receiver.

"Moe, am I glad it's you."

Before I could get to my reasons for calling, Tom told me his news. "Dad's dead."

The story was gruesome. Two weeks into the new year, the old man, in pajamas no less, had wandered out of the house in sub-zero weather.

"It was midnight, for Christ's sake," Tom said. "How would I know?"

Apparently, Sis was blaming Tom for dad's final walk. The doctor, just shy of ninety-five, made it halfway to the garage where his missus had ended her life nearly thirty years before. He fell into the snowbank where the next morning a neighbor walking his dog discovered the body.

"The animal was sniffing dad's bare foot sticking up into the air," Tom said. "He'd been dead for hours, frozen solid."

I thought better of my purpose. This was not the time to discuss plagiarism. "I'm sorry to hear it, Tom." I got the details and told Tom I'd call back after the funeral.

"Roger, Moe, over and out."

For the next week, I contented myself fixing errata and smoothing Tom's meaning in difficult passages. At some points, not really meaning to foreshadow, he referred to events that were yet to happen. Those I massaged into foreboding pieces of dialogue. The story needed more of the ironic that ill-fitted Tom's character. Instead of the text referring to P-a's impending death, I had the Tom of the story saying, "I'll be the first to go, P-a. You know how risky I am." The fact that they had both survived in real life spoke to me of the miraculous. I let two weekends pass before I called Tom again. The phone rang nearly twenty times.

"Oh, Moe, I'm glad it's you," Tom repeated as if in a nine-day echo. "My sister calls incessantly. I wasn't going to pick up."

"What's going on with her."

"Fighting. What else? She wants the house emptied. I tell her I'm working on it. She threatens me with lawsuits." I let him go on for a while, and he finally talked himself out, realizing that I had likely not called to discuss family business. "So, what's up, Moe?"

"Tom, do you know a guy named Mangold? Tom Mangold?"

He didn't hesitate. "The British asshole? Heard of him. A real user."

"Do you know his book?"

"The *Tunnels of Cu Chi* I suppose you're talking about. Yeah. I've seen it. Mostly it's a bunch of pro-VC bullshit. Ho Chi Minh couldn't have done a better job of canonizing the Cong."

"You know why I'm asking?"

"I suppose because I quoted the b.s.-er."

I held my peace. I wanted Tom to be the one to discuss it.

"Okay, okay. Yeah, I took a bunch of stuff from the book. So what? I'm the one who fought those bastards. Mangold was actually their pal."

"Yes, a propagandist. I understand that, Tom, but you know better than I do how those (and I used his term) bastards feel about someone using their work."

"What the hell. Who's telling this story? You want me to kowtow to some civvie chump? A Bulldog no less. Fuck you. Fuck him. All of you . . ."

"Don't hang up Tom. Please." I waited for his spate of anger to subside. "Listen, Tom, you and I are friends. I don't want your good work to be attacked." When he didn't immediately agree, I tried to reassure him, "Hey Tom, I am on your side. Your book is better than his."

That brought him around. "What do you mean? Attacked?"

"As soon as this is reviewed, anywhere, Mangold and Penycate will know. And they will howl."

"Pennyworth is a pansy."

I ignored his name-play. "Sure, Tom, but he'll raise hell. They will poison the book. You could be sued, and will surely be ruined as an author."

I hoped Tom was thinking about it, but he was still angry. "You mean *you* could be sued, don't you. Some friend. Aren't you thinking about yourself?"

Now I was mad. "Tom, don't insult me. I wouldn't let the book be sold with their stuff in it. If you want to write about the subject, it has to be in your words from your experience. I'll help you."

Given enough time, Tom would come around, my experience told me, but I was unprepared for what came next and how rapidly he conceived it.

"All right. We'll work on it together. Come home to Cloquet. I'll put you up here, and we'll finish it."

I pictured myself huddled at a desk with Tom amongst heaps of his father's newspapers and stacks of medical files, shivering through a month or two of writing punctuated with wrangles. "I lost my job, Tom. I'm broke."

Tom didn't hesitate. "I'll send you some cash."

I knew it would be a warm winter in the north before Tom remembered his offer. I'd never see the money. "Include that fifty you owe us. DeLorr wants to buy some groceries for the kids."

I finished reading Raci's comments, the last of which was to cross out "groceries for the kids." I retrieved the takeout from the hall. I wasn't hungry and put it in the fridge. I set the manuscript on the desk once more and sat on the couch where I'd last seen Raci. I was drained.

That morning I'd risen late, spent a good deal of time in bed, some of it napping, but I felt exhausted. It was only 8:30, but sleep was my best escape from the tonnage of guilt and confusion that was weighing me down. I stretched out and slept.

It seemed like fifteen minutes when I woke to the phone. Their voices were alike, and for an instant I hoped it was Raci and started to speak. Nettie saved me from gauche mortification saying, "Dad, are you awake?"

I looked. It was nearly one o'clock. I struggled to stand on parental legs, "Sweetie, it's two in the morning there in Minneapolis. Is everything all right?"

"I have the same question," Nettie said. "I just got off a long call from Mom. What's going on?"

"What do you mean?" I struggled to wake fully, to buy time. "Listen, can I call you back?" She didn't answer. "In a few minutes," I offered.

"Okay, Dad, call me."

I went to the toilet. I splashed water on my face and looked in the mirror. Tell me this is a nightmare. I drank some water and tried to shake off that horror that collects around long, ill-timed naps, especially those bent on an escape that ultimately is quashed. I lingered as long as I felt

I could without upsetting Nettie, shuffling again to the desk phone. I sat and punched in my daughter's number.

Even though she picked up on the first ring, I was ready. "Ella says, 'Hi,'" I said. "And Gabby, too." I hoped I could feel my way around with her.

"Great, but later. First, what went on with you and Raci? With Mom?" She was serious. She mostly used Raci, seldom Mom. "I am worried about you both."

Raci had called frantic and in tears.

"What did you say to her?" Nettie wanted to know. "Did you tell Mom about Ella. About Gabby?"

This had been her fear ever since she had reconnected with her mother. I hadn't been communicating with Raci then, and Nettie couldn't at first bring herself to tell her mother that Gabby had filled in the vacancy she'd left, or that Ella had become her new younger sister, replacing Siiri. Since the whole country separated those two at the time, Nettie decided Raci needn't know.

"Oh, Sweetie, I would never. No. I *did* go out to check in on Gabby and saw Ella there. But to Raci, I just mentioned an appointment."

"It had to be the book then," Nettie said. "You let her read it."

I explained, in part, what had passed during Raci's visit. "I'm guilty. I suppose I wanted her to see, even though it really was accidental. When I left to see Gabby and get food for us both, she read it through."

"She did, Dad. The part about Siiri and Michael."

"I know. She marked that page."

"Well, that explains the raving and crying, then." Nettie had read the book twice. And when she'd asked me about Moe's kids being alive, I said, "It's fiction, Nettie." She had not criticized their inclusion.

"I was careless, Nettie."

"No, Dad, you were selfish. Think about it. Raci woke from

a two-month coma missing two children, not to mention another now living with her new ex-husband. Twenty-some years later those kids show up alive in a book written by said ex-husband. How should that make her feel?"

I squirmed. "I didn't lead her to that part. I actually warned her about coming."

"Dad, listen. I love you, but aren't you overlooking the reason Mom called you? And why you agreed to meet her?"

I said nothing.

"I think you are still in love. I know Mom still loves you."

"She said that?"

"Absolutely. But she couldn't handle the denial."

I had no idea what she meant. "What denial?"

"You know better than anyone the power packed in a story. But, Dad, stories can't bring the dead back to life."

"I hate that book. I'm not publishing it."

Nettie's breath whistled into the phone. "Do not destroy that book." She knew well enough that it need not be said. I'd never thrown anything out. "I don't know what you should do, Dad, but this is a chance you shouldn't miss, and I'm not saying it to make my life better." She gave me Raci's hotel number. "I'll send you her itinerary in a minute. And you might consider that even in her twenties Ella may soon benefit from knowing someone who has handled tragedy."

That struck me speechless.

"I'm going to tell Raci about it when she gets back. Unless you tell her first."

I could not answer.

"Sorry for the late call, but I had to talk about it. I'm going to bed. I love you, Dad."

My daughter was willing to reveal her own mendacity, deceit that spanned a dozen years, to clear the way for her mother and me. It was generous and dangerous, too. Nettie, though, was certain of her own influence. She could navigate troubles. She also wanted to give Ella something of what Gabby had been for her. A steady older woman familiar with loss and survival.

Great. Nettie could sleep soundly. I was sure I wouldn't. Up all night? I did not know what I would do. I touched the manuscript in front of me. I could finish reading.

. . . Toady was waiting for me the following Friday. He had the coffee going and was already sipping a cup, so I could tell he'd been there for a while. As soon as he saw me at the door, he hopped over.

"Burt called," he said.

Over a month had passed since Roxie went back into treatment, and with all that had been going on in my life, I hadn't given much thought to Burt. That was how fast times changed. Some of the newcomers at *Today* hadn't even heard of him. I suppose they thought the meeting was my invention, or Toady's.

"What does Burt have to say?"

"He wants to come back. He's ready."

My feelings about my former mentor—had I really considered him my savior? I had—were a muddle of disgust, admiration, love, gratitude, and anger. "I suppose he needs help."

Toady nodded. "We have to shell out bus fare and, two months' rent for his place here, and a month for his place there."

I wondered about the wisdom of sending an addict any amount of money.

"I hope you can get Muckey to help," Toady said.

I laughed. "I don't know. He's as broke as I am."

"No, I mean we can send him some funds. He can pay the rent Burt owes in Compton and put the old boy on the bus. Maybe buy him a sandwich for the trip."

"What's this going to cost?"

"Rent is one-o-five in Compton, seventy-eight altogether here, and seventeen dollars for the bus fare. Express."

I looked at Toady hard. "Two hundred and some. Any chance we'll get something back?"

"We'll get Burt," he said. He bounced and smiled. "Maybe *Today* can chip in."

"If you mean the treasury, let's not even think about that." Most now attending would not understand.

"Listen, Moe, we'll put out the word, create a special fund, and see what happens."

I consented to his plan, but it had to be aboveboard.

It took only a week to raise the money. As I had thought, *Today* did not chip in much, but I was surprised how generously other groups gave. Burt had a long-time and widely-spread reputation. He had sponsored hundreds and had kept many sober. I was relieved. DeLorr and I were hanging on to the severance for all we were worth. I didn't want to raid that fund for this.

Muckey agreed to clean up Burt's mess in LA and see that he got on the bus. He'd always been a soft touch, but he also needed to get Burt out of Roxie's vicinity. He had Burt move up to JJ's. Made him clean up. Searched his luggage for contraband—those two watched him constantly—and set the date for his return, three days ahead so one of us could meet Burt at the station. Not being employed, that was my job. I was also in charge of clearing Burt's rent at his place just down the street from *Today*. I said, without looking first, that I'd clean Burt's apartment up for his return. That was a lavish promise and a gargantuan mistake.

NIGHT

How dirty could a one bedroom kitchenette really be? The answer came with two full day's worth of scrubbing, polishing, and arranging.

Burt lived on the third story of what had been a stylish family home in the early 1900's. The apartment was likely a servant's quarter, one of two on the floor, whose stairway had originally led to the kitchen. Sometime in the fifties the owner broke through the back wall at the first floor landing to make an exterior, private entrance.

The place was entirely wooden: floors, walls, ceiling, and cupboards, all built in place, were fir or redwood. It had been a handsome room but uninsulated. It was now quite chilly, even for a Minnesotan, and must have baked during summer. The three windows, each set in its own dormer, sticky but openable, allowed me to air the place out. Even after I hauled out the garbage, its two-month fermentation hung on the walls. Everything needed to be washed. Other than trash, garbage, ripped newspapers, tatters of shirts and bedding, Burt's place was bare: no books, no radio or television, no carpet or throw rugs, and, of course, nothing hung on the knee walls which caught the slope of the roof only four feet off the floor. Burt owned two oaken straight-backed chairs, a single lamp by the Hollywood bed, a dark-stained ancient oak dresser which could have belonged to his grandmother. There was nothing in the refrigerator other than a rotted mass of vegetables in a hydrator. A glacier of ice crystals occupied the freezer. The bath was a stained and filthy shambles.

"Why are you doing this?" I asked myself. "Good question." It was more than I had bargained for. Over the past quarter century I had managed to live life, helping only myself. I hadn't the altruistic sensibility that I believed came to other people who had always had enough. Growing up without, or with little did not encourage me to give anything away, certainly not labor. Once deprived, one can never have enough which forms the core of alcoholic syndrome. I had settled on beer, wine, spirits, and aperitifs to fill my want and could never drink enough to satisfy it. Now I was learning, teaching myself as best I could, to give however little it might be, to serve others. If I could do that, all in moderation, I could remain sober. So, for Burt, the man who showed me how to live unjuiced, I brought buckets, mops, brushes, gloves, rags, a ladder, and cleaning supplies to the apartment and started in. I kept thinking how pleased Burt would be to come home to a sparkling clean place.

I'd put in one full day and needed another to finish the job. Burt would arrive in two days. Returning home from the first spate of scraping and sponging, I'd opened a surprise letter from Tom. Inside were a one-way Northwest Airlines ticket to Minneapolis and cash: Two twenties and a fifty dollar bill. Tom's note said, "Hop the next flight." Across Grant's portrait Tom had scrawled, "For groceries."

Obviously, I couldn't take the next plane. I called him. The phone rang incessantly. I hung up and tried again. Just about to hang up, the receiver on the other end was picked up and immediately dropped. It bounced, rattling my eardrum. "Tom? Tom, it's Moe. Hello?" I finally shouted into the phone. He wasn't there.

I tried again a few minutes later, busy, and again after two hours, still busy. I was certain he'd passed out after fumbling with the handset. I'd try again the next day. It was the same story. The phone was back on the hook, but Tom wasn't answering. He would just have to wait for me to get there, and it wouldn't be soon. I had other issues like Burt's return.

Muckey called to give me the lowdown on Burt's arrival. "I watched the bus leave. There is one stop, but since he doesn't have money, he shouldn't get into trouble. I bought him a box lunch before he left."

Burt was due at two in the afternoon at the San Francisco bus terminal. I drove to pick him up. I felt nervous. I did not know what to expect and the sobriety sweepstakes between us had been turned on its head. Still, I couldn't shake the idea that Burt knew more than I did about living and prospering away from the evil of dope and booze.

From my car I watched the buses arrive then sat on the front fender as passengers alighted. Burt was the last off his Greyhound. He wore a white short-sleeved shirt draped over pressed slacks, all of which hung from his frame. He was thinner, perhaps a bit gray-looking, but still the man I knew. He stepped to the ground, looked right, looked left, winding up and loosing that sinewy neck of his, and finally caught sight of me waving from the car. He picked up his suitcase the driver had retrieved from the bus belly and sauntered toward me. He moved in that tentative way one does just entering the streets in a rain.

Burt looked right and left as he moved very slowly to the car, as if searching for someone, anyone but me, to talk to. He approached, did not cast so much as a smile, not even an embarrassed smirk, and nearly upon me raising his bushy brows, said, simply, "Shall we go?"

I found as much to talk about as did Burt. I couldn't rightly ask how Muckey was, or Roxie, or about Maggie, or how he, Burt himself, had been. I knew, and Burt knew, all that. And other than Toady, to whom he'd talked already, only a few at *Today* were looking forward to his return. He would be a member-only for the foreseeable future. So, we rode in silence across the bridge.

When we turned into his neighborhood, he turned to me, blinking his eyes slowly and grinning, "My grandmother warned me there would be days like this. 'Keep your eyes wide and senses keen,' she'd say."

"Sound advice, Burt."

He poked his head out the window as we drove by *Today*. He pulled back in and said, "There's a place I won't be going again." Then he clammed up as before.

We parked right in front of his house. Burt simply left his bag in the back seat and wandered oblivious of me toward the rear of the house.

"Let me help you with your bag, Burt." I grabbed it and followed. I had the key, something he'd left behind. His ancient landlady had found it in the door when coming for the rent.

I dragged the bag up three flights, wondering if this was the kind of helping that would set me free. It seemed more servility than service. Burt tried his apartment door.

"Shit. It's locked."

"I have the key, Burt. And we've taken care of this month's and the back rent. It's the least we could do."

"Oh, no matter," he said, "you could always do less."

I wasn't sure at that moment how to take his quip. "Is that what your grandmother would say?"

"My grandmother was not a fool."

"I didn't mean that," I said.

Burt pushed through the door. Once in he stopped dead. "It stinks of Lysol in here."

I mentioned the cleaning. He pulled a large

handkerchief from his back pocket and covered his nose and mouth. "Makes my eyes water."

I slid the suitcase inside and stood by it.

"Flop that on the bed, Moe." I was too deeply in already to stop now, so I did as Burt asked.

"It's the least I can do, Burt."

He didn't answer. I closed the door and waited. What I waited for, I'm still not sure. It didn't seem right to leave him there alone after all the trouble we had gone to getting him back.

I stood and watched Burt wander around the place like he had never seen it before. He looked out each of the windows—glass I had cleaned for its first time in years—checked the refrigerator which Toady and I had stocked with a few necessities, milk, eggs, butter, and the like.

After examining the bathroom and exiting shaking his head in some sort of disgust, he went to the bed and opened the suitcase. Burt looked at me and grinned, not his usual friendly wide smile, but a mischievous, more diabolical smirk. "Here, Moe, take a whiff of this."

He tossed a white frilly pair of panties up in the air, arcing them across the room at me. Not wanting to, still I caught them.

"Go ahead, take a snort," he said.

I shook my head and put the drawers down on the nearest chair. "No thanks, Burt."

He took them up again and breathed through the crotch. "Hey, boy, you don't know what you're missing."

That was it. I'd cleaned the man's toilet and tub, washed his walls, and lugged his travel bag. I'd donated, driven, and put up with his indifference and then his insolence, but this was too much. "Let me know if there's something else you need. I've got to go."

I left him standing in the middle of his barren

room a pair of white panties to his nose, brows lifted, and eyes wide open. It was the last I saw of Burt.

Much to my detriment, though not too often, in moments of weakness I've wondered whose they were: Linda's, Maggie's, Roxie's, an unknown lover's, or something snitched off the rack at J. C. Penney's. And what that underwear meant to Burt I never wanted to understand and did not ask about. To me they and his action represented just another addiction as desperate as swilling the juice or shooting up a vein, something to take him out of himself, away from the world, to hide from his life and maybe even from his grandmother. He used them all—booze, drugs, sex—as a shield, a barrier, a bower. That moment, I decided, Burt had used those lacy briefs as a weapon, like shooting an arrow. He kept help and health away from his tender parts, mainly from his broken and damaged heart.

From that, for him, I could offer no protection.

Tom wasn't answering. From what I knew of him, I wasn't going to fly into the Minnesota winter without a definite, agreed-upon plan, especially since DeLorr and I had battled about the whole idea. I understood her point of view: I was unemployed, and, though I was looking for a teaching position, my prospects were slim in the middle of the year.

"And how are you going to interview when you're two thousand miles away, housed with a crazy man?"

"I can handle Tom."

With that she went wild. "Oh, you can handle Tom. Listen, Moe, if you go there, I can't guarantee I'll be here to sweep up the pieces when, no, *if* you get back."

"You haven't read his book. Have you?" I had her there. "Have you?" She wavered, and I struck hard.

"It is great. It will sell fifty thousand copies. This is a wonderful chance. This is what I want."

Chasing rainbows had been a favorite pastime in my life, and DeLorr was right to wonder about this big opportunity. It looked to her like another boondoggle similar to the one I was still recovering from: corporate life in California.

"I'm just saying, Moe."

"If I can't raise him, I won't be going to Tom's anyway."

That very night, at two in the morning, Tom called.

"Hey, Moe, are you coming?"

Even ripped from a sound sleep and groggy, I could tell he was blitzed. "Are you drunk, Tom?"

"What's this? Some sort of gestapo interrogation?" He said. "Christ, I sent you a ticket two weeks ago. You could've at least called."

"I did. You dropped the phone in your beer."

He didn't remember but took my word for it. "The weather's getting good. This is the time to come."

I changed phones, and after DeLorr hung up the bed phone, we talked for a while. He said he'd been working since our last call two weeks after the funeral. His revisions were going well.

"Getting rid of all that Brit stuff. It was crap anyway," he said.

"I want to spend the weekend with my kids, and I have to find a replacement for my Friday meetings. I'll be out the first of March or so." I'd have to tiptoe around DeLorr, but leaving the following week would give us time, I hoped, to reach accord.

I was glad of the break. All the suffering

I'd witnessed weighed on my spirit. After Burt's homecoming, *Today* was tarnished for me. Once again I was amidst lost souls and strangers. Susan had drifted off, leaving only her ennui on the table, and though Toady kept coming and leading, he'd been unsuccessful in his efforts to bring Burt back into his own creation. Now I had to go.

"Sorry, Toady, this is an important step for me."

With the equanimity of a prince, Toady let me out easily. "Moe, you've done your share. The meeting is going well, Burt at least returned to town, and your trip to LA was outstanding service. Do your thing. Please, though, stay close to the fellowship out there."

"Sure. There are drunks everywhere," I said.

I replaced myself at the Friday meeting, sat through Oscar's first go at a meeting and blessed the job he did. It was important to me to leave with all in order. I'd arrived at *Today* with almost half a year sober, in August, celebrated my first birthday there and spent nearly seven months practicing good works. I felt fine.

Tom seemed right about the weather. An early thaw had sprung up that week. I hoped it would hold, and I took it as an omen of a warming in my relationship with Tom. If I could keep him away from booze and work side by side peaceably with him, the editing would be done by the end of April. I'd already made favorable contact with an agent who was waiting for the full manuscript. He'd loved what I had sent him. I was hopeful.

March, however, played the lion. I flew out Tuesday early morning, packing Monday while DeLorr was at work, the kids at school. But by the time the plane reached Minneapolis my connecting flight north had been canceled.

A blizzard had struck the northern counties of Minnesota. Accumulations of up to two feet of snow were predicted. Half of it had fallen by my arrival mid-state, and Duluth, my destination, reported gusts of ninety miles per hour. Snow piled in drifts high enough to bury a house. Everything shut down, including the phone lines.

Such storms had been common there, much to our glee in childhood. They swirled over the frozen Canadian plains, bent south at Lake Superior's far north end to barrel down the shore like runaway tractor-trailers on the two-mile descent of Thompson Hill that ran down the cliffs, funneling furious energy straight at Duluth. I waited out the storm at the Curtis Hotel, downtown Minneapolis. It took two full days to bring the area back to a minor semblance of order, to partially clear runways and roads, and to restore power to some of the stricken towns nearby. The weather, as it often does following a Canadian storm, turned frigid, ten below zero past sundown.

Getting from the Duluth airport to Tom was another chore. The marooned visitors in Duluth were lined up to leave any way possible. I finally caught a late evening Greyhound, the fourth of the day, and arrived in Cloquet near eleven. The temperature had by then dropped to minus twenty.

During a half-hour-long trudge following narrowed city streets lined by snowdrifts and piles heaped by plows clearing the streets, I had to scramble up the bank when cars approached or risk being mowed down. Once I slipped, dropped my suitcase, and came close to disaster. I'd dressed for the weather too lightly, and when my pants and long-johns grew wet from falling and sliding down snowbanks, my knees and shins ached with cold.

Tom's street, Chestnut, was a single lane wide.

There was no traffic there at that hour, and the neighborhood was completely dark, still awaiting the restoration of electric power. Woodsmoke hung in the still cold air. I hoped Tom had his fireplace warming up the living room.

Only for a moment did I stand in front of old Doc McIntyre's house. The white clapboards and Ionic-capped columns seemed to grow out of the drifted snow up three stories to the attic dormers where Tom and I had played Hitler and studied the Cub Scout motto thirty years before. All windows were blacked out. Loose crystals of snow, but not a wisp of smoke played about the chimney stack. The walk and the driveway were drifted over. I walked down the neighbor's shoveled drive and waded across shallow snow piles under the eaves of, as I'd always thought of it, Mrs. McIntyre's garage and edged into a drift that towered over my head toward Tom's back door. Never in my life had I gone in the front.

Once in the big snow past the garage, it was more like swimming than climbing. With every step, I broke through the thin, icy crust the cold had laid atop the drift and was forced to use my suitcase as a buoy in front of me. I was a snow snail humping up and over a mountain. I slid down the far side of the drift right onto the porch. The storm had blown both the porch and kitchen doors open, depositing a hundred shovelfuls of snow into the vestibule and, swirling into the kitchen itself, sleeted the floor. Some of it had melted then frozen into a sheet of ice that sent me slipping onto my back in the middle of the linoleum. My suitcase slammed against the oven.

I groaned and called out. My voice sounded hushed in the leavings of the storm, the cold, the muffled surroundings, and, as I later saw, the stacks of newspapers and books which, even frozen stiff, attenuated my call. I needed light. The blizzard murdered electricity.

In old houses, especially occupied by ninety-somethings, conditions, other than piles of refuse, change slowly. Innovation belongs to youth. It was so here, for a full box of matches kept for lighting the oven was exactly where I remembered it from scouting days here, "farmer" matches we lit on our pants zippers or sometimes on a plaster wall down in the basement. I lit the oven first. Then I used a closeted dust pan to shoo the snow out enough to close the kitchen door but for a crack. I'd called out for Tom twice more to no reply. I'd take care of myself first, look for candles, then search for Tom.

I spent some time warming myself before the open oven, widened the entry door a bit being mindful of monoxide, and stood to dry my pants and long underwear. Over the range hood, I found candles which I fixed to cup saucers. The kitchen was large but heated up fast. I lowered the oven dial, closed its door, and warm enough to venture forth, I passed into the dining room, looking for Tom. I closed the swinging door against the kitchen's heat, and with the candles aloft moved along a maze-like path of papers stacked neatly, solidly, and closely to shoulder level. I passed down several dead ends, searching methodically for my friend. I soon exhausted the dining room paths, went past the wide stairway into the huge living room. More papers and magazine paths led to a sun porch stuffed solidly with more. Tom was not on the main floor.

When we were boys, Tom occupied the smallest bedroom on the second floor at the back of the house, its single window overlooking the garage and backyard. I headed there first, but stopped in front of the closed bathroom door at the head of the stairs. I tapped lightly calling his name. "Tom, are you in there? It's Moe."

He was there. And he wasn't. I'd tapped twice and tried the door, which opened narrowly, stopping with a thud. I pushed and shouldered in enough to bring the candlelight and my head around the door. Tom's body, for I immediately knew he'd died, lay, pants at its knees, in a pool of frozen excrement and, having flowed at his other end from the gash in his head, darker blood soaked a bath mat which had frozen and curled at its edges. He and, thankfully in a way, both spills had frozen solid sometime in the last two days. I pushed in, lowered the candle toward Tom's stricken face. Were his eyes open?

At once, the electricity was restored. I dropped the candle when the lights blazed.

In the months following Tom's death I had stopped believing in anything, though I immediately grew much too busy to know it. Sounds phony, but I had what became the inevitable divorce roaring inside my ears, *Tunnel Rats* to finish, offers for more books and the movie. Besides, who can realize he's lost faith while living at the center of the universe?

Leaving Tom and Minnesota, I was finished. Too much death, too much alcohol, and too many drugs, which no one else seemed to be able to stop drinking or taking. Why me? What had I done to make it easy for me to stay off the booze. Two nights later in Minneapolis I drove by the automat where I used to buy my evening wines. For the first time ever, the car went straight by. I looked but could not turn.

That is what mystifies and in the night plagues me. I've not downed a drink in twenty-five years. How did that happen? Maybe Tom insured my sobriety by launching my career. I don't know. All I can say for sure is that each person I came across at *Today* had earned his liberty in his suffering way.

I did not deserve to be freed, and look what it got me.

I sit reading through the night at my blood-money, cherrywood desk, feeling sorry, looking out the dark windows seeing my own lamp-illuminated face, looking much like Tom's own the moment the lights sprang up in his winter house.

Through it all: six novels including *Fallen*, *Careless*, and *Boozer*, all of a kind as this, *Twelve*, my last report on the drinking-front, I still cannot face loss. Does it matter now? Does one need faith when there is fame and money?

Finished reading, I toast my lost friends with my ice water. I name them all: Hillside-Glenn drowned in this stuff. Maggie left behind her broken body, her liquid spirit seemingly intact. Tom died, as he knew he finally must, ingloriously in blood and excrement. Len likely returned to the sea, and Susan, so thin already, perhaps lost more flesh until she turned to the side and simply ceased to exist. Burt, I have known for years already, succumbed to a new bulge in his knotty neck, a sort of throat cancer for which they say he refused to seek treatment. Muckey followed Roxie back to Montana, the pair having four kids on the slag heaps. None have heard from or looked for my sponsee, Gael, who I called Jude. Toady stayed at *Today* for quite some time. Two years after Burt returned to Oakland, I stopped by on a book tour swing through California. He was there. The next time less than a year later, gone. My sweetest friend played cello for years in the Riverside Symphony. Gabby had grown huge, lost her looks, but kept her music and self lovely, even after her own disease wasted her down.

Who among them drank once more? Outside of the deceased, Gabby, my lovely Gabby, and myself, I don't know. Likely, some.

Through this night, I do what I'm best at. I wait. As soon as Nettie's information came, I acted. I wrote my editor, telling him I'd take another month with the book. I wouldn't be sending it to him. I checked seats on a flight to Dublin.

Now, I wait at my desk. I look out toward dawn.

I finger the numbers I jotted as Nettie had spoken them. I wait for light. I wait for it to be time to make just one last call.

Author's Note:

Part of the job of life is to find oneself.

There are those who find this a simple task, easier than falling off a bicycle. It is hardly worth thinking about them. They will take care of themselves and of others, too.

Then there are those, among whom most of my characters dwell, who founder and fall away. Most remain lost throughout their existence. It is to those, whose every turn is an effort and a pain, that my heart goes out.

They are the Toms, the Burts, the Maggies of our earth, moving inexorably to their sad and dismal ends, shaking off the warmth of friendship and family. Even with help along the way, they do not, once tottering, seem fit to right themselfs again. This is especially true if they drink or drug.

For all those, I am sad and thankful, too.